Robinson Crusoe 1,000,000 A.D.

By
John Argo

Clocktower Books, San Diego

Contents

First Glimpse

A cold layer of sea fog masks a beach early one morning, a million years from today...

A figure appears on a sandbar just offshore. As the tropical sun slowly burns off the fog, the figure resolves into a lightly clad man fishing in the shallows of the ocean bay with a simple but effective spear. He is young, lean, and bearded, with long hair. He frowns with concentration as he walks about stabbing the water in sudden lunges. His blue eyes glitter with determination to stay alive. The young man is an anomaly, an evolutionary afterthought. Nobody will ever come to rescue him. There is nobody. He is the last human—a Robinson Crusoe with no Friday and no hope of ever being rescued, for mankind has been extinct for eons.

Alex (so he names himself, after his long-dead genetic source) keeps a wary lookout over a half dozen rippers, predatory animals who squat across the water waiting for him to make one fatal mistake. His alert senses hear the sea gently churning, the slap of ocean water onto clean white sand, palm trees rustling, and seagulls cawing. He smells saltwater and fresh air. The rippers watch Alex's every move from across the water. They fear saltwater, which is why he knows they won't swim across to kill and devour him. Nature has filled the world with many strange new things, including huge saltwater flowers with tree-trunk bodies that dot the shallows in which Alex fishes; and butterflies as big as a man's head, dodging among the strange new flowers. The spear stabs suddenly. Alex exclaims sharply and hauls out a wriggling coppery-scaled fish.

Survival is easy. Understanding the enigma of his existence is a much harder mystery he has not been able to solve.

Yet.

1. Alex Kirk Marooned

The world was a mystery to Alex Kirk, and his own existence was an enigma within that mystery.

He kept a wary eye on three rippers as he hunted and fished along the shore of his tropic domain. Nature had made some changes in the past million years. New flowers had grown fantastically large atop stems resembling tree trunks, growing in the ocean's edge. Some were carnivorous, with sticky surfaces to trap insects and small birds, so the flower's petals could close up while it slowly digested the struggling prey. Multicolored butterflies large as Alex's head fluttered about—in reality evolved, diurnal bats. They had pink bodies covered with a light gray fuzz of hair, and their four limbs straddled those wings (resembling the bright yellow and red tree-flowers) with tiny claws at the elbow and knee joints. These butterfly bats fed on certain types of non-carnivorous tree flowers, but there was a gray variety of bat that were blood drinkers. Alex loathed the latter with the same primordial human instinct of repulsion by many-legged crawling things. He avoided the nocturnal bloodsuckers.

The rippers constantly shadowed him from the beach across a run of cold, foamy seawater, looking for an opening so they could kill him. They would not reach him out here on the sand bars and on the stumps of these fantastic new tree-flowers. A sea breeze made palm trees rustle as Alex foraged so he could eat and stay alive. Sunlight intensified colors and made him squint, but he never lost track of his enemies. The rippers were afraid to cross the fast-flowing tidal stream or they would long since have made a quick meal of him. He had taught them to stay out of range of his deadly, poison-tipped arrows. Several piles of bleached ripper bones lay half buried in sand—a reminder to stay out of his bow range.

Hot sand crumbled between Alex's toes and warmed his bones. He'd fashioned a hat of skin and feathers to shield against a blinding sun in a powder-blue sky. He was a dark-haired, wiry young man with soldiering in his blood. It showed in the alert, confident way he carried himself and the weapons he'd fashioned from stone and wood.

Alex loved being alive despite life's dangers and its loneliness. He liked the warmth of the sun. He liked the smell of vegetation and ocean, the wind in his hair, the thunder of surf. Seagulls uttered raw screams as they kited overhead in moist air under billowing white cumulus clouds. He loved life itself, and vowed to make the best of it, although sometimes despair nearly drove him to end it all. What he would not give for another soul to speak with, but there would never be another. It was tempting sometimes to just swim across a narrow channel of water and let the rippers take him, but he had a strange faith that something more was meant for him in this existence.

Every day, Alex hunted and fished along the tropical beaches of his small domain. He wore a stone knife in his belt and carried a bow and arrows as he hunted under a powder-blue sky with a few high cirrus clouds. Every afternoon in the tropics, huge billows of white cumulus clouds on the horizon would send brief but intense rain showers, but other than that it was humid and clear under a blinding sun.

Each evening, he would eat comfortable supper by a fire after dark, in the safety of his little redoubt high on the bluffs overlooking a nameless sea. The magnitude of his misfortune was so incomprehensible that he brushed it off, but deep down wondered what had gone wrong. More than once he asked the unanswerable question: *Why?*

A full moon floated in the blue sky over reddish mountains. The moon looked hazy citron among spindly palm trees that shimmered in wet air. Near the moon hung, always, a gray smudge whose explanation Alex could not find in his memories.

As he went about his simple work, Alex sometimes remembered images and sensations that half drove him mad: cities and roads, skylines and jet airplanes, the touch of other humans, especially the woman he loved, Maryan...He could not find a shred of evidence that she or any of it had ever existed.

In his dreams when he slept in his hut at night, he floated down rainy neon streets of a lost world. Those dreams were filled with the scent and the music of Maryan Shurey, the woman Alex Kirk had loved.

The dreams were always about the same. Sometimes he spent a long time floating over a cityscape to get there. He floated through the sky in some fantastic vehicle they must have had back then. The skyline was filled with massive buildings that shimmered lightly in a fog of light, and in that shimmering mist were thousands of tiny square window lights making a sprawl like some alien alphabet that must have meant something to someone, some comforting but exciting message loaded with promises and urgency. Then he lay beside her in a room where they had made love. She slept by his side, with a contented look on her face. He lay awake, savoring the moment. Nearby stood a metal ice container from which protruded an empty champagne bottle. The remains of a fine seafood and pasta meal were hardening into a crust on expensive heavy cream hotel china near the window. In the blue-black darkness, a television set flickered silently, its volume set to Mute. On the television, an ice cream truck slowly turned a corner. On the corner, a store front said Ito's News. The scene was from a picturesque little town in upstate New York someplace, a slice of Americana. One could see the rustling elm trees of Beacham on one of those summer days when the air is filled with scents of mown grass and hot melting tar. A little girl leans out from the ice cream truck. She is cute as a button, with missing front teeth, freckles, and reddish bangs. The sound cuts in: "Hey, what flavor would you like? Chocolate? Vanilla? Or Strawberry?" She'd fold her hands together, incline her head to one side so her locks bounced, cute as a button, and she'd say: "Personally, I prefer strawberry. That's because it's my favorite color. Don't you think?"

Those dreams were so vivid he sometimes woke up thinking he'd made love to this woman who must have died a million years ago. Her very dust had turned to atoms and by now floated among the stars.

Later in the day, Alex headed home with the plump bass he'd caught among the tree-trunk flowers. Huge butterflies fluttered overhead, sometimes briefly blotting out the sun with their undulating movements. The rippers' rankness wafted toward him across the narrow saltwater channel as they bounded along growling at him. The smell of his fish, and their long patient waiting, had made them hungry. They took turns to paw the water's edge, urging him with hooting and barking noises to come over to them. He ignored them.

A faint shadow briefly dimmed the sky with sizzling, crackling noise. Alex nearly dropped his fish, and the predators scrambled for cover.

Startled, Alex looked up. He stared across the wide bay with its rippling tidal waters. He heard a loud bang that echoed from horizon to horizon. A chrome streak appeared and instantly vanished into a forest on a hill two miles across the bay. The sky was bright as ever, and a fine thread of vapor quickly dissipated, drifting away in the powder-blue sky.

The world looked as though nothing had happened, but some instinct told Alex his life had just become infinitely more complicated and dangerous.

2. Caves

Unaware of the horrific danger that suffused this place, a pale young man floated nakedly and motionlessly in a stone tank full of water.

The walls of the tank were smooth like rubbed, bluish-gray slate. The silence was deceptive. The air around the tank was dark—caverns full of darkness, galleries and tunnels full of darkness, ceilings dripping with stalagmites from ages of patient time. Horror and innocence together stalked these corridors.

The liquid in the tank and on the floor all around had a faintly greenish absinthe tinge that blurred the man's still features. His eyes were closed, his handsome features serene as if he were dreaming in these days before his birth.

And nearby, someone waited. Something. Someone. Breathing hungrily.

The light was dim in the birth cave. Light did not shine here so much as it flowed slowly and thickly, like a turgid polymer up one side of a glass beaker and down the other. The light was thick, a matrix of vivid memory routines that randomly invoked themselves, one now, one then, and just as quickly vanished, in this place where time had lost all meaning.

The air was very still—hardly moving at all, just when a droplet of dew fell from a stalagmite pink as coral, or ran like candle wax down some shimmering stalactite. The echoes of these drippings traveled back and forth in the caves—the sound of a droplet landing above the sleeping man's face, sending rings outward in tiny lapping waves.

The young man lay in this cool, mossy broth with his arms at his side. Each delicate fingertip was whorled with perfect skin poised against exquisitely detailed thighs, for he was in every way a complete human, down to the very capillaries that glowed in his pale skin. On the backs of his arms and legs were strangely hard, dark patches more resembling wood than skin. Time had lost all meaning long ago, except in the quickening of his pulse. If stones and water and floating slime had ears, they might have heard the growing thunder of his heartbeat while the walls dripped ever so steadily and quietly with the patience of a clock that never lost spring compression.

Nearby, giving off muffled breaths, was the hungry Watcher who moved clumsily in the shadows. He wheezed with effort and sometimes sobbed with need. The Watcher eyeballed that growing body so warm in its tank, with the mass of umbilical tubes trailing out of the tumor-like, warty bioexchange mass covering the abdomen. The Watcher knew: that stuff was richer than gray brains and would make his hunger stop hurting and his own thinking a trifle less fuddled. Did not want to eat this, knew he shouldn't, but could not stop himself. Again. And drawing closer, crawling, ever so quiet so as not to wake the young sleeper. So sad, the lovely face. Already, the Watcher's mouth snuffled as he swallowed the freely flowing saliva of his famishment. So bad, to do this, but could not help himself. His fingers twitched as he reached out for the tangled tubes that brought life to his brother.

Alex Kirk lived down the street from a little girl with dimples and white teeth. Her name was Maryan Shurey and they often got into trouble together.

They ran away one afternoon. A bright blossomy afternoon, the autist might have said as a young man, a moo-day, so winsome the ifty leaves and crowny trees, all green and hackathorny, the magpies dancing their cartoon dance under white clouds {glued cotton on Popsicle sticks} on the refrigerator door in the kitchen.

Later that afternoon, Alex and Maryan came back riding in an ice cream truck waving waffle-cones piled high with scoops of vanilla chocolate and strawberry music—Pop Goes The Weasel!

The dreams were like a narcotic, filling the young man with warmth and pleasure as he slept in his stone womb.

The Watcher, too, dimly remembered Maryan Shurey and Alex Kirk.

Maryan stood on a stool and leaned out of the truck, telling each kid who came close: "Hey, what flavor would you like? Chocolate? Vanilla? Or Strawberry?" She'd fold her hands together, incline her head to one side so her locks bounced, cute as a button, and she'd say: "Personally, I prefer strawberry. That's because it's my favorite color. Don't you think?"

Thus, in nature's complex and odd ways, nothing was lost. The sleeper twitched briefly. Maybe his eyes flickered just a bit, the lids lifting as the lashes trembled, while the Watcher tore open the rich cheese containing the fishness, the yolkness, the momness, the thick bloody pudding of oxygen and iron and life flowing into the newly formed young man. The sleeper was days away from being born, and his perfect fingers closed once, twice, silently in the water. His hands fluttered and grew still even as the tank's color turned from transparent green to wine red, then black and the water roiled. The water bubbled and foamed, filled with the violence of the watcher now eater who reached in with both hands and tore out the tubes, tore off hunks of rich life, stuck his head into the very water and groaned with need and pleasure as the orgasm of satiety filled him like a sick full tide. Leaving his dead prize to dry and mummify, the eater, now Watcher again, staggered away from the feast still steaming with the warmth of the tank and the bloody fatty sweet creamness of a dead summer morning that would never see its afternoon.

When the Watcher finished what was left in the tank, it belched noisily and wandered off, getting lost in the lower galleries for days. Sleeping off the fullness. Dreaming of another boy's summer days. The Watcher who now slept on a soft sandy corner in the stone caverns knew *hungry* because of the ice cream truck. He could see in his own dry dreams the boy and the girl smiling. Alex and Maryan. The taste of vanilla ice cream lingered on the side of the watcher's tongue from a long sucking slurp a million years ago. The tongue like an icebreaker cut through floes of chocolate to reach the steaming frozen vanilla meat wrapped around the clean little pinewood stick that smelled like a forest or a wood mill.

After sleeping a long time, the watcher awoke feeling that hunger again. He lifted his misshapen head and raised himself on hairy arms that were brawny but not quite the same length. In fact, the left side of his body was much smaller than the right, and even his head was oddly shaped with a large right side and a little left side, except the two frog eyes were alike.

The caverns smelled of love and mint and freshness. Sponges glowed faintly on the walls, some more yellow, others greener, with bacterial luminosity. Eating sponges helped soothe the hunger, but they were not the meaty food that made the stomach feel good. The Watcher remembered how scary it had been to run away with Maryan and began crying—its howls resounded heart-brokenly among the stalagmite/stalactite galleries. Maryan gone forever. Better to have stayed home and watched cartoons rather than this dangerous adventure. Daddy coming home with the evening newspaper—where? The Watcher was alone and wanted its mother, but that was long ago and she might have forgotten by now. Maybe the ice cream truck would come again? And maybe the little girl? Would she taste good?

In another tank in another cave not far from the last, a young man slept in a tank, awaiting the hour of his birth. As he slept, he dreamed warm and comforting dreams of Maryan and Alex.

Pop goes the weasel! The ice cream truck came around the corner. Impulsively, Alex grabbed Maryan's hand and ran, towing her along. Always up for adventure, she squealed and ran along with flying pigtails. The truck turned the corner and disappeared from sight. The boy and girl ran after it, but couldn't find it, and got lost. The morning grew hotter as the sun arched up above the towny roofs, and tar began to run black and liquid on the asphalt streets. They ran and ran, growing tired and scared, until they heard the distant chimes again on a faraway city block: Pop goes the weasel! Now they knew which way to run, to catch the truck, to be borne home grinning and licking cold vapor-wrapped ice creams on sticks. What fun!

The dreams inside the new, good copy of Alex were sweet and efficient. The deoxyribonucleic acid polymers had long unraveled according to their programmed instructions. His genome/phenome had sparkled in the tank like an intricate glass spaghetti about six feet long and roughly in the shape of a human being, at least seven or eight months ago. The ancillary cellulation had grown in a steady process, all at once, dermis and epidermis forming at one level, striated muscle tissue under that, spongy bone at the core, and nerve filaments snaking through the entire structure according to some astronomically complex bioelectrical blueprint. His brain unpacked itself rather like a blow-up rescue boat inside his dura mater. Plop, went one cortex, plop went another, until the whole skull cavity was quite packed, while leaving nice room for the sinus cavities that would soon receive their first breath of air.

The Watcher could smell new life forming in the caverns and tunnels. He snuffled about, licking clean weedy water and eating mushrooms that glowed on the walls. He was often scared, and hungry anyway.

Waiting...

Wee Alex, he stumbled through the darkness crying for his mommy. Or for the little girl with the nice smile. His tummy really hurt now, pounding like his heart. His wailing filled the coal-black air around him and came bouncing back like scary beasts pouncing. Scared, he waved his arms and yelled and ran, and the more he yelled the more the wails and screams and snorts followed him, pressing from all sides, until he hid in a blacker-than-black corner and shivered quietly and soon the bat-like noises stopped flying toward him.

Ah, then he rose. He smelled the flower smell, the sweet smell, the mommy smell, the nursing hands and feeding tubes of where it was good to eat. This way! the good smell seemed to say, and the mushrooms glowing on the walls looked like big smiles as he stumbled, faster and faster.

In the ninth month of the new young man's gestation, specific nanofactors started executing.

Some of it was RNA, working its way along natural zipper strips of genetic polysaccharides. Other bits of it were synthetically engineered machines no larger than molecules, building up protein sequences that would structure his memory for him. Even after such a vast time, a lot of it still worked. It all worked, and it worked at all, because the process had taken on a life of its own. The drive of life, tropism to the light, the push of root through wall, the symbiosis of coral and a thousand darting guest species, had won here too. He dreamed blissfully of Maryan Shurey as the specially programmed protein chains released their artfully packaged data, reel after reel of film, into his memory. Maryan was a slim, athletic blonde with an angel face and blue eyes. A dancer, a skater, casually tanned and even a bit wind-chapped as she whirled around him in tighter and tighter arcs while taking off, one piece at a time, every item of clothing except of course her skates. Her blue eyes and white teeth smiled into his soul. He was about to be born.

The chamber had been almost perfectly still for such a long time that the stalagmites rising drip by sedimentary drip from the gallery floors had time to touch, and in some cases meld with, stalactites hanging drip by longer drip from the gallery ceilings. Now it was the turn of the young man to be a brief drip in the unimaginably ancient life of this semi-darkened place. The water stirred in ripples, distorting his features, as he moved his hands in tiny twitching motions. Was that a faint smile on his perfectly formed lips and face? He had light brown hair, medium coarse, just long enough to fluff lightly at the edges as the water moved around his head. Everything was perfectly formed—the muscles in his shoulders, the biceps on his upper arms, the thick veins in his strong forearms. Now a fleck of blood drifted by his face. And another. The water stirred. His expression changed to one of displeasure, then pain. Thick gouts of blood swirled around him, looking more black than red in this faint greenish light.

The moment of his birth must have been barely hours or minutes away, and it was a good thing, for something unexpected was happening that he could not explain. He was not quite ready to open his eyes, but he knew that he must. His dreams of Maryan Shurey had fled; no bringing them, or her, back. He felt a searing pain, a terrible tearing in his gut, as if pieces of him were being torn out. He was not quite ready to take his first breath, but already he was screaming. Great silver and brass and ruby bubbles erupted as he doubled over, clutching his midsection. As he doubled over, he felt a slippery, slimy strength and realized it was someone-not-he, some other, for he could push against it and he did not feel anything, so it was not part of him. The Other pushed back when he pushed. The Other grew angrier, hungrier, more frantic, he didn't know what to call it, but the pain doubled.

The Other tore at him, and he could feel parts of him shredding like cloth. He tasted his own blood as he screamed in underwater bubbles. He blared with excruciating, blinding agony as he struggled to hold his insides together. The Other shook him. He was flung up and down as the Other tore at him. He felt his teeth in him. He banged his head on the hard side of the birthing womb. As he rode up and down, his head bobbed into the air several times. Involuntarily, he took his first breath. He was pulled under and nearly drowned. Desperately, he made a fist and beat against his pulpy head, and he backed off for a minute or so, long enough for him to be born.

And so he was born, struggling for his very life before it was properly infused and inspired into him by contact with the air.

Lightning bolts of adrenalin surged through him in those incredible minutes. He could see in the dark; his pupils must have been fully extended. He hung back in horror, with his elbows pulled over the edges of the birthing tank, his body up his lowest ribs above the water.

He saw the thing that was eating him—it was a man not much unlike him, though covered with blood and gore, and staring with white hungry insane eyes. The Other's teeth were bared, and its angry red hands held up like claws. The Other's mouth made slobbering, anguished noises. The Other's long hair was a mass of blood and strands of skin and gore. The Other wore some kind of simple hide cloak that steamed wetly in the poor light.

Terrified, the young man sat up splashing water from the tank. His pale new hands gripped the slippery marble-like stone rim of the tank or tub that surrounded him like a sarcophagus with no lid.

This was the moment of his birth, and he was shot through with a million volts of adrenalin for he was being eaten alive.

Screaming, he flailed at the predator his wet white hands. His hair lay back slick and shiny, and his eyes were dark holes of terror and anguish. He beat his fists on the hairy, powerful creature mauling him. He saw its wild eyes, the blood rolling out of the corners of its mouth, the blackness of its slurping tongue. He smelled the stink on its hide, the stench on its fur, the rot in its folds.

He saw what hurt on him, his gut, the mottled and bumpy mass that covered his stomach like a tumor. Coming from various parts of his torso were long tubes. Some were diaphanous, like cellophane (good Twenty-Second Century word! even through this, his memory kept sturdily building, those proteins just programmed to keep whaling away at his brain). Other tubes were rubbery, white, venous. Many were slim like little snakes or spaghetti strands. But out of that pile of warts and bread loaves on his mid section came a handful of these thick blackish-brown tubes, and they must have been ripe with nutrients, for the killer's hands fastened about the remnants of them. The Other had consumed much of his connections to the birthing tank, to the galleries around him, by now, but its greed had no end, and the closer it got to his belly, the more intense was the pain for the newly born young man, the Alex who now struggled with slipping heels and sloshing water to rise to his feet in the tank.

He screamed, pushing at the beast with his feet, but it returned a bare-knuckled blow at his face that stunned him. He almost drowned as he sank down into the water. As he went down, still clutching the slippery stone rim, he carried with him a glimpse of the mingled malevolence and innocent fury in the starving predator's eyes: and a wink of intelligence. They knew each other. They were of the same blood. Somehow, they were brothers.

Desperate, filled with adrenalin, he rose out of the water like a violent cork. He wrapped one arm around the Other's head and gouged at the Other's eyes with the fingers of his other hand. He didn't have strong nails yet, and those he had were waterlogged, or he would have gouged the Other's eyeballs out. He must have hurt it, for the Other bellowed with pain and shot a sharp elbow into his diaphragm that left him feeling winded. He sank back into the water, and he saw the Other's hands coming down for his throat. He saw the insane glow in the Other's eyes, the arctic sheen of its teeth, the primordial expression of the predator. He felt the Other's powerful grip around his throat, and realized that it meant to kill him right then. He pulled in his chin so that it would not have a good choke on his neck. He felt the bruising strength of the Other's fingers against his exposed collar bones, but his windpipe was intact—if only he could go up for air!

He raised his arms and shoved his forearms into the crooks of the Other's elbows, making its arms collapse. It still had a powerful grip around his throat, but with its arms bent in, its face was closer—just within reach above the surface. Everything was a blur as he reached up. Young Alex worked his hands into a firm grip on the edges of the cloak around the Other's neck. He pulled the cloak tight around his neck, starting a choke on him. Immediately, he felt his grip weaken. He let his back sink to the bottom while he planted his feet into the Other's stomach and thrust upward. At the same time, he pulled sharply down with his hands.

The Other came crashing helplessly into the water, banging its head on the edge before it went under. As it went down with a massive plash that showered the floors all around, Alex came up. He felt weak, limp, and took a rasping hungry cry for air. While his lungs filled, the Other's hands rose like claws out of the opaque water and scratched his face. Its fingernails rasped down his neck, down his chest, seeking someplace to grasp, to harm. It still had a choke on his neck with both hands.

Alex wrapped his legs and arms around it to keep it under water. He felt it weaken in two or three abrupt increments. Was it a trick, or was the thing now actively dying? He felt its fur rasping against his tender new skin, and recoiled. It stank of rot and meat and vomit. Its foul orifice was close enough to kiss, and it stank of deep garbage and offal. Alex head-butted it and it weakened another increment, sinking under the water.

As he held the Other, Alex felt it kick and punch. He felt the thud of its fists against his ribs, and nearly let go. He knew if he gave it even a hand-span of freedom it would find a way to kill him.

So he ignored his deep aching pain and tightened the way his arms wrapped around it. He knotted his fists together, wrists pressing its head, and ignored the pain as it bit his hands. Its fingers clawed desperately, trying to break his fingers.

One of the fingers gave with a soggy snap, breaking backwards, and Alex screamed loudly, filling the cave with his electric anguish, but he managed to tighten himself around his enemy even more tightly.

He had no choice. In another minute it gave up clawing him and struggled with its hands to push up from the bottom. Alex wiggled into position, placing one knee on its ribs, while bracing his other foot against the tank wall. This way, he pinioned it against the corner and bottom of the tank, and it weakened quickly.

Alex's heart pounded. He saw spots. He gasped for breath, again and again, while his body started to shut down the searing adrenalin that would soon burn it up. He waited a long time after the last bubbles rose, after the last twitches subsided, when the Other was still as a piece of rubber, growing cold, and he was sure it had drowned.

Alex waited for a while, still holding the Other's corpse down, while listening to the caverns around him. He heard the dripping in its darkness. He saw the glow of sponges on the walls, the ripple of biolumes in the stony creases of the natural ceiling, the gleam of dim reflections in the still waters covering the floor.

Then he heard a new terror, in this unknown world of terrors into which he had just been born. The new terror came in the form of savage roaring from somewhere far away yet near enough so that Alex could almost hear spit crackling in the pink and pulpy throat of whatever wild and savage predator waited outside the caves to make a meal of him. He let go of the dead body underwater and stepped sobbing from his womb, holding himself, shivering as he danced cold and naked from one foot to the other. He hugged himself and chattered teeth behind blue lips as he stared about with newly terrified eyes.

There! He heard it again, the hungry roar of a large mammal looking for him. He sensed that it was looking for him, looking for a way in to come tear him apart and eat him, something more powerful than this weak and misshapen copy of a human being he'd just killed.

Even as he stood hugging himself and chattering, the dead thing floated up in the pool. Its face floated up, just barely breaking the surface enough for its outlines to be clear. The water was blackened and made opaque by Alex's blood, and in its surface tensions emerged the bizarrely malformed but still recognizable features of a Neanderthal-looking carbon copy of Alex Kirk.

So why am I Alex when I am not? As he looked down in wonder at who and what he was, he vaguely understood that something terrible had been done to mankind and that he was supposed to be where he was, but this poor deformed brother of his had interrupted his birth process, and he could only hope that the proteins in his brain would continue their work without the precious nutrients. In the dim light, he could see the trunks of the tubes still hanging out of his midsection in fragments, about six of them, none longer than his hand could grasp, most too short to grasp. Pulling on them caused pain. Leaving them alone made the pain subside. He staggered about, reeling from the pain of his one touch, and almost wished he'd let the Other kill him. It was a wish he would have many times again as the realities of his new world became starkly plain.

Then he had no more time to speculate, for he heard the first of several prowling and hungry beasts trying to get in. It roared with a terrifying power that echoed loudly through the sunken galleries and corridors. He realized it had already smelled him.

Alex didn't know how long he stood in the gloom beside his birthing tank, with water plashing around his ankles.

Nor did he know where his mother was, nor why he was Alex. Or if he was Alex, and he was sure he was not. So who or what am I, he wondered.

He hugged himself and cried like a small child, though he was a grown man. It wasn't cold exactly, but the water droplets drying on his skin made the still air feel chilly. Nothing happened except his nose got stuffy, and he stopped crying after a while. Nobody came to help him, which was sad. Then again, nobody came to eat him, and that was good.

Sniffling, he remembered the Other's cloak. The Other's body floated on the surface as a tangle of indistinct lumps. Alex walked with sloshing ankles around the outside of the birthing tub to grab hold of the Other. Alex worked the cloak loose of its cold rubbery corpse, pushing it away. The garment was repulsive. It was wet and heavy and smelled of decay. Only Alex's own pitiful state caused him to overcome his revulsion and slip the garment over his head. It was still faintly warm from the Other.

Far away, as if outside, an animal roared hungrily. Was it getting closer? Was it finding a way in?

Alex slumped in a corner and wrapped his arms around himself , shivering as needles of cold invaded his bumpy skin. His teeth chattered, and his vision came in rocking bursts. He was cold and terrified and hungry. Where was he? What was everything? He knew part of it—a small part—but not enough to make sense of it. The memories of Alex Kirk came rushing like faint, flickering holograms through his bloodstream, the way subway trains went crashing through a lighted station and one could see right through its glass windows. What was glass? What were windows?

How long did he sit there? Probably a day or two. He slept.

The roaring woke him several times. There were animals somewhere nearby—big ones, from their sounds—and something in the way they circled outside (if this was inside, there had to be outside, he could only guess). From something in the way their roars triangulated in on him, he knew they wanted to taste his flesh. He didn't know his name, but he wondered if somehow they might. He called himself Alex but knew he wasn't. He was only a few hours old. Surely even in the wild dumb beasts knew more than he did. But they did not have the meme soup of Alex Kirk rushing along the metro rails of his inner grand central union station where the lights were going on, one by one. Or was he hallucinating at that?

Stiffly, he dragged himself erect. The cloak had dried to a warm dampness by now from his body heat. It smelled faintly of rotting meat. It was roughly square except at one corner, where the Other must have chewed on it in its hunger. Alex wondered if he would be reduced to the same. Remembering fine milled soaps and warm baths and freshly folded linen shirts, he wanted to cast this abomination from him, but he needed it to stay alive.

Alex's eyes adjusted to the dim light.

Glowing things were stuck to the walls. At first he thought they were Art Deco wall sconce lights. When he examined them more closely, he found they were glowing sponges or fungi. They were glowing mushrooms; he recognized their layered shapes. He drew away in disgust. But he lingered a little, fascinated by how his hand glowed in their eerie light. He went from mushroom to mushroom, waving his hand—here yellow, there green, in a few places amber. He wondered if they were edible, and remembered horror stories of poisoning. Never eat wild mushrooms, a voice said in him. Then again, perhaps it would be better to end his life here, now, as it began, before any more pain, any other horrors.

Outside, if that was the right word, somewhere, the beasts roared his name in their language.

The water around his feet fascinated him. It was neither warm nor cold—it was almost exactly human body temperature, and filled with fine, lacy green kelp that resembled stringy spinach. At first he was repulsed, but when he touched the water and sniffed his finger, he found it had a faintly pleasant, clean taste almost like parsley. Yes, somewhere between parsley—and oats. They had oats in their barn in New York... what was he thinking? Heart beating fast with longing, he had a fleeting glimpse of a barn, and a horse with a girl on it—Maryan Shurey at 14, long-limbed, blonde, in jeans and a flowing white shirt, laughing as she waited for him to mount his horse Baldwin—how did he know these things?

His hands hurt where the Other had bitten him, his stomach bled where it had gored him with its teeth and claws, bits of his intestines hung out along with rotting chunks of torn umbilical cords and cheesy cakes of that wart-like mass through which the feeding had gone. At times, he doubled over with pain, holding this squishy pulp that sprawled on his gut like a twenty-pound tumor.

Always, whenever his mind wandered into the past, into his past or someone else's past, he wasn't sure, he heard that powerful throaty roar. The beast was somewhere close by. Its roar was strong enough so he could feel it in his frame. It sounded as if it had its snout to the ground— was there an opening, a door, a way in and a way out? He sensed its terrible and one-track intelligence. It had him and only him on its dog or bear-sized mind.

He was thirsty, so he knelt and drank. If the water wanted to kill him, let it. But it was sweet water, pleasant tasting, with a faint almost anise tinge, just enough to seem astringent without burning. Because of the dim lighting, he could not see well, but now he realized there was a film on the water, a bubbly sludge, that smelled like sweet kelp. The sludge had the same pleasant taste as the water. After a while, when it didn't kill him—in fact, he felt great—he knelt down in the water and ate handfuls. He ate slowly, gingerly, and with increasing gusto. It didn't feel much different from eating watery vegetable soup, or maybe oatmeal, and it filled the stomach.

With his most dire needs met, he explored around his environment more and more. He now realized that he was not yet thinking clearly. For example, did he not hope somehow to find sunlight and fresh air? He was a newborn, and he longed for a mother's touch more than he cared about breaking out of the safety of this dark cocoon.

Perhaps he already sensed the utter hopelessness of his situation, and wanted to avoid confronting the truth.

The caves, as he came to think of them, although he was not sure that was accurate, extended for great distances.

Most puzzling was the fact that he saw no evidence of human artifice. Were all the memories that were unfolding in his head fictions? Had there never been a human race, a Beacham University, an upstate New York?

As his eyes finished developing, and his pupils dilated, he became accustomed to the soft bacterial lighting around him. Taking his cue from bite marks on the mushrooms, he peeled bits of them off the walls to eat. They tasted dry and oaty—not bad at all when washed down with floor water.

Something else he noticed—his wounds were healing incredibly fast. He readily guessed that the water was more than just runoff—it smelled so fresh, it must have antibacterial and other fabulous healing properties.

Alex Kirk—who he was and wasn't—had been a smart young college student—and he was his clone, yes, that was it—but how? And why? And where?

First he explored in the gallery where he had been born. He was depressed and lonely, but he was human, he lived, and therefore he had hope. He could not be the only one like Alex!

But he was disappointed. In the other birthing tanks floated an assortment of creatures like in a medical museum. In one tank floated a dead child the color of chalk, covered in bubbles. In another tank floated a mass of undifferentiated tissue, resembling a large nautilus shell covered by human skin, and in its side the hints of a sleeping face with sightless depressions for eyes. In another tank floated the longitudinal half of a person—alive! Along the tissue-thin wall down its center, healthy blood coursed in the veins, and he could see a heart pumping strongly. Its head, however, had no face, and the brain case was collapsed and anencephalic. Its well-formed arm and leg lay in an attitude of rest, and it had a faint erection. But it would be dead within hours of its birth.

He turned away from these horrors, hoping to find another like him, but the other tanks were dry and empty. The water on the floor was ankle deep, but the marks on the walls indicated it had once been waist-deep—almost up to the rims of the birthing pods. Perhaps it had once filled the entire gallery to the ceiling, and this whole place might have been one giant womb, nurturing dozens of copies of him.

Those clones would have been released from their umbilical cords, would have swum up toward the light, and clambered out on the dry floor of the caves above.

There were caves and caverns, and then more, but they dwindled into darkness and he could only go so far, no farther. He smelled oddly different air wafting his way, some of it smelling of decay, some of it vegetal, some of it almost like fresh air.

As far as he was able to explore before the wall lights and ceiling biolumes waned to nothing, he found that the caves were a disappointment. The ground rose out of the birthing area about ten feet to more galleries—but these were bone dry. He found other birthing areas, all of them dry and dusty, a few with bones in them, others with specks of mummified organic matter that crumbled to the touch. Whatever this was, it was dying. This whole place, this mother organism, was wasting away and he perceived its immense long age with a sense of his own insignificance.

He returned always to his place of birth, to his stone mother, in which now floated the uncorrupted loser of his birthing contest. He'd read once—or, more properly, Alex Kirk had read—of saints whose bodies had been immured and when the tombs were opened decades or centuries later, they were preserved in perfect blush, as if they were still alive. So floated the hideous copy of him, on his back, with streaks of the green healing vegetal matter growing over its skin. Ah, he could see now: the caves were dissolving and absorbing, consuming, the Other's corpse to keep the birthing area antiseptically clean.

As it would eat Alex once he died. How long had this all been going on? Were the caves themselves alive? Tumid possibilities brewed in Alex's unfolding consciousness as he prowled about the confines of his birth. In nine months he'd grown from a seed to a man. Now he was becoming restless in this blind paradise. He felt hormones exploding in his neural network, enzymes foaming over with mindless purposes which, he could guess, had to lead as all things in nature did to procreation, but if he were Adam, where was Eve? There wasn't any, he suspected. He was alone in this universe with its dead or malformed copies of himself, in this cave of nightmares at the forward end of time.

Depressed, he sat on his haunches and whiled the hours away in fantasies of Alex Kirk's past life. He picked at the hard material on the backs of his arms and legs until the surrounding skin bled. For while this place was not only giving him his body and brain, and filling that brain with his memories via some piggyback nanotechnology, the memories were not complete. The synapses had failed in places when the scientists were recording them. Maybe the process of recording in itself destroyed ten percent of the subject matter—so he had a pretty good knowledge of all that he had learned in school, perhaps from specially grown and specific cultures, but his personal life was a frustrating blur. Most of all he wanted to know who his parents were, so that he could claim them for his own, but memory of them seemed to be confined to early childhood. They were large shapes with comforting arms and pleasing voices that made him feel good inside, but he could not make out what they said.

He hoped in time he'd know what they had said to him to make him feel so good inside.

One day he grew angry.

The very air around him seemed charged, as with some hormonal injection. He must get out! It was time to be born from the outer womb, now that he had been born in the inner womb of the tank. He rampaged through the upper galleries, throwing rocks, breaking stalagmites. He ran back down into the birthing gallery—and stopped.

The half-creature was gone. A trail of slime and wet ran up the corridors where it had crawled, propelled by instinct. And the same instinct forced him to follow to where the animals outside roared.

Leaving all that he knew behind, abandoning safety, Alex groped his way along through the darkness, uphill, toward the smell that was so good. He knew it almost before he saw it: Outside. He smelled the green of the trees, heard the low stately back and forth of fresh wind sighing in heavy tree crowns, heard the twittering of so many birds, and smelled the very sap flowing in the branches. He could almost already feel the warmth of the sun as it beamed down on the smooth brown skin of the trees.

He ignored his own fears as he pressed forward. Somewhere out there was Maryan Shurey, and he must get to her.

Sometimes he thought he could hear the half-creature slithering along, pulling itself by one hand, pushing with its leg. Perhaps its half-head was turned toward the light as it followed some plant-like phototropic impulse.

Already, a faint bluish glimmer was visible far ahead. The walls began to glisten with a hard new light. At the same time, Alex began to feel odd little crumbling somethings on the walls as his fingertips crept along ahead...and then the something began to feel more like...veins...He frowned, looking closely. He rubbed his fingers over the uneven stone surface. He felt the relative smoothness of cool stone underneath, but on top he felt strings of sandpapery material.

As he pressed forward, the ground leveled off. He smelled water again. He smelled a tinge of rot and yet a freshness on top, as if the wind were blowing over stagnant water.

Not once yet had he glimpsed a single evidence of human artifice. There was not a shred of evidence that mankind had ever existed. That struck him suddenly, in this unlikely place, at this unexpected moment, as he stood in the first glimmering of contact with the world outside his cave.

The nearby roar of a huge animal startled him out of his thoughts.

3. Daylight

Daylight!

The cave mouth was open, and for the first time he could see the world outside the birth caves.

Alex rounded a corner and stumbled through a wider gallery of caves, then into a blinding blue luminosity. Rubbing his hurting eyes, he glimpsed puffs of laundry-clean white cumulus clouds over the red cliffs opposite. He glimpsed birds, and things that looked like huge yellow and red butterflies.

He had never seen blue sky, sunshine, white clouds, but remembered things like that from Alex Kirk's memories. This must mean some of his memories were valid. If some were valid, then maybe all of them were.

In that same instant, he also reacted with visceral terror to the sight of three animals feasting on the half-man's body.

The animals, *rippers,* were a cross between wild boar and bear, with curling yellowish tusks and vicious little eyes. They had powerful furry dark bodies, with ruffles of hair hanging from the back of each of their four bear-like legs made for climbing and running. Their small oval ears perked up as he came around the corner.

The half-man had dragged itself onto the sand in the middle of a wide gallery, and these rippers were now feasting on its dying body. What had made him so eager to crawl toward the light? Probably the same great urge that was causing Alex to venture here, he figured as he crouched behind a crop of boulders.

Alex glimpsed what the caves were about. The string-like attachments on the walls were the farthest tips of a vast root system extending from a tree-derived life form that had evolved around the cave entrance. More than anything, the life form resembled a huge root system, coiled like a mass of anaconda snakes on the floor, under the ceiling, around the entrance. Situated on leathery brown muscles attached to the inside of the cave itself, as tendons attach to human bone, a large chitinous door plate had slid open to allow animals from outside to come in. There could only be one reason for this, Alex saw even in that single sweeping glimpse: the cave lured animal life into itself, like a giant Venus fly-trap. Perhaps it used the Alexes growing in their tanks as part of the lure. Or perhaps it used the waters lingering in pools just inside the cave entrance to trap animals, drown them, slowly digest them, and let the stench of their rotting carcasses draw in more animals to become the next victims in an endless chain. The half-man had crawled partway through the maze of deep pools (each pool just wider than a man could straddle), when the beasts from outside pounced on it.

Two of the rippers were about the size of grown lions, while the third was smaller—most likely their cub. He saw also dozens of scattered bones and skulls on the ground outside, some whose eye sockets were half buried in loam since years ago.

Just as the rippers spotted him, Alex turned and fled.

One ripper detached itself in a few sparse, frugal motions and darted after him kicking up dust. He just managed to scramble up a wall, onto a ledge, from which he threw sharp rocks. It shied away, snarling and roaring. He struck it on the flank with a sharp stone, and it darted away with a frenzied wail of pain and anger that promised a return bout soon.

His legs trembled. He saw other rocks he could throw, bigger rocks, but he was scared rigid and could only hold on to the ledge around him. The animal joined its partners in a dusty fight over the remains—and then there was a cry of alarm from one of the rippers. He heard the rumble of the door. He heard their exchange of snarls, and the dragging of body parts, while the door slowly closed. It made not quite a rumbling sound, nor a metallic one, as much as the loud grinding of carapace surfaces, of horn on horn, a crunching shut of claws.

With a final thump of the door, he was in complete darkness, and alone—He hoped. It took him a long time to gather the courage to climb down. His knees shook for hours. He hurried back to his birthing gallery, where he sated himself with cleansing green and mushroom fare. He knelt and drank deeply of the water, feeling its comforting and pleasurable coolness on his skin.

Now he understood the precariousness of his situation. There was no barrier to come stop them if they wanted to enter the galleries, only their fear of being trapped if the door closed on them while they were inside. He figured it out slowly: this place had been birthing clones for (how long? Eons?). When it was time to leave the cave, the clones knew instinctively to head for the door that led to life; but which led to death, because from the evidence he'd seen, generations of rippers had grown up feasting on the delicacies released by that door. No wonder they'd been roaring eagerly, probably smelling the blood of his birth!

These animals would be the bane of his existence, the constant companions of every waking and sleeping hour, the ever-energetic predators who dreamt of eating him alive. He called them rippers, not knowing if that had ever been an animal contemporary to Alex Kirk. He was sure the animals he'd just seen had not existed in that form during Alex's time. That in turn suggested that a huge amount of time had gone by—perhaps eons.

He considered the problem from every angle as he trudged back down into the darkness of his birthplace.

First, how long would it be until the door opened again? Would the mountain know when another of him was born? Already, forms were shaping in two birthing pods. It would be weeks, months, something like that, before the next rush of instinct. He must be ready by then. But what did he have? He was naked, and had only the shabby cloak he'd torn from the brother he'd killed. He could throw rocks, but how long before they jumped around him faster than he could throw?

He searched and searched, but there was no high ground to which he could run, where they could not also climb. In the birthing gallery was a ledge high up, not much bigger than his feet. It was the highest point he could find, and also the farthest from the door. In an emergency, he could perch precariously for a while, but he'd grow tired and eventually slip down. His only hope was that the rippers would not venture this deep into the cave system.

He waited patiently, hoping to find at least one more brother like himself growing in the tanks. He would have a friend then, someone to talk to. He would cut his cloak in half and give him the other half. But the dozen or so remaining tanks, surrounded by ankle-deep water, remained empty and silent.

He woke up with a scream and jumped to his feet.

Clean greenish water splashed around him, filling the air with a wholesome oat smell. He felt adrenaline pumping through him. The door was calling! He rushed to their tanks, but those were empty.

He heard the animals roaring before he even smelled them. This time he peeked from a safe distance—sick to his stomach. The rippers had caught a smaller animal, some sort of wild cat, and torn it apart in a gory, bloody mess.

One of the rippers spotted him and came loping in great strides. Its movements reflected the utter confidence and arrogance of a king predator. They probably owned that valley out there. And yet it kept stopping, hesitating. Then, as it heard his running steps, the animal must have forgotten its fears about the door closing. Scenting his terror, it ran after him. He could hear its powerful paws digging into the dust, and its raspy breath getting closer behind him. It panted like a person, almost as if asking to reason with him, but he understood its deadly intentions.

The birthing gallery was no sanctuary anymore.

Alex's heart pounded, and he tasted the bitterness of adrenalin and fear as he climbed on the edge of a tank and from there to the ledge above.

The ripper entered the room, its magnificent tail switching, and its head scenting left and right. Then its yellowish eyes spotted him and it snarled.

Alex slipped, releasing a small cloud of debris, and the ripper backed away hissing. Its hackles stood up.

Alex recovered at the last moment, and pulled himself up.

The ripper was cunning. Already it patrolled in circles on the edge of the tank he'd jumped from. It snarled at him and seemed to be gauging a jump.

He looked up and spotted a tree root growing out of the ceiling. Any moment now the animal would come flying. It probably weighed 250 pounds, and could knock him from his perch with one paw. Then he'd be gone.

He bent both knees and leapt, stretching one arm as far as he could. It was his only chance.

At the same moment, the ripper leapt.

He grasped the tree root and pulled himself up with both hands.

At the same moment, he felt the rush of air under him. He felt the hot, wet breath on his calves. He heard the click as a set of claws missed him and struck the wall, then a scratching sound as the animal slid down, and finally a splash as it landed in the water.

The ripper roared in fury and jumped back on the edge of the tank.

At that moment he felt the root above him sag and then give. He felt a fine trickle of sand on his face that turned into a torrent of small rocks and then medium rocks and finally boulders. He heard a brief scream below, then silence. When the root first gave, it swung him face-first against the rock face. There he clung more afraid of the ripper below than he should have been of the avalanche coming down from above.

A few more rocks shifted and then it got quiet.

He coughed in the chocking dust. He hung on blindly until his hands could not grip any longer. Then he dropped—a mere foot onto the dry yellow clay and gray sedimentary rocks piled under him.

The sky above him was visible through a thick fog of dust. Blue! And golden sunlight! He held his hands over his eyes to shield them until they could adjust to the blinding light.

As the dust began to drift away, he saw that the entire gallery was choked with rubble. No clone would ever be born here again. The delicate balance of water and herbs and mushrooms and hormones that had evolved over the eons had just received its death wound. He imagined the door, with its muscles, would die soon too.

The ripper lay pinned on its back, only its face showing. It was still alive, whimpering feebly. It looked at him through a cloud of pain, moving its tusks back and forth as if still trying to gore him. He picked up a boulder the size of a bowling ball and walked over to it. It whimpered in fear as it saw his intentions. He smashed its skull in and it died there before him. This would be the tenor of his relationship with the rippers.

There were more of them abroad, and they had his scent, so it would be only a matter of a short time before another came looking for him. They'd be extra hungry now that their food supply had run out.

Bathed in cold blue daylight and no longer sheltered from the world, he looked up toward the sunlight. He would be fighting for his life time and again. He started climbing up the rocks to his new world.

For a moment, before the next ripper attacked, Alex forgot his fear and his pain and his hunger and stood in awe of the natural world.

It was the first time in his life that he could feel the air on his skin, smell the trees and flowers, hear the snap of a bird's wing above. The reality was far better than he'd imagined from the memories he'd inherited from Alex. For the first time, he understood the urgent love and wonder of being alive.

He turned and was able to get a quick overview of his world. He was on a hill about 100 feet high and lightly covered with pine trees and scrub bushes. Behind him loomed a cliff of sorts, with more pine trees on top, about 300 feet high. Down below, he could see the two surviving rippers tearing apart the prizes that would be their last. Directly opposite—across a valley of tall deciduous trees with a river flowing through the middle—was another cliff, and beyond that lay a forest. The river came from a low mountain range to the right, and flowed out into an emptiness on his left in which shone a silver thread, which he made out to be an ocean horizon.

The river that flowed through the valley was about 60 feet across and looked a cold, choppy green—ice melt, he figured—flowing fast. On either side were sandbars, and on these lolled a pride of rippers with their young—He spotted ten animals before losing count. And running out of time.

One of the rippers below had spotted him. It dashed out of sight, probably around the bottom of his hill, and he could hear its rapid thrashing motions in the brush.

He ran in the only direction he could think of—toward the tall cliff. He ran across some logs and thick layers of dead brush that covered a fault about 50 feet deep. He ran desperately along a narrow ledge around the cliff. He saw now that it was a pillar of sandstone, like a natural tower, that had separated from a long stretch of cliff.

Just then the ripper came bounding into view, magnificent-looking with its powerful paws and flying leg manes.

He looked desperately about—He could go down or he could go up.

In his downward glance, he saw forest below, with jagged boulders sticking up on which he would impale himself if he fell on them. Around the edges of this cliff standing up like a tall finger from the forest, he saw the sandy beach, and beyond that the crashing white foam of sea water torn up by rocks away from the shore.

Looking up, he saw what looked like a small patch of trees on a plateau, blindingly x-rayed by sunlight so that it looked as if the light were a dazzling white liquid amid which the trees looked like black sticks and the leaves themselves appeared to be afire without burning up.

The ripper ran across the bridge of logs and brush—and started to crash through. For several moments it hung precariously by its front hocks and claws, straining its neck to pull its dangling lower half up.

Alex spotted a set of serrations in the cliff and began climbing.

The ripper crawled laboriously onto a log and inched carefully after him. He climbed, feeling the wind blow through his rough leather garment. The animal stood on the ledge below him and bellowed. He could almost feel its breath on his heels. It was afraid to jump, for fear of falling the 50-60 feet into the jumbled rocks below.

He kept climbing, until he reached a larger ledge that tilted sharply upward to his right. Careful not to slip on loose sand, which would land him in the animal's mouth, he continued upward until he found himself on an undulating green plateau. His position relative to the sun had changed, and the sun in fact seemed to have moved in the sky. There was a semicircle of tall, thin trees around the back edge of the plateau, and their crowns were still bright green with sunlight. He glimpsed the vast expanse of bluish-gray sea over the opposite edge.

He looked down and saw the cat prowling along the ledge, looking for a way up. As luck would have it, he didn't think there was. But up here, there were about 30 feet separating the edge of the plateau from the range of hills, opposite, from which it had separated. Several fallen logs spanned the chasm (which was hundreds of feet deep). He was able to run from one to the other, throwing several smaller ones to one side until, with a screech of wood, they tumbled end over end and crashed on the boulders far below.

The ripper slipped away, looking for another way up to make a meal of him. He was down to two logs spanning the divide. One was about a foot in diameter, but rotten and light enough to move. He labored on that one until he had almost no strength left. The root end was on his side, so he dug furiously with his hands. He kept looking up afraid to see one of the rippers running toward him on the opposite hillside—not yet!

He felt the soil yield and was almost pulled down with it as the tree emitted a loud cracking noise and went down into the chasm with a load of soil and rocks.

The other tree was bigger, but what he had on this end were the tips of its crown. He rocked up and down, testing—and found the tree had been dead for some time. It was rotten in places, but still fairly formidable. No way could he budge this monster.

As he had feared, the ripper stood on the opposite edge, sniffing at him and challenging him with snarls.

He stepped out onto the one big member that hooked over his rim and began jumping up and down.

The ripper started to cross at the other end and stopped, backing away.

He kept jumping, and a major branch thrusting into the hillside made a cracking sound. There was hope! He must not stop rocking, or the ripper would be upon him.

The tree cracked again, and brown chips rained down from its trunk.

The ripper was starting out across the log again. It moved silently, hissing at him, its yellow eyes greedy, and its claws digging into the sides of the log while it kept its belly low.

The log gave a mighty crack and started to move. He heard soil beginning to rain amid a clatter of stones. He ran and just barely caught hold of some bushes to pull himself up. The tree crashed down about twenty feet and then stopped, jammed against the rock face below him. He must move it another dozen feet, and then there would be no more bridges for the beasts to cross.

On the other side, the ripper had retreated back to the rim and was looking for its next opportunity to cross on that remaining log that partially spanned the divide. Alex was exhausted, but he was so close to safety—he must not quit moving. He pushed several boulders over the edge until one crashed into the tree crown, and with loud cracking noises the tree renewed its final descent. The boulder plummeted down, twirling, while the tree swung down toward the other side. As the tree did so, it leveraged its root ball out of the earth. The ripper let out a yelp and tore away as the tree's bottom bounced out of its hole, pivoted on the rim, and then fell sideways into the forest below.

As daylight began to fade, Alex made a feverish run around the edge of his new domain. Huge butterflies flapped languidly around him as if mocking him. Their tiny bat-faces with inscrutable, their eyes like large, luminous buttons. They seemed wise enough to stay out of reach.

It appeared this tower of stone had long ago separated from the cliff face, tilting toward the sea. It had sheer reddish sandstone facings on all sides, and it did not appear there was a path anywhere for the predators to climb up. The area was about the size of a football field, tilting higher at its forested end, and undulating down in grassy hillocks toward the sea end.

Never mind he might not be able to find a way down, for he would have to live here, to feed himself, to hunt and fish. For the moment, as evening approached, Alex was safe from the rippers—but for how long? He was beginning to hunger, but even more, he needed to sleep. Dreading what else might live up here, he found a large, fallen tree and dug himself a depression between its roots. He laid leafy branches across the roots, which acted as ceiling struts. He surrounded himself with dry, rustling leaves and promptly fell into an exhausted sleep full of fearful dreams. He kept seeing those four-inch incisor teeth aimed at him from hissing mouths. And then, too, he dreamed of a luscious blonde named Maryan Shurey who rode by on a horse, smiling...

She wore a baseball cap and a light blue sweater, same color as her eyes. Alex Kirk had been in love with her.

During the night, the horror of his situation sank in as Alex lay huddled and shivering in his earthy hole.

He had sunk to the lowest level imaginable—by comparison, his stay in the birthing caves had been paradise. Here he had nothing but the stiff, cold hide he wore, which chafed his skin raw and at times actually made him colder. He was about to die from loss of body heat.

His misery enveloped him in layers. He was starving and his stomach was in constant pain as its acids began digesting the stomach itself. More immediately, he was about to die from loss of body heat. He shivered through the night, convinced that he was losing so much body heat that he would not awaken in the morning. As the ambient temperature dropped toward the dew point, moisture formed in the leaves around him. His protective shield of radiated body heat shrank perilously close to the skin. Soon his feet and ankles were stiff and numb.

All the while, he kept getting flashes of his long-ago Alex Kirk memory, in some impossibly wonderful paradise in upstate New York, where the lovely Maryan Shurey rode by on a horse and smiled at him while he sat on his porch drinking lemonade and waving. Had such a world ever existed? There was not a shred of evidence anywhere today, but the thought of finding his way back to that world offered the only glimmer of hope in this lost existence into which he had fallen.

He discovered he had company in his burrow. Lines of ants kept crossing his torso, and he kept crushing them when he felt their hundreds of tiny legs tickling and burning.

Something slithered past, hunting, and stopped. A forked tongue probing sent airwaves around him as the snake dispassionately examined what he was. If it were poisonous, he prayed that it would take him quickly. But it slithered on, perhaps seeking something smaller that it could wrap its mouth around and swallow down the corridor of its body.

Something large emerged to his right and plopped onto his face. Instinctively he reached up—and found a beetle almost as big as the palm of his hand. For a second its hard, armored feet started to hook into his skin. He screamed and tore it off his face in rage and fear and anguish as he crushed it in his palm. Instinctively, he pressed the shattered, still twitching carapace to his mouth and sucked out the eggy-tasting slime inside. He threw the empty shell away into the night.

Strangely, that calmed him. He could feel the lump of matter moving down his esophagus and into his stomach, which calmed down as it began to digest. He chewed on dry grass—*hay*, he thought, *like cows eat*—in the hope of adding some bulk. He crawled through the brush and licked dew off large curling leaves on the ground around his lair.

Then he burrowed deep and fell asleep.

A roaring sound woke him in the morning. He sat up, startled, throwing leaves in all directions.

It sounded as if it came from ten feet away, and made his hair stand on end. Was this his last moment alive?

There, across the canyon, stood a mother ripper and two cubs. She projected those loud roars with such power that he thought he could already feel her licking his crumpled corpse before those 4-inch incisors tore him apart.

He hid from them, terrified. Meanwhile, the warm yellow sun burned down on his limbs, and he soon exercised the stiffness out of them.

Then came his defining moment.

Angered at his helplessness and the animals' predatory selfishness, he decided to begin educating the rippers. He was not just going to die—he was going to fight back. He was going to take charge of his world or die trying! Let them feel some respect for him. He gathered a handful of rocks—round ones that would not curve in the air during flight—the size of large marbles. He could throw them easily, with the coordination and skills he had inherited from Alex Kirk. He could aim them, for Alex had been a good athlete, especially in college at Beacham University.

The first shot missed, but startled the ripper, who jerked her head up and took a half step back. Then she glared at him as if outraged at his daring. The next one clipped one of her cubs, which ran off wailing. She watched it go and then stood with her side to him, growling at him. He could see the fine lines of her ribs under that shiny, well-fed brown fur. He could see her sides compressing and decompressing with every breath she took. The next shot clipped her in the ribs, and she sidled away. She thrashed a bit, alternately licking her side and roaring and spitting defiance at him. He let go another shot, which went wide. His arm was getting tired. When he bent to pick up another rock, she abruptly rose, nudged the second cub, and off they went. Had she learned not to come roaring at Alex? Maybe she would come silently next time. At least she had that much respect for him now, that she would sneak up rather than bully him with roaring.

From the look of the sky, the weather was going to be nice for a while—but he could not bear the thought of going through another night like last night.

He must provide for several things: he must be warm and dry. He must have food and water. He must make a complete exploration of his little niche here atop the valley.

It took just a little while to walk one exploratory circuit around the edge. The cliff dropped off sharply on all sides, and he began to feel hopeful that he was safe here. Every so often he would hear a snort or a roar, or a crashing among bushes very close, and that told him his enemies were relentlessly working to catch him, as if it were some birthright of theirs—not entirely incorrect, as he was later to learn. They sounded hungry and annoyed by now. Sometimes he would see their dark forms gliding through the shadows below. Once he looked down and, unexpectedly, saw one looking up at him, its paws as high up against the crumbling sandstone as it could reach when standing fully erect on its hind legs. He was too shocked to react. It looked up at him expectantly, wondering if he would come down to it. He was so surprised he nearly fell. He threw a melon-size boulder down, but it twisted out of the way with plenty of time and then bounded away. He missed with two other small boulders.

Alex began to think of the cliff top as his sky island or fortress.

The cliff top was a rectangle about 500 feet on its long sides (including the edge overlooking the sea) and 200 feet across the beaches it overlooked on the two shorter sides. Though it was a tower tilting away from a ridge of hills, its top gently sloped down on its seaward side, lower by about 50 feet from its landward side.

From the movement of the sun (shining from the south, and apparently moving east to west, Alex figured out that the sea was south of him.

The north side overlooked the rift below, full of trees and bushes and ferns, in which the rippers prowled. Beyond that lay a wall of brownish-red cliffs topped by the same sparse woods as his tower. He could plainly see the hole in the top of the cave system, and the overturned tree whose torn roots waved at the sky. As he climbed up here to explore, he spied the fearful face of a ripper looking hungrily his way. Alex and the animal looked at each other across a distance of less than 100 feet, and he could read the merciless calculations in its bright eyes and hear the flick of its tail amid sun-dappled ferns.

To the east and west was a sheer drop of about 300 feet into impenetrable deciduous forest and sandy beach front.

There was a high spot on his island in the sky, about fifty feet higher than the rest of the little plateau. Up here were one or two trees and a mass of lush ferns populated by butterflies. From here, he could see over the ridge opposite. He looked past the hole in the ground where the tree lay, exposing the caves below. He looked beyond the ridge and saw a valley about a mile wide basking in late sunshine. He could see another wall of reddish cliffs glowing beyond. As best he could tell, the cliffs enclosed an alluvial plain, for he saw a waterfall pouring from the hills in a mass of foam, throwing out a small rainbow. He cupped his hands and stared through them, wishing he had binoculars (another memory from Alex). Through dense forest, he spied a series of small cascades dropping down the stepped sides of a 1,000-foot high mountain. He could only catch glimpses of silvery water from his vantage point, but to the southwest he saw evidence of a strong current emptying into the ocean, so he guessed that a river flowed through the valley.

There was no source of fresh running water. The largest four or so boulders were weathered on top, however, and he found small puddles of condensed water there. Alex Kirk had been a Boy Scout, and he immediately began to think of schemes for building a solar still. With no materials like plastic or metal, however, that might prove very difficult.

The central part of his cliff was a slope covered with grass and flowers—in some areas high grass full of dandelions, their wispy gray balls shedding flyers into the fresh wind. In some areas, small carpets of yellow and red flowers covered the ground. There were a few large boulders, but other than that, there were no surprises in the topography. Birds and butterflies abounded. There was a clean, healthy silence except for the rustle of wind in his ears.

Climbing down, he was reasonably satisfied that it would be hard, if not impossible, for the rippers to climb up the sheer cliff to get him, though he realized they were resourceful and relentless, and all it would take was one success on their part to spell the end of him. Every waking moment, every sleeping nightmare, he would live in constant fear that he was about to have his neck torn open in an attack from behind. Trembling and feeling puny, he picked up a stout stick as he crossed back to the ocean-side of his fortress.

He stood overlooking a spectacular vista of the sea that stretched to the horizon. There was a beach about 250 feet below—flat, just as he remembered beaches from Alex's time. To the east, flat beach sand gave way to dark marshy soil, and in the marshes he saw grazing cattle sort of like small buffalo—they had very small manes and not the huge hump that buffalo and bison had had. He stared as hard as he could, and determined that some had udders, which meant milk. But they were a long way off, and he would probably die getting there, for his friends the rippers were never far away.

On rocks offshore, he saw gatherings of sea birds and otters sunning themselves, and he envied the otters their shiny coats and fat sides. They appeared well-provisioned, while his stomach continuously rumbled with fear and hunger. He watched an otter slid down into the sea with a splash and emerge a minute later with a fish. Clearly, there was fishing to be done—and somehow he must overcome his dread of the rippers to get at that rich source of food.

He had not yet discovered a single shred of evidence that mankind had ever existed. He stood in the afternoon heat, which bathed him with a delightful pinkish-yellow glow, and he leaned on a long, sturdy stick, surveying the world. He remembered that book—a childhood favorite of Alex Kirk—titled *Robinson Crusoe*. He remembered a picture of Robinson: a bearded man dressed in furs, with a parrot on his shoulder, a pipe in his mouth, and a musket over his shoulder. He had several muzzle-loading pistols in his belt, and a coconut canteen of water. How silly that all seemed, he thought, reflecting on his own situation. Robinson Crusoe had had a shipwreck to which he swam and brought back raftsful of gunpowder, food, supplies, even a Bible, until the ship was washed away in another storm.

Alex had no ship, no gunpowder, nothing. He would have given anything to have an axe or a knife.

He must make everything from scratch, and hope to remain safe from the rippers long enough to succeed.

There was also the lurking question: *why bother?* If there were no other humans in this world, then why not just throw himself off the cliff, or let the rippers finish him off? Surely he was the loneliest human being who had ever lived, isolated in time eons after the last of his kind had perished, if they had ever existed. He suffered not only from fear and hunger. He suffered from a terrible, incurable loneliness. He had no hope of rescue, for there was nobody to rescue him. The last of his kind had died a million years ago—so his instincts told him, and he accepted their wisdom. If he could find a shred of evidence that the world in his head had ever existed, he'd be at least a slightly happier man—anything; some small artifact like a spoon, a piece of glass, a shred of paper, a fragment of a wall; anything at all. But there wasn't even that.

He drank judiciously from his meager water supply. He had found several sheets of broken slate with suitably smooth faces, and stood them up on edge in the niche. During the day, warm moist air would drift in from over the sea. When it brushed against the cool slate, its temperature would drop, and the moisture in the air touching the slate would run off, dripping into the trough. This way, he might collect as much as a quart on a good day. Leaning in to carefully slurp a few mouthfuls without draining all of it at once, he smelled earth and watched spiders dancing around his head. Now he had a source of drinking water.

On his cliff there were several kinds of birds, ranging from those that fluttered in the tree tops to a kind of wild hen that strutted about. He are wild berries, and chewed small wads of wild wheat. He looked carefully for plants whose roots might be edible.

Keeping his stomach full with whatever edible bits he could find, he built a shelter for himself out of fallen tree limbs.

He propped these up, as many as he could find, against the largest of his rocks, which stood head-high to him. He found also in the forest two kinds of covering that he could lay upon his lean-to. He found sheets of damp leaves that had decayed into crumbly layers and then dried out, which he laid over his dwelling. He was well aware that one good rain could wipe out his work and leave him soaked and chill—somehow, he would overcome that problem also. He found a wonderful kind of moss in the forest—sheets of it, hanging from tree limbs—just not very much of it, though he glimpsed huge harvests of it across the chasm where he'd struck the ripper cub with his rock. Soon, he thought, he would outgrow the resources of this island of safety and would have to venture out as Robinson Crusoe had—just not with a musket, but maybe he could fashion other weapons. He spied the cattle again and thought—the Native Americans had fashioned their lives around the buffalo—what if he could do the same with those animals?

He now had a semicircular shelter, three or four layers of limbs and twigs thick. Into its crevices he packed leaves, soil, and moss. He laid as many flat stones as he could over the top, and between those fine stones, without taxing the roof too much. He covered this with palm fronds and broad leaves to prevent rain from gouging the roof apart in minutes. He made two rows of large rocks, one on each side, to prevent the flow of rainwater around the front of the boulder. He left a small opening along one side of the boulder, just enough to wiggle in and out.

Now he had a shelter. It was getting late in the day, and with the light gone, and just a dim sliver of the moon visible, he would soon be unable to function. Fortunately, it was near summer, and the daylight shone longer than the hours of night. The weather was mild, though a tall white wall of puffy cumulus moving in from the sea did worry him a bit. He wasn't sure the roof of his abode would survive an intense rain. He would have to continue building and reinforcing.

He found three more of the huge beetles, which he cracked open and sucked empty after flicking away the detritus of their digestive organs.

So, as dark fell on his first full day, he filled his shelter to the brim with dry leaves. He was pleased at the small progress he'd made. But he dreaded the night ahead. And he was not disappointed in his fears, for he suffered for hours with the cold, shivering violently, at some moments wishing he could just die.

The next day was overcast and chilly, and he had little incentive to go exploring.

Luckily, there were only short periods of slight drizzle, and during those he stayed in his shelter. He patched a few leaky spots, but overall the shelter was dry. He realized by now that he must get down to those cattle and make a hide for himself, or he would die here from hypothermia next time it really rained.

He was pleasantly surprised that his primitive water-still yet seemed to be working. When he inspected the bits of slate he had stood on edge in his water puddle, he found that the puddle was nearly overflowing.

The wind from the sea, moving past the slightly angled rock, had cooled it sharply, making the plentiful moisture in the night air condense on the surface and flow into the puddle. He drank deeply, savoring this small victory. He came to treasure the beetles as a delicacy, and between them and dry grass, he managed to keep his stomach, if not full, then at least from pain. He tracked down a nesting spot of his flightless birds. They laid their eggs in the thatch between groups of coarsely separated fist-sized rocks on the eastern edge of the clearing. He managed to grab one egg and run before the violently squawking chicken chased him halfway across the hill. This wouldn't do, of course. He'd have to figure out some way to mine that resource without driving its providers off, or depleting it. He resolved to limit himself to one egg a day, which he slurped with great satisfaction after punching a small hole in the egg. The yolk went down intact in a mass, leaving him to savor the slick egg white. He took the broken eggshell and laid it back where he had found it. His theory, which proved correct, was that the chickens (except perhaps the one who had chased Alex) would think those were eggs that had hatched, and therefore this was a great nesting spot. No matter that the eggshells smelled of predator (me)—plenty of nests were invaded after the hatching and inspected too late.

By and large, he ignored the big butterflies, and they ignored him, forming as innocuous a backdrop as the trees and the cliffs. At night the things he called moths came out, and once or twice he awakened to swat at one feeding on his blood, but they came out mainly at night, and kept to sea level where they had evolved.

Even as he kept exploring this new world, he kept having those dark dreams of the old. He kept reliving certain moments from that other man's lifetime, particularly that haunting nocturnal scene in the gloomy bedroom: *curtains blowing in the breeze, TV flickering, Maryan sleeping nude beside him, and the night sounds of a city wafting in: a car horn, a shout, distant music, and more wind...*

Soon, he thought, he must begin to venture off this rock.

Also, he must have fire. In anticipation of whatever tiny spark he managed to make, he created the means to capture it. On a boulder that had no water puddles, he placed three stones the size of his head. Over this he placed the largest flat rock he could find. This would be the most important spot in his world—its Los Alamos, where he would harness fire.

Under this primitive rain shelter, he built a small chamber out of pieces of slate that he stood upright and topped off with another piece of slate. He kept one upright aside as a little door. There would be plenty of draft through there, but in a high wind he could block it somewhat. He must maintain a steady flow of air without letting his tinder burn itself out. He collected straw and bits of dry wood. He was overjoyed to find a huge tree that had been clipped by lightning and was full of charcoal. If he could create a fire, he thought, he could also create more charcoal. It would be a primitive variety, not the refined product of an industrial kiln, but it would burn reasonably well if dry. The driest place on the cliff was in his shelter, so he took an armload of charcoal there.

It took him hours of sitting patiently, clicking rocks together, rubbing wood until it was hot enough to sting his fingers. His back ached, and his arms and hands were raw. He also had several disappointments, where he got a little smoke, but in his anxiety his breath blew the fire out instead of creating a flame.

By the end of the second day, he had created a small bow, using a strip of hide from his coat, and a foot-long sapling. He found a straight stick about a foot long, whose end he rubbed into a point. He twisted it into his bow and placed the point of the stick into a depression in a tree log. He surrounded this with the finest tinder, including an abandoned bird's nest. Then, steadying the stick in a fold of his coat, he ran the bow back and forth for a long time until smoke began to puff up. He blew into the tinder gently, and whooped when tender little tongues of yellowish fire curled up. Quickly he added more tinder, then coarser tinder, until he had a dry limb whose end was aflame. This he took to his little chamber on the rock, and lit the charcoal within. He had to douse the fire in the log with sand, so that the whole cliff would not go up in flames. Now he had his fire! With the bow and stick, he could make fire as often as he needed.

Now he'd begin cooking. He built a campfire not far from his shelter, in a depression surrounded by round rocks. Here he laid by a heap of dry wood and got a regular fire going. He found two Y-shaped sticks and sank them into the ground on either side of the fire, and across this he laid a long, straight stick: his spit!

He made himself a spear from a small, green sapling that he cut down using a sharp rock. He rubbed its point sharp, and then hardened it in the fire. Now he went hunting for a chicken. The matter was done quickly, and it was a bit gruesome, but it was necessary for his survival. Having speared a chicken, and finished it off with a rock, he carried it back to his campsite. He plucked all the feathers off (a tedious job). He cut it open and carefully removed the organs associated with waste, to avoid poisoning the whole innards. He was so hungry that he did nothing more to prepare the bird. He stuck the spit through it and roasted it over the fire. After an hour or so, during which he sat in great anticipation, and during which fat dripped down into the fire and rose in sparks, leaving a greasy smell in the air, he was ready—and he was not disappointed. This was the first meat he'd ever eaten, and he gorged himself. He knew he could not store the excess, and that poultry could become poisonous quickly, so he ate until he threw up. His stomach was not yet producing the enzymes required to digest meat, and it would not accept any more for now. Yet he felt good after drinking some water, and surely some of the meat stayed down. Also, from the way the fat burned, he knew he had another source of fuel.

He was pleased with his progress. Now he had fire, and meat, and water, and he was dry—but never warm enough. He was afraid to build a fire in the shelter, lest it asphyxiate him. He was surprised, however, how much longer he stayed dry when he went to sleep with a full stomach. Early mornings, before dawn, were still the worst—He huddled and shivered desperately for several hours until the sun came out to warm him.

Then came the rainy day he'd been dreading. He sat in his shelter, dodging one leak after another, but the main mass of it held, or he would have died from cold. He shivered all day long, and the night was so terrible that he got up in the dark and hobbled about in order to burn some energy. He waited, minute by painful minute, until at long last the sun, taking its time, laid a gray line across the horizon, and then its yellow ball rose, and he just kept walking in circles, mumbling hysterically and shivering, until its warmth began to bring his temperature up. This had only been a mild foretaste. Autumn and winter were yet to come, and he had no idea what the weather would be like at this latitude in this epoch. Life was not worth living this way. He must foray out to do battle with the world. He must learn somehow to work around the rippers and whatever other enemies he might have.

Immediately he set to work, building his arsenal.

Arsenals alone did not win wars—one needed intelligence.

So, as he planned and built and tested his weapons, he sat first here, then there, whittling, twirling, blackening, licking a hardened wooden tip, and all the while observing his environment—including the enemies that inhabited this world.

He made a large bow, using another strip of his garment as the gut string. He made himself ten arrows, each two feet long, whose tips he hardened with fire. He made himself a stone mallet by placing an elongated rock on a short, thick stick and tying it tightly with yet another strip of his garment. He found a bit of granitic rock that he chipped until he wound up with a knife about six inches long with a sharp piercing-tip and one reasonably sharp cutting edge.

He noticed that, busy as he was, the rippers were not paying much attention to him the past day or two. Frequently, taking a break, he'd wander up to what he called the north tower on his cliff and look out over the valley. He studied the rippers' habits and, since he himself had become something of a gruesome predator, he could almost admire their successful rulership of a much larger domain than his own. There seemed to be a pack of about six rippers. At least once a day, he watched the rippers parade on the beach below. He noticed that the buffalo or cattle would edge out into the sea, and the rippers would not follow them. One time, they captured a calf in the shallow surf near the saltwater marshes where the cattle congregated, knee-deep and chewing while looking watchfully about. Two big rippers held the calf down with their massive paws and teeth, and then dragged the carcass out onto the sand so the smaller four could participate in devouring it. Unlike certain large cats and bears of his own time, these beasts did not seem to like being in deep water. Or maybe they disliked salt water. In any case, the otters and birds further out paid no attention, indicating they had never experienced a ripper attack. Alex had been an excellent salt water swimmer, and he reasoned that, if necessary, he could run into the water and swim up the beach.

He saw them on the beach one other time, hunting buffalo. Three big adults had walked in magnificent aloofness, every muscle rippling with self assurance, their very gait a kind of music. They stampeded the cattle and then brought one down by snapping at its hind legs to tear the sinew and then, when the animal stood lowing in pain, finishing it by taking its neck in a vise-like jaw grip and twisting. They took turns doing this until finally, the bull weakened and rolled over. Within seconds they had torn its belly area open and were tearing out huge yellow and red masses. The three cubs slipped in join them. Within a short time, they wandered back to their valley, carrying bloody chunks of meat in their mouths for a later snack. The carcass lay in the sand until the tide got hold of it.

To get down to the beach safely, without sacrificing the security of his cliff top, and to allow himself a swift return if need be, he built himself a primitive drawbridge. He made a kind of ladder of two fifteen-foot long, four-inch diameter specially cut saplings. He cut about twenty foot-long sticks, each an inch in diameter, which he lashed onto the saplings as steps with the last strips of his coat. He was now naked and by God had better get a piece of the dead bull's hide. He was risking everything in a gamble because it was better to try this than not. He worked on this ladder it until it was perfectly smooth, in part, because his life depended on it, and because he was stalling—his courage kept giving out on him, and he would rub at it endlessly with round, flat stone with a rough face.

When the time for his expedition came, he left the mallet behind. He made a belt for himself of leather, which he tied in the front. From this hung his bow and arrows, neatly tied down, and his knife.

Finally, he went to check his intelligence. From the north tower, he could count all six rippers lying in the sun on a sandbank by the swiftly flowing river a half mile away in the alluvial plain. They looked as if they had eaten well, for they were lazily licking themselves and did not seem to have a care in the world. Perhaps, he thought, they were the top of the food chain and did not have a predator more deadly than themselves to worry about. If there were more of Alex, he could change that for them, but that would never happen.

He was the only one of his kind alive.

Making sure that his weapons were well secured, he placed his ladder so that one end rested firmly on a rock two or three feet above a ledge in the cliff edge and the other rested on the nearest bread loaf of dark, mossy rock covered with white bird droppings.

He was lithe, and thin, and in good condition. This first gap was the riskiest, because if he slipped he'd fall to his death. Luckily Alex Kirk had never experienced any fear of heights, so he should not either. He climbed down on the ledge and tested the ladder. It was firm, with very little bounce, and slightly declined at an angle toward the first bread loaf. He swung himself down so he hung high over the beach, then hand over hand lowered himself to the first rock. He landed feet first. Never looking back, he spanned the next two gaps, which were smaller and lower, by walking on the ladder until he stood on the beach. He left the ladder between the lowest of the rocks and swept his bow and one arrow into the ready. In this posture, he ran as fast as he could across the beach to where he'd seen the carcass wash in the tide.

No sign of any ambling rippers on the beach.

His heart aflutter with fear, he raced through the sand until he came to the water. The buffalo were a few hundred feet east of him and lowing in mild alarm, but not prepared to give up their greens for a panicked run.

He smelled dead decaying meat and wrinkled his nose, but must push on. He left his weapons, except for the knife, on the dry sand so the gut string wouldn't get wet. Splashing into the water for a look, he beheld the most amazing sight in the glass-green water that glowed with captured sunlight.

The carcass floated in about six feet of water. It was surrounded on all sides by silvery fish that nibbled at its contents. There must be hundreds, ranging from tiny ones in schools to fish easily as heavy and as big as I. He knew that if there were sharks about, these fish would run for it, but he studied the lay carefully. Looking nervously up the beach, he took out his stone knife, dove down, and joined in the frenzy. He was after the hide, pure and simple. As he dove down repeatedly, working hard on the skin to sever it from the meat, he opened more opportunities for the fish to feed. They swarmed unabashedly under his arms, brushing against his ribs, and bouncing repeated on and off any spot where there was a bite to chew off.

The hide wasn't quite dry yet, but it had been picked quite clean. He scared a flock of birds off as he rolled the hide up. The salt water had stiffened it and perhaps ruined it to some extent but he figured—live and learn.

He carried the hide on his shoulders like a carpet as he ran back to the boulders. Up he went, throwing the hide ahead of him, and ran to safety. He pulled the ladder up and finished his climb up, which went without incident.

Once at the top, he spread his prize out and gloated over it. There were a few gouges where beaks had gone through, and it was a bit stiff, but he had a wonderful blanket to wrap around himself tonight.

He needed more hides.

Soon after, as he was crossing the beach, he could only think about that second hide he wanted very badly.

He had his big bow, ten big arrows, and a stone knife. He wore only a leather loincloth so that he could move unencumbered.

He had planned his day's work very carefully.

He jogged down to the cattle, and predictably they stampeded a bit. A few ran into the water, and that was where he shot a medium size bull. He was still a bit leery of his predatory lifestyle—Alex Kirk had disliked hunting, saying he'd only do it for survival—and he would rather choose to kill a male than a possible mother with young who would be left behind.

The bull took his arrow through the neck and stood lowing in pain, stunned. He put another arrow through his neck, hoping to sever arteries, but the animal just turned to face him and put its horns down as if to attack. Then he saw the poor beast was staggering. He ran close and put another arrow into him from underneath, as close as he could to where he guessed his heart must be. The bull toppled over and he danced out of the way.

Still no sign of the rippers.

Alex emerged from the water with this incredibly wet, heavy square of hide. He managed to drag it onto the dry sand above the tide line, fleshy side up, and decided to leave it to the sun and to carrion seekers to clean it for him. He was tired, and it was too heavy just now. Heavy arrow at ready, he sprinted again across the sand. All the while he heard his ragged, panicked breathing as he felt the sand sucking in every footstep, slowing him down. He stumbled over a sharp rock and cried out in pain but kept going. He looked more carefully where he was going— he'd be dead if he stumbled and sprained an ankle. He hopped up to the first rock, raced across his ladder, and pulled the ladder up for the next hop. Already, he was out of reach of any potential rippers. Slowly and carefully, he made his way back up the rocks, one by one. The biggest rock loaf had a surface about ten feet by six feet. He could rest there a few moments and look back. The hide lay on the beach, covered by birds that pecked it clean for him. Some of the birds had sharp beaks for poking open shells—He hoped they wouldn't damage the hide too much. He was already daydreaming about the things he could do with that hide, from fancying up his water still, to dressing more warmly.

He decided to walk back to the cliff. Halfway across, he slipped and fell. He managed to grasp the ladder and hold on. The ladder turned once, but then stabilized. Then the rung he was holding came loose. As he struggled in midair, he smelled ripper. Horrified, as he twirled in space, he saw their tusks and their tiny eyes just a few feet below him. They must have been watching the whole time, waiting for him to make a mistake. Now it looked as if they had him. He could see the cold determination and triumphant hunger in their eyes. He could see the wetness in their pink snouts as they salivated for a taste of him. The hide wasn't strong enough to hold his weight. He grasped the poles with both hands and shimmied as quickly as he could to the ledge. The wood crashed down below him, just as he got his heel out of reach—but not before he heard the snap of jaws and felt the hot breath of a ripper on his foot.

He clambered frantically up the rocks, scrambled onto the dry grass atop his sky island, and lay down sobbing in relief that he was alive.

As time went by, Alex resolved to avoid any more such close calls. He always carried his weapons, and never left his back exposed. He went out each day to hunt and fish, and he always made a point of knowing where the adult rippers of the valley pack were.

In a way it was comforting that they shadowed his every move. There were usually at least three, sometimes five, beasts following him at a distance. As long as they shadowed him, he knew where they were and could feel reasonably safe from surprise attack.

One day as he walked along the beach, under palm trees rustling in a sea breeze, he kept a wary eye on these evolved mammals, whose upper halves reminded him of wild boar, but whose shaggy bellies and clawed limbs were thick and fast like those of bears. They paralleled his path, staring hungrily from a sandbar across a swiftly flowing run of cold, foamy tidal seawater. They were afraid to cross the fast-flowing salty water or they would long since have made a quick meal of him. They had also learned to stay out of range of his deadly, poison-tipped arrows, and there were several piles of bleached bones on their side of the water to remind them what happened when they got into range of his bow.

Alex liked the warmth of the sun. He liked the smell of vegetation and seawater, the wind in his hair, the thunder of surf. He tolerated the raw screams of seagulls, who kited overhead in moist semi-tropical air under billowing white cumulus clouds.

He liked being alive. Despite his predicament, which included the enigma of his own solitary existence in a world where mankind had been extinct for eons, he enjoyed life and planned to cling to it as long as he could.

In a patch of blue afternoon sky among puffy clouds, the full moon floated among spindly palm trees high up on the reddish cliffs covered with vegetation on the landward horizon. The moon's smudgy lime plains and powdery *maria* gleamed a faint lemony-silver. Near the moon hung a mysterious little grayish smudge, an elongated cluster of tiny lights and shadows, whose nature Alex could not coax out of his ancient memories.

Alex's memory was filled with images and sensations that half drove him mad: cities and roads, skylines and jet airplanes, the touch of other humans, especially Maryan... He could not find a shred of evidence that any of it had ever existed.

In his dreams he floated down rainy neon streets at night, and sometimes he could smell, almost taste, the way rainbow gasoline slicked the curbs, the way rubber and discarded fast food buns stank in gutters, but had any of it ever been real? He floated among glowing computer screens. A white-faced geisha's oval face wore a veiled expression as she stared down with wondering eyes at her *miso* soup and seaweed while *koto* music swirled in a mix of breathy jazz. He rode in elevated silver trains among dots of light made hazy with fog and smoke, high up, to that one dot of light that was Maryan's window, behind which she waited while applying after-bath perfume in slow motions with pale hands and steam roiled over her naked form. Later he lay among tangled bed sheets with Maryan, while nearby a mute television screen flickered unwatched; its bluish light danced in empty glasses and in a wine bottle and amid the abandoned China plates of a finished dinner. He could almost feel her silky skin and hear the passion in her rapid breaths as he and she touched each other.

No matter how deeply he managed to sink into these cinematic and evocative dreams, he always awakened to the monotonous cawing of sea gulls and the thunder of distant surf. He was utterly alone on this earth.

Sometimes he awoke in the middle of the night to the crash of thunder and slashes of lightning amid a downpour. He would lie awake inhaling the rot of the jungle and think how the stalking rippers were probably at that moment scheming about ways to eat him, and then he'd drift back into a cheerless sleep that was entirely of this place rather than that long-gone place.

Sometimes on a sunless day, when there was no hunting or fishing and all he could do was sit in his doorway chewing dried fish and stoking a smoky little fire, certain shreds of that extinct world might float by—a whiff of cold beer, a laugh on a street corner, the rumble of a passing truck, two shop girls teasing each other. In a blink of the eye, all that remained was the distant crash of surf invisible in a blinding fog that kept even the sea birds on their black wet slippery jags.

He did not fully understand who he was or how he'd gotten here, but he did understand how utterly alone he was. He was a castaway marooned beyond the end of time, the last human being, a final Robinson Crusoe.

Hot sand crumbled between his toes and warmed his bones.

He'd fashioned a hat of skin and feathers to shield himself from the blinding sun in a powder-blue sky. He wore a stone knife in his belt and carried a bow and arrows. He thought it ironic that mankind had begun in the stone age and was now ending its days in the same manner.

As he walked on the beach, Alex kept a wary eye on several rippers that shadowed him from just across a sliver of fast-running tidal water in the bay. There were plenty of smaller mammals, but this was the top of the food chain, except for himself. They were a species that had not existed in human times. A typical adult weighed 120 pounds. It was thickly furry, brown, with claws like those of a bear on which it loped when excited or hungry. It had a smallish cat-like head with curling dirty-yellow tusks like a boar's.

Here on the beach, a family of rippers trundled hungrily, a short distance beyond his reach, and he beyond theirs. He could smell their rank odor and hear eager snorts from dripping, glistening black nostrils. Their dark gaze followed him with hateful interest.

Alex had determined they would not rule his life. He kept his deadly bow handy. His arrowheads were coated with fecal matter that would cause massive infection and death upon the slightest wound. If they took him down, they would not go easily themselves. Every so often as the weeks and months dragged by, and these tormentors kept after him looking for their opening, he'd loosen a well-placed arrow that might connect with a thigh or neck. Then he'd take perverse pleasure over the next few days in watching the animal sicken and die in pain while its pals circled around it waiting for a meal.

Alex was lucky that day and bagged a gleaming golden sea bass with copper and silver scales that might have been manufactured by the finest of watchmakers—but this was nature at work, the master artisan.

He laughed as he splashed through warm ankle-deep water. The rippers were afraid of saltwater and stayed on their side of the sandbank as he made his way home to his own beach and then to the cliffs above it where he made his home. It would be good eating tonight and for days to come. He could already imagine how the fish would smell as it slowly roasted, and how its crackling skin would taste.

At that moment, a faint shadow briefly dimmed the sky.

Startled, he looked up. He stared across the wide bay with its rippling tidal waters. Before he saw anything, he heard an odd sound—a brief rumble and sizzle like a burning thing streaking through the air, like the rattle of a lightning bolt, echoing from horizon to horizon.

The rippers too were startled. They cringed, looking over their shoulders and then loping away into the bushes above the beach.

A chrome streak, like a fine silver or glass thread, appeared and instantly vanished into a forest across the bay two miles distant. He watched for any signs of fire or smoke, but none came. Nor was there an explosion. Alex had never seen anything like this before. Was it a natural phenomenon? Everything he'd found in the world turned out to be an illusion created by cruel nature—like a stone surface that resembled a road but turned out to have been made by glaciers advancing and retreating during the ice ages following the extinction of mankind, or like a distant skyline that turned out to be a rock formation after he'd hiked for days to get there at great peril to his life, or like a figure waving to him from a distant hill that turned out to be a sheet of moss caught in a tree and fluttering in the wind.

The sky was bright as ever, and a fine thread of vapor quickly dissipated, drifting away in the powder-blue sky.

He sighed, resuming his trek home. It meant another dangerous expedition to investigate, of course—he couldn't pass up even the faintest hope of finding another human being alive somehow. Already, he was planning his journey: perhaps by raft this time, to avoid the predators on land. A quick trip up the beach, into the woods—it would probably turn out to have been a fist-sized meteorite, another dead end, another disappointment—and he'd make his way back to the only safety he knew.

He replayed the image of the streaking object over and over in his mind, down to the sizzling sound and the odd ozone smell. Did it have anything to do with that other mystery he'd so often pondered on moonlit nights: the unnatural-looking smudge that hung frozen in space beside the Moon? He resolved to find out as soon as possible.

The next day he was intrigued by thoughts of swimming parallel to the shore to explore the impact area of the mysterious sky object.

After making sure the rippers were busy in their valley, he clambered down from his sky island carrying his ladder. He used the ladder as a bridge between the sky island and a large boulder. He laid the ladder aside to prevent any rippers from crossing over and surprising him on his own turf.

Arrow at ready, he sprinted across the sand toward the water, where he would again be relatively safe from the rippers.

As he was halfway to the water, he saw them streaking toward him down the beach: two adult rippers in full sprint, moving like the wind. He dropped his bow and arrows on the sand, where he could retrieve them, and dove into the water.

He swam as hard as he could straight out.

He heard the rippers splash in the water behind him, and redoubled his efforts.

A rip current suddenly caught him and pulled him out.

He tumbled head over heels at the bottom of the water, rolling on the silty sand, suffocating for want of air—

—everything moved in a daze, and he heard the underwater mumble of waves and the rumble of crashing breakers above and the whisper of sand abrading his body—

—And then, past the breakers, the sea flung him clear, and he bobbed dazedly in three foot swells in an otherwise calm sea.

He was now about 150 feet out, comfortably treading water, getting his breath back. The two rippers had given up their pursuit and were tearing into his kill. He prayed that they would not completely tear the hide apart, though he could use scraps to make small pieces of this and that—for example, ties to bind the halves of a tunic together along the edges.

Should he wait until they were done? The rest of the pride was racing in for the feast. No telling how long they would lie in the sand, digesting. Now one of them left the dead animal and paced along the shore, looking after him. That answered his question.

He broke into an even, measured long distance stroke parallel to the shore. Once he warmed up, he was like a machine laying down yard after yard. The water was calm and pleasant and it actually felt warm. That was a commodity he could appreciate. Every few minutes he'd take a look around underneath, looking for aquatic predators, but saw only swarms of little fish and one grouper who ignored him.

Gradually, he was in line with the valley. He paused for a rest, treading water, and studied the lay of the land. His intended goal, the peninsula jutting out to the west, was still at least two or three miles off. It would be a long swim. Without his weapons, he might be best off returning to his beach—but the rippers would be busy on the carcass for a while. Even at this distance he could see the greenish-silver glow of fish feeding at the carcass. Best to wait it out, maybe swim a bit farther west and look things over.

In a million years, what would be left of civilization? Probably just about nothing. One or two good ice ages would race across the ground, scraping buildings off their foundations, leveling cities, leaving gouge marks. The earth might shift poles, or even reverse them. The South Pole could be in Hawaii, and southern Africa might be the new North Pole. A million years, a million possibilities. Even his own place of birth showed absolutely no sign of a human touch.

His cliff was a quarter mile to his right as he faced land, looking north. His cliff had split off from a long, low coastal range of foothills that ran as far to his left as he could see. Beyond those were more hills, each range twice as high as the first, until in the distance there were mountains. Everywhere he looked, he saw thick deciduous forestation, much as Alex had known in upstate New York. Only this was the ocean—had it cut its shore somewhere near Syracuse? Were Rome and Albany beachfront property?

The river that had cut out the valley he was looking at probably ran pretty fast in the spring, when the snow melted. It had carved its way through the foothills, opening a canyon a quarter mile wide.

As he rested, he turned playfully and did a somersault in the water.

The dark shapes below him in the sea at first glance resembled a pile of buoys.

Swimming down, he saw they were on the ocean floor below, and far too big to be buoys. Whatever they were, there were a half dozen or more and they were approximately the same size, 90 feet long by 20 feet wide, give or take, and roughly bullet shaped.

He came up for air, and then dove down again, about six feet. Yes, there was a jumble of huge cylindrical shapes down there. Could they be evidence of something manmade? Or were they just another cruel illusion, a hoax of nature played on his wishfully thinking mind?

He couldn't get near them—their tips loomed up out of the shadows at least two fathoms down. They were heavily embossed with all sorts of sea life, and glowed uniformly dark blue-green in the sunlight that penetrated so far and no farther. Perhaps they were just giant rock formations.

As he dove down repeatedly, he noticed a shadow racing past him. The shadow flitted by so fast it was just a flicker. Alex stopped in the water, backpedaling with his hands and feet.

Now he spotted several sharks among the cylinder shapes. The sharks glided in wide circles, cruising, and he could see their dark eyes panning for targets.

Time to move on, thank you.

If even one of them took an interest in him now, he'd be finished. To speed his way, he dropped his knife and his belt, so that he was stark naked.

His heart beat rapidly, and he could feel a cold sweat breaking out on his torso even in the water. He thrust one arm forward, lay on his side, and crawled rapidly away on the surface in a smooth scissoring swim that he hoped would earn him as little attention as possible.

The band of sand looked far away as he kept crawling toward it.

Once or twice he looked back, noticing the sharks swimming in agitated figure eights around the colony of upright cylinder rocks.

Looking forward, he saw that the land was still agonizingly far away.

He kicked and stroked until he was exhausted, but in time he felt warm sand in shallow water gently melting under the touch of his hand, and he staggered ashore with a cry of relief.

He was safe from the sharks, but was unarmed and defenseless on land as well, and he quickly scanned about for signs of the rippers.

He staggered naked and choking on a sandbar 100 feet offshore.

Winded and blinded from his encounter with the huge sharks, and from his hard swim, he threw himself on the hot sand. There he lay on his stomach, coughing and spluttering water while slamming his palms down on the sand as he regained his

Slowly recovering, he rolled over onto his back. He half sat up on his elbows, scanning the horizon on all sides. The sea looked mystically still, hiding its secrets. At the moment, he appeared to be safe. He was on a bar of sand in the middle of the mile-wide bay. On either side of him flowed a noisy, turbulent arm of blue-green water pushed to the sea. Each of the streams was about 100 feet wide and not a place the rippers liked to venture into.

He looked at the sun, which stood high in the sky. Must be around midday, and the time would be growing short for him to make any long explorations toward the southwest, much as he was curious to learn what had slammed down to earth the other day.

He coughed again, spurting water convulsively from nose and mouth. Effortfully, he raised himself, hands and knees on the sand, then up on his feet. He'd lost his fine knife in the water, and he cursed roundly. He'd spent hours chipping away, sharpening and polishing until the tool had been almost like a thing of steel. And yet—he had all the time in the world, literally—he could start on a newer and better one, maybe a little longer and better balanced. He chortled to himself, almost cynically, as he started to turn around to dive in and swim back to his stronghold.

Then he froze in place.

His eyes grew wide as he looked down at the sand, and chills ran up and down his spine.

There was a footprint in the sand, not his own.

4. Footprint

As Alex looked down at the footprint, and then around him, his stomach contorted with a mixture of emotions, ranging from fear to elation, back and forth. The search for the mysterious sky object would have to be postponed.

He made fists and crouched, as if he expected to be hugged or attacked any moment. And yet that was impossible. The spit of land on which he stood was surrounded by water on all sides. The sea whispered to one side, while palm trees rustled on the other. Birds wheeled overhead. The distant thunder of surf, and the nearby roar of water rushing past the spit, almost drowned the birds' raucous cawing. A broad swath of calm, deep water separated the spit from firm ground in the valley. There was no place for another person to hide.

He was not, after all, alone in this world. He could have spent a lifetime here, marooned and alone, never knowing there was at least one other human being anywhere near.

Should he call out? Should he make his presence known? Or should he run and hide?

He knelt down, as his common sense returned, and studied the footprint in the sand. Then came his second surprise, a shock almost as overwhelming as the sight of that footprint itself.

It had been made by a woman.

He frowned and looked at it closely. The narrow shape, the long delicate toes, the shallow impression, all pointed to a female—probably young, probably graceful. He bent close to inhale any scent that might be there—but he only smelled the faint decay of a dead mussel fragment, a bubble of rotting kelp. He saw tiny insects scurrying inside the footprint hauling out miniscule debris to eat, for the sand was loaded with nearly invisible life forms washed in by the tide and left to die, probably after reproducing in time for the next tide.

Dazed as he was, it occurred to him that if there was one footprint, there must be more.

Like a man walking underwater, he rose and looked about. Sure enough, he saw the faint impressions of more footprints. The one he had found was a perfect impression left in the dark brown, wet sand just under the higher, dry white sand baking in the hot sun. He found faint impressions that seemed to lead up from the water.

Again and again, to make sure he wasn't dreaming, he compared his own foot. He made an impression near the female footprint, and almost cried for joy when he saw they were not the same. Not at all. That one footprint, the first one he'd found—it was so perfect that he could almost see the whorls of the skin, but of course that had to be an illusion. The sand was too coarse and grainy for that, even when wet.

The footprint must have been made during the most recent low tide, for water rushing in with the incoming tide would mar and disturb such a delicate and perfect print. He studied it some more: seemed to be adult, from a woman of average height and build, walking with a strong and healthy stride.

As he looked at the foot prints, he noticed the wavering line of dark droplets on either side of them. Some of the droplets had not yet soaked into the ground.

Blood.

He rose, trembling, and looked about. It seemed as if the ground were whirling under his feet. Was it possible? Was he not alone after all? Could there be another human being alive? Wounded? Or had she bagged a kill and was running with it? Or was it some added cosmic joke—a new kind of ripper, raising danger to new levels?

He began to get hold of himself. Now, if ever in his short life, he must keep a cool head. He knew instinctively: contact with another human could mean any number of consequences for himself, from losing his life to gaining a partner, or in-between some level of friendly cooperation.

Where did the footprints lead? He followed them eagerly up onto dry sand in the middle of the sand bar, where they became quickly blurred. Even as he walked desperately in circles, a light wind drove up a foot-high wall of dust. The footprints led nowhere.

He ran down the other side, and saw one or two more descend into the water.

No! he wanted to yell. A pang gripped his stomach as he looked about on the other side for signs of the rippers. Sure enough, he saw a shadowy figure slink from one dark area to another among the tall marsh reeds. If the woman had gone in there, they'd tear her to pieces in a minute.

There was nothing he could do now. He was unarmed and defenseless. He stared desperately, shielding his eyes from the sun with both hands and standing on tiptoe. He edged backwards up onto the highest point on the sandbar to gain an extra few feet of vantage to scan the valley from one side to the other.

Nothing. The woman had vanished. If the rippers had a kill, they would be silently trashing the tall reeds as they milled around the corpse and tore off pieces. They'd fight over a body, perhaps even killing one of their own number, like sharks in a frenzy. No sign of any of that.

Then he saw the keel line in the sand opposite.

He dove in, hard, without another thought, and swam against the fast-flowing current. Gasping, struggling, he dragged himself ashore a hundred or more feet downstream, almost where the narrow channel opened into the sea. Keeping an eye out for rippers, he raced back toward the keel mark.

He saw also the giant flowers, where she must have run. Where blood had dripped, the large yellow and red petals were curling up hungrily, making low squishing sounds like groans of satisfaction as they digested their treat. Butterfly bats sailed in close for a bemused look but kept safely out of range.

Yes! He ran along the edge of the sand bar, feet splashing in the water. The woman had come in a small boat. She'd pulled it ashore here for some reason. Alex knelt and ran a fingertip gently along the edge of the sharp depression in the wet sugary sand where the keel had cut like a knife, and drawn along like the runner of a sled in snow. *An honest to goodness boat*, he thought. The keel was four inches wide and sank in to its full depth of six inches. No sign of a fin, though if there was one she might have pulled it out to get the boat on shore. No sign of a heavy weight either coming or going. She'd probably come alone or with one other person at most; or children. *Children?* Could one dare hope?

He rose and stood shielding his eyes with one hand as he looked out to sea.

There! He saw the sail. For a moment he whooped and jumped up and down. It was just a small sail, drab and ugly, the tip of its triangular shape just visible as the boat rocked in deep pockets of water going into the rough water near the breakers.

He stopped jumping and grew silent. Pangs gripped his gut. What if it were someone dangerous to him? He must observe first. Must find the woman. Maybe there was a man, or men. He must find out who they were, what they were like before he exposed himself to their mercies. Maybe the woman was a prisoner and he could free her. Maybe she was just another loner like herself, convinced she was the only human being on earth. Anything was possible. He must find out, and decide from an informed position how to behave.

He saw more blood on the sand. He heard the low growl of a ripper, probably the beast he'd spotted running from one hiding place to the other among the bushes. Alex backed toward the channel, ready to dive in if the ripper came out after him. As he stared toward the dense vegetation further inland where the sand ended and the marshes began, he saw the trail of footprints and the spatters of blood. Big droplets of it, almost a dark vermilion color, congealed like thick-flowing oil, lay spattered on the sand. Some of the droplets had rolled a bit in settling, and had picked up a partial coating of fine sand grains.

No time to look more closely—two rippers came loping out onto the sand, probably some of the beasts that had been shadowing him further up the coast for some time now. They appeared to have some fear of him—though he didn't have his weapons with him—or they'd be running full tilt. Instead, they loped toward him with a kind of exploratory posture, waiting to see what he would do.

Alex whirled and dove into the water to swim back to his own place. The rippers stayed on the sand, watching him with enigmatic gazes.

As he swam, hugging the shore to avoid sharks, Alex reflected on his exciting find: whoever had a fine boat like that would not go away anytime soon. It had taken time and civilization to build a boat like that. The boat was too small to go very far, so they would be nearby.

Then he thought: would they accept him? He was, after all, not the man Alex Kirk had been. If she was a real woman, capable of all that a woman could do and be, then what place could he have with her?

If she were alone, and hoping for a miracle, would he be more disappointment than joy?

Now everything was changed. He was no longer alone in the world.

A thousand times, he relived the moment of finding that footprint. He dreamed less about Alex Kirk's lost past, and more about his own hope for touching another human soul. His emotions were in high kilter, running the gamut from fear through joy. What if they were cannibals? What if they weren't even really human? He paused at that thought, in the act of building a small boat, and wiped his brow. The more he thought about it, the more he realized he must be careful.

Some things he could not help. For example, he kept a fire going as he hollowed out a log in the safety of his sky-island. The tree he'd chosen for this purpose had been struck by lightning and lay folded over. It had a long, slender trunk of which about twenty feet were usable. The trunk was about three feet wide, and he estimated he could squeeze in there if he managed to hollow it out. Because it was folded over from where it had fallen over, it was up off the ground and he could get a fire under it. The trunk had begun to dry out, particularly with wind constantly blowing around it, so it took readily to the fire.

Alex worked on the boat throughout the daylight hours, using a row of small fires elevated on stones to get each flame's optimum point of heat focused on the underbelly of the trunk. As the wood charred, he used a stone chipper to chop away at the resulting charcoal. The charcoal itself would be useful in future fires, and he wasted nothing but stored it in a black pile with the rest of his charcoal in a dry bin behind the hut.

As always, he wished he had the steel tools, particularly power tools, he remembered the real Alex as having had. They had it all, those ancient people, he thought, and why did they have to blow it? Sweating, dirty, covered with wood chips and smeared black, he chipped out his boat inch by inch.

The result, after five or six days of relentless labor, was a misshapen, blackened hulk of lumber. In one place, he'd burned a hole right through the hull. He fixed that as best he could by chopping out a plank from the outer rings of a nearby tree, wedging it in so that the wider surface was on the outside bottom of the boat. He cemented this in place with liberal amounts of very sticky tree sap from a stand of pines. He had no nails, not even the tools to make holes for pegs, though he could have shaped dowels with some ease from saplings. Truth was, he didn't want to take a year to make this thing.

While he labored, he lived on rainwater and eggs and an occasional roast fowl. He felt his body emaciating as he worked on all day and lay awake half the night worrying and scheming. In great part, he worried about being alone in the open ocean in this vessel he was making.

He had no idea as yet where to look for this woman and her people. Every evening, he'd step to the edge of his cliff and look out over the sea in the direction where she'd gone.

One night, he thought he spotted a light far away. It was just a wink of a light, but it persisted. Of course, it could have been a reflection of moonlight or starlight on the water; but, he reasoned, the Earth was turning, spinning fast, and in five minutes such a reflection should have stopped shining his way. This little wavering point of light—like a star fallen to earth, the tiniest of stars—winked on and on for a long time. Most likely a fire someplace, he thought. *Where?*

As he stood on the edge of the cliff, he reflected on other nights when he had done this, looking blindly at nothing in particular. Evenings, when he was tired from the day's hunting and building, and when a warm dinner of broiled hen wrapped in vegetables filled his gut, he would sit by the red embers of his fire. He'd made a guardedly secure home for himself high up in the cliffs. In his memory, he would explore a long-vanished world and remember the warm touch of Maryan Shurey and the comforting presence of other humans who had inhabited picturesque little Beacham township in upstate New York. It caused him piercing anguish to know he would live and die without ever having experienced the touch of another human being, or a comforting voice, or a friendly word. The memories of long-ago Alex's life were his only real treasure.

He stared down at the white breakers thundering on the beach rocks 300 feet below. A disturbed wind drove whitecaps across the sea and made tree crowns rustle in the forest. He held one hand up to shield his eyes from the grit and bits of leaf sailing around him in the brisk, fragrant sea wind.

He stared across the wide bay with its rippling tidal waters. He contemplated the dark forests waving back and forth under a full moon. There was no shipwreck for him to visit on a raft to collect supplies. There would never be a passing ship.

Now he stared eagerly, with some trepidation, at the tiny red ember that signaled intelligent life. The fire was probably on some island. He triangulated as best he could using the far cape to his right and the slope coming down into the sea about two miles away. It looked as though wherever that fire was burning, it was two miles offshore. Not a good place to go in shark-infested waters, except in desperation.

It also occurred to him: was someone signaling? To him? Or to others?

He told himself: What do I have to lose? A life lived alone, when I have a 50-50 chance of either being eaten or meeting other human beings I can share my life with?

With that resolved in his mind, he went peacefully to sleep and awoke at midmorning the next day, well-rested and eager to finish his boat.

It took another day or two of scraping, and he added more pine sap to the wound in the hull. Even if it leaked, which he was sure it eventually would, the whole thing was buoyant enough to keep him afloat. Two miles each way, one time—that was all he would ask of this little sailboat.

He'd spent hours contemplating how to build a sail with the materials he had at hand. It occurred to him that his own body would serve as a primitive obstruction that the wind might ram against without any ability to tack or guide. He remembered ancient images of windsurfing. Many ways to skin this cat, if one were inventive enough. It would be simpler to do that than to try and embed some sort of mast in the hull. In the end, he fashioned a primitive sort of wind sail using a twenty foot upright, and a sturdy enough sail woven together of reeds and vines. His sail looked more like a basket on a frame, but he figured it would take him the two miles and back.

Getting the boat down off the cliff without shattering it was a great ordeal leading to bruised ankles and knees as well as torn elbows and bloody hands. At one point, guiding it down from a higher boulder to a lower, he slipped and landed oddly so that his elbow smashed into his chin, rattling his teeth so that he was afraid he'd loosened one or two, but he only ended up with a sore jaw and a cut tongue. Cursing, swearing, he lowered the two hundred pound vessel down until it landed in the beach sand with a healthy resounding sound. The only damage was to the foot-square plate covering the hole he'd burned in the hull, and he had to re-glue the whole thing. He warmed his pitch with a torch, until the resin sizzled and blackened. To this he added handfuls of fresh pinesap until the whole mess fused, holding the plate tightly enough. He made a floor of thick deciduous tree bark and laid that down to cover the hole, so that he would not accidentally step on it and push it out, thereby sinking himself. As a final precaution, he made himself a kind of life preserver that he resolved to tow behind, just a block of wood with some good handholds carved in it, and vines attached for more grips.

All the while, of course, he had to be on the lookout for his arch enemies the rippers. They appeared to be busy with a herd of wild oxen a mile up the beach, and were avoiding him for the moment.

All the better, he thought, looking up longingly toward the peace and security of his sky-island before pushing his boat down toward the incoming tide.

5. Island

Alex stood in the boat holding up the sail and aiming it so that he could tack along the sides of the wind. It was a good day for sailing. A moderately brisk wind pushed the boat along at a nice clip. The boat was slow to steer at the helm, but the rigging worked enough to make turns.

At first, Alex tacked back and forth in zigzags near the coast until he was past the cape and out in rougher seas. There he rode up and down on eight-foot swells, and the boat took it well. He was up to his ankles in water, but the boat was solid and kept pushing out to sea.

For a while Alex was a bit scared, scanning the horizon and not seeing any signs of land. He hoped to see a wisp of smoke or even a flash of flame, but there was nothing. If worst came to worst, like if the boat sank, he could swim the mile or two back to shore. It was not a prospect he liked, but he was determined to find out what lay at the end of this journey.

After he was about a mile beyond the cape and heading steeply out away from land, he saw a smudge on the horizon. He stood as best he could, rising up and down, and held his sail so that the wind threatened to push it from his grasp. He buried his face in his hands as he held the mast, and prayed it would not suddenly spring apart in his grip. Many of the reeds had already snapped and were loosely snapping in the wind, some making low whistling and twanging noises. The boat tended to ride too much to the left, to port, and he had to keep correcting by leaning far to one side, but the island grew larger. Still no signs of smoke.

Too late he noticed the breakers around the island, and the sharp teeth of black gleaming rocks over which washed foaming water. Garlands of kelp lay strewn among the boulders, and the ocean crashed rhythmically so that he could hear the shuddering under the water as all the boulders shifted with the rocking sea. The boat shot through a wall of breakers and became logy, slowly riding along, saturated with water. Alex lost his balance, went to his knees under water on the boat floor, then rose suddenly on a great curling head of foam. "Whoa!" he shouted, realizing that he was headed toward the tip of a groin whose bluish boulders rose like a crocodile's mouth out of the sea. He dumped the sail over one side and jumped out the other, just as the boat was carried high and then dumped, smashing, onto a ledge six inches under water.

He didn't have time to worry about it. For a moment he felt the silty, abrasive churning of an undertow. For a minute or so, he was thrown in cartwheels underwater. He heard the tuba-sounds of water channeling among the boulders as he spun helplessly. He felt the sand on the bottom and then found himself being carried away. A moment later, he surfed belly-down over a ledge and would have gone right back over the other side and out to sea, except he was able to wrap himself around a protruding stone and aikido himself into a crevice, where he stuck, during a moment when the sea paused for breath before plunging onward.

Gasping and pouring water from his mouth, nose, and ears, he pulled himself up out of the water. He could see his raft was finished, but he felt too battered to think about how he might get back to the mainland. He felt the weight of the water gliding off him, and the balmy wind drying his skin already as he hopped from stone to stone toward the sodden beach. There were few of the giant butterflies in view, most likely because the tree-trunk flowers that nurtured them were absent on this island. The sand smelled of rotting kelp, and swarms of insects buzzed over piled desiccation from various tides ago. There was a faint smoky something in the air, stale, not an active hearth fire, not a healthy wood smoke, but something puzzling and industrial, cold and unwelcoming. With a feeling of dread, he climbed up a slope of round rocks. The rocks lay packed tightly like a road. Again it was hard to guess if man or nature had laid them so perfectly in a carpet.

Then he saw the boat. Someone had pulled it up onto the rocks and into the shelter of an overhang. It was a squares boat with uplifted fore and aft, sturdy as a rowboat but lively as a little shell. In it, neatly furled, lay a mast with sail. Alex bent down to feel the sail. Surprisingly, it felt like wool. He rubbed forefinger and thumb together, feeling the oil there. He smelled it, a lanolin kind of sheep odor. He found the sheep minutes later, a herd of them, grazing unattended. He casually counted a dozen in plain view and a few more hidden shadows that promised to be more, standing in the rocky grassy ledges above where they'd gone to graze. They looked down on him, chewing comically, as if they were thinking something witty.

Alex climbed up a winding path and came to a small meadow about the size of his own sky-island. Several of the sheep followed him, and one or two ran ahead making their *bad-a-a-a-h!* noise. All they lacked was bells, he thought, and this could be some Irish or Alpine village a million years ago. He smelled the smoke, more strongly now, at the same time he saw the ruins. Down in a little valley nestled inside a ring of huge boulders (like teeth sitting on someone's lower jaw, with thorn bushes and plum trees growing from the gums) were nestled some six houses, none with roofs.

As Alex stood overlooking the village, a light fog was creeping in. The sunlight, which he hadn't particularly noticed before, illumined the growing milky haze from within like light inside a lantern. But it promised to be a fading light, for already down under the fog, on the cold and dripping walls of abandoned houses, black shadows were gathering. The stones dripped coldly with dark water.

Alex walked down into the ghost village, heart sinking as he noticed the absence of windows, doors, roofs. When he stepped into the houses one by one, and saw the worm-eaten gray timbers so fragile that they crumbled at the touch of a foot, and when he saw the deep soil that had gathered where floors had once been, and when he saw several wide tree trunks that had taken shelter here long ago, he got a picture that this place had been abandoned not yesterday, not last year, but generations ago.

He held his head and cried out with disappointment. "Hello!" he called. "Hello!" He walked over a mass of moss and ivy and brambles a yard deep in places covering what must once have been the village square. "Is anyone here?"

No answer—he heard only the wind, whispering in the leaves, and saw how the sun silently gilded the rocks, painting them with a kind of bright, tortured irony that made all the sadness in him well up, all the loneliness of his hopeless existence. Tiny butterflies fluttered over green and yellow lichen and nuzzled bright yellow flowers. Bees, probably descended from domestic ones, buzzed around an irregular dark comb in a tree. Birds twittered and hopped from branch to wall to boulder, unmindful of whatever tragedy had occurred here. Still, there was that cold aftertaste of smoke in the air, a faintly sour odor.

Alex clambered up the opposite side of the protective hillside and stood overlooking the seaward shore of the island.

Nothing.

The sea was becoming enshrouded in mist, and the light was losing its golden luster. The island was only about half a square mile in area and roughly oval. It reared up from the sea on stone pillars, a primordial lava up flow through a long gone mountain worn away by wind on some plain long since drowned in the ocean. Now, on the scrubby meadows high up, with their scraggly bushes and trees, fog was rolling in to soften and obscure the view.

Worried about becoming trapped for the night, Alex rushed down to the sandy beach on the seaward side.

Amid cawing sea birds and crawling crabs, he found a bundle of rags lying half in and half out of the water.

He smelled the foulness of death from a distance, and heard a loud buzzing of insects.

"No!" He hurried up close, while shreds of fog blew swiftly past, and his face dripped with condensation. Shivering, he stood and looked at the body on the beach. The stench was enough to knock a person back, but he forced himself to get near. Brushing aside scuttling crabs and swarming flies, he lifted the large wool cloak in which she was rolled up. He caught a brief glimpse of the ravaged face, the hollowed empty eyes, the lipless mouth, the clean young teeth. He glimpsed long black hair still with a trace of gloss in its healthy young fiber. Pulling the cloak open further to expose a torso laid open to whitish bone and purplish flesh swarming with the greenish golden carapaces of insects, he saw that she had her bony hands clutched together over her abdomen. The claw marks in her gut were still visible. That would explain the blood on the beach weeks earlier. She'd gone to land for some reason, to get something, to do something, and the rippers had attacked her. Somehow, she'd fought them off and managed to get to the boat. She'd managed, perhaps with the last of her strength, to sail away and make it this far. She'd beached the boat and staggered around the island, too weak to go over the top, and collapsed here. But where had she been headed? Surely not to those ghost houses.

Holding his nose, he groaned loudly with dismay and let the corner of the cloak fall back to hide her face. Backing away, holding his hands over his face, he recognized the delicate narrow foot sticking out from among a rumple of wool. As he backed away, a large sea bird landed and strutted up to the cloak, pecking at it imperiously.

Alex turned and started to run.

Then he smelled that oddly cold smoke again, and followed the smell several hundred feet around to the northern end of the island, which he realized he might have seen from his aerie atop the cliff several miles away.

There he found the likely cause of his fire. Someone had stored wood here in a kind of wall-shape fifty feet long, and anywhere from five to ten feet high. The logs had been broken from young, small timber and left to dry for firewood over a period of years. Recently, for some reason, someone had set the whole thing on fire. There were still a few spots faintly smoldering, though the dampness was rapidly quenching the last hot spots.

Beyond this wall of wood, nestled in a fold in the central hill on the island, was a cottage. A strong smoke house smell surrounded it, as if it were a place for preserving fish and meat, aside from the burned wood outside.

Alex was torn between running for the boat and getting off the island, and staying to learn more. Certainly, he couldn't just make off with someone's boat.

The air was filled with fresh drizzle now, and the rocks gleamed as though dripping with rain. Water ran down his hair and splashed coldly on his damp shoulders, making him shiver. The air was growing darker, and he knew there would be no more sunlight that day.

The cottage door was tightly closed. He approached carefully, noting its dark and lifeless aspect. The cottage was built of good-sized gray and brown blocks tightly fitted with a crumbling mortar made of straw and mud. The cottage was more of a lean-to, built hive-like against the stone surface of a cleft in the hill. Its thick roof consisted of rough beams overlaid with layers of tightly bundled straw and clay. A stone chimney protruded, dead, leaking not a shred of smoke from under its clay rain-cover.

The cottage had no windows, and the door was tightly woven from interlaced saplings.

"Anyone in there?" Alex called out. *No answer.*

The door was held in place somehow on the inside, and Alex had to kick and pull for several minutes before he got it loose. A crossbeam finally fell down, and he staggered back holding the door in his hands.

The same smell of rot and death greeted him as he stepped inside. In the twilight, it took a few minutes for his eyes to adjust. In the meantime, he spied a table with objects on it, including striking stones and tinder. He worked feverishly, with trembling hands, striking the stones together until he had straw and tinder going. From this, he lit a handful of straw torn from the roof.

The single room lit up, revealing a garish scene. The floor was stone, polished from much walking, and strewn with clean sand. To the right was a rough wooden bench against the wall that seemed to be loaded with objects and serving more as a table than a place to sit. More toward the center was a fireplace built of many small flat beach stones like bricks. To the left was a bed—a wooden enclosure filled with straw and covered with a thick wool blanket. On this blanket, propped up with her back to the wall, was the corpse of an old woman.

In the dry, smoky air, her leathery features seemed to be in the first stages of mummification. Her cheeks were sunken, her toothless mouth open, her eyes big hollows with whitish eyeballs glimmering from tiny shriveled eyelids sunk way in. Her hair was white and sparse, but wild and long. Her body was clothed in thick woolen garments, and only her thin neck and bony hands were exposed. Her gnarly hands were crossed over her knees, which were slightly drawn up as if she'd died sitting up. In her lap and strewn over the bed were scraps of white material.

Looking more closely, Alex saw lines of ants crawling up the bed on both sides and entering separate holes—one in her left cheek, the other in the middle of her neck, a third directly into her mouth, and he stopped looking to see how many more holes the ants had made. As he looked, a beetle crawled out from her mouth, and he quickly jerked back.

The fireplace was overflowing with ashes, and when he looked more closely, sitting on his knees and twisting around to look up, he saw that the chimney had been tightly plugged with straw.

Alex formulated a good guess as he stepped from the cottage. For some reason, the woman had committed suicide. The chimney had been purposely plugged up. Fire had burned long and hard in the fireplace, maybe for days, filling the cottage with carbon monoxide and smoke, and soon killing the woman. She'd sat in bed awaiting death. *Why?*

Perhaps the other woman, the younger one, had left. Or perhaps the younger woman had died. This older one had been overwhelmed by grief. Alex could certainly understand. Much as he wanted to flee from this place, Alex realized he was stuck for the night. Fog roiled in so thickly now that he could hardly see his hands before his face. He could hear the sea, but couldn't see it. The birds and insects had fallen still. The last rays of daylight moved through the fog. The light grew still, copper-colored, fading, as though Alex were at the bottom of a well.

Alex went back into the cottage. He lit a wax candle set in a clay cup, and placed it by the door on the bench. In a strange way, even though there was only death here, it was at least a testimony to life that had been. Could there be more? Or was he making of himself the greatest fool in history? He rolled the woman's body up in one of her blankets and carried her outside. It was like carrying a husk. She weighed hardly anything. He realized that the insects had most likely carried away what was edible inside, leaving mostly bones and tendons. He took the body down to the water. Blindly, he walked into the surf. He felt the icy water crawl up his legs, up around his groin, up to his waist. There, he released her, pushing her away with one foot. He heard a splash, as from a fish, and knew she'd be well taken care of. Dragging the sodden blanket with him through the water, he sloshed back on shore.

In the cottage, which still smelled of smoke and death, he pulled as much of the straw down out of the chimney as he could. She'd been weak, and had not plugged the chimney up badly. Alex held his candle up until a blaze started in the chimney. In minutes, it had burned through. He waited outside, watching sodden yellowish smoke pour up from the chimney, over the top and out from the clay rain-cover, and then down along the roof as if the smoke itself were wet. By now, a light steady rain was falling in long quiet strands, like a tightly woven tapestry, at a slight angle.

Everything was wet, the whole world, Alex thought as he picked up the broken door and leaned it against its doorway. By now, occasional wind gusts blew up the beach, and the rocks in the hills made low moaning and keening sounds as thick damp wind pushed through.

Alex found a modest woodpile under the bench and soon had a roaring fire going. The cottage warmed up and dried out. Fresh cold air sucked in through the door opening, swirled around the room taking away the stench of death and decay, and entered the fireplace, where wind and stench ignited in a healing and cleansing fire that pushed up through the chimney and away into the stormy night. Alex fed all the straw from her bed into the fire, burning away more of the death that had taken over the cottage. The floor was littered with flakes of white material, and he kicked them heedlessly about.

Alex made one more trip outside, reluctantly. He carried her blankets out, five of them, and swirled them around in a puddle of rainwater to cleanse them. As he did so, he rinsed soot and dirt from his own body, no matter how cold it felt. It was good to be clean. Then he brought the blankets inside, wrung them out, and laid them around the fire to dry out. It was good and warm inside by now, and slowly the floor and the walls themselves became warm, warmed through by the good clean reddish bluish whitish fire.

He repaired the door, putting the stout cross-timber in place to hold it from inside. It would keep any rippers, ghosts, sea monsters, or other unwanted guests out long enough for him to awaken and use the old woman's good supply of stone utensils to fight them off. The smell of death grew faint, though it was still present. He stopped smelling it, and it seemed to fade away. From a storage nook high up, and he pulled out more straw and filled the wooden bed-square. He found dried fish and dried fruit wrapped in leaves, and had himself a meal. He filled a clean cup several times with pure rainwater, to wash down the dry food. Feeling contented, he fluffed out the blankets and waved them one by one for a long time before the fire until they were dry enough to wrap himself in. It was hot in the place, and he was content to just lay the blankets into the bed.

Then he wrapped himself up and quickly surrendered to exhausted sleep.

He felt fire in his eyes and awoke with a start, throwing blankets aside. He remembered the dead faces he'd seen, and the losses they meant to him, and let out a muffled yell as if coming up from a drowning well.

Sunlight stabbed through the reed doorway in dozens of thin shafts, and had found him on the bed and caressed his eyelids.

He sat up rubbing his eyes and slowly remembered where he was. The fire had gone out, and the fireplace overflowed once again with white and black ashes.

He rose and stumbled to the bench, where he found half a clay cup of water and drank it to relieve his thirst. He found a few bits of dried fish and chewed on those while pulling the door open.

Outside, the rain and fog were gone. The normal semitropical warmth filled the air, hot and moist. The air smelled bracingly of the sea, and the wind itself was fresh and cooling. Alex walked down the beach to the edge of the sea, which was at low tide. There was no sign of the old woman. He walked around the long bend in the direction he'd come, and found the young woman's body still on the beach. A half dozen pelicans were working around it, scooping up the crabs that had come to feast, while swarms of insects filled the air and covered the sand around her.

He sat on the beach cross-legged for a long time, chewing on his fish and holding his cup. At times, tears welled up in his eyes when he thought of what could have been. If only he'd been here a few weeks earlier. He wiped the tears away. If nothing else, he knew now there were other humans, and maybe he'd find more. Just realizing he had not been alone—even if perhaps these had been the only other two humans in the world, and he was perhaps again alone—changed everything somehow. It did not make the world any less tragic or awful. It did not make it any more or less beautiful and mysterious either.

It was extra scary now, in a way it had never been before. He'd been resigned to his loneliness. Now he was starting to let hope torture him. If he never met another living person, that would be a crushing disappointment he could not bear. He thought about this, and decided it would be worse not to try. It would be worse not to hope.

He knelt down in the soft, creamy sand near the water and dug with both hands. By trial and error, he found just the right consistency of sand so that it was wet enough to stick together and easy enough to dig without collapsing constantly inward. In a short while, he had dug a longish depression in the sand. He tested it by rolling into it, and found it was just deep enough. He walked over and carefully, assailed by the smell and the angry buzz of disturbed insects, dragged her to the hole. He tried to avoid touching her, and pulled her by two bunched handfuls of her wool cloak. She was empty, and light, like the older woman, and moved across the sand with a soft sighing sound of grains moving under material. When he dragged her away from the indented and stained place she'd lain, he saw a fine stone knife in the sand. It was of smooth blue stone, with no markings. Even the chippings had been polished smooth over many hours of fond rubbing.

He slid her into the slot and used his feet to push sand over her, while pinching his nose shut. When he had her fully covered by six inches or more of sand, he brought some rocks down from the upper beach, until he'd covered her with a loaf-shape of stones. *Done.* He picked up the knife and walked down to the tidal strip. He rinsed the knife and put it in his belt. He washed himself in the sea, though he was sure it was more symbolic than hygienic. He paused for a minute over the grave to think about who she might have been, and how he might have spoken or laughed with her.

He hoped she had had a good life. When there was nothing more to think, he walked away.

Alex walked around the circumference of the island, and it did not take overly long.

He followed a sandy beach most of the way, except on the landward side where it was broken up by surf and boulders, and there was that rocky landing with the boat still parked on it. He walked uphill to the sheep meadow and looked out toward the land.

He got his best view of the world yet. At this distance, he could make out distant mountains with white tops. Closer, he saw the valley in which the rippers lived. At the narrow end toward the forests and jungles, he saw a high waterfall tumble down. Even from here, three or four miles away, he could see the plume of mist drifting away from the tumbling water, and he could make out a faint rainbow as sunlight mingled with the water.

The water formed a fast-flowing river that cut though the valley, and it was clear that at flood-times the entire valley was the mouth of a huge, raging river that blasted out to sea. Most of the time, it was a flat marshy plain cut by one main channel and several smaller channels of fast-flowing water like the one he'd dived into to swim across to shore and look at the blood and keel cuts on the sand. On either side of the valley were long, medium rows of hills with rocky faces and vegetation on top.

Somewhere in those hills on the right, he knew, was the cave in which he'd been born. It was part of the enigma of this whole place—and who he was, who the old woman had been, who the young girl he'd just buried had been.

He knew he could not stay on this island. Maybe one day he'd be strong enough, but not yet. He wanted so desperately to be around living people, and being around the dead would bother him all the more. At the same time, he knew he would be back here, maybe often. It was the closest thing to civilization that he'd ever know.

Even if he stayed here alone, he could be the keeper, passing this dead world on to anyone who might come after, if anyone did.

He made one more foray down into the central part of the island, the sunken village.

Clambering over the undergrowth, he saw signs of fresh water below. Was there perhaps a spring somewhere in this depression, though it was no more than a few hundred feet across and contained half a dozen stone houses packed tightly together? Nobody could answer his question now. They were all gone, buried in a moss-choked columbarium at the end of the village street.

Tucked away into dozens of wall niches, under a large rock overhang, were the funerary urns of the inhabitants. Alex had to stoop to climb in over the mossy rocks. He counted several dozen niches, all of similar size. At one time all the niches had been covered over with stone slabs, but most of the slabs had fallen down. Almost all the slabs had illustrations and inscriptions, carved in a primitive manner most likely using harder stone to chip at softer stone. The slabs had been held in place by narrow ledges cut by human hand, but winds and earth tremors had rocked them loose. Tongues of moss ran down the recessed Cliffside, oozing from open wall niches like a kind of water of time. The middle niches were the oldest, and the urns inside were the most pitted. Pushing carefully in until his head and shoulders were in one of the niches, Alex found that the number of urns continued inward for at least ten feet, each urn being about a foot high and half as much around. The word amphora came to mind, from Alex Kirk's meme trove, except these urns had rounded instead of conical bottoms. They must have burned their dead, Alex thought, for only ashes could fit in a vessel that small. When he saw into the back of the niche, he was shocked, because the style was different—more ornate, smoother, finer made, and so delicate they crumbled to the touch. That was when he realized he was looking at a culture that had existed her for centuries, maybe a thousand years or more, before vanishing. He saw a number of interesting things, and then one shocking find.

He left the village, feeling more overwhelmed at what he knew than puzzled by the enormous amount he didn't know. The passage of time, the coming and going of lives, the drizzle of countless lifetimes like sand through an hourglass, weighed on him with a depressing heaviness. There was something else that he reflected on, which had not occurred to him, but which he realized afterward. There was no sense of family about the urns. Each bore at most a name, written in language he could readily understand from Alex Kirk's memories: Robert, Martha, Sandra, Keith, Leigh, Vasco, Lars, Kim, Shinko, and so on. Furthermore, some of the names repeated. He counted several Keith's, several Brains, several Johns, several James, innumerable Mary's, two or three Workups. But no family names. It was as though they all belonged to one great family— even the Alexes, who might have taken the name Kirk. The shocking find was that the most common names were Robinson and Friday. And variations like Robin or Robinette and other days of the week. Did it mean there had been many brought into the world as he himself had?

He had a feeling the answers to some of his questions lay near, but he wasn't sure he'd feel any better once he learned more about the truth.

The island loomed around him almost as mysteriously as it had during the fog and rain of night.

Daylight did not shine deeply into its dark shadows. He felt himself in the presence of ghosts as he circled around to the old woman's cottage. Though the house stood empty now, he felt an obligation to leave things in order, if only for himself when he returned. He straightened things out, fixed the door so no animals could get inside, and prepared to close up the cottage. He would think about using it as a hideaway, after some time had gone by and he'd digested what he'd seen and felt here. Before he closed up, he noticed a couple of slender wooden sticks lying in a corner, along with a small clay jar. He knelt down and examined the jar. It was filled with a black paste, and the tip of the sticks were black. Crawling on all fours, he began to take an interest in the pale scraps lying around. Most were blank. They were paper, evidently created by chopping vegetal matter up fine and mixing it with wool in water to make a pulp which was then pounded flat and left to dry in the sun, maybe stretched over a flat rock or pressed between flat rocks. He resolved to explore the art of paper making on his next trip. Right now, he was more interested in the old woman's writings, which he found on several of the scraps that had been in her bed. She must have composed some thoughts on her last day, until the light faded and the deadly gas from the fireplace took her away. Alex sat on a rock on the beach and read the scraps, repeatedly and out of order, until some logical threads took shape in his mind.

I am Kathryn, bearing the memories of Kathryn Bellwood, an instructor of History at Beacham University. In many ways, I am Kathryn Bellwood, who lived eons ago. Yet, I am my own person, so I call myself simply Kathryn or Bella. We write because we feel we must leave some record, even when it is not clear anyone will ever read it. To you, years in the future, maybe a thousand years from now if this record survives, greetings. If you wonder why you live, know that we wonder also. Know that it is good to live, and to love life, and to enjoy the world despite all its evils and hardships. In that sense, I have no regrets. Like Dorothy, my dear friend Dot, I am a clone. We are sterile and cannot bear young. We are born in the cave and very few of us ever escape from the devils who eat us. I was strong and smart. I was quick and got away, finding my way to this abandoned village where nobody has lived in centuries. I tried often to return to the valley, but the devils frightened me off. Finally I did rescue Dot, who bears the memories of Dorothy Chin, who taught Chinese Literature at Beacham. Dot went back to the valley despite my objections and has not come back. I fear the devils have taken her, and I am so old and sick that I don't think I can go on. But know that life was good, such as was able to live it, and maybe in some ways we have had it better than the millions of true humans who lived and died in their cities, with their wars and other horrors. They accomplished great things, but there is no memory of them in the universe except what we unfortunates carry in our genes. The night is coming and I can smell the smoke now. It reminds me of Kathryn's childhood, and it makes me sad that I never was able to sit with my (her) parents at the fireplace at Christmas and tell stories. I did have a kitten once, and it lived to an old age but was taken by forest animals. I am growing drowsy now, and I have so much more to tell about...

With that, the account ended, and Alex sat for a long time staring at the words on the crude paper. They were inked in stiff, uneven print letters and did not resemble the fine script he knew Alex Kirk had possessed. He rose and took the papers into the cottage, where he carefully hid them in a dry cubbyhole high up. He laid them pressed between stones so rodents could not make a meal of them. They were perhaps the last written testament of mankind. At the same time, Alex had learned enough, reading between the lines, and knowing what he himself had learned in his short life so far, to know there was a place he must go look for more answers and possibly for his own purpose in life, his own salvation.

Alex took the women's boat, the new knife, and several blankets and set out for the mainland. He had to sail carefully, aiming through an opening of calm water among the boulders, but he managed without damaging the boat.

Just outside, he tied the boat up for a few moments on a rock while he dived down to retrieve his own knife and spear from the wreckage of his raft whose image lay shimmering and trembling one fathom down among kelpy rocks. His bow and arrow he found also but they were waterlogged and probably ruined, though he tossed them in the bottom of the sailboat for possible salvage.

The sailboat looked much as he'd first seen it, when the young woman was still alive and sailing back to the island some weeks ago. It had a tall mast and a woven sail made pliable and airtight with lots of grease. The whole boat smelled pleasantly of lanolin and pine tar. It had a clean, dry, smooth bottom with evidence that straw had once served as a seat, though he had not thought to gather any for his journey. It had a wooden keel-fin, which he dropped through a central slot whose rim rose to gunwale height. It had a rudder of flat wood polished from use and rubbed with oils to make it water resistant. He could sit in a rear corner with one arm over the tiller and the other hand holding a spar that controlled the sail's pitch, and off he went rocking up and down in the soupy sea as the wind pushed him crisply along. The wind was strong and he kept the sail angled so the boat would press forward on her slightly raised bow.

Pulling the boat up on the sand, he hiked across the hot beach and up the sandy cliffs until he was on a meadow nearly 200 feet above sea level. The meadow was covered with red and yellow flowers, and the air was fresh. For hours, he hiked about looking for any signs of the crashed sky object. He widened his search to include the mix of palms and evergreens growing in the foothills of low mountain ranges, but found nothing—no crater, no burned area, no debris. He began to think the phenomenon must have been one of those fist-sized meteorites that often drop through the atmosphere and burn up without a trace before striking the ground. Gradually he let it go from his mind and returned to his sky island.

In the next day or two he repaired his bow and arrows. He rested an afternoon long in the warm sunshine, sleeping on his promontory after eating well—eggs from his hens, and two quail that ventured too close for their own good. But he kept looking toward the valley, restless to discover its secrets and see what it was Kathryn and Dot had sought there. He had a good idea of what he might be looking for.

Only that prepared him for what was to come next.

In the early morning, right after dawn, he eagerly set sail for the valley in his new boat.

Rather than sail directly to the sandbar fronting the middle of the valley, he tacked away toward the hills opposite his dwelling. He noted with pleasure that one could not make out his sky-island from the sea, which gave him a sense of security. Better not to advertise his location, but to use the island as bait for any other possible souls stranded in time as he was, and he resolved to visit the island regularly. But today his quest lay in the valley where the rippers lay in wait, the beasts that had cost Dot her life and in consequence the life of Kathryn. Alex resolved they would not take his own.

By the sun and the time of day, he noted that he was heading more or less westward. He realized that he had just had confirmation that Beacham University was not an artifact in his head, but had once been a real place. Kathryn's use of the words "eons ago" did not cheer him as much.

This still did not tell him whether the area around here was that which had long ago been called Upstate New York, or if Beacham had somehow conducted its genetics experiments on some tropical island. There was much still to be learned.

He rode into a tiny cove surrounded by high cliffs. There, he beached the boat on a thumbnail beach, securing her anchor line under a heavy stone.

From this protected cove the valley was well out of sight around a long bend to the east. He waded around rocks, through shallow water, and came into a larger cove closer to the valley. This cove had a larger beach leading to forest above the rocks. He clambered up into the woods and discovered fruit trees. Birds twittering excitedly among the dangling fruits signaled the orchard-like nature of this area, and Alex looked for a good tree to climb.

Sitting in a tree atop the cliffs, chewing on a juicy sweet pear of delicate flowery flavor, he promised himself to come again and take home a few fruit trees.

Day after day he returned, each time growing bolder as he got to know his terrain.

In the hills above the valley, the forest was sparse and level, and sound traveled well over the mossy, leaf-strewn ground. That made it hard for him to be stealthy, but it also played against his adversaries. If a pack of rippers were to try and stalk him, he was pretty confident he'd hear them in time to react, whether that meant to stay and fight or to run. Perhaps there had been a fire up here in recent years, for the trees had thin, young trunks. Between that and the ground cover of ferns and low bushes, there was little place for him or anyone else to hide.

He trudged the mile or two of ridges carefully, holding his bow and arrows ready to shoot.

Good thing too, for one day a large ripper did rear up suddenly from nowhere, it seemed. The animal had been lying in wait in a depression, very still, until he drew near. With a roar it loped toward him. He could see the triumph and hunger in its mean little eyes. He could see mucus bubbling in its black nostrils, and he could see the furry pinkness of its tongue amid serrated inch-long teeth. He managed to unload two arrows into its neck and jump aside as it faltered on and came to a crashing end in the leaves behind him.

Close call; he stood trembling and breathing hard. He was glad he'd had the sense to come armed to the teeth and tense as his bowstring itself. The animal lay gasping its last ratcheting breaths, staring up at him with accusing eyes, and out of mercy—and so it wouldn't summon any more of its fellow travelers—he loosed a third arrow hard into its heart. It died in mid-breath, growing limp, and he kicked dirt over it to slow the spread of its blood and innards smells in the air.

He was nearly unnerved enough to leave here and never return. This had been one of his closest calls ever, but then again he rarely ventured this far into their territory. He told himself he could not give up if there was any hope of finding what he sought.

Day after day he returned, and he managed to outflank or avoid any further ripper meal-seekers.

One day, his perseverance paid off in both the brightest and darkest of ways.

He still had only a vague idea where to look for the place Kathryn's writings suggested was around here, and he was covering the area methodically, one part at a time, skipping nothing.

On this particular day, he sailed beyond the valley as usual, moored the boot, and proceeded back toward the valley on foot carrying his weapons ready. Today was going to be different. Instead of exploring the ridge on top, he was going to venture into the mouth of the valley.

As he made his way along the beach, he listened with the greatest caution for signs of danger. Twice, when the beach ran out, when the woods came right up to the water front, he swam out about 30 feet until he could come back up onto clean beach sand. On open sand, he could spot anything that moved.

Once again the beach dwindled and narrowed—this time because the foothills meandered right up to the sea. The hills above him were not wooded, but rather bare sandstone pitted with age. The narrow strip of sand led around a corner.

He considered swimming out, but the water near shore was full of boulders and looked uninviting.

Cautiously, he made his way along the narrow strip of sand, clinging close to the steep rock face on his left.

For a moment he did not recognize where he was.

He stared at the river flowing past, at his feet, into the sea.

What a tranquil scene!

Then he realized: He was the valley of the rippers. He had arrived where he'd planned to be. *Now what?* His heart pounded rapidly, and his hands were clammy with fear. The leaves around him rustled gently in the breeze, and he expected a beast to explode upon him at any instant. So far, no sign of trouble, but the stillness was more frightening than if there had been any actual commotion.

He resisted the impulse to dive into the water and swim away as quickly as possible. To his right was the ocean. In front of him rushed the swiftly flowing, powerful jade-green water covered with foam caps, about 30 feet wide in its channel. Ahead was the alluvial fan-mouth of the river, mostly dry at this time of year, a sandy plain dotted with tall brush and saltwater reeds. It was again obvious from this perspective that, in the spring, this river was several times as large with melt water.

Cautiously, he peeked around the bend of the hill, which had been torn out ages ago by rushing water. He looked up the valley and saw lush vegetation stretching upward toward the second line of hills a half mile away.

As he looked along the river bank, he spotted something in the sand—something that looked familiar. Compelled by a curiosity so intense his heart pounded, he walked along the sandy beach—at a moment's notice, he could throw himself into the water and be carried out to see by the headlong current. He knew the rippers were afraid of rushing water and the salt water to which this led, so he hoped he was doubly safe. Still, he had visions of being torn apart on the very edge of the water before he could throw himself into it and be swept away to safety.

He stepped over and around numerous round, buried stones.

He approached the long white object with a sense of trepidation.

The letters BEACHA were raised in high relief in the granite. It took him several minutes for the realization to sink in: before him, rising from the sand, was a weathered lintel of one of Beacham University's portals.

It had probably lain facing down for eons, and had in the past few decades or centuries been rolled over by a high river current.

He could reasonably figure out now that at some time in geological time, a sea—probably an arm of the old Atlantic—had forced its way over parts of what had once been New England and New York State.

He stood, stunned, looking at the lintel, thinking that with a few more points to orient himself, he could probably even figure out where Alex's house had once stood. His knees trembled at the thought. More than ever, he knew the cinemas playing in his head represented a real past that had existed, not some fantasy world. The next step would be to find out why. Why was he here? Why had any of this happened? Kathryn had figured out that she was a clone—that should be a vital clue. He shook his head slowly, overcome with amazement as his understanding underwent a world shift. He was where he had started, eons ago—the very place where a young scientist, one sunny afternoon had approached Alex and Maryan to ask if they would be willing to contribute blood and cell specimens for some routine research.

Alex loved the touch of her hand. She might be a champion figure skater, but her touch was soft and feminine. The sun shone warmly, and he felt the ripping sexuality of springtime as he kissed her hand. Her eyes reflected the same hunger, and she ran the fingers of her other hand through his hair. Their picnic lunch, as they sat beside Mirror Lake, remained packed and untouched, and it would soon be time for them to split up to go to their afternoon classes. Alex was on a three-letter scholarship—swimming, baseball, and track—majoring in Chemistry and minoring in Literature to get a nice spread. Maryan was on a track scholarship and was majoring in International Relations and minoring in Linguistics; she also spent several hours most days practicing figure skating. They really had to make the most of every little hour they could squeeze out together.

"Hello," said a man's voice.

They looked up. Alex saw a long-haired, smallish man, probably in his mid 20's, with the look of a grad student. He wore a white shirt open at the collar, dark trousers, and his hair back in a pony tail. He had a full reddish-dark beard, and on a leash at his feet scampered a puppy.

"Oh how cute!" said Maryan.

The man waved a metallic clipboard. "Hi, I'm (name forgotten) in Biochemistry. We're doing some routine experiments, and he wonder if you'd be willing to donate some specimens."

"What kind of research?" Maryan asked.

"Just routine stuff," he said. "Genetics."

Alex was a bit puzzled. "You want specimens—for what?"

"To run some genome sequences," the man said glibly. "It's a statistical thing."

"Oh," Alex and Maryan said in unison.

"You get a free dinner at a nice restaurant." He waved tickets.

"Oh well," Alex and Maryan said, laughing as they looked into each other's eyes, "in that case, sure!"

And here, a million years later, he knelt as the tradeoff for that dinner. He was grateful to be alive—He had the great spirit of Alex Kirk, after all—but wouldn't it have been better if they'd said no? And what had happened to mankind, anyway? What had killed them off?

As he slowly rose, relieved that his memories were most certainly real, he recoiled in horror. He backed up quickly, stepping over the round stones buried in the sand.

They weren't stones at all, but skulls. He realized that when he saw that several were upturned, and their empty eye sockets stared at him. And he recognized as well that these skulls were different from those he'd glimpsed outside his birthing cave—these were smaller, finer, narrower—as Maryan's had been compared to Alex's.

This was his bright discovery that day. The dark one was about to follow.

No time to stand there in shock.

He heard a rumbling sound.

A terrible scream rent the air.

He caught a glimpse of a naked woman—her body hideously deformed into round puffs of flesh, her head flattened on one side with no ear or eye or hair, her remaining eye blank with terror as she ran to the water, her hands vainly thrashing in the air... she was a poor sister of Maryan Shurey—He was sure of it—and almost himself screamed in horror and revulsion.

He remembered his own poor brother, whom he'd killed. The valley was full of skulls of his brothers and her sisters. How many perfectly beautiful copies of her had come into the world, only to be horrifically devoured like the wretch whose brief life he had just seen end?

A second later, two adult rippers were upon her, tearing her apart.

He dove into the river, partly from fear, partly because he could not bear to see more. The cleansing water took him out to sea, from where he numbly swam back to his boat.

He was sure the rippers would be busy in their valley for the rest of the afternoon.

6. Friday

He felt a terrible urgency now that he knew where the women's birthing cave was.

Maryan Shurey filled his dreams with memories of their intimate nights together. He could almost look over his shoulder and follow the latest detective drama or comical commercial, except that his passion kept bringing him back into her arms even as he awakened at night, filled with need. The purpose of things was falling into place in a vague manner. He knew that Beacham University had been pivotal in gathering genetic material. He knew something terrible had happened leading to mankind's extinction. He sensed the desperate manner in which things had been done, to land him and his fellow clones in this far-distant exile beyond time. He knew, most of all, that he must find a copy of Maryan Shurey, though the realization weighed heavily on him that something in the unseen master plan had gone wrong: all the clones were sterile. Was there a point in going on at all?

Yes, because I am lonely, and I have a right.

He spent every daylight hour patrolling the cliffs from a safe distance away from the valley. His most immediate task now must be to neutralize the rippers so he could get close to the birthing cave.

He studied the individual rippers, getting to know them and their habits. How could he get over there—and how get into the birthing caves without being seen by the rippers?

What if he hunted the rippers one by one and killed them? How many days or weeks before the next pride entered the valley to take charge? Not a worthwhile plan. But maybe he could thin their numbers for a while, keep them on the run, fill them with fear if that was possible, maybe even scare them off for a time until their natural hunger and greed got the better of them.

How long until the next birth in the caves? A day? A month? A year? A century? This process had been going on for ages.

He must get into the opposite hill and make a determination, once and for all, if he had any hope of having a sound, sane mate in this world. What would he not give for her sweet company, her warmth beside him at night, someone to talk to? Just think—he'd never ever gotten a hug, a kiss, a kind word. He'd been struggling so hard to survive that he'd forgotten the depths of the misery he lived in.

He made himself a deadly new bow, stronger than the first, and a set of arrows. He would carry two bows—one a back up if the first failed. He would carry thirty arrows, each two feet long with a fire hardened point dipped in excrement. He would tie them in bundles of five, and five bundles together into one roll on his back, with five arrows in hand for quick use. These weren't the all-purpose hunting arrows he'd been making. These were beast-killers.

At dawn, after eating a good meal, he climbed down from his plateau. He jogged across the beach carrying his weapons. Quickly he pushed the boat into the water and jumped in. He sailed along the coast with his bows and arrows on his belly neatly bundled, his spare arrows slung together and trailing in the water.

He passed the valley and came ashore on the other side, in a slightly different place as he did each time to keep potential stalkers guessing. He clambered up the hill, one hump at a time, until he came to the top of the coastal hills. He followed the canyon edge as slowly and noiselessly as he could, with one arrow ready to cock and fire and more at hand.

He stayed out of sight from the river. He saw the rippers lazing in the sun, unaware of him. Something long and white lay tattered among them, and he felt revulsion at the thought of what—or who—that might be. One of the adults was gnawing on something Alex was almost sure was a torso.

He searched up and down the ridge, going back finally away from the rim. He was becoming more paranoid by the moment, thinking he'd been crazy to come here. The more time went by, the more likely the rippers would come up here, as had that recent big one he'd slain. He kept checking the wind, which was very light and blowing northeasterly. Damn, it could shift just as easily and blow east, and they knew his scent. God, they loved his smell. It must be like an aphrodisiac, their holy grail.

Then he found something.

About 200 feet back in the woods was a pile of brush that looked oddly as if it had washed up somehow. He pulled some of it away, and found underneath a kind of slate slab. There might have once been a handle on it, but that would be worn away by now by the simple night wind over so many eons.

Looking over his shoulder constantly, he labored at the slab.

It wouldn't budge.

He heard a distant roar.

He lay down and pushed against the slab with his hands, pushing his feet the other way against a tree trunk.

Nothing. He threw himself on the slab and frantically brushed off several feet of dirt and rocks.

Then he stretched out again.

He heard another roar, and froze listening.

Nothing. His heart pounded in his ears and his breath came in gasps.

Silence.

He pushed, and the slab moved aside. It made a stony noise almost like metal dragging on stone. Then he realized that it was what was left of a manhole cover.

A wan shaft of light fell inside, and he saw a hill of earth piled up. Over the ages, tiny rivulets of sand and water must have leaked in. But the tanks were still active. He lowered himself in resolutely. With an arrow cocked, he waited just below the hole for his night vision to return. He saw dim glowing objects, and knew what they were - mushrooms growing on the walls.

The cone of soil on which he stood yielded a bit, sending down a shower, and he sank a foot or so into it, but then his feet hit firm, compressed soil. He sat on his haunches, arrow ready, and waited.

He listened intently.

Wind moaned faintly across the hole above him.

Below, in the caves, he heard splashing. He heard a dull sound, like a voice.

He went down, cautiously, one step at a time.

He heard a murmur. Laughing? Crying?

A sharp cry. Pain? Fear?

Step by step, he made his way forward. In the darkness, his pupils opened wide, and the soothing light of the mushrooms began to let him see how his skin glistened a faint bluish-white.

He heard laughter, crying, then a scream.

He inched forward, his heart pounding.

Then he heard Maryan's voice: "Please, no!"

He ran forward, splashing through puddles.

Here were the birthing galleries still active. He smelled the familiar freshness of the greens, and his ankles sloshed through liquid. His soles began to feel soft and comfortable—hadn't realized how hard they'd become.

Despite the healing fluid, a smell of death hung in the air.

He took it all in, in a flash: three galleries... one dark and empty... The second with a shape in a tank... in the third, three figures: two mutants, one normal...

With a yell, he stepped into the room.

They barely looked up, the two puff-girls gnawing at the viscera of Maryan who lay naked and sprawled against the wall. She was immersed six inches in the healing green water that could do nothing for her now.

Using his bow as a whip, he beat the two unfortunates until he saw red welts on their backs. One tore out a piece of meat and ran cowering toward the front of the cave. The other he had to kick and beat before she would take her arms out of the torso.

He kicked the second mutant out of the way and knelt by Maryan, but there was nothing he could do. He touched her—she was still warm—so this was the one who had begged for mercy.

Numbed with horror and disappointment, he staggered out of there and went into the second gallery.

The figure he'd seen was a mummy. Her shriveled face and hands peered out of a dry, empty tank. He saw what must have happened—her killers had devoured the nutrient rich abdomen with their umbilical cords, and must have been so rough that they tore the stem of the umbilicus out of the bottom of the tank, so that it drained. The mummy's bottom half was missing. As he went by, the wind of his passage made her topped over forward like a chunk of papier-mâché.

"No!" he yelled. "No!"

He had risked his life for nothing, chancing the rippers to come here.

He went from tank to tank—nothing.

Then he heard a rumbling sound. He felt a rush of adrenalin, and clung to the nearest tank. A slat of light stabbed into the cave.

He listened for roaring noises, but none came.

His curiosity compelled him to rush toward the cave entrance, though his mind screamed for him to stop.

He saw the two misshapen creatures run out side. Rippers pounced on them.

He just rounded the corner into the front cave as a ripper loped out, carrying in its jaws the body of the women who had just died.

He heard a squeak that sounded like fabric tearing: the tendons on the wall were moving, contracting the giant brownish muscle tissue that operated the door—and the door slammed shut, sealing him in darkness.

He wanted to cry, but he was beyond emotion, in shock. He staggered dimly about... realizing that he could stay here, that he could kill any mutants that developed, that he would rescue the next Maryan.

He broke a piece of mushroom off the wall. He knelt on the floor and drank the healing water. Between bites and gulps, he made a meal of the liquid and the mushroom bread.

Then he climbed up the mound and pushed the slab back into place, shutting himself in.

He would stay here as long as it took.

He would die here if he did not succeed. He wasn't worth going into the world again alone.

He sat down with his back to the wall and began the wait.

Slowly he sagged downward until he was lying down. His thoughts began to drift, and he must have fallen asleep...

Alex was with Maryan, holding hands and running along the shore of a lake. She was so beautiful, with her healthy red cheeks and fine face. Her blonde hair hung in pigtails—ah yes, that trip to Lake George in 2010! They'd made love there for the first time, after two years of intense petting. They'd already vowed to marry, and this was their first vacation together. They were both 20.

It had been dim in the bedroom at the motel, with the Venetian blinds drawn, and the summer sunlight filtered to a honey-brown glow. Alex had held her thighs against his ribs, feeling the softness of her knees under his armpits as he thrust, so wonderfully, and thrust again, and each time she moaned. She clutched the rumpled bed sheets and turned her head from side to side...

...Not moaning, but sobbing.

Cold wet hands shook him, and a bloody tangle waved before his eyes.

He threw himself against the wall in recoil at the horror before him.

The monstrosity fell over Alex; he felt its cool flesh against his; and it landed with a splat of flesh in a shallow puddle of green parsley.

He could smell blood about it. Had it been feasting somewhere in the darkness?

He stood over it, his bow raised to come down on its neck and kill it.

It turned, raising one hand in supplication.

"Please," it said.

He sagged in wonder. It was she.

"Maryan?"

"Alex?"

"I can't believe this!" He was on his knees, hugging her. She felt slippery and wet, and cried out in pain.

He looked down and saw the torn umbilical dangling from her.

"Where are we? What's going on?"

At that moment he heard the door again, crazed with the ardor of giving birth again and again.

A stab of light.

A cautious, questioning growl rumbled powerfully through the caves.

He looked down the corridor, through the open cave mouth, and saw a ripper prowling on the distant river bank. Another of the powerful animals just then slipped into the caves with searching eyes and open, hungrily dripping snout.

Alex held a hand over Maryan's mouth. "You have to be absolutely silent," he whispered.

Wide-eyed, she nodded.

He took her by the hand and they retreated deeper into the cave. He chambered an arrow and looked watchfully behind. The majority of the rippers were busy on the river bank or in the entrance and had not yet scented Alex and Maryan. The rippers were busy chewing on white puffy objects, and their muzzles were red.

Alex noticed that Maryan was doubled over in pain, and he kept his arm comfortingly around her. She was perfectly formed, and he knew that the tree-knot of umbilical matter should fall off soon as her abdomen healed. He examined the ends briefly, saw teeth marks—the mutants had gnawed them off, causing her to birth prematurely as he had. "We have to stay in the caves until you are healed," he told her. "You need the green water to heal you."

He didn't mention his fear that a massive infection would kill her as surely as the attentions of the rippers.

The cave door closed and the rippers were shut out.

The caverns resumed their timeless quiet. Water dripped into birthing tanks. It was too dark to see in which tanks another Maryan or other woman might be growing, and in which some monstrosity, and yet which other tanks were past the point of ever giving birth again.

Maryan grew very sick, and Alex nursed her hour after hour, bathing her in the healing water, cradling her in his arms which she breathed in labored gasps and her body was racked with fever. He kissed her cheek, touched her face and her arms with his hands, tried to keep his tears from spilling over her. He should be grateful to have had her for a few days, he thought. At least he had for the first and only time in his life felt the nearness of another human being. Slowly, she improved, and they lived in the eerie tranquility of faint green light. They ate wall mushrooms and sat talking together. They embraced each other and explored what it meant to love another person, both in the body and in the soul. They reminisced about the ice cream truck and other memories of growing up in Beacham University. Each had some extra memories to contribute that the other had lost, and so Alex learned that Alex Kirk had been a Special Forces commando during one of the Middle Eastern wars.

As he remembered the healing atmosphere and healing waters of his own cave, the brilliance of this place fill him with a solar clarity. He understood: Eons ago, there had been the university, and this cloning center. For some reason, mankind had vanished. The earth had shifted, tearing the male and female wings apart a quarter mile. The river had pushed through, clearing out a valley. The cloning facility was so powerfully intoxicated with the life principle that it had evolved, become an organic thing. After all, here was a breeding ground of human stem cells, a loom that wove constant tapestries of DNA.

Time passed, and he slumbered by her side as she lay in her birthing tank. At some point, he awoke, filled with a sense of urgency. He looked down into the tank, where she floated like a shimmering mosaic image at the bottom.

The very next moment, she sat up in a fan of flying water and gasped for air. She gripped the sides of the tank with her fists and looked straightaway with wild, wide eyes.

He thought his heart skipped a beat, and he took a step backward.

"Ah!" she cried, and started breathing in loud gasps. Water, blood, and mucus flew from her nostrils. Her breathing gurgled as if through a tube.

She grasped her neck and writhed in the tank splashing water everywhere. She was choking on something.

He grasped her from behind, linked his fists, and pulled them sharply upward into her solar plexus.

She started coughing violently, crawling about, but whatever she'd been choking on was loose and gone now.

At last she rose, calming down, exhausted from her ordeal.

The mass of tissue on her belly was smaller and pinker. The bite marks were gone—the necrotic tissue had dissolved. She was healing!

And the tank had kept her alive through the deepest coma, when he'd thought she was dead.

They whooped and laughed and held each other, for quite a while. And they spoke. Did they ever speak! they chattered like two kids.

They had become so accustomed to their unchanging existence that they nearly did not notice the creaking sound that signaled that the door was about to open.

Alex gathered his weapons and had Maryan hide as far back in the caves as possible, right in the piled soil he'd slid down from on his entry.

He strode through the galleries to meet his fate.

He even bent to take a few good drinks of the healing water of life.

Then he strode to the entrance. He felt the roaring before he heard it, a deep exploratory growl. He armed himself and made his way forward into the daylight that now bathed the forward chamber.

As he entered the first gallery, fitted his best arrow to the bowstring. The door had partially opened, just two or three feet—a twitch, perhaps? No reason—nothing about to issue forth.

And there stood two of the devils, breathing hard. He could see steam coming from their mouths. Their mouths hung open in what looked like a fiendish smile. Their eyes interlocked, and they could read each other's minds.

He drew back with all his strength and let fly, right into the torso of the closer.

Without waiting, he reached for the next arrow, chambered it, pulled apart with all his might, and let fly.

In seconds, both rippers were thrashing on the ground, making their wounds infinitely worse. Their screams and snarls were so deafening that he reeled back holding his ears.

He should have had another arrow ready, for one of them rose in a flash, turned toward him, and leaped.

He saw it coming at him, and barely managed to move out of the way.

But it fell short, with a loud thump, and lay dying at his feet.

He put an arrow through its neck.

Then he stepped over it and put another arrow through the other one's neck.

He drew his knife and attacked the sinew of the door.

He thought he heard a thin, distant scream come from the living cave as he tore out its fingernail, one might say. He carved and carved until blood ran down the walls and the door slowly rumbled shut with a helpless bounce. He found heavy rocks and piled them against the edge so that the door could not slid open again. Then, using another large rocks, he smashed the skulls of the two animals he had just killed.

He would wear their pelts as a sign of triumph.

But first—the most important matter of all. He must bring Maryan to her new home so that they could make a life together.

Alex and Maryan talked and talked, of nothing and everything, chattering constantly, never growing tired of touching one other, yet each still very shy with the other.

They sailed to the sky island together, delighted to have each other's company. She asked questions about this strange new life, and he told her his story and his theories about the world in which they found themselves. When she saw his dwelling on the sky island, she said: "Hmm, this is going to require some work."

He put his arm around her. "It's not much, but it's our home."

After showing her around the cliff, he became anxious about the hide in the water. He was even more anxious about parting from her side, but she lay down to rest. She fell asleep in minutes, and he lay beside her. He watched the even rise and fall of her shoulder, the strong and steady pulse in her neck, even the fine down along the line of her cheek. He felt good having her here, and the shelter felt warm and secure.

A little bit of light leaked in, and for those moments it might as well have been a motel room at Lake George a million years earlier.

While she slept on her first day in her new home, Alex climbed down and crossed the beach.

The buffalo carcass had moved out a bit, but the tide was low and it was stuck on the sand, covered with birds. The ribs and spine were clearly visible. The fish had done a good job of cleaning it, alternating with seagulls and pelicans. He sharpened his stone knife as best he could on a thick piece of bone, and then carved away what he wanted of the hide. There were ripper teeth marks throughout, and this particular hide would be good only for odds and ends. But nothing would get thrown away. He left the hide exposed for the birds and fishes to clean it up.

Climbing back up to the cliff, he looked in on Maryan. She slept soundly and evenly. A good long sleep would do her good.

He went to the north edge and surveyed the valley. The surviving four rippers appeared restive—one adult and three young. They knew their numbers were dangerously low to defend their territory. The cubs were probably up to about 100 pounds by now, and quite powerful looking. Perhaps, with the birthing cave no longer such a safe and lucrative feeding source, they would move on in search of other food. Or they might intensify their efforts to get him. And now that he had Maryan, he must make the world safe for his kind.

As he sat watching them, he figured that he had their movements down pretty pat. In the afternoons, after hunting down and devouring the morning's kill, they liked to sun themselves on that spit of sand that protruded into the river. They were surrounded on three sides by dense, old brush, and it was pretty dry. He formed an idea, and went to his fire chamber.

Some time ago, he had idly fashioned the first of several clay vessels. This was shaped like a cup, and contained stray bits of tinder and fat. He had also made a candle from buffalo tallow. He emptied the cup and inserted the candle. Making sure his sacred fire was well fed, he lit the candle and placed a stone lid on it. With his bows and arrows and stone knife, and holding the cup carefully in both hands, he made his way down to the beach.

This time he did not swim, but he walked through the marshes in the alluvial plain. He'd never been here before, and saw plenty of small game and wild life. If he could keep the valley clear of predators, he could live well here with his bride.

He jogged along, careful to stay downwind of the rippers.

He had a tricky time crossing the river outside its fan, where its current was weak. He had to keep the cup above water at all times—the bottom of it was wet by the time he paddled ashore on the west beach, but the flame still flickered. If that went out, his trip here had been in vain.

He climbed up the rocks and made his way into the woods above the valley, not far from where he'd found Maryan. There he gathered just the right kinds of torch materials—goodly sticks, and dry moss to wrap around them. He fed the little fire carefully with a bit of spare tallow and a new wick. He also built a small campfire using what he could find—some cow dung, leaves, dry wood. The fire was hot and not very smoky—it would take them a while to smell it.

Even at that, as he watched from above, he could see their muzzles sniffing—but they would do that all the time. They lay lazily on their sides, ribs showing, heaving with sleepy breathing. They blinked into the sunshine and soaked in the day's warmth.

He was working hard, and perspiring.

When he was ready, he had about two dozen torches lying in a row, and a nice fire going, about a foot in diameter.

He laid five of the torches in the fire, head first, and waited a moment until they were ablaze. One by one, he threw them down. Another five. Same thing. And another. And then the last.

By now, all four animals were on their feet staring dumbly.

A wall of fire was growing faster by the second, a wall of smoke and heat about 100 feet long, cutting off their escape. They milled nervously, snarling, and kept to the edge of the water.

The water boiled by at a furious clip, bringing branches and other debris from the mountains. It looked green like jade and cold, with foamy teats and a mean disposition. The rippers seemed to fear it as much as they did the smoke on their other flanks.

He must act fast to capitalize on the situation. Recklessly, he slithered down directly into the valley. The adult female was trying desperately to cross through the hot embers as the fire began to die town. He put three arrows through her and she went down, twitching.

He circled around the north side, coming down in the sand just at the edge of the fire. With the greenery burned away, the three cubs had a similar idea to come his way. He shot the first one and it fell in the water. The other two turned to run, and he followed them up onto their skull-laden inner sanctum. There, he shot the second, and it lay down helplessly, taking deep twitching breaths as it started to die with his arrow protruding from its side.

The last cub snarled and got in a stance ready to spring at him. He shot an arrow down its open throat, and emptied his quiver into it.

Alex cooked a bit of ripper meat over a small fire and washed it down with cold river water.

Then he skinned them, one by one, until his hands ached and his arm felt numb and wooden. They would make nice pelts for his bed. Maryan's bed. Their bed.

He even forced open the women's birthing door and there, amid the stink of decay, pulled out the two other carcasses and dragged them to the river. He watched them catch in the current and float swiftly toward the sea.

He recovered about half his arrows—the animals in their death throes had mashed the other half.

Leaving the three skins to dry in the sun and be picked clean by small animals and birds, he now bravely ran through the heart of ripper valley toward the sea.

He found the other three carcasses near one another. He found a small log and floated it in the water. He tied the rippers' tails to the log and pushed it through the current until he had it on the east side. There, he walked in the water, pulling it along until he came to their beach. He pulled the load as far ashore as he could so that the log was anchored while the carcasses were in the water. Already, silver shapes moved visibly about in the water, ready for feeding.

He pulled the hide from the buffalo carcass up on dry sand to finish its first curing.

Out of habit, he still looked over his shoulder every minute or two.

This time, it was not a ripper that came bounding toward him, but Maryan. She looked sleepy but rested. "I'm starving," she said.

"We have some great beetles here."

She made a face.

He sat in the water and carved some meat off the cubs. "Let's go have us a steak dinner."

She stood arms akimbo. "I was mad because I thought we missed that one."

Alex laughed. He knew what she meant—that student who had taken samples from Alex and Maryan. "I hope old Alex and old Maryan enjoyed their dinner as much as we are going to enjoy this."

"Wish we had a bottle of wine."

He told her: "I saw fruit trees along the coast. If we can make salt from the sea water, I think we can make just about anything we want, including wine. Just not for tonight."

"Aw darn." She snapped her fingers.

Alex and Maryan had two good years in their little world before everything changed.

They walked arm in arm along the beach. They sailed up and down the coast, bringing back fruit trees. For a while, they kept a monkey as a pet, but eventually it got lonely and ran away, probably looking for a female of its kind; Maryan and Alex missed him, but they couldn't blame him.

They wanted to create a memorial in the valley, to put all the skulls and bones in one place, but after a short effort they realized that there must be hundreds, if not thousands, of them and they gave up. They had a small pile of skulls, and they threw those into the river with great reverence.

For a while they moved to the island, where they managed a small sheep farm on the high meadow. Then the fog and the eeriness of the sunken village with its burial vaults, and the old woman's cottage where she had committed suicide, and the beach where he'd found Dot's body...it all got to be too much and they moved back up to the sky island. They only returned to the village periodically to cull the sheep, to get wool, and sometimes to overnight when they were tired from fishing.

Before they killed the caves once and for all, Alex took Maryan on an exploration of his birthplace. The dead child still floated in its brine, as if made of chalk. Maryan held her palms to her cheeks and was horrified. The clone he'd killed was barely a skeleton anymore, for the healing waters had absorbed him. The birthing tanks were empty. He finally realized that the cave-in had injured the cave so much that it had died. Only the healing waters still showed that same spunky freshness. The area where he'd been born, which was choked with soil and rocks now, was lushly overgrown with grasses and vines. Tiny animals skittered about. Birds marched around, picking and pecking. The hole above was too large to close—he'd thought about bringing the manhole cover from the other place, but the cover was much too small. He did not have the time or the energy to fell trees and drag them over...he'd have to let this go.

The mushrooms still grew here and there, but it was obvious they were dying out. With them, and the miraculous water, Alex knew something precious had been lost that could never be recovered.

The decision to kill the caves came one night when they were sitting around their campfire. They'd had a good day, because they'd located a small field of wild wheat and they'd brought back a basket full of seeds—yes, she knew how to weave baskets, and they made pottery in their kiln—and they were talking about planting fields so they could bake bread and have oatmeal and so forth.

From the darkness came a faint cry that might or might now have been human.

Maryan rose and said darkly: "It's a sister."

"Maybe it's only some small animal," he said.

They listened, and did not hear anything more.

"I want to destroy the facility," she said.

He thought about the nutrient mushrooms and the healing water.

"We can't allow anymore clones to be born, Alex."

"Okay..." he could see her reasoning. "But then we'd lose the water that saved your life."

She thought about that. "Then you'll have to do what's necessary."

"And that is?"

"Go in regularly and abort anything that's growing."

They thought about this in silence for a while, upset and hurt by their difference of opinions. He had a horrible image in his mind. "I could destroy the mutants without much problem. But what about the next you?" he finished in a whisper: "I couldn't harm you."

"Then the right thing is to destroy the entire place," she said finally.

"Why not just let the healthy clones live?"

"Alex, you are the science major. Think! There is no gene pool. We are doomed. We can only beget inbred idiots—which brings me to the next thing. I've been thinking—I don't want to have children anyway."

He scratched his head. Of course she was right. He had been so busy surviving that he had not thought about the future much. There was a long silence during which he stirred the fire between them, adding a small log to keep it alive. "You realize that if we don't let any more clones be born—."

"I don't want any more clones born," she said with finality.

"Okay, then. It means you and I will live our lives out here together and then one of us will probably die first, leaving the other alone."

She came and embraced him. "I'm sorry, Alex. That's why we can't permit another human being to suffer like this."

They held each other, perhaps loving each other more than any two persons ever have, because they were each all there was, or would ever be.

The next day they set out together for the female birthing caves. The boat needed some repair, so they left it on the beach and walked through the alluvial plain. They each had a bow and arrows, but saw no rippers.

The cave door swung loosely, and the interior smelled of death. "I'm pretty sure the cave itself has died," he told her.

"Let's make sure."

"Okay."

They inspected the birthing tanks—nothing new growing. He had his heavy mallet with him, and now he smashed the tanks, one by one. When the mallet broke in two, he discarded it. He upended the remaining tanks. If none of them could hold fluid, nothing could grow there.

He knelt down and sniffed the water—it had a flat, greasy smell and debris floated in it. The cave was dead.

They made sure the manhole cover was secure, and on their way out they closed the door and barricaded it with rocks so it could not open again.

They left great smoky, roaring fires burning in the caves, that could be seen for miles at night, in order to eliminate any possibility of further unfortunates being born.

The days were getting a little shorter as the Earth moved far from the sun.

Alex worried about winter coming, or what would pass for winter in this semitropical place. He had no idea what that would bring, but if they were unprepared for cold, they'd die here. They had a half dozen ripper hides, which were fairly pliable and kept them warm. He supposed they could always move over to the island if need be.

Every morning, they'd begin their day by climbing up on the north face of his old cliff, and surveying the valley. He knew for sure that one of these days they'd see new rippers or even worse predators moving down into their domain.

They loved each other very deeply, and their sex was passionate and long. At first they hadn't thought about pregnancy. Then they used condoms that he made from intestine from their cattle herd. Finally they realized after a few accidents that the infection had probably left her sterile—or perhaps they were both sterile from a genetic standpoint. They stopped worrying about it and enjoyed what time they might have. They relished every day. They worked and played hard, and talked often about the dimly remembered lives of young Alex Kirk and Maryan Shurey.

They built a wooden house around a central fireplace that they made of stone and mud. The autumn and winter, when they came, were not too severe. They had warm clothing (though no wool yet; they doubled hides and stuck straw between them). They had warm, waterproof (greased) boots with soles that he carved for them out of wood.

They built a boat and went fishing, using rodent gut for lines. They took their boat up and down the coast a mile or so, and finally located a flock of woolly animals similar to sheep. They brought several males and females home with them and left them on the cliff, where they could not escape. They used his old shelter at night, and pretty soon there were six or eight of them. They spent their days happily chewing on anything green, of which there was plenty, and in season they began to leave puffs of fur in the hedges as they moved about. They had only to gather armfuls of the material to spin into wool. He had not yet found any metals, but that would come. He did find a way to melt beach sand and pour a sheet of glass. You could not see through it, but he took several sheets up on the cliff to make improved nighttime water stills for the sheep. He captured a queen bee and soon had a thriving bee hive. He built a pottery wheel and threw any kind of vessel that Maryan or he needed. They brought in more fruit trees and planted them around their house. They had grapes, apples, pears, and various kinds of berries. The vines grew nicely around the house. He could take, say, a few handfuls of berries and a cup of water and boil them in a clay pot, stirring constantly with a wooden ladle, until a kind of hot jam was left. Then he could seal this in clay jar using beeswax to seal them. They could store these in their three-room cave storehouse.

They made more glass and created a refinery where they could evaporate seawater and obtain a respectable amount of salt—more than they could immediately use. They became experts at brining and smoking meats, using their excess salt and a smokehouse he built in a few days near their home. They had several racks of smoked meat in their store house, hanging from a wooden rafter to make it hard for scavengers to get to the meat. It was tough and salty, but it could tide them over in a pinch. Some days he'd go out and catch a dozen or so respectable sized fish, and they'd smoke some of those for storage.

No new rippers had yet settled in their valley, though they did hear coyotes and wolves howling at night. They wanted a good dog, but dogs had long ago returned to feral pack life. Most wild animals would not become reliable pets. Besides, there was no better watchdog than a group of geese—cantankerous and dangerous birds, but they wouldn't hesitate to attach a marauding fox and drive it from their young. After two years, Alex and Maryan were doing very well.

7. Siirk

One day early in summer, Maryan and Alex were out on the alluvial plain.

The sky was blue and cloudless, though it was a whitish blue that sometimes meant lots of moisture. The moon had seemed real large the night before, like an omen, though it probably meant moisture was magnifying it. So even though it was sunny, they weren't excessively warm, and thought that was just all right.

They were gathering berries and flowers, always looking for new herbs. She was about a hundred feet from him, when they heard a noise.

They looked at each other, then around, and at each other again.

"Did you hear something?" she called. He could still picture her as she stood there, wearing a wool kerchief over her head and a long leather dress. She looked beautiful in a lean and grave manner, holding her basket with both hands.

He put a finger to his lips and snapped an arrow to his bow. Cautiously, he walked through knee high grass toward her, cocking an ear for further noises, and looking north for signs of their old enemies the rippers.

Then more noises—voices?—they ran toward each other, but it was too late.

A man-like thing burst into the clearing coming from the sea. He was covered with short dark fur and had a head somewhere between human and animal, with black human ears but less a face than a boxy tapering snout covered in the same dark fur. He bled dark red blood from gashes along his torso, and appeared weak.

Maryan screamed and dropped her basket.

In the same moment, several other beings came into view riding on smallish horses. That was the noise they'd heard—the clatter of hooves, muffled on the beach sand, occasionally clanging against a rock. The men on the horses were no more men than their quarry.

As the victim burst into view, several deafening shots rang out. The creature fell on the ground and slid in the dust, dead.

Maryan and Alex tried to run, but the riders were upon them, circling them. Nets flew through the air, fell heavily upon them smelling of rot and fish. Alex struggled, but the riders had ropes through the net, and it tightened with him inside like in a purse. The riders dragged him some distance over the sand before stopping. Maryan was being similarly manhandled a few yards away. Alex glimpsed her white figure in a net being dragged. She was on her back, head slightly raised off the ground, and hands helplessly raised to her chin.

Now Alex got a better glimpse of their captors, who dismounted and strode, swaggering and grinning, toward them. The Siirk were chilling to look upon, a mix more of reptile than anything else, though they had streaming white manes that hinted of some long-ago mammal in the stew. They wore fancy, well-tooled leather and cloth clothing, with wide belts and guns. They had leather leggings and boots. But they were lizard-like—men with lizard teeth and leathery faces. They were covered with a random mix of gray and white scales, particularly from the lower lip down, on the pale softness under their chins, along their jowls, down into scaly necks. Their eyes were like dark buttons that radiated a kind of gloating ruthlessness. What made them all the more scary was their similarity rather than dissimilarity from humans. Alex shivered to think what genetic experiments by man or nature to produce these beings.

Their leader presented himself before him and rubbed his belly. The rasp of scales over scales was audible. "Si-i-r-k," he said in a loud hissing voice (sounding sort of like "silk" or "seelk," with a nasty kind of self-satisfied drawl on the "ee" as if being a Siirk tasted good). "Siiirk!"

The Siirk wore an amulet—a plain disk, dark brown, maybe metallic, about six inches long and as thick as his index finger—on a leather thong around his neck.

Alex was terrified that he meant he and Maryan would taste good. He looked at Maryan fearing for her composure, but she sat stolidly, even bravely, waiting for their next move. They'd talked often about the dangers of their new world, and in one glance their eyes agreed that most likely this was the end. She made a small kiss with her mouth toward him, which he returned, trying to smile. If they killed them, he hoped they would kill her first, quickly, and then him just as quickly.

"Siirk!" the leader bellowed again, and someone kicked Alex in the side, below the kidneys, sending him doubled up on his elbows and thighs. "Siirk!" the creature yelled; he looked upward and gesticulated with his hands. Downward. Something would come downward. Rain? A bird? An arrow. He yelled at him, and stamped his feet in frustration.

The next Siirk they were to meet was Omas, the overseer, who had a stick with a leather thong on the end. *Ouch!* That thing bit! He had another leather thong on the other end, and that one had a brass ball in it a third the size of a small marble. He never did use that on him, but he now understood what had torn gouges in the body of the fleeing Thuga. For that was their name, the slave people—Thuga, which he took to mean "I spit on you," because whenever the Siirk spoke that word, they made as if spitting.

The three Siirk they most dealt with daily were Omas, the overseer; Nizin, the paramount chief; and Kogran, his equally swaggering son.

They opened the nets so they could set their feet on the ground and walk; but they kept the nets over them, and each of them tied by a twenty foot rope to the saddle of a horse. On the two horses wrote Siirk warriors in brass-studded leather armor, their white manes blowing from under leather helmets.

Omas gave them each one taste of his lesser lash, across the buttocks, and he felt a pain like fire. He heard Maryan suck in her breath and gasp, but she did not cry. Omas walked around them, brandishing his lash and giving them "haw, haw" 's that sounded threatening and educational all at once.

They walked them down to a fleet of boats that lay beached. These reminded him of Viking boats Alex had seen in pictures, but the boats were smaller and wider. They had a simple square sail that could be angled for tacking.

The boats had simple wooden seats—for Siirk only. Alex and Maryan were made to sit on the floor, getting their butts wet with the thin bilge that rolled back and forth.

It seemed the Siirk had come for slaves and cattle. They appropriated their entire herd, and planned to walk them eastward to Siirk territory under the guidance of horsemen. There were a dozen boats, 100 heavily armed Siirk, and maybe thirty Thuga, most of the latter in leg chains. Of this party, about ten Thuga walked among the cattle, for they were cattle themselves in the eyes of the Siirk. And they appeared to be docile, unintelligent creatures. Half of the Siirk were land-based, and 20 of those were mounted. The rest carried pikes and walked—foot soldiers, he presumed.

Nizin, the paramount chief, sat in the boat with Maryan and Alex. Nizin gloated over them like a great prize. He saw the intelligence in their eyes, and laughed, nodding, as if to say, *yes, I know you're bright, but I'm always going to be a step ahead of you.* His smile had something dirty about it, and he wasn't sure if he planned to eat them or to molest Maryan.

Soon the expedition set off, for the Siirk were not ones to waste time. The dozen boats sailed slowly in the quiet sea about 100 feet off shore. The lazy pace of the cattle, which had to be whipped to move along, slowed those on shore. The Siirk sat in middle of the boat where the rocking was least, while the six Thuga rowers sat in the back of the boat, and a Siirk with a whip behind them. The cracking of that whip happened more frequently than he think was warranted. The Thuga had a bovine, mute quality and they kept rowing. They never spoke with one another.

Soon the boats began to outpace those on shore, particularly when the cattle had to be transported through the water to go around outcroppings. Nizin waved the boats on impatiently, looking at him like a child who'd just gotten a new electric train set for Christmas. It was just the dozen boats then, with their Thuga rowers and Siirk soldiers, and them, heading into the unknown—and no good, he was sure of that.

He managed to whisper "I love you," and Maryan whispered the words back to him, and Omas brandished his whip, but Nizin brushed him off. Nizin came and sat down on his haunches and stared into their faces. He motioned with his hands: *Speak, speak! I want to see you speak!*

"He wants us to speak," Alex said.

"Careful, he may understand English."

Nizin bounced with delight and pointed at her. "*Ingish! Ingish!*" he nodded and motioned for her to say more.

"Go screw yourself?" she opined.

Nizin shrugged. "*Ingish.*" he shook his head and mumbled several times, "*Ingish.*" He pointed at Alex and laughed and yelled: "*Geedeen!*"

"English?" Alex asked.

He nodded joyfully and looked over his shoulder at Kogran, who laughed and nodded. "*Geedeen!*" they both said.

"*Geedeen,*" Alex said agreeably, but that seemed to make them mad.

After a while—how often and how many different ways can one say "English" and "*Geedeen?*"—they tired of this game and retired to their bench.

The hours went by, and the monotony of the shore was unbroken—forests as far as he could see.

Alex began to notice some odd things. For one thing, one or two of the Thuga appeared to be feigning dumbness. They had bright, furtive eyes that they kept pointing downward.

Secondly, the Siirk had a strange ritual whose true and horrifying nature soon revealed itself.

As the daylong cracking of the whip continued, and Alex's ears tired of it, suddenly, on a nearby boat, a Thuga jumped up, threw his oar in front of him, and dove overboard.

Instantly, all the Siirk rose to their feet and began cheering while those Siirk in the affected boat took turns taking pot shots at the unfortunate. They watched his body float mutely in the waves as the cruel armada kept on course.

The Siirk, one by one, took turns slipping quietly overboard, and furtively swimming to a boat in the rear that was completely enclosed by leather curtains. It was being towed by another boat with a double complement of Thuga overseen by two Siirk with whips and other Siirk with guns. Each of the Siirk made this trip, spending a bit of time back there, and just as quietly slipping back into the water, swimming back to his boat, waiting a moment, and then sneaking on board. The practice, so strange at first, was so constant and so commonplace, that Alex began to ignore it.

Maryan and he managed to sit close to one another, so much so that they could link index fingers and communicate their love in silent little tugs.

They made landfall in the noonday heat and the Siirk sat down to rest in the shade of some great trees overgrowing the beach. Several Thuga built a fire. They produced a huge cooking pot, which they filled with water, and into which they emptied sealed jars of some powder—instant soup, Siirk style. The Thuga made deep lowing noises, looking often at the fire. At least they could express their hunger.

One of the Thuga spooned out a bowl of soup intended for the others, and took a furtive sip. Instantly the lash of Omas descended. Cursing and kicking him, Omas smashed the heavy ball down on him several times. He cringed with what pain the animal must be feeling. The Thuga lay silently for a few moments, with nobody tending to him. He thought he was dead. Then he began to move, slowly, with his arms wrapped around his torso. Staggering painfully, he brought two bowls of soup, one for him and one for Maryan. As he knelt to set the bowls down, and Omas let them lift their nets to eat—showing his brace of muzzle loading pistols in the process, as a warning—He saw that the wounded Thuga glanced sideways at Maryan with a look of cunning. He was one of the bright ones who were somehow different from the rest. They always had water by their side, and Maryan used her jug to wash down one of the creature's worst gashes, which was not only open to the flesh, but actually dripping blood. He had a bruise around his eyes, and she dabbed that gently with the hem of her dress. He was afraid for her for a second, but the Thuga acknowledged her gesture with the faintest nod and then rose to shuffle back to help feed the others of his kind.

He was slurping the salty, greasy liquid that tasted sort of like pineapples and fish, when he heard a shout.

Several shots rang out.

The Thuga—he'd overpowered a Siirk, and shot that Siirk and another Siirk, threw the empty pistols aside, and ran on powerful legs back west along the beach. Instantly, the Siirk began shouting and betting, while several of their number aimed long rifles and fired. Miraculously, the Thuga moved sharply leftward and vanished into the bush. He had no idea if he'd been hit or not.

Instantly, the overseers got to work, using the lighter end of their whips on the cringing Thuga, until Nizin signaled enough. Couldn't whip them dead because then who would row?

After two days' journey, they came to a Siirk settlement on the coast.

This was a rude frontier community hewn from the plentiful lumber in the surrounding forests. No sightseeing for the Thuga or them. He glimpsed a wooden wharf, and unpainted wooden houses rising up a hillside beyond that. Siirk walked about, barely noticing their convoy. Boats larger and smaller than ours seemed to come and go here. He noted several barges towing logs out to sea, and could only guess that they must let them drift west or southwest on some current.

The group went ashore a mile or two southwest of the village. Only one boat went aground, held by its Thuga rowers while they and Omas, Nizin, and Kogran debarked. Nizin led the way, and the other two Siirk walked behind them. The ever-present nets hung over them, and they had to hold them up with their hands to keep from stumbling over them. As usual, Omas brandished a pistol to warn them against trying to escape.

They walked up a twisting path so poorly defined that he doubted many souls had gone this way. But Nizin seemed to know his way.

The path led up through moderately thick woods, up onto a lovely grassy hilltop, into more woods, still climbing, until they came to a flat clearing in the woods. In the middle of the clearing was a wrecked spacecraft.

The wreck was a cylinder about 100 feet long and 25 feet in diameter—He thought immediately of the cylindrical shapes he'd seen piled up on the sea floor. It was a skeleton, really—much of the upper part was missing, though all the ribs were still in place. Where the skin was intact, it gleamed like a mirror—something he only remembered from Alex Kirk's life. It gleamed like liquid mercury under a sheet of glass. It gleamed brighter than chrome. It was blinding in its beauty. They marched right up to the wreck and they could see the inside now— instrument panels up front, pilot and co-pilot seats overgrown with vines, and then twin rows of seats like in a bus toward the front, and an empty cargo compartment in the rear half.

"It doesn't have any wings," said Maryan.

"Could have been slung under an airframe," he guessed. "Maybe dangled from a balloon?"

The Siirk said agitatedly: "*Geedeen!*"

Nizin grabbed his net and towed him into the ship, making him stumble. Tough old bird. He staggered over the debris—moldy carpeting, soil, vines, weeds up to his thighs. He towed him to a shiny square of the wondrous mirror-material. He slammed his fist against it, several times, and a broken image appeared. A human—talking... "Greetings. This is a robotic rescue appliance. To ensure that this machine has been summoned by a bona fide human, please speak aloud the name of this continent now, in English."

Static kept corrupting the image.

The little spiel played over and over again, and Nizin threw himself against it in fury, pounding both fists against the speaker's face. Then he shook him so violently that he nearly passed out. He could smell his last sweet, greasy meal on his breath, and the stench of corruption rising from his gorge where it was being digested. "*Geedeen!*" he shrieked. "*Ingish!*" he threw him against the bulkhead and pointed at the screen.

He knew what he wanted him to do.

Kogran and Omas held Maryan between them. Kogran pulled out a knife whose blade glinted a dull leaden color, and he pointed it at her neck.

"Ingish!"

"Okay," he said.

Nizin grinned. He waved for Kogran to lower the knife. He recognized Nizin's cunning—he knew he could control him by using her, and that suited him in the desperate sense that, if anything happened to her, he'd kill himself and then they'd have what they really deserved— nothing at all.

He faced the still babbling screen and cleared his throat. "North America."

Nothing happened. Sweat broke out around his neck. "North America."

Nizin gazed at him in wonder. "*Nofameka?*"

"North America, you stupid mutt," he said to the speaker, and pounded on it with his fist. "*North America,* you pile of turds."

It was clearly broken. He looked at Nizin and shrugged. He was scared. "Broken. Kaputt."

Nizin seemed to take this in stride, to his surprise. "*Nofameka? Boken. Kambutt.*" he nodded thoughtfully.

Then he turned around and kicked the broken craft. He waved to his followers to return to the ship, and gave him a shove with the flat of his foot for good measure. "*Geedeen!*" he yelled as they marched at full tilt down to the boats.

He was sure Nizin had more up his sleeve than reptilian scales.

Once again they were on the water. They headed southwest, hugging the coastline.

Alex suspected that the coastline roughly followed the old Atlantic contour, but several hundred miles further inland. Occasional Siirk fishing villages drifted past. He saw little evidence of technological progress—they were roughly in the 15th Century because they had guns, yet they seemed not to be great explorers or inventors. But they were sharp—Nizin clearly knew that the ship they'd visited had come from the sky somehow, and he wanted to trace its route back to raid whatever he could.

He witnessed his first fight between Siirk. It happened in the water as one swam back to the curtained mystery boat, and the other was just coming from there. They had a brief staring contest, then knives came out—thin, mean, personal dirks they were, not like the broad utility knives they carried on their belts—and one or both were about to die when Nizin stood up and yelled at them to grow up.

Finally, all the boats ran aground, as if to stay a while. Alex gathered there was a Siirk city further along the coast, but this was as far as they were going for now. This looked like one of Nizin's permanent camps.

The Thuga were herded away somewhere. Nizin, Omas, and Kogran led Maryan and him through a forest, down through a canyon where they had to ford a small river, and back up the other side. The forest water was cold and his feet hurt. He was glad to be back in the sunlight, which warmed him back up.

They followed a broad trail of beaten earth, surrounded by thick forest on both sides. Occasionally, Siirk on horseback passed. At one crossroads, they saw two Siirk warriors in chain mail, leaning on their axes and chatting. These Siirk greeted Nizin with feral respect, deferent but proud, and there was always some loathsome undercurrent, Alex thought, in the way these reptile-men sized each other up.

The group turned on a narrower trail and entered an area of cliff dwellings. Passing there, they left the Siirk town and came to a beautiful wilderness. It was a mountain meadow full of gorgeously colored flowers. They marched toward a forest on the other side, and now the aim of their journey became clear.

Sitting at the edge of the forest was a giant ball with the same blinding, shiny material they'd seen in the wrecked spacecraft. Only this one wasn't wrecked.

As they approached they came up to the ball, for it sat slightly elevated; they had to climb up a rubble wall about ten feet high to actually reach the ball. He noted the finely slitted vent grills that ran horizontally along the bottom. An array of broken tools littering around the base told him Nizin's people had worked hard to pry this nut open, and had failed.

It was perfectly round, a ball he estimated to be fifty feet in diameter—the size of a small house.

"*Geedeen!*" their three Siirk officers yelled, all banging on the sides of the device. "*Ingish!*"

Nizin took him by the shoulder and pulled him close. Nizin lifted the amulet he wore on a thong around his neck and tapped it against the ball. He touched the skin, and a panel appeared in the otherwise perfectly featureless surface that captured the blue of the sky, the white of clouds, the light of the sun, and swirled them into a blinding abstraction.

"Greetings," said a man in a suit, holding some papers as if he were a TV anchor. "I'm Vector, your friendly transport and communications expert. This automated boat has landed to answer your emergency call. First, we must determine if you are truly a human requiring assistance, or if the call was the result of some natural phenomenon such as lightning. Please state the name of the first President of the United States in English."

"*Ingish!*" the Siirk yelled. Besides Omas, Nizin, and Kogran, a half dozen Siirk officers clustered around.

Noticing that Omas had the knife out, and Maryan in a headlock with the other arm, he said: "George Washington."

"Thank you," said the man brightly in his well-modulated announcer's voice, "That is correct."

The Siirk gaped as he continued: "Please choose from the following menu by reading out loud. If you are injured and cannot speak, please wait until the next scheduled orbital patrol can make a pass over your location."

Orbital! They had something in orbit that sent out patrols? Yes, but a million years ago. If there were still someone up there, they would have long since come by to investigate. He felt safe betting that nobody would come to help them.

The Siirk were beside themselves, staring at the list of written items.

He now had a little bargaining power. He stripped his net off and threw it on the ground. He motioned for Maryan to come stand beside him. Omas let her go after a reluctant glance toward Nizin, who gave a hooded nod.

They stared up at the menu, which included: Injured?, Need Police?, Need Food & Water?, Lost?, Value Added Tax?, Voice Line, News Update, News Archive, More Selections.

Alex pressed *News Update*.

The Siirk stepped back, gasping, as an elderly woman anchor read slowly and painfully from a note pad in her trembling hand: "This is Jill Claymore with World News Incorporated aboard the orbiting city *Yuri Gagarin*. I am the last anchor person alive, and this will be my last broadcast. It is March 13, 2090, and I have been told that I only have a few weeks or months to live with my cancer. I don't know if there are any people left on Earth. I do know there are fewer than 100 of us left here on the station, and all other points in space shut down years ago as we ran out of young people. I expect this generation will be finished in the next five years or less, because I am 86 years old and one of the youngest persons here.

"It may well be that you are a freshly born young person, a clone of someone who lived before his time. If so, we wish you well. You are the only hope for mankind's future, and we send you all our love."

The Siirk were wide-eyed, mute, with mouths hanging open as they clustered around to hear this strange monologue.

Alex felt a frantic sweat on the back of his neck. What had happened to his ancestors? Why were they extinct? How had they managed to make him be born so far into the future? How far was this into the future? He was full of questions.

Maryan clung to him and helped him navigate through the menus.

The last thing he wanted was to send armed assistance to Nizin, but he had to produce something for them.

"*Archive*," he said.

A different menu appeared, with hundreds of tiny pictures. He ran his finger along (Nizin imitating him by drawing a finger through the air) and the sound kept changing, until he came across *Why Mankind Is Extinct*. He repeated this clause, and the picture switched to a newsreel while an announcer spoke in voice-over.

Picture of a deserted city, windows broken, streets empty, papers blowing along, birds lined up on sagging telephone wires.

"After more than a million years of human progress, it took just one virus to destroy the human race."

Wide shot of outer space, with the Milky Way majestically sprawling like a sea of light from one end to the other.

"The virus was too small to see or detect. It came stealthily, and it acted stealthily before anyone had any idea."

Pictures of test tubes, microscope, genes, chromosomes, DNA double helix, stick and ball model of complex molecules...

"By the time science tracked down the cause of the spreading human irreversible infertility syndrome, or HIIS, it was too late."

Picture of a busy European shopping mall, with men, women, and children thronging the busy stores.

"Humans were concentrated in huge urban centers, where the virus spread insidiously in two or three generations before being identified as HIIS."

Montage shots of similar malls in China, India, the U.S., and Africa.

"Within 25 years, one can see the difference: an aging population, and fewer and fewer children because the birth rate is plummeting toward zero."

Picture of a special school outside London, protected by barbed wire, high walls, and guards.

"A small number of humans appear to have an inherent immunity. Their children continue to be born, coveted by a vast population that has become sterile. For a while it looks as though mankind will carry on. Are these brave few souls a new super-race?"

Same school, looking depressingly deserted.

"Even these hardy genes cannot withstand the rapidly mutating virus that opportunistically assails human DNA wherever it finds it."

Montage: police raiding buildings; grainy black and white footage.

"For many, the last days of mankind were an ordeal of looting, pillaging, and other crimes. Law and order broke down."

Montage: scientists at work. All of them look frail, white-haired, as the last surviving humans age away.

"Scientists continued to the last day, looking for solutions. Some theorize that cloning, if postponed for a thousand years or more, can leapfrog the virus's deadly assault on the Earth."

Pictures of cells, bloodstream. Virus attacks cell, pokes a hole in it, spews its genetic material inside. Virus sloughs off and drifts away, spent.

"The attacking genetic strand attacks the chromosomes themselves, forever altering the message from which the human being is copied billions of times. Once the host has died out, the virus should become inert and possibly break apart over decades or centuries of lying in the soil, where the four seasons and other natural phenomena can destroy it."

Picture of a newborn baby in a laboratory among test tubes.

"Here is Alvin Montefiori of Albano, Italy, born December 13, 2071. He is the last human being known to have been born alive. A variation of the virus, thought to have joined with influenza viruses, attacked and destroyed even those brave new humans born *in vitro*."

Here the presentation went dead. It was enough to give Alex a good idea of how the human race had ended. Shaken, he stood back. What had they meant by "leapfrogging?" That must be the clones, engineered to appear thousands of years later.

Impatiently, Nizin began to bellow and bang on the sphere. *"Geedeen!"* he pointed up. It was clear he knew the thing could take him up into the sky. When he saw the look on Alex's face, he seemed to relent, and signaled for Thuga to fetch food and drink for Alex and Maryan.

Meanwhile, a series of images rotated randomly on the screen. The President declared an emergency... children cried and went unfed... riots in the cities... families in mourning... cells trying to divide, and failing...

He rose and found another archive clip of interest to him (and he imagined these might still be beaming down from a source in orbit).

Thuga brought bowls of steaming soup and lumps of savory bread. Maryan and he ate their first warm meal in days while watching.

Picture of a building in a valley, scientists at work in a lab.

"This is Beacham University, where much of the final cloning research was carried out under an urgent Government program."

Picture of interior of building: gleaming floors, high ceilings, tastefully decorated walls, men and women in white coats walking importantly.

"Here, in the only state of the art facility of its kind, scientists are racing to perfect an automatic cloning complex. This complex is considered mankind's last hope, though many detractors don't think it can possibly work."

Picture of graduate students walking around campuses taking samples from cooperative, nodding young undergraduates.

"To avoid contamination with existing human cells, the source cells that will be used were taken around the turn of the millennium for earlier, unrelated genetic experiments, and left sealed in test tubes long before the HIIS outbreak."

Picture of a long hallway. From a door on the right, a young man emerges. From a door on the left, a young woman emerges. Both are naked, their bodies airbrushed for modesty. They meet in the middle of the hall, link hands, and walk away.

"To further avoid the possibility of contamination, the project will not become active until the year 3500, when all humans are long gone, and their cells effectively destroyed. The cloning is expected to continue for up to one century and then dwindle after some 10,000 new humans have been created."

Picture of birthing rooms with stone tubs, tubing, objects on walls.

"These 100% automatic birthing rooms will provide everything tomorrow's children will need. A kind of benign fungus will provide bioluminescent heat. Multiple umbilical cords will feed blood and other nutrient fluids, including nano-engineered memory enzymes so that the clones can share the memories of their source individuals."

Repeat picture of a long hallway. From a door on the right, a young man emerges. From a door on the left, a young woman emerges. Both are naked, their bodies airbrushed for modesty. They meet in the middle of the hall, link hands, and walk away.

"Each of these perfectly formed human beings will be created from a vast cocktail of genetic material to ensure a diverse, healthy, and robust gene pool."

Maryan and he looked at each other and nearly laughed.

"It didn't quite turn out that way," she said, chewing her bread.

"Yeah." He eyeballed their keepers. All but Omas had drifted off to rest from the noonday sun, or presumably for lunch someplace.

Alex rose stiffly and stretched. Feeling the need to relieve his bladder, he stepped down from the mound. Omas nearly had a heart attack, but relaxed when he made urinating motions. He glanced craftily at Maryan, no doubt noting that he wouldn't run away without her.

As he wandered into the sun-dappled forest, he heard a noise—a deep, low groan of contentment.

There on his left, not twenty feet away, was a low-ceilinged cabin. It was curtained like the mystery boat.

Alex froze, compelled by curiosity.

The curtain blew aside in the wind.

Inside sat a Siirk with his back to the wall, holding something to his chest.

At first Alex thought it was a female, nursing a baby.

Then Alex recognized the face of a sleeping Thuga.

Only it wasn't sleeping. The top of its head was missing, and the Siirk leaned his head forward to eat. The Siirk uttered another low, intense pleasure-thrum.

A twig cracked under Alex's feet.

The curtain fell back, and Alex glimpsed the Siirk's expression flown apart in a hiss of deadly rage.

But the Siirk left Alex alone, because the Siirk probably knew Nizin would torture him to death if he harmed Alex at this time.

Alex returned to the sphere, shaken. It took him an hour or so to realize he'd forgotten to do what he'd gone there for.

Nizin and Kogran had returned from— Alex could just imagine! Alex could hardly stomach being near them.

But he pointed to the amulet on Nizin's chest, and at the sky.

Nizin looked down at the amulet, nodded, and pointed skyward.

Alex asked to see the amulet, and after several minutes of gesticulating and haggling, Nizin let him hold it, but kept hold on the leather thong with both hands.

Alex found the amulet was light, as if hollow inside. It was made of metal, probably steel, of a brown or matte olive color. As Alex turned it over in his hands, he discovered that it consisted of two halves that could be twisted in opposite directions.

As Alex twisted the amulet's ends, suddenly the screen lit up in the side of the sphere and a woman said: "Sorry, only one rescue boat per site. Please contact Emergency Services if you are having trouble with the lifeboat they went." Then a man in overalls appeared: "We're sorry, all technicians are away from their desks right now. Please leave a message and we'll answer as soon as they can." The woman's voice returned: "The default time before another boat can be automatically sent to your location without intervening human attentions will be—" (and a mechanical voice cut in) "1200" (and a different voice said:) "Months."

The screen went blank.

A century before they'd send another boat!

He thought of all the cylinders in the valley of the rippers—how many centuries had it taken for them to be washed out to sea and pile up like that? Were there any of the cylinders left up in orbit? How could he get one, if any were left, without putting it in Nizin's hands?

"*Ingish!*" Nizin yelled, waving his scaly claws. "*Geedeen!*"

"Geedeen," he agreed. He motioned: "Go away. I'll call you."

Well, he didn't like that at all. Before he left, he put Omas on the case, but pressed against the whip to be sure Omas was gentle on Maryan and him.

He brought the main menu back up and played around with all the options.

He tried calling orbit but nobody answered.

He listened to more information about the end of the human race.

Omas stirred patiently but anxiously nearby where he hovered to make sure he didn't hop in the sphere and fly away. He kept Maryan seated on a rock out of his reach.

Then he came to an interesting sequence of options titled: "Fly To Orbit?"

Oh yes, please!

He checked the sub-options: Quick Emergency Evacuation? Medical Evacuation? Cargo Lift (Non-breathing)? Passenger Lift (Breathing)? Open Door - Shut Door. Power Up. And more....

His heart beat faster. He was about to take a big gamble, but he had to risk it. They couldn't spend another day with these cannibalistic beasts.

"Maryan, darling."

"Yes, sweetheart?"

"You know he love you."

"Yes, and you know he love you."

"We're about to take some action."

"I understand. If They don't see each other again..."

He was unable to complete her sentence. "When I give you a wave, roll over the edge of that embankment, all the way to the bottom. I think I'd better act now, while there are almost none of our pals with them."

"I'm ready," she said, blowing him a faint kiss.

He said: "Open Door."

A female image appeared. "You have asked to have the rescue boat door open. To ensure this is a valid action, please identify the largest mountain range in North America."

"The Rocky Mountains."

"Thank you."

A hatch slid open—a rectangular opening appeared in the shiny material where nothing, not even a seam, had been before.

Omas began to shout. "Nizin! Nizin!"

The inside of the sphere appeared to have three stories; all Alex saw was the middle one. Alex quickly guessed: the automatic pilot/astrogator was above the flat aluminum looking ceiling, and the power drive was below the aluminum looking floor. In the middle section was a circle of simple leather seats, about 8 of them, with webbing to strap into. Alex thought about the vents along the bottom of the sphere.

Nizin and Kogran came running, and behind them a crowd of Siirk.

Alex said: "Close Door," and the surface was shiny and featureless as before.

Nizin puffed up the slope. Omas told him what he'd seen.

Alex opened and closed the door several times.

Nizin tried: "*Opador,*" he said.

Nothing. The gadget was cued to Alex's voice signature.

"Open Door," Alex said. The door opened.

Nizin and four other senior officers stepped inside. At first they were fearful, but then, when nothing bad happened to them, they climbed in to see what was what. He wished all the Siirk, the entire race, would get inside. But in the end, only Nizin and three of his lizard-men were inside, testing the seats. Omas, Kogran, and about ten others stood outside looking in.

Alex surreptitiously made a sign, and Maryan quietly slipped down the slope. Nobody seemed to notice.

Good.

Alex said: "Close Door."

At that moment, there was an outcry. Nizin and his three companions started yelling and gesticulating. The three companions made it, tumbling out of the boat, while Nizin was trapped inside when the door closed.

It was now or never, Alex thought, watching the three elders stumble away from the craft. Kogran and the others began to shout at Alex.

"Quick Emergency Evacuation," Alex said.

Omas was on his way toward him, and Kogran also, a little more slowly. The three elders were still lumbering away with upraised arms.

The sphere began to vibrate. The ground under their feet began to tremble. Several Siirk tumbled over. They wanted to run, but Kogran had a spear in his hand and threatened them with death if they ran and left his father.

The sphere uttered in a booming, male loudspeaker voice: "Ten seconds to lift off. You are advised to seek cover at least 1000 meters away to avoid being heat-blasted."

The echoes of that voice traveled around them, startling both Alex and the Siirk, though he'd expected this.

"Eight, seven, six..." ran the countdown.

The engine sounded as if it were starting to go millions of RPMs.

"...Five, four, three..."

He dove for cover, rolling over the edge and down toward Maryan.

"...Two, one, lift-off!"

A tidal wave of pressure and heat radiated away from the sphere.

The sphere rose straight up, dwindling rapidly into the clouds.

The heat blast—the temperature so high that the air glowed bluish-red—streaked out in a growing disk in all directions, and he saw several Siirk flying through the air, including the elders, at least one of them coming apart in pieces.

Kogran and Omas were among the few Siirk who were kicked over the edge and avoided the worst of the blast.

They lay unconscious and spread-eagled.

Alex took Maryan's hand and they ran as fast as they could into the forest.

Alex had killed Nizin and many of his men.

He'd made the mistake of leaving Nizin's son and his overseer alive, when he could have killed them while they were unconscious. Alex berated himself for the latter mistake. What saved him and Maryan, at least for a while, was that everyone at the site was out cold, and that the site was far from the settlement. It must have taken them hours to get together a search party with nets, guns, and Thuga porters.

Maryan and Alex headed away from the coast. Alex dreaded being weaponless—another mistake—and there was no time to sit around making anything more than a sharpened stick for a spear. They found two good cudgels that would have to do—They'd be helpless if they ran up against any rippers, but they were free for the moment. Free of the Siirk and their horrible ways.

They would expect them to head northeast to their valley, perhaps to the island which by now must be known to the Siirk also.

Talking it over, Alex and Maryan agreed to go home. Where else could they go? For now, they must simply get away in an unexpected direction. And they did. Jogging east in forests that had no trails other than those of small animals, they covered about 25 miles a day. They ate what came to hand—eggs, worms, beetles, roots. They drank from streams.

To confound any sniffer animals they might bring, they walked west a distance in one stream, then east a distance in another.

Alex could read the sun and the sky pretty well, and he kept them going as directly north and east as possible, as far from the coast as they could go.

They never did hear the hoof beats of any pursuers.

"What are they going to do?" asked Maryan as they sat huddled together a few nights later, afraid to go to sleep.

"I don't know. I'm hoping this wilderness runs on forever and that we're not trapped in some Siirk society." he told her about the sight he'd seen in the veiled tent, sparing her the details. She shivered, and he held her close.

He was wondering privately if they should just take their lives together, maybe go back and jump into the sea holding hands. It would be quick, it would be mutual, and it would be the end of their suffering.

He must seemed very down just then, for she embraced him, still trembling as she was, and held him silently while they listened for Siirk death to come down the trail.

But it didn't. Not yet.

Within a few days, he hunted a few smaller animals by hurling rocks at them.

Alex and Maryan dared not make fire, but ate the bleeding, greasy meat cold right off the bone, like animals. As humans, they did not make good carnivores, and they retched up some of it, but enough stayed to keep them in protein and fat.

Alex used the intestines to fashion several bowstrings. Soon, he was armed with a light bow and some arrows sharpened by rubbing on boulders that they passed. The boulders looked as they might have eons ago, light green in various shades of lichen on top, and dark, mossy green on the downward facing facets.

One time, from some heights, they did see a solitary ripper in the distance, but it was traveling laterally from them, west, as if tracking some game, and they didn't make its acquaintance. "They can't go back to their valley," Maryan said with a sigh.

They'd had this conversation a thousand times. They could go back, and perhaps nobody would bother them for a while, but it would be suicide in the long run—Kogran was now presumably chieftain, or Omas if he had killed Kogran—and they'd be cruising back in their boats looking not just for revenge, but for some way to wring or torture a new sphere out of them.

Never once did they pass any sign of past civilization. That always amazed him. A million years could wipe out all traces of humanity. A dozen or so ice ages could scrape Manhattan clean of everything from skyscrapers to subway tunnels. He'd bet not even the contours of their cities could be seen anymore from a plane or from space. They must have gone 200 miles west when a longing made them turn north along a wide river—a child of the Mississippi? This far north? No signs of civilization here. That told him much—this world had more than one intelligent species now, but they had not spread very far. Which left a lot of wilderness for them to hide in?

They became nomads—new Native Americans, carrying their few possessions as they went. They made a few simple bowls out of wood, and knives out of stone and bone. He made stronger bows and arrows, and on one occasion had to kill a ripper and her cub. He'd stumbled on the cub, and the mother attacked—no choice there. They had enough hides to make a shelter at night, and they were not afraid to light a small fire. They knew how to make their fire as little smoky as possibly—burn very dry wood, cook fast, put the fire out, and bury it.

Then the days started getting shorter, and they began to think about winter. They had only one place to go, and that was their home in ripper valley. He hoped the Siirk did not travel much in winter.

It was time for them to go home.

They had wandered in the wilderness, by Alex's calculations, for three months, heading due northwest.

Now they headed east, and in about 20 days reached the coast. The trick now was—which way to go? Which way was the valley? His guess was that they had come to the coast far beyond the valley, in Thuga territory. No sign of life, Siirk or otherwise, along the coast. He remembered how, in the early days of his life, he'd always looked over his shoulder for rippers. Now he looked for Siirk, and he realized he would be looking over his shoulder like this to the end of his days. And the Thuga? Too early to tell how they felt about yet another race sharing their territory.

Alex and Maryan killed a deer in a sandy cove washed by the sea, dressed it, cooked it and ate it. They sat back as evening came and listened to the wilderness: the wind in the tree crowns, the ocean piling onto its breakers with a roar. What a magnificent world! Alex told Maryan: "I just want to take one more look at our valley, see if there is anything we need before we leave."

"We'll have to spend the winter," she said. "It will be too cold to travel."

"For the Siirk as well as for us, I hope."

She laid her head on his lap and embraced him dreamily. "If the time comes, we go together. We don't live our lives in fear."

They walked down the coast, taking their time.

Within a few days, they came to their valley. Scouting carefully, they found no sign of Siirk, except that their cattle were gone.

A new ripper couple had moved into the valley. With the birthing facilities gone, there wouldn't be room for more than those and one or two cubs. Alex noticed that the rippers looked fat, as if they grew a layer of fat in the winter to keep warm, perhaps even to hibernate. Privately, he planned to kill them sometime during the winter if they needed the food. He eyed their pelts longingly.

Maryan and he settled in somewhat uneasily. Every morning, noon, and evening they went to the beach to scan for signs of returning Siirk.

Alex was sure the Siirk wanted his hide as badly as he wanted the rippers', but maybe the Siirk would not return this far north. The silent sky, with thick layers of gray winter clouds, brooded above as if in enigmatic answer.

Sometimes when Alex and Maryan went hunting for berries in the upper forest, and the fog crept around them in silent shreds, Alex got the feeling that someone or something was watching them. Maryan got the same feeling at times, and she'd stiffen up and stare into the mossy darkness among the trees. Sometimes it was just a bird that would snap aloft from a branch, or a squirrel darting along a tree trunk.

Sometimes it was a snap of a twig, unexplained, magnified in the damp air, never repeated, but hanging there in the silence like a barbed question mark in the gloom of the deep forest glen.

Then, one day, Alex and Maryan had visitors.

They were on the sky island, tending to their flock of chickens. Alex was constructing nests in which the chickens could lay eggs. It was an overcast day, late in the morning—the early fog had burned off, and the sun was trying to struggle through the pearly cloud cover—when Maryan shrieked.

Alex dropped the rocks he was juggling,

On the cliff with them stood about six figures.

Thuga!

Around the cliff stood at least a dozen more, all armed with shields and spears. They were an eerie, frightening sight, with their massive heads and powerful bodies, and their oddly angular snouted faces. Some had short fur completely dark, while others had dark fur with white patches. The middle one stepped forward. He wore a white circlet on his head—a kind of crown or coronet, he thought. He also wore a white linen cape, unlike the others, who wore only loincloths.

Maryan and he clutched each other.

Was this the moment they would have to choose their destiny? He pictured them stepping off the cliff together at the 300 foot side and plunging to their deaths, holding hands.

The Thuga in the white cloak held something in his hands as he stepped closer and closer.

He was walking directly toward Maryan, who clung to him with a ferocious strength born of terror.

The Thuga walked directly up to Maryan and stopped. He raised one hand in a gentle, calming gesture while holding the other behind his back. Carefully, calming them, he came closer and closer.

Then he bent down, took the sleeve of Maryan's tunic, and touched his eye to it. He made a kissing gesture to that spot on her tunic. Then he genuflected before her, on one knee, and held his hands out. In them was a mass of white flower petals.

Maryan moved from fear and shock to utter surprise. She held one hand over her heart as if to quiet it.

He said: "He's the one you comforted. The one who ran away."

The man—He must call him that, for what else can he call him? And were they not all descendants of the true men here—turned his gaze to him, touched his chest with a leathery dark hand, and said in a deep, resonant voice: "Kumar." It sounded like Shoe-Mar.

Maryan took the flowers and sniffed them. "They're wonderful!"

She let him smell. Jasmine, he thought.

She held out her hands and urged him into a standing position.

Xumar was slightly taller than I. He pointed to himself and repeated "Xumar." Then he pointed to the people around him and down on the sand. "Takkar." he walked past them and pointed to the mountains in the north. "Takkar."

He pointed to the mountains. "Takkar."

He nodded.

He pointed to him. "Xumar."

He nodded.

He pointed at his people. "Takkar."

They all nodded.

He pointed at him. "Chief." he made circling motions above the heads of the others. "Xumar Chief Takkar."

Xumar pointed to himself. "Xumar Sif Takkar."

He nodded. And so it went. They introduced themselves ("Abex" and "Meddiun").

He pointed southwest. "Siirk." he held his nose.

He learned then that the Takkar could smile and laugh, for they did both. All held their noses and said "Seelk."

One of the chiefs stuck his gut out and rubbed it in circular motions as he strutted around. "Mmmm. Seeeelk." And they all laughed. Maryan and he were doubled over with laughter. He imitated the chief, rubbing his stomach and repeating the way the Siirk spoke their name in utter self-adoration. More laughter.

Xumar pointed at the ground, and then made a circling gesture over the land around. "Takkar." he stamped his foot. "*Takkar!*"

He understood: the Siirk raided Takkar land to take cattle, slaves, and whatever else was not bolted down.

He took a spear from a warrior and brandished it toward the southwest. "*Takkar!*"

So he meant to protect them, for they were guests on his land.

He grew excited and intense, motioning for all of them to sit down. He pointed up, way up, and made a whistling sound as he pointed with his finger, starting way up, and slowing and steadily dropping to the ground.

A space ship of some kind. Maybe a rescue boat or supply cylinder.

He rose in a crouch and pointed to the valley, and repeated the descending fingertip, the whistling noise.

There! he'd been right! Every century or so, a ship came down. But why? All the ships had eventually been swept out to sea and sunk during spring floods, he surmised.

Xumar cleared a sandy patch with his palm and drew a cylinder with his finger. Then he made twisting motions. The amulet! The amulet that Nizin had shown them!

Xumar, still crouching intently, pointed to the mountains. "Takkar!" he made twisting motions, pointed to the picture of the amulet, and then to the valley. Then he motioned for them to come with him.

For the first time in his life, Alex felt utterly safe.

Maryan felt the same. Forces out did not surround them to kill them at a moment's notice. Xumar's people were prepared to fight the Siirk to keep them out of the Takkar people's territory—maybe. Alex and Maryan would be able to live their lives out in their valley after all, for which by now they had a kind of grisly affection—it was the place of their birth, and the burial ground of a nation of the clone people.

As they hiked through the forest with their 20 armed companions, Alex and Maryan began to learn a little about them and their language. There were actually two Takkar races—which they called the Big Takkar and the Little Takkar. The Big Takkar were an intelligent humanoid race, while the Little Takkar were an offspring whose intelligence was in the bovine range. Unlike the Siirk, who used the Little Takkar as cattle, the Big Takkar protected them, cared for them, and employed them in a kindly fashion. Their fondness for the Takkar grew the more they learned about them.

They began to pass through Takkar outposts. The first were sprawling forts on hilltops, with walls of thick upright logs that would resist anything but heavy cannon fire. Alex imagined during a battle they'd wet the wood to make it less likely to burn. Dark figures cheered and waved spears as they passed each of the forts, for Xumar was king over all of them. The Siirk hadn't had any idea of the prize they'd captured some weeks before they'd captured them. Xumar had been on the water, fishing with several colleagues—he'd stayed and battled the Siirk raiding party while his friends escaped to seek help.

After several days' march, they came to Xumar's capital, Takkar. This was a city in the forest, sprawling over several hills, containing maybe 1000 wooden structures. Some of these were quite long and reminded him of Native American long lodges Alex Kirk had read about.

Everywhere they went, they were received as heroes. They went with Xumar to his magnificent palace, which was built of logs and plaster, and white-washed. It was two stories tall, and must have had fifteen rooms. They had cold running water, but no hot water or toilets. It was still an outhouse society, but what the hell, he figured, can't hold it against them. Give them a few hundred more years and they'll build St. Peter's.

Alex and Maryan were given bowls of warm milk with honeyed rice and a mint leaf—very tasty—and shown to an enclosed tub of water. There, in privacy, Maryan and he were able to soak in luxury for what seemed like an hour. A pipe running in from a stove provided a steady trickle of hot water to keep them warm—They had to avoid going near that pipe to prevent a scald.

Xumar had five wives and a crowd of children, all of whom presented themselves at a lavish feast. The Takkar obviously loved life—they loved to eat, and they ate well, as they found out. "A few weeks here and they won't want to leave," Maryan whispered, nudging him in the ribs, while they ate.

Their stay in Takkar lasted about ten days, though he wasn't counting closely. They felt safe at last, and relaxed. It was a vacation for them.

But Xumar was a restless man, always planning something, always thinking of new ways to affect the world around him. One day, he introduced them to Mixic ("Mishik"), a priest of the Eagle cult. Mixic was an older man, gray around the head, and wrinkled around the mouth.

Alex and Maryan followed Mixic into the inner sanctum of the Eagle lodge. This was a mysterious, hallowed place. The entrance corridor sank into the earth and was lined with tightly woven poles and topped with a thatch roof. The corridor was gloomy, lit only by stray threads of sunlight filtering through the poles, and this ended as they got deeper down. There, torches flickered along the walls, and stuffed eagles sat in wall niches—altars, he guessed, with candles flickering before them.

They came to a round hall about 30 feet in diameter. The wall all around was about 8 feet high, rising in a slight dome to 12 feet at the center point. Under the center point stood a wooden table or altar with ritual objects on it—feathers, leather pouches, wooden containers of powder, and more. They all had to bow before the altar. Mixic told them to wait. He went to the altar, took an object in both hands, and brought it to them. Alex gasped.

It was an amulet like the one that Nizin had worn around his neck.

Mixic took the amulet back and laid it on the table with the utmost care. He tried to explain about its function, making twisting motions with fists close together. Xumar joined in, making motions of objects coming from the sky and landing ... He held up both hands, palms facing each other...in a valley.

Alex grew excited, and inquired in pantomime if this valley lay near the sea.

Xumar nodded vigorously, lighting up because he could see the comprehension on his face. He pointed at him, signaling he understood that he understood. Then he pointed at the amulet. They *must walk*, he signaled, *back to the valley where there is a sacred place of the Takkar at which they will call a silver house down to earth. The silver house is the home of the Eagle God, and the Takkar wait months beyond number for another visit. When the silver house is in the valley,* he signed, *the hunting is always better and enemies stay away.*

How did the Siirk obtain an amulet? Alex signed.

They raided an Eagle cult lodge ten days' march south of here. That was several years ago. They found a sacred spot in their own territory and brought down a silver house.

Xumar signed: The silver house killed some Siirk.

Mixic signed: *It displeased the Eagle god greatly that they took a silver house.* He added: *We go soon, show you.*

Alex and Maryan returned to the valley with Xumar, Mixic, and ten warriors.

Xumar rode bareback on a horse whose long, magnificent blonde mane curled in the wind.

Maryan looked healthy and strong, a far cry from the woman dying of infection that Alex had rescued from the monsters in her birthing caves. In her ankle-length, flowing dress, she looked positively regal. The Takkar had given them some blankets and clothes of wool that they appreciated very much; Xumar carried them for them on the back of his horse. The Takkar tended to weave very fine wool in dark earth-tone colors. He thought several times that they might have to travel to their city to trade their furs for their wool and other goods; but since they were the last of their kind, he did not feel a great ambition.

They both felt a tangle of emotions as they entered the valley, coming down from the mountains. Maryan sniffled a few tears away, and he felt a horrible pang as he saw the late afternoon sun glint like blood in the water, and on two dozen or more skull-tops that stuck in the riverbank sand like cobblestones. The Takkar looked about with misgivings and made the Sign of the Eagle—a fist with index finger and thumb spread, held to the forehead while looking to the sky. Xumar pulled his cloak tight around himself and gripped his iron-tipped spear harder.

They came down on the east side of the river, opposite the bank of skulls. There were fewer skulls in the middle of the valley—testimony that few clones had ever gotten that far on their first run out of the birthing cave doors.

Mixic unfolded a soft leather map, which he consulted in a conversation with Xumar, holding the map against the horse's neck. He saw a drawing etched in burn marks: the river, the plain, the cliffs on either side. In the center of the map was a circle, and lines radiated from it in all directions. At the end of each line was a notation—a landmark of some type. Guarded by the warriors—for Xumar carried the sacred talisman in a bag that hung from his neck—They moved closer and closer to the center of the radians. It was getting dark, and they had to break to make camp. They did not light a fire, but posted guards all around.

In the morning, Xumar rode out to do a fast reconnaissance along the seashore. He returned saying the shore appeared safe. He sent several warriors to the east and west to carefully scout the area.

With Mixic and four remaining warriors, they came to a tangle of brush. They set to clear it at Xumar's direction, and discovered a slightly raised surface of concrete, badly weathered and pitted. It was an oval about 100 feet long and 40 feet across—a landing platform? This was a human artifact he'd missed in his desperate search long ago! It was impossible to read the lines the map said should exist on the surface. Perhaps centuries ago, when Takkar ancestors had brought down the first rescue ship, the concrete had been in better shape.

The platform was completely cleared within about two hours. By noon, a vast pile of brush, thorns, and torn-up grass lined the sides of the platform. The warriors had been able to use their stout spear-handles to simply push the brush off. In a few places, the platform was cracked, and thick trunks had to be sawn off. Two or three real trees had also poked through, and these had to be cut down with great effort, down to the surface so nothing should stab the ship.

Mixic alone stepped onto the platform, his layered clothing blowing in the wind, his dark, angular ox face enigmatic. He moved with great dignity, holding the amulet up like an offering. Then he gave it a gentle twist, laid it on the platform, and walked off with the same dignity. They waited.

Alex noticed after a while that a shaft of glowing light, very faint, stretched from a center point in the concrete right next to the amulet. The Takkar noticed it too and a murmur went around. The ancestors had been right. Several men fell to their knees. Xumar stood holding his horse's bridle and looked up, shading his eyes. Maryan and he did the same. It must have taken nearly an hour, and Alex grew impatient, puzzled, even disappointed—then several warriors shouted, pointing into the sky.

The 'silver house' fell down like a drop of water, like a splash of mercury.

Alex wasn't sure it was even a solid shape until the spacecraft descended in a crisp, quick motion. There was a whoosh of air, like a subway train arriving, and they were pushed back several feet, all of them, their clothes and their hair blowing, grit getting into their eyes. The boat almost materialized rather than landed. There it was, a 100 foot long cylinder, 20 feet in diameter, devoid of any markings. It steamed where its hot skin burned the condensation out of the air.

The silver skin was very hot now. Mixic motioned for the group to wait.

Just then the first gunshot rang out.

The Siirk had killed the warriors Xumar had sent out.

They had been lying in wait, probably for a long time. Very likely they'd lain in wait in the valley even as Maryan and he made their long trek. The thought of them hiding in their valley in the days of their return sickened him. But the Siirk weren't after Maryan and Alex or the Takkar—the Siirk were after the amulet they assumed either they or the Takkar possessed.

"Thuga!" a Siirk voice yelled full of contempt.

Arrows nicked in, cutting down the four warriors. Gun shots from Siirk muzzle-loaders boomed, and Mixic fell down mortally wounded. He turned him on his back and saw that he was already dead from a massive chest injury.

Alex saw them come running—a skirmish line of reptilian devils in their leather jerkins. He recognized Kogran, their chief now that Nizin was dead, and Omas, the overseer of the slaves they derisively named "spit people."

A Siirk stopped to aim his rifle, and Omas angrily stopped him, berating him not to harm the magnificent ship that gleamed before them all. Alex bent over at that moment, which saved his life. Maryan ducked while arrows peppered the one remaining guard.

Xumar moved with blinding speed, grabbing the amulet from under the ship, mounting his horse, and galloping away. Several shots rang out, and Xumar's horse fell dead under him.

Omas and Kogran shouted for the shooters to stop.

Five or six Siirk at the far end of the skirmish line fell on Xumar, beating him.

"*Sii-iirk*," Kogran slavered with deep satisfaction, rubbing his belly as he stepped up to the ship. He wished he'd hug it and be fried to toast, but he wasn't that dumb.

Maryan and Alex were surrounded by Siirk who had sheathed their weapons and merely meant to keep them from running. A heated discussion erupted between several Siirk, including Kogran. One camp apparently wanted them to touch the ship immediately, while the other wanted to wait until it was cooler. He noticed the ship had stopped steaming. After some debate, Omas brought a Little Takkar slave to the platform. Several Siirk spread-eagled the poor thing and slammed him full-bodied against the ship. He bounced off harmlessly and walked away dazed.

A big rattle of laughter and cheering rose. The Siirk waved their fists. Xumar was brought back, his wrists bound with thick rope. He had another rope around his neck, and the other end was tied securely to the waist of a burly Siirk who wore a thick leather belt studded with nail-heads. He was the biggest, meanest Siirk of the lot and he gave the rope an occasional yank that sent Xumar staggering. Xumar bled from several wounds, one on his temple, the rest on his torso. Two triangular flaps of brown, furry skin hung from his chest, revealing white muscle and bloody tissue.

"Ha! Sii-iirk," Xumar's captor growled with a vicious grin, running its paws over itself. This was not a subtle creature, and Alex read its intentions from the hungry way in which he regarded Xumar. The other Siirk were more fastidious about their eating habits and looked away.

Kogran motioned for Alex. Already, Omas once again had Maryan by the throat, a knife blade flashing dangerously by the delicate skin of her neck. "Geedeens," Kogran growled. Kogran was all threats and no nonsense. "Geedeens." he said and motioned Alex closer. Kogran shoved Alex roughly along the sleek hull of the ship. Kogran repeatedly pounded on the ship with one fist. Alex understood what Kogran wanted him to do. Dazed by the sudden turn of their fortunes, and the deaths of Mixic and the warriors, Alex tried to think clearly and couldn't. Kogran grinned and kept the knife on Maryan's throat. Maryan squirmed helplessly and wide-eyed. What to do? Alex wandered absently back and forth, letting his hands drift across the warm skin of the ship. "Open," he said, "Greetings."

Nothing happened.

The Siirk all around him were hostile and impatient. They growled at each other and snarled, exchanging rakes of their clawed hands.

Suddenly, a large square of ship's skin changed from chrome to glassy, and a picture screen appeared. Against a dark background, a balding man in a sort of business tunic spoke soberly: "Greetings."

"Ahhhh!" the Siirk said. "Geedeens."

"If you are a human and understand English, please name the world's highest mountain top. If you do not speak English, please name your language. *Si non hablas Ingles, por favor...*"

"Mount Everest," Alex said.

"Thank you. Please speak the option you desire, or touch it with your hand." The list of options, accompanied by symbols, stretched several feet, beginning with he Need Rescue. He looked for the Immediate

Evacuation. He noticed options that included calling for more assistance—no, he didn't want to bring more of these precious ships down for these beasts—and the Siirk held Maryan on the platform with a knife by her throat so that he wouldn't get any ideas about repeating the performance that had cost them Nizin.

"If you are unable to speak, press your hand against the options..."

Alex had to do something quickly, but what?

At that moment, a terrific growl went up, so loud and fierce, so desperate and powerful that it made the skin on his spine rise in gooseflesh. All eyes turned away from the ship, away from Maryan and Alex, and toward Xumar. In one move, Xumar had turned around, twisting the thongs that held him down. Xumar had pulled his Siirk jailer up on his back and trotted off. The Siirk, now looking terrified, squealed for help. Alex heard the soft rattle of wood and leather as a number of arrows found their way onto bows. That sound was followed by the rattle of several guns, and then by the twang of arrows flying loose. The Siirk rolled up his eyes and went limp, looking like a pincushion full of ordnance. Xumar trotted on powerful legs.

Alex seized the opportunity and pressed Full Immediate Evacuation. The door slid open, unnoticed by the Siirk who remained captivated by the drama with Xumar. Alex took a step to his right and poked his index finger into the eye of the Siirk holding the knife. Kogran dropped the knife, screamed, and held his eye. Alex grabbed Maryan around the waist and they dove into the open cargo bay together.

The Siirk bellowed as they noticed this new drama. Several shots sounded, and bullets ricocheted in the cargo area. Kogran screamed for a cease-fire.

Alex yelled: "Close doors!" Omas bellowed something outside, and the bullets stopped. Just as the door was half closed, one arrow sailed in, bounced off the opposite bulkhead, and fell harmlessly to the floor. From the sound of hooves, some of the Siirk were going after Xumar. Those near the ship fell quiet in one groan of frustration.

The door winked shut, leaving Alex and Maryan in darkness. Alex smelled stale oil and dust that had not stirred in eons. The boat inside was a mix of rust, dust, and shiny surfaces. Parts of it were crumbling, while patches of skin retained their silvery flexibility.

Alex faintly heard an object hit the outside of the boat—a rock, he imagined, thrown by an angry Siirk.

At the same moment, the boat jerked free and rose. Alex's stomach yawed, and Maryan shrieked, holding him tightly as they slid along the floor. Lights winked on, and huge panels played in full color in several places. The boat moved sickeningly without regard for dimensions or for their stomachs. The movement was fluid, quick, remorseless—yaw, pitch, and roll all at once—and Alex thought he was going to black out. They settled into a fast, steep, steady climbing motion.

A man's voice, modulated almost musically, said: "If you are unable to command, the boat will take you directly to the Emergency Receiving Medical Station, or ERMS. There, in the hospitality of the world's largest space station, you will receive a full medical assessment from professional medical staff before entering the main colony, where all your needs will be met." The voice exaggerated its pleasantness: "Have a pleasant journey."

A woman's voice cut in with similar unctuousness: "If you are able to command, please speak the ten digit official command sequence now."

Alex had no idea what she was talking about...a key to the computer that ran the boat, he supposed. "We don't know the sequence," he said.

"That is not a lexical command."

"We don't know!" he yelled.

There was a silence while it processed. "You will be taken to Emergency Receiving Dispensary ERD-151 at Rosa Parks Hospital on West 59th Orbital Stack. Please stand by."

In the ensuing silence, Maryan and he studied the boat that could become their tomb or their liberation...their fate could be seconds away, hours, days...or until the oxygen ran out.

Weak lights flickered brownish in the walls. The boat bucked a few times, making groaning noises. They clung together, scared for their lives. The seat cushions had fallen apart eons ago, leaving a brown dust that blew away and exposed age-dulled metal surfaces. In places, the floor was ankle-deep in russet powder. The air smelled dry and stale. Alex began to feel a sort of metal band around his head, and his vision grew blurry. Alex felt Maryan sobbing in his arms, and realized they were probably dying from asphyxiation.

Then, as he slipped into unconsciousness, as if falling asleep, lights came on, clean air started blowing, and an entire wall opened up into a spectacular view that picked up millions of pixels of light on one side of the steel hull and sent it to corresponding pixels on the inside surface, giving the illusion of a window. His headache faded, leaving a residual kern of unease somewhere around his brain stem. Maryan stopped sobbing and composed herself.

"My God," she said.

Maryan and Alex were airborne, and sailing faster and faster while rising into the air.

At first, they could almost count individual leaves and branches on the millions of trees below, then the individual whitecaps of waves on lakes and bays as the boat went faster and higher. Soon they were skimming along under a mass of cumulus clouds, through a blue sky gilded with sunshine, while below, under a thin haze of brownish-gray rain cover, glittered the tangled new beaches of the brave new world that Earth had become with rising seas. Maryan and Alex flew westward, popping through the sound barrier. They hung on as best they could. The boat flew smoothly, except for an occasional jolt through twisted layers of turbulent air. They flew westward, into the sunset, which perversely looked like a sunrise gilding the wide, shallow waters of new seas where a million years ago had been the deserts of the American Southwest. They flew over the Pacific Ocean, angling toward the equator, and Alex guessed the autopilot was readying for—what? Orbit?

Their course veered south, with the sun rising toward their upper right. They sailed over the ruddy Mars-like continent that had once been Australia, and then upward.

The sky darkened and grew black as they entered space.

The stars shone in carpets all around, and the moon lay like a cool light-disk to one side. The smudge in space beside the moon twinkled with borrowed light like a lane of broken glass. That was where they were streaking with increasing speed, and Alex had a sense of foreboding. The smudge began to resolve into a terrifying picture of broken structures surrounded by miles and miles of scattered debris. This looked like a place of death.

"A space station. Or what?" With the deep black of space as a backdrop, a vast hulking form waited for their approaching boat. At first he thought it was a maze of lights, but soon he realized the lights were reflections. To one side was a slightly curved wall—the horizon of Earth at night, glowing with rainbow colors.

As the boat traveled in orbit, another sight began to emerge: the full sphere of the moon, dazzling in reflected sunlight. On the clearest day on earth, Alex had never seen the detail on its surface with such exquisite clarity. For a few moments, he gazed at the craters and rilles with hungry fascination. Then he realized the bright light hurt his eyes. The pseudo-window wasn't translating the heat involved in the reflected sunlight, but the brightness seared his eyeballs. He staggered back, rubbing his eyes. "Dim!" he said. "Dim!"

A bell chimed. A woman's voice said: "Do you require service?"

"Yes, *blazes!* Make the display dimmer before we fry like fish in here."

"I will adjust the settings using the default contrast values for the cabin. Please wait a moment." A woman's shape was dimly visible in a tall, narrow side panel rippling with interference. Hers was the soft, sensuous voice of ancient spokeswoman; he recognized it from Alex Kirk's memories. How he longed to be back in that lost world of comforts and mass civilization! Maryan squeezed his hand as they waited. Sure enough, the display dimmed by several shades of gray. Still, the growing station was overwhelming in its size and complexity. As they drew near, they began to see the extent of its damage and isolation.

An enormous cylinder about 20 miles long and five miles in diameter made up the vast bulk of this world orbiting a world. Capping it at one end was what looked like a city-disk a mile thick and at least six or seven miles in diameter, that might once have housed up to two million persons living on the food grown in the cylinder. Clustered around the cylinder were other mile-big structures—cubes, cylinders, spheres—and clustered around those were smaller and smaller aggregations of shapes into dizzying degrees of smallness.

He looked for signs of life, but could not find any. Not a moving body in a spacesuit. Not a moving vehicle. Nothing. Worse yet, there were broken areas where bent girders showed through. Clouds of debris hung in frozen orbit, moving with the main mass of the station. Worst of all, it appeared that one end of the cylinder had taken a massive hit of some kind...a mile-long tongue of atmosphere was slowly leaking out into space, visible by millions of tiny white specks in its debris field. The station might be a million years old.

"Will we be able to breathe in there?" Maryan said with a pale face and large eyes, holding her hands over her mouth. She didn't address the question to Alex; she was just thinking out loud. He felt helpless and frustrated, unable to protect her.

The boat flew toward the hull of the station at flash speed, and Alex instinctively closed his eyes and expected to die in a silent explosion. Instead, the boat penetrated through the station's chaotically shattered skin, which consisted of thousands upon thousands of silvery squares that had once made one continuous, smooth surface and now resembled a puzzle falling from a table. Each square seemed to have its own shade from dark gray to gleaming silver, depending on its orientation toward the sun. Many were curling at the edges or bend double. The whole station looked as though a clumsy child had glued mirror-shade confetti all over its skin.

8. Space

Eons ago, this must have been an impressive city in space, Alex thought as he stood with his arm around Maryan, as they stared at the approaching starscape of broken marvels.

Now the great station was a gray ruin, illumined mainly by reflected light from the Earth's atmosphere and basking beside Luna's bluish-green stencil rays. Everywhere Alex looked, debris hung frozen in the thin atmosphere. On the outside, the silvery metallic skin of the station was peeling off in huge squares and rectangles, exposing shadowy girders and tangles of cable underneath. One could see into the station at various impact points, where small objects had slammed through, and the interior was an absolute shambles of suspended debris and dust.

"Greetings," a male voice said behind Alex and Maryan, and they whirled. Alex tightened his arms around Maryan, who stiffened in his embrace.

On the wall behind them had appeared the image of a genial man with white hair, of indeterminate race and age. He wore dark, comfortable clothing and appeared to be in a comfortably gloomy study. "Sorry if I startled you. My name is Spector, and I am a librarian with added functions as a host. I can book rooms for you, hire a rental car, suggest a good podiatrist, whatever you need."

"Are you a real person?" Maryan said, separating herself from him and advancing toward him with curiosity. "Were you?" she amended.

"Oh no," Spector said in a mixture of kindness and condescension that Alex found irritating. "I am a composite of numerous people, but primarily I am an avatar of the chief librarian of our time, Dr. Grant Genovese. Have you met him yet?"

Alex said: "I think he's been dead and gone for a while." *Ages,* Alex thought. *Eons.*

Spector's image flickered an instant, and a brief look of bafflement fleeted across his features as the entire scenario refreshed itself via a warm boot. "My name is Spector," he said, which was when Alex realized Spector was broken, like most everything in this gigantic orbiting tomb.

"Try to understand this," Alex said. "The station is in ruins. We need help. Will there be breathable air where we are going?"

"Let me check for you," Spector said. "Where are you going?"

Maryan said: "Wherever it is possible for us to survive." She added: "We'd prefer to go back to the surface of the planet."

Spector looked puzzled. "This station has every amenity. Would you like me to book you a hotel room, a massage, a swim party at one of our themed pools? Do you prefer Polynesian, Icelandic, or Arizona Desert?"

"Spector," Alex said, gesticulating with frustration, "please be a good host and listen. Listen carefully."

"I am listening," Spector said, inclining his head with warmth where he sat behind his desk.

"A million years have passed. The station is a wreck. There are no more human beings. We are extinct."

Spector rose, putting his hands in his pockets. He looked rumpled and academic in a gray sweater, white shirt, and beige linen trousers. "Logic tells me that I am speaking with two human beings." He smiled cozily, as if enjoying a joke they'd made.

"We need air, water, food," Maryan said. "Spector, the station is a wreck."

Alex told her: "My guess is we're overwhelming his functional database, what's left of it."

"Maybe he's just a librarian as he says," she said.

"I am a librarian," Spector said. His image flickered and he appeared once again to reboot. "My name is Spector. Can I be of service?"

The boat shuddered, and Alex and Maryan hung on to objects around them as the floor rose up as the boat ran aground. They turned away from the streaked, fuzzy screen where Spector had been, and faced the large view screen.

"Look, oh dear God," Maryan said, pointing. Alex could only stare numbly at the overwhelming scene that played out before them. They were in a vast space full of frozen debris. Some of the objects still twirled slowly, and had perhaps been twirling thus for eons. Radio lifts were everywhere, as were silvery skin squares and glassy wall tiles. The boat had run up on the ledge of a huge curving platform forming a ring miles long inside the main structure of the station. From a thousand feet up, indirect sunlight streamed in, a smoky pillar of light that cut through torn structural elements and stabbed downward. Where the light entered, torn metal gleamed like worn copper and brass, almost a dark golden color. The beam itself was filled with a dust of microscopic debris that glowed bluish in places, light yellow in others, and in a few rare spots as though it contained miniature rainbows. The space around it was almost entirely dark, except light glittered on slowly twirling broken surfaces and loose objects. Light bounced off distant curving walls that were still intact, whose portholes and railings were dimly visible. The beam of light drenched a section of the ledge near the ship with near daylight intensity, seemingly dripping off the edge and plunging another thousand feet into unfathomable depths full of ancient architectures and geometries that steeped in a somber olive-drab and coppery-brown gloom. Paper had gone out of vogue in the early 21st Century, replaced by very similar looking sheets of an environmentally friendly bioplast called radio lifts. These were biodegradable sheets containing pixons whose color could be remotely programmed, so that they could "say" whatever one wanted them to, and each sheet had enough intrinsic memory for a library of older tree-books. The drained atmosphere inside the station held a jumble of drowned debris that looked holographic and disembodied, illumined from behind by brownish-green fingers of light.

Maryan gripped Alex's side, painfully, getting his attention. She pointed silently to a form lying suspended in midspace as though asleep. It was the frozen body of a long-dead young woman. Her skin looked bluish in the light, as if she had been a denizen of some watery world created out of rainwater and cigarette smoke. Her hair, what was left of it from eons of bumping about, was of a dark and indeterminate color but might once have been blonde or even reddish. Hard to say. Even the corpse's expression was hard to read—was it peaceful, or was there some slowly dawning horror that had never had a chance to fully burst on her features? Her eyes were closed and her mouth was slightly open as if she were uttering some words, and was stuck on one long syllable that just wouldn't come out.

One by one, they counted at least a half dozen bodies of young men and women, or parts of them, looking like broken statuary. Aside from a few shreds of ancient clothing, all were naked.

The mere presence of the boat had created infinitely slow ripples of nudging among the drifting objects, which ultimately began to affect the nearest corpse, the young woman's, which turned slightly and in so doing revealed the desiccated texture of the chalk-white skin. But her eyeballs still glittered from under partially open lids, and her arms lay relaxed by her sides. Her legs were intact and also relaxed, slightly bent at the knees.

As the boat drifted at a glacial pace, they passed a row of dead, dark openings that loomed above dust-blurred walking platforms. High up, still dimly visible in dark blue on light gray, were the letters *L5 Port of Entry & Dep*. The rest of the sign had been torn off by some long-ago disaster, and the entry point of a missile or fist-sized meteorite through the station's had collapsed somehow, sealing itself off. Alex frowned in puzzlement at the airtight pucker of ripped metal, spattered glass, and melted materials far overhead in what must once have been a lovely dome with stained glass-like effects.

A sudden jarring of the floor made Alex and Maryan cry out and reach for their balance, forgetting the view outside.

The boat ran slowly aground, bow first, a bit sideways, and sat firmly on the metallic ledge. The boat had bent a handrail down and now hung frozen on that ledge, looking across a wide walk space toward a series of doors and shop windows. "Like a huge mall," Alex said.

"A shopping mall," Maryan said wonderingly, from some ancient memory of her Shurey ancestor.

Alex noticed that it was getting hot in the boat, and the air seemed to be leaden. He touched his throat, which was slick with sweat. "Oxygen is running low."

"Maybe it only did a quick replenish in the atmosphere," she said, "and there is little or no backup in its tanks."

"We'll suffocate." He walked in a panic up to the opposite screen and banged on it with both fists. "Spector!" He said again: "Spector!" But the screen kept flickering, and only shadowy hints of the librarian's form appeared in short takes.

Maryan held her throat, coughed, and sat down abruptly on a steel bench from which dust flew up.

Alex pressed his fingertips against the Spector screen and moved his hands about as if he could force the elusive advisor to step out. Then he noticed a red sign to one side and brushed his wrist over it. The faded white letters "Emergency Screen" became visible. He touched the sign, and a fractured blue enveloped the screen. Only partially legible, it portrayed a map of the space station. As Alex touched various parts with his fingertips, they popped up in detailed 3-D relief, holographically, inches outside the screen surface. When he ran his hands over the models, they turned at his bidding. "Spector!" he cried. "Help us! We need air!"

Maryan rose and stumbled toward the screen pointing. "Look, there is a green area in the center of the station." She pressed her hands against it, and the area rose in relief. They saw a forest at the heart of the station.

The display did not seem to be aware of the ship's wrecked state. The station was a cylinder about twenty miles long and five miles in diameter. Their boat had entered a larger end-cap section filled with tier upon tier of shops, streets, hotels, a whole city—empty of life. The external skin of the cylinder, ruined and airless, encompassed several decks of living and working space on a vast scale—each deck several hundred square miles in area. The innermost deck, facing into the open cylinder, apparently had been designed as a series of parks and farms but was now a jungle of forests and swamps under a glowing internal sky. It was a dark-green wilderness with reddish sunlight looming behind huge trees; so the interior had become a huge forest, a jungle, and therefore must contain some breathable air as it reprocessed carbon. It was a rash guess, but they were running out of breathable air by the minute.

Alex took a look at Maryan, who had slumped with her back against the screen and was holding her face in her hands. Could they get there in time? Desperately, Alex strode to the front of the boat. There, he waved his arms, cutting through layers of hanging cloth and dusty cobwebs. Coughing, he cleared his way to a forward view screen, under which he saw a panel that looked as if it might be a cover over manual steering controls. He tried to pry it open with his hands, but the cover stuck. He picked up a loose bar of composite steel, like a crow bar, and pried at the panel until it snapped and fell off. Inside was a small bank of lights—all burned out, dull amber and red with a few greens mixed in—and control buttons. A few of the buttons shattered under his touch, and the plastic-like material dribbled away under his fingertips. But the underlying steel shafts were intact—apparently made of a corrosion-resistant alloy or composite—and he boldly pressed them, testing their function.

At first he felt nothing and was afraid that the boat's controls were dead. After all, how many eons had she lain silent and unmoving in frozen sleep, her materials weakening from the sheer passage of time?

Then, a sudden lurch—and the boat slammed against the deck, worsening its injuries. No telling if the new structural damage was letting air out faster—but this boat would never fly in space again. Alex worked the controls feverishly. "Hang on, Maryan. I'm going to try and get us to that forested area."

Suddenly the boat lifted smoothly, and for a moment he thought he had its controls in hand. The next moment she lurched, left with her stern, then slammed down on the steel deck again. Alex groaned. He could just imagine slamming this thing down until it broke open and they lay dying like gaping fish on the inhospitable steel walkway. With both hands, he continued pressing buttons as he learned their functioning. He was beginning to feel short of breath, and his arteries were pounding in his throat. How much longer? Maybe just minutes. God, something had to happen, and quick!

As if reading his mind, the boat floated up a finger's breath, so it was free of friction, and accelerated in a leftward sideways motion.

"Alex!" Maryan cried, watching the wall of shop windows approaching.

"I'm trying—" he started to say, pumping the buttons, but he couldn't control the boat.

The windows and walls approached in a blur of speed.

Alex and Maryan felt the shudder, but did not hear the slam of shattered glass, as the boat spun through department store windows. Still spinning—in fact, accelerating—the boat bashed through great empty halls in which decayed signs hung overhead and dusty counters vanished in puffs of dust. Effigies—mannequins male and female, some near naked in faded pink, some holding a pensive finger to a lip or touching what had once been a hat or a hairdo, or holding a hand near a hip where once had been a trouser pocket, toppled out of the way as the boat crashed wildly and careened about. Ancient lights flickered on, then winked out just as quickly as their circuits smoked under the load. Some vanished in showers of sparks as their wiring was torn out of the ceiling. The boat rocketed on like a carnival ride gone wild. She crashed like a ballistic cigar immersed in a bow wake of flickering blue lights and reddish flames, then slammed through a rear wall, across a silently frozen street in a night scene without neons, and into another level of stores. From there, she changed direction, spinning counter-clockwise, and down through a mezzanine, partially weightless, down multiple balcony levels, and through a gloomy courtyard, down an alley framed in faux brick, through a plate window—and into a mass of trees.

There, the ride came to an end as the boat couldn't navigate through the dense trunks, turned upward but couldn't mount the traction to climb into the interior central sky, then burrowed nose down until she came to a stop in the ground. At that, the engine died. Breakers slammed, the lights went out, and fire sparked. The boat would never fly anywhere again.

The cabin was dark and smelled faintly of rubber and smoke, making Alex and Maryan choke.

They rushed to the side door by which they had entered down on Earth. They pounded on the door's hard surface. Alex noticed a red and white striped area above the door and pounded a fist there. The door slid open a few feet with a tortured creak and then died in its tracks. Maryan and Alex held hands and stumbled from the opening. Cool, fragrant forest air enveloped their senses as they fell to their knees on thick moss several feet below door level. They rubbed their eyes to clear them, and then looked around at this orbiting wilderness.

An animal howled loudly, and eerie echoes reverberated through the forest. Goosebumps rippled on Alex's back, and Maryan gripped his arm with steely fingers as she looked around terrified. The ground started trembling, and the boat lying nearby began to shake. "Let's find a safe spot," Alex said. He looked up, frowning, as a wind blew around them.

The air smelled fresh, of pine and water and soil, even aromatic from mosses and flowers and fresh grass, but the atmosphere itself seemed to be becoming more disturbed by the moment.

Alex took in the vastness of this place. It appeared to be an enormous cylinder coated on the inside with forests. The opposite surface was almost too far away to see, lost in haze and distance as if on another planet. On this end was a narrow pinch of windows and balconies leading to the deserted and airless stores and avenues of that long-ago downtown to which the agrarian residents must have gone for shopping and entertainment. The other end of the cylinder was twenty miles away, lost in a fog of light and atmosphere. Along the center of the cylinder were clouds, and at times they flashed with lightning. Some areas were dark and foreboding, as if full of rain. It was such a dark, roiling, disturbed area that now seemed to be closing in on Alex and Maryan and their beached boat.

Minute by minute, the swirling wind doubled. Surrounded by forest on all sides except the grayish walls and blank windows behind them, they couldn't see the countryside around them. The wind tore through the tree crowns, making their branches and leaves sway. Even more puzzling was the fact that dark shapes seemed to be lifting up, like blankets, twirling in the wind, and angling in toward the boat. Heavy, wet bunches of leaves were spinning through the air toward them, and when the first ones started hitting the boat, Maryan tugged at his hand. "Come on, we've got to run for cover!"

Alex hesitated. Should they get into the boat? As he stared at it, the boat trembled as the wind shoved it a bit, and a thick dust of loose soil swirled up around it.

"Come on!" Maryan yelled. Her voice was almost lost in the din.

Together, they ran uphill, through a maze of trees, while leaves shot around them and whipped their faces with cutting ferocity. They had to help themselves along by pulling themselves along the trees and taking turns helping each other. There was only one logical direction to take: toward the wall behind them, but away from the boat, away from the broken window through which they had crashed.

The wind was audibly howling now, and Alex couldn't hear his own voice as he yelled for Maryan to grab his hand. She was clinging to a tree, trying to make it the last fifteen or twenty feet toward an opening in what looked like a stone or concrete wall. Alex ran toward her through the wind that practically tore his clothes off. Together, they ducked and ran down hill, into the opening, into a dank but quiet cellar of sorts. There was a slightly rancid smell in there and it was dark, and their feet stood in water up to the ankles that felt cold and unpleasant, but Alex felt safer than outside. He rumpled his face squeamishly at the feel of running slime between his toes. Outside, small whirlwinds danced about. Leaves and branches raced in circles.

The boat lifted up at the bow, bounced a few times, then swung around. For a second it rested facing the opposite way. The boat slowly rolled over, turned sideways, and rolled out of sight. There was a loud tearing, smashing noise, a rending of metal and shattering of glass. There were a series of slapping noises. Alexa and Maryan hung on in the darkness as their refuge shook. The air was filled with dust, and they had to hold their hands over their faces to protect their eyes and to minimize breathing in debris.

Then, some ten minutes after the wind had started, it began to subside. The howling faded, almost reluctantly, as if the atmosphere had enjoyed a good, mean brawl. Branches and leaves fell to the ground. The wind wasn't strong enough to sustain heavy objects now. The air was still brown with dust. Leaves ran in circles, but the wood debris lay still. In another ten minutes the wind had almost completely subsided.

Glad to get back onto dry ground, Alex and Maryan held hands as they emerged from the muck and scrambled onto dustier, drier ground. They clambered back up that small incline through the trees, and emerged coughing and waving their hands before their faces to face what had happened. Now Alex understood, he thought. The smashed window was virtually sealed off, and no more air could escape. The boat was totally wrecked. The boat was wrapped around one edge, twisted in the middle, and partially draped across the opening so that its other end rested against the opposite side of the window frame. The rest of the window was covered with a thick mat of tree branches. The blanket-like objects, which proved to be of a stiff, dark material like the moss on his sky island back on Earth, formed a barrier.

Maryan stiffened and pointed upward at the wall.

Alex jerked his head up to look, and saw large crab-like or spider-like creatures descending. They were as big as human beings. Each had legs six to eight feet long, and chitin-covered body sacs the size of a human torso. Alex towed Maryan along as they sprinted away from the wall.

They ran up a long, gradual incline into the forest until they came to a ridge about ten feet high. It was covered with brittle leaves and other debris, and afforded them an outlook point over the dust-choked canyon leading down to the building wall. The spiders were too busy to pay any heed to the two humans. The spiders' mandibles worked furiously as fine ropes of sticky grayish fluid came from an orifice each had in the base of its torso and curling up for ready access.

"They're weaving a net over the hole," Maryan said, catching her breath. She wiped a dirty wrist over an equally dirty face.

He nodded. "It's all part of some damage control scheme, looks like. To keep the atmosphere in. To repair holes. The station is sealing up the hole we made coming through, using any material at hand including the boat we came in."

"The station must take a good number of micrometeorite hits," Maryan said. "That's part of the answer how any of this has survived." She bit her upper lip pensively. "Alex, it almost seems as if the station itself is intelligent, doesn't it? Do you suppose it's been repairing itself like this for a million years from all those little micrometeorite hits?"

He remembered the smudge of light, and the plume of debris they'd seen while approaching the station. "I suspect you're right. I just hope it doesn't think we are the enemy."

"At least the air is still breathable."

"It's actually rather pleasant," he said, looking around. "This place has survived for a long, long time."

She stepped beside him, putting her arm around his waist, and for a few minutes, they were able to gape at their surroundings together. They stood higher than before, but still couldn't see over the tree level, which reached a hundred feet in an endless cascade of forest leading away from the wall.

She pointed up at the distant, hazy opposite wall of the cylinder. "That looks like forest up there, above the clouds."

He nodded, squinting in the indirect bluish sunlight that filtered through from the distant end of the cylinder. "I think I see some water glittering. How do you suppose it stays flat against the cylinder wall?"

"We can't tell from here, but I'd guess this whole station must be spinning," she said. "This structure seems big enough to have some slight gravity, and probably has more mass than a fair-sized asteroid." She did a few quick guesses and calculations. "Although the cylinder is mostly hollow, its walls have mass. It's five miles in diameter, so (multiplying by π, or very roughly three and one seventh), it's over 15 miles in circumference. Twenty miles long, so the inside surface, if it were perfectly flat along its curvature, without hills and dips, would be about 300 square miles. God, that's huge."

Alex shook his head. "Amazing. And yet—they were dying out. They had all that genius, all those tools at their disposal—"

"All dressed up and nowhere to go," she concluded.

"Or going nowhere," he said more ironically.

"Don't forget the city at the end. That's a disk about a mile thick, and as much as seven miles in diameter, so it's got an inside surface area of 20 square miles, not counting multiple floors, which could make it dozens of square miles more."

"The scale is mind-boggling," he agreed. He thought of the floating bodies, the debris, around their landing zone. "No gravity in the center, I imagine, so they would have lived on the inside surface."

She said "It wouldn't be the same as natural gravity, but close in some ways. I have to wonder about the health effects."

"Like on the vascular system."

"Exactly."

"So how will it affect us?"

She shook her head. "We'll probably be okay for a while, but I would think long-term it might affect our blood pressure, our sense of balance, the way our organs function, I have no idea. Still, we may be safer here than down on Earth with the Siirk and who knows what other predators."

"You have a point there." He looked back at the wreckage of the boat. "We'll need to find water, shelter, food, weapons—with luck, another boat. Then we can choose whether to live up here or down there." He grinned and added: "We can commute back and forth."

She took his arm and started to say something affectionate, but they heard the trumpeting scream of a wild animal again, echoing across the forest and losing itself in the freely floating inner atmosphere, and he could feel her freezing against him in shock while her features blanched. He imagined he probably looked just as terrified to her, as he cradled her against himself. His hair stood on end, and he felt goose bumps rippling up and down the back of his neck and spine.

Even as he held her close, he glanced about seeking higher ground for them.

The atmosphere had a wild, rank freshness, with damp, loamy undertones.

The light was changeable and surprising. At times it could be wild, with gray rain clouds forming stormy, slow-motion corkscrews above. At the moment it was muted, as was the air around them. It was almost restful, a kind of greenish glow like that inside an ancient bottle toward evening, sepulchral, churchly, mesmeric—but Alex knew the dense vegetation around them could be harboring instant death for all he knew.

In a golden, dappled glade they broke a pair of saplings and used rounded stones lying in the lumpy hillside to grind one end of each sapling into spear points. Alex missed his sky island. So far, he had not spied any significantly high ground. Maybe up in the galleries under the city...? He looked up at the pinkly glowing round stone or ceramic wall that separated the city from its agricultural zone, several dozen square miles of so of the wall, pitted with age around the windows that were still intact. He wondered if any rooms up there that contained air. The city seemed to still have some atmospheric pressure, even if its air could not sustain life.

Alex and Maryan heard that trumpeting scream again, and returned to the urgency of fashioning their weapons.

A snapping noise, a twig breaking, came from the forest nearby. Maryan grabbed him by the arm, and they ran for cover behind a berm near the city wall.

"What was it?" he said.

"Did you see anything?"

"I didn't."

"Sounded like a fairly large animal," she said.

They waited. They minutes went by. They lay side by side, peering over the top of the berm with their newly made weapons ready. Sweat rimmed Alex's forehead, stung his eyes, ran down his cheeks.

Nothing.

Slowly, they rose. "Can't stay here forever," she said.

"Wonder if it gets darker or lighter," he said looking into the distance.

She put one hand on his shoulder and pointed with her other hand. "Look through the haze, far away."

He did. "My God." Distantly, he saw a dark smudge, and a number of spattered lights. "There it is. Outer space."

She pressed his shoulder lightly. "Keep looking, Alex. See it? We're turning. This whole thing really is revolving."

"Looks like were not going to point at the sun directly," he said. "They probably have mirrors and filters down there so they can control the amount and quality of light coming in."

She pointed up. "There are some secondary light sources."

His gaze followed where her finger pointed, and he saw big squarish shafts of light that seemed to come right out of the ground near the city wall a few miles further along. "Maybe we should head toward the light."

She shrugged. "What have we got to lose?"

Jogging at a light clip, they carried their spears loosely at the ready, on a constant lookout for danger. Keeping the wall to their right seemed to offer at least some kind of protected flank. Alex noticed that their Earth-toned muscles carried them forward with considerable strength for now, although they might lose their tone in the lesser gravity here. The air was rich and didn't tire them. They were used to surviving off the land, and this space-bound forest seemed to consist of vegetation remarkably like that they'd known on the planet. Soon enough, they became aware of small birds, insects, and tiny mammals scurrying among tree roots. Whatever dangers one might fear, at least this place was teeming with life.

They came to a place in the wall where water gushed out in a strong, thin stream. Approaching cautiously, circling around to outflank any possible predators, they found that the life forms enjoying the water were small and looked harmless. The water splashed out from a hole in the wall, jetted about six feet in a glittering, twirling arc, and splashed into a small pond the water had long ago carved out of rock and sand. The pond was covered with lily pads and contained fish that raised their open mouths to capture insects that buzzed loudly in a sepulchral glade under thick tree cover. Alex peered into the cool gloom and noticed vines knotted around each other above, with huge thorns. Other than that, it was delightful to listen to the splashing of the water and watch small birds taking turns flying up to the fountain and fluttering their wings as they drank in mid-flight.

"Looks safe to drink," Alex told Maryan. Covering each other's backs, they took turns drinking thirstily. Alex wished they had a container to carry water with them. All in good time, he was sure. From the rust stains around the mouth of the water source, he deduced that there had once been a metal pipe there. At that moment, another snapping sound echoed through the forest paths nearby, and Alex felt that creeping feeling again. "Something is watching us," he whispered.

"Or someone," she said with a shudder. "I feel my skin crawling."

"We shouldn't hang out around a water hole. The whole neighborhood comes here to drink."

She snapped her fingers in a sudden insight. "We can lurk nearby and see what lives in this area."

"That would be a good safe thing to do. You hungry yet?"

"Starving."

The station had its succession of days and nights, though unlike anything Alex and Maryan had seen on Earth.

At periods resembling Earth days, the light would fade and grow strong again. This happened in a slow, mostly imperceptible fashion. It was noticeable in the way that central mass of clouds seemed to darken, and the light grew murky. It was noticeable in the way the air would lighten again at the same slow steady pace, until some corners of the clouds sparkled with light. There was a lot of moisture in the clouds, and large patches of them were dark bluish-gray, almost black in certain angles of light. Others were pleasant billows of white cumulus with golden highlights when the noonday sunlight poured through whatever mirrors and filters closed up the far end of this world cylinder.

Sometimes it rained. Usually it was a misty drizzle that descended into the treetops and seemed almost to emanate from the ground. At other times it was a brief but driving rain that seemed to curve slightly even while falling straight. Sometimes a wind, reacting to changes between hot and cold areas in the atmosphere, would drive spiraling, needle-like droplets that stung the face and neck. Most of the time, a near-tropical stillness sweltered over the dark forests and swamps. The stillness was punctuated now and then with an animal cry, and there was a perpetual low twitter of birds and rustle of air in grasses and leaves.

Here and there, thick billows of mist roved over still ponds and streams. Parts of the station were more thinly forested than others. In some places, particularly on low rolling hills, the trees were sparse and the ground tended to be covered with lower bushes and patches of flowers. Always hovering on the periphery, however, was the thick forest. Some of it was pine. Many groves of trees were deciduous. The hillocks varied from high to low by a matter of as little as six feet or as much as sixty feet.

Then again, in places, the hard undersurface of the station had become visible near the bottom of a ravine or in the side of a hill covered by tree roots and hanging moss. It a stony, battered fundament that was very durable like ancient concrete, and helped explain the station's longevity.

Alex and Maryan began a roving existence that reminded him of how they had lived after their escape from Nizin and his horde. After several days of climbing up and down hillocks near the wall, they found themselves back at their starting point. By Alex's estimate, they had traveled a little over fifteen miles. It had been at times tortuous going, to get past swampy, thorny, impenetrable areas. In several places they had found holes gouged in the wall long ago. The holes were so old that their edges were rounded and blackened. Their edges were softened by years of soft wind and water. As a finishing touch, the holes were sealed with that spider goo to a texture like dirty glass and beeswax. In several spots, Alex and Maryan found the pitted skeletons of boats similar to the one in which they had arrived. Two such boats were embedded in the wall along with vines and flying blankets and other debris sealed with spider-spit superglue. Other wreckage (so ancient and jumbled it wasn't clear if it represented one or two craft) lay half-buried in soil and flowers on a low hill over which butterflies fluttered. Nearby was a balcony cocooned in debris.

Alex's mind turned elsewhere as he found his breath short and his legs aching. "Our strength will decline as we get spoiled by this gravity," he said. "We need to get back to Earth."

"Meanwhile," she countered pragmatically, worriedly watching thunder clouds a mile away, "we could climb up the wall and reconnoiter."

They clambered up the sloping wall in low gravity to a place where once a series of balconies had stair-stepped, giving city dwellers lovely views of sunsets falling in long over orderly miles of farmland, neatly tended orchards, country roads, rivers and ponds, the entire vista. Alex and Maryan climbed up the balcony ledges, aware that they would be visible to any predator like tiny specks from miles away on the vast grayish expanse dotted with other specks that had been windows and portals. They went slowly, putting their fingers in the little square holes in the stone where long-gone railings had rusted and disappeared, blown away like dust in the breezes of eons. Here and there, they surprised a flying thing that flew off in a sudden explosion of flapping wings and angry cries. Now and then, a rat-like animal scurried away with finely rippling long tail.

"If we can find one of those silvery boats," Alex said, squatting on a high ledge and squinting toward a distant amber dawn, "we could be back on the Earth in an hour or two. I really miss a fresh breeze and the wide open blue sky."

"Me, too." Maryan clung to a half-crumbled balcony nearby, as they hovered 200 feet above the jungle treetops. "Maybe there aren't any more boats."

"It's possible," he said grudgingly. "The station has been sending them down for ages. I'm surprised they lasted this long. That last one was a wreck on the inside."

She nodded. "You'd think they would have crumbled from age."

As they sat outside the lair they were considering living in, daylight grew brighter. The proposed new home was little more than a niche with a leafy, overgrown collapsed hotel room behind them. Alex peered in and dreaded to think what might dwell in such a black place. He could make out thick glass, dark with age, that fronted on the near-vacuum of the city beyond.

Alex and Maryan gazed at the emerging new day. Unlike the other days they'd experienced so far, the light did not stop growing in that bluish haze they'd come to know as daylight. Instead, a yellowish brightness flared. It made the long cylinder of the station look more like a dark tunnel. Clouds swirling in the center obscured the vision somewhat, but Alex and Maryan recognized a looming apparition beyond the far, broken end of the cylinder.

"The moon!" Maryan said.

"Look how close it is. You can look down into the craters."

"Looks so close..." She frowned as she pondered. "Fifty thousand miles, I bet. You can see the curvature up around the top, and space beyond."

"No atmosphere, no haze," he added, "so the transition between moon and space is abrupt." The distant mountains stood out bright and stark against the black nothingness beyond. Stars spattered the blackness in close and endless profusion.

Maryan said: "I think it pretty much confirms what I've been thinking. The station sits at L5. That's one of the two major Lagrange points, caught between the gravity fields of the Earth and the Moon."

Alex added: "Can't go up, can't go down, and if it drifts sideways for any reason it gently drifts back into position at L5. No orbital decay, no gradual flaming descent into Earth's atmosphere...perfect design for a station meant to last forever."

She pointed. "Look, something is happening."

As they watched, a dot of white light moved in a straight path over the surface of the Moon.

"Definitely is a line down there," Alex said. He'd only begun to notice the fine hairline because of the dot moving with increasing speed among pale rays and olivine plains. The line stretched over gray dust fields without touching any craters.

She said: "Looks like a long road or a track maybe. I can't make it out for sure."

"There goes that dot of light," he said. The pinprick of light seemed suddenly to lift from the surface and wink out of existence. "Think it blew up?"

"Possible. Could be a meteorite that somehow flew just past the Moon at a low altitude."

"Or a ship? A boat maybe?"

She looked at him. "You think they are launched from the Moon?"

He exhaled, baffled, and shook his head. "Anything is possible. Our people are extinct, or they'd be around, inhabiting their city, this whole station, growing crops, and they certainly wouldn't have surrendered Earth to the Siirk."

"Are you hungry?"

"Ah..." He looked down at his stomach. "Back to reality. Yes. And thirsty. I hate to keep climbing down to that watering hole every time we need a drink." He sighed. "Starting over again is a drag." He brightened. "We can probably scavenge some simple things like knives and cups if we can figure out how to get into the dead city."

She nodded. "Yes, without suffocating or imploding or whatever."

He grinned. "You can do it. Just hold your breath."

"Your mama, pal. You're the one that's full of hot air, so you go." She made a wry face. "We don't even have enough sunlight or heat to fire a clay pot or two. We'll have to use a hollowed tree trunk to store water."

"If we can find a sharp rock suitable for scraping and cutting."

"This isn't easy," she said with a long sigh, casting her eyes down.

"Cheer up. I'll go down and hunt a little lunch. That will make us feel better." He started down the wall.

"I'm coming with you," she said with a near-wail of anxiety. "If we go, we go together." She looked nervously over her shoulder. "I don't even want to think about being alone if those spiders come climbing down."

He dreaded the big crab-like creatures too, but he brushed his fear aside. "I think they just fix things. As long as we don't look broken, they won't come to lick us with their goo."

"Ee-yoo-www," she said, wrinkling her face.

They climbed down the face of the wall in the light gravity. Alex felt the momentum of the massive wall and the jolt as he jumped to the spinning inner surface of the cylinder. They followed the dry higher ground, avoiding the mucky dark marshy lower areas. They held their spears ready and moved carefully through the gloom with its drifting wisps of fog. The silence was interrupted by a low susurrus from insects humming over the water, and the scurrying of tiny feet—mammal and otherwise—in the trees around them. The light above was almost sunny as it shone in the laundry-twirl of clouds at the gravity-free center of the cylinder but down here it was still that somber coppery twilight. The leaves, however, were turned fully upward and glistened with the light that drove the photosynthesis in their veins. Lower to the ground, the leaves were huge, to catch as much light as possible, while higher up they were small as the plants optimized their exposure to the wan light.

Alex and Maryan had long ago overcome their ancient prejudices. They considered it an invigorating treat to capture a large beetle, mercifully kill it by tearing its tiny head off, and break it in half. Holding the broken carapace up, they could suck the liquid from its interior the same way they treated any lucky finds of bird eggs. Anything to get the protein and fat their bodies craved. "I'd really like a chocolate Easter egg sometime with vanilla filling," Maryan said wistfully as she tossed a large, empty beetle aside. "Or a nice ice cream, you know, vanilla on the inside and dark, brittle chocolate around the outside."

"Stop torturing us. Maybe we'll get lucky and find some cacao plants," Alex said. "I'm not sure we'd recognized them if we fell over them."

"Do you smell something odd?"

He sniffed and wrinkled his nose. "Something faint. Dead."

"Let's be careful," she whispered.

They trod one step at a time along a grassy ridge. They went up a slope and emerged in a wide brushy area. For a moment, Alex had the illusion of being earthside. The intense moonlight flooded the air, making the clouds shine bright-blue with whitish trailing wisps. The hillock smelled of flowers, and the ground felt firm and dry under Alex's feet. In the same moment, both he and Maryan caught a stronger whiff of that dreadful smell.

"What is that stench?" she said holding her nose.

"It's coming from over here," Alex said. Against his will, curiosity and instinct drew him to an area of taller grass along one side of the hillock, and there he spied what looked like a reclining form. "Here it is."

"That's it," Maryan added with finality as they clung together and stepped closer. The corpse in the grass was that of a tiny person, maybe half of Maryan's size. It was neither Siirk nor Takkar, but a new species. At first glance, this looked like the body of a young boy, with fine silvery hair on its limbs and chest as well as its head and face, but the head was large in proportion to the body and the shape was like that of the Takkar, blunt and angular. From the wrinkles on the cheeks and around the eyes and mouth, as well as the webbing of fine scars on the coarsened hands, Alex suspected this was a full grown adult. "Look at the skull," Maryan said, still holding her nose as she stepped around the body.

"Nizin or some of his people," Alex said. "That has to be their handiwork." The creature's skull had been severed on top and its brain was gone. The skull was empty except for a mass of silvery ant-like insects swarming around the remaining edible scraps inside. Alex knelt and examined the edges of the skull. "It was bashed open, then pried apart. Look, you can see gnawing marks around the edges."

"Can it be?" Alex whispered with a pang of horror. He pictured the Siirk leader with his amulet, rubbing his belly in cruel and ruthless self-love.

"Do you suppose Nizin is alive?" Maryan said in a hushed voice. Her eyes were large, no doubt remembering the horror of their capture and journey with the Siirk.

Alex nodded reluctantly. "It's possible. We just thought he vanished into space but it makes sense—if we got here in one piece. I almost hope it's just him, and not a whole bunch of predators like him."

"I will bet he's up here, looking for a way down and killing everything he finds for food or fun."

"I almost hope you're right," Alex said rising. He held his spear close. "If we can find him before he finds us, we can probably have him for lunch instead of the other way around."

Maryan made a face. "I don't mind eating bugs, but I wouldn't want his meat in my stomach."

"Yes, I think I'd rather go hungry too."

They slipped back down the jungle trail heading back to their roost. Along the way, she said: "We can't really go back up the wall. We're too visible."

Alex shuddered. "What were we thinking, exposing ourselves like that?"

"What we really should do is go to the other end of the station. If he's operating down around here, he might never get to the other end."

He stopped and pulled her into the shade of a large tree. "Let's try our best to find a boat. I think they are all down here, on the city end. There is probably nothing on the other end."

She looked uncertain. "You mean in the Reception Center we flew past? It's all dead in there."

"The boats have to be controlled by an automated process, particularly if it turns out to be true that they get launched from the moon somehow. There can't be humans left alive. All we've seen has been these canned Spectors and Nectars."

"But I'm afraid of Nizin. We can put twenty miles between ourselves and him."

"And a possible boat."

"You may be wrong. So how would we get into the city?"

"There has to be a way." He looked toward the forest. "Those flying blankets now...and the spiders. I have an idea."

"If there is any hope of finding another one of those silvery boats to take us back to Earth, I think it's going to be in the city."

"You may be right," Maryan said, though her eyes were clouded with doubts. "I'm scared of that dark, gloomy place with those dead people floating around in it."

"So am I. But I'm more scared of spending the rest of my life wandering around in here eating bugs and looking over my shoulder every five minutes for Nizin."

"Yes, I'm definitely ready to go home," she said, taking him by the hand. Together, they wandered close to the breach in the wall, which by now had thoroughly sealed itself. They ran their hands curiously over the surface of the self-created plug. The plug was about the size of a large show window. The last of the huge spider crabs were just then scuttling away, receding into dots far up. The combination of smashed metal and glass plus spider saliva-glue plus the flying blankets had created a seal that was now hardening into a glassy mass. The flying blankets grew naturally nearby like a grayish-pink groundcover. The blankets were about an inch thick and stiffly fluffy, like very light felt. The resulting smooth finish and seemed to level out any lumps and uneven spots where materials had been welded together by the force of the wind and the adhesive power of the spider glue. The result was a resin finish impervious to scratching by fingernails or rocks.

One corner of the old plate window was still there. It was a scratched, milky triangle shape of ancient glass. Its thick greenish core had somehow survived the eons, although the surface had taken on a metallic sheen. The surface was bumpy and bubbly from all the vegetation that had attached itself and then died and fallen off, giving way to more generations of the same. In one or two spots the glass had thinned. Cracks ran through those spots, and Alex felt it was a miracle it hadn't shattered under the wind onslaught a short while ago. Like much in the orbital cylinder, it raised more questions that he had no time to puzzle over. Through a thin spot, they could see the dim frozen landscape beyond. There was some sort of atmosphere in there, though he was sure it wasn't breathable. Somehow, they must attempt to get to the station in hope of finding an undamaged silver boat.

Maryan pointed to a shadowy corner of the big store. "Looks like a protective suit of some kind." As he squinted and moved his head about, he made out the words *Fire Department Emergency*. "Fire departments in outer space would care about hull breaches and fires. Wonder if we could grab one of those suits?"

She nodded. "Probably fall apart in our hands if we touch one, but worth a try."

Alex and Maryan made a kind of emergency breathing apparatus from what they now firmly called 'flying blankets.' They hiked half a mile inland to a high grassy tableland, where they spotted the grayish material growing amid the grass. "It's some kind of moss," Maryan observed.

Alex pulled up a towel-sized swath of the stuff. There was a root ball in a corner, with veins running up into the felt and foot-long stringy roots dangling full of soil. The root stuff proved easy to separate from the felt-like material. Alex and Maryan learned to pull the felt off without damaging the roots. They had soon harvested a good pile of the felt, which they carried in two bundles back to the breach in the wall.

The material seemed sticky and, when they applied any pressure to it, it seemed to ooze a sap-like syrup.

"This feels as if it has glue in it," he said.

"You're right." She smelled it. "Sort of a cross between turpentine and vanilla."

He wrinkled his nose. The smell was faint and delicate, but definite. "Probably make you see stars if you smell it long enough."

"And you want to breathe this stuff?" She regarded him with alarm.

"You have any better ideas?" He didn't tell her he was having a scary vision of ending up forever drifting among the mummified corpses in the station.

They came back to the breach and threw their bundles down. She leaned nose-first against the wall. "Can't smell a thing. Maybe the spider goo neutralizes it." She looked up. "Want to help me catch a spider?"

He grinned. "Are you that brave?"

She cocked her fists on her hips. "Anything to bring my man back alive from the city of the dead."

"Funny, I was going to send you."

"Sorry. No chickens allowed."

He sighed. "I should have known." Truth was, he wouldn't have permitted her to go, though it was a tossup. If something happened to him and he didn't come back, she'd be stuck here alone. The other side of the coin was that he couldn't imagine letting her get stuck in some horrifying situation, maybe meeting a lingering and painful end, which would be bad enough for her; but then he'd be stuck here wondering about her, maybe driven mad and forced to go looking for her. As though reading his mind and understanding that train of painful thoughts, she said: "We never figured on lasting long, Alex. You know that. When we go, it's over for our kind."

He shook his head. "If one of us goes, we're both gone." He couldn't bring himself to say the next sentence: "I couldn't bear to go on without you." The tearful look in her eyes told him she was thinking the same. He regarded the opaque sky, the unreadable clouds, the secretive forests opposite. He remembered the sudden raging wind and the flying blankets, and shook his head. "Somehow, sweet thing, I don't think we have a choice. We have to go forward."

She yanked at a pile of flying blankets. "Let's get this over with. I've got the creeps."

"Me too." He pitched in, and together they rigged a primitive breathing device. The pieces of blanket overlapped slightly and could be pressed together; their sticky sap made them stay glued. "I think," he said as they feverishly worked pressing edges together to form a three-dimensional shape, "the spider glue hardens it like epoxy into that glassy condition."

"Might be overkill for us," she said.

"I hope that's right. If this thing comes apart out there, I'll be sucking nitrogen or CO_2 or who knows what kind of crappy air until I go balls up."

"Don't even say it, Alex."

"I'll be back," he promised. He took her in his arms, feeling her soft curviness against his body. He'd never longed for her more than just now. He felt gooseflesh along the backs of her arms. He felt himself tremble in her tight embrace. He was more scared than she, but he was afraid to let her know it for fear she'd go herself.

The trip into the department store was bad enough. It was a gray place of ghosts and dead air. Alex got to the emergency cabinet, dragging his ungainly air bag. Through a window, he saw a space suit staring back at him. It was surrounded by small oxygen bottles arranged bandolier-fashion along the wall inside the cabinet. He broke the glass and reached for the gray suit with its dark faceplate. As he had expected, the material crumbled to dust in his hands. The metal parts stayed intact. In a fit of impatience, he pulled the entire composite cabinet out of the wall and dragged it toward the breach. A great cloud of dust followed him. He pulled the cabinet into the breathable atmosphere of the cylinder. Blankets rose up in a slight wind and floated ever faster, closer, and slammed against the wall to seal the hole he'd made.

He and Maryan cobbled together a breathing apparatus using the metal parts of the fire emergency spacesuit. All he really wanted was the head cover, which they replaced with sticky blanket material. The stickiness hardened in minutes, and he had an eerie-looking globe with a faceplate to cover his head. Any gaskets were long gone in the breathing cylinders and connectors, but most of it was metal and with a little help from the blanket material they had Alex breathing ancient air—a bit stale, but it kept him alive.

Now he was ready to enter the city.

It wasn't the atmosphere in the dead city that scared Alex.

It was the gloom.

The air was a mix of ghastly-smelling and tasting oxygen and inert gases left over from eons. Perhaps the machinery of the city still limply functioned, producing a weak positive pressure, recycling unused air; or perhaps, yes, this made sense: stealing air from the vast green jungle cylinder and recycling it under solar power. In any case, the pressure was sufficient to prevent Alex's primitive breathing apparatus from exploding.

Alex walked about the ancient department store testing his breathing apparatus.

"Take your time!" he heard Maryan's concerned voice say from a new opening they'd forced in the plate glass window. He saw her frightened pale face hovering beyond the marred glass. She couldn't see him, but he could see her face and her hands looking as though she were swimming underwater in some coolly lit aquarium. "I'm good," he called back. "Go take a rest and I'll be back soon."

"Be careful!" she called in a tiny, scared voice.

"I'll run like the dickens at the first sign of danger."

Each of the small breathing cylinders was good for about 15 minutes, and he had enough for several hours. He carried them in a bag slung over one shoulder.

He went back to say goodbye to her once more, just in case. He pushed through the cover she'd made and was glad to be on the other side again. The air was richer, moister, kinder to the skin and lungs and eyes. She wiped his face with damp leaves while he sat against the wall gasping. Dirty sweat ran down his face, and his skin felt gritty. His eyes felt irritated. "Are you sure you want to do this?" she asked.

"What choice do we have? Just think how cool it will be if I come flying back in one of those silver boats."

Her eyes lit up and she cradled his head in her hands. She bent to kiss his forehead. "My hero. Oh wow, I'd ride with you, everywhere."

"I'll take you to the beach," he said. "Our beach. We'll catch a nice fat pheasant and bake it in hay, with some tubers around it and those juicy mushrooms, and maybe some nice sharp radishes..."

"Stop!" she said laughing. "My mouth is watering."

He rose. "Okay, time to get it over with." He turned and eyed the hole in the wall through which he must again step with his breathing apparatus.

All their laughter faded immediately, and she appeared to be fighting back tears when he stepped into the stale darkness lugging his ungainly life support system.

He made slow and careful progress through the ancient shopping arcade.

Sunlight filtered through the dirty atmosphere in the abandoned city and shone on dusty surfaces. The air was filled with frozen dust motes, and, like in a scene underwater, the glowing motes began twirling around him.

In one eerie moment, he turned a corner around a square, metal pylon and confronted a nude flesh-colored mannequin. It was a female figure with daintily poised hands, frozen seemingly in the act of taking a step toward him. He caught a glimpse of faintly red fingernails, one blank white plaster eye socket, one dull blue eye, and rouged lips turned black with age. He jumped backward, startled, and threw himself against the pylon. In that moment, the air of his passage disturbed the figure and it crumbled into dust.

Alex hugged his crudely sealed mouthpiece closer to prevent dust from getting in it. He stepped over the thick metal platform on which the mannequin had stood and pressed forward.

Gravity in the store was the same as in the cylinder. He was maybe two stories higher than the forest floor in the cylinder, but the artificial gravity created by the cylinder's spin was nearly the same. An object resting on a surface generally tended to stay there. An object not resting on a surface was not appreciably attracted by any gravitational mass, since there was hardly any, so most objects would continue to hang in the air, or to drift once set loose.

Alex came to the smashed doorway where the boat had entered. He stepped noisily over shattered glass and other debris and came out on a mezzanine facing a great plaza below and the transit center opposite. He had little time to admire the stunning view in the sepia light pouring through glassy surfaces high up. He barely glanced at the shadowy lifeless streets snaking below, with a few vehicles still parked haphazardly as if they'd been abandoned suddenly. He took it all in with one glance, remembering that some of the last humans must have died here of old age—and the abandoned vehicles had probably been left there by programs. Most likely none of the vehicles would ever start again, given that their batteries had rotted away and their wiring had corroded.

Grasping the handrail with both hands, Alex pushed off gently with his feet. He found himself balancing with his wrists while floating in air horizontal to the deck. Grasping his sack of air bottles, he maneuvered himself into position, closed his eyes to mouth a prayer to whatever gods lived here, and pushed off.

He sailed through the air above the plaza for several minutes. It was both terrifying and relaxing—terrifying, because with every yard he floated farther away from his source of life in the cylinder; relaxing because he was helpless, and all he could do was breathe with concise precision while watching the debris pass. A waxy looking mummy turned her face toward him, and it struck him as odd that she had been an attractive young woman. Perhaps—his skin crawled—she had belonged to some later group of people who had blundered up here and lost their lives. What stories these dead people could tell!

He turned in mid-air and landed feet first against the railing before the transit center or entry point. Hands on the rail, he vaulted down so that his feet were in contact with the floor again and, with a gentle jerk, he was caught up in the false gravitational motion of the space station.

Changing air bottles periodically and discarding the empties, he entered the domed inner hall of the transit center, which resembled an ancient train or bus station. There were ticket counters to the left, vendor shops to the right in which food and other goods had crumbled into dust. There was a broad, circular, rubbery floor ahead, and beyond that the narrow toll gates leading to the various docking ramps. Overhead, shreds of electrical wiring and broken boards still hung where once arrival and departure information had been displayed along with, probably, advertising, announcements, and news.

Alex knew he had only about ten minutes before he must return. If necessary, he could make the trip again, since it had gone so smoothly, but he didn't want to. The best-case scenario now would be to ride out of here in a silver, bullet-shaped hot rod, pick Maryan up, and zip back down to Earth.

As he looked around, his heart sank. Dust was piled everywhere in heaps, particularly in corners and under counters. He went to the edge of the loading docks and looked out. No need to venture farther. Two smashed boats lay on their sides against each other after some ancient collision. They weren't even silver anymore but had a blackened look as though fire had done them in, followed by millennia of tarnish.

Another boat, with its front half missing, hung down over the edge of its dock by several thick, graying cables.

Beyond the docks, in the core of the station, glowered a vast, black pit of nothingness. No starlight, no sunshine, no light of any kind emanated from that black hole in the bowels of the city where perhaps once there had been repair shops. In what dim light there was, Alex gradually figured out that some space object had penetrated long ago, blasting through the station's skin like a bomb and gutting numerous levels of the center of the city itself. Bits of white and gray debris hung suspended in a whirling cloud over that coal-black abyss.

Alex saw no usable silver boat anywhere to get him and Maryan back to Earth. He would be out of air soon, and must return to the green cylinder. There was a lozenge of metal, a kiosk, and Alex approached it on his way back. The kiosk sparked with a tiny light, maybe a short circuit. A figure appeared on its dimly shimmering surface. "Greetings."

Alex patted his limp air sack as he slowed. "Greetings, fool."

The man in the business suit waved. "My name is Vector. I am the automated transit coordinator. How can I help you?"

Alex stepped up to confront the image, which flickered and was so faint as to be almost invisible against its grayish background. "I want a boat here right now to take two people back to Earth."

"Wonderful," Vector bubbled happily. He raised an electronic clipboard. "Let me check on the availability of the next transit cruiser."

"Be quick about it."

"Thank you for waiting patiently." Vector frowned. "Gosh, I'm sorry. There is not another boat available today." He looked up from the clipboard and regarded Alex with sympathy. "However, in the meantime, can we offer you coffee and donuts at the vendomat behind you?"

"Oh screw yourself," Alex said bitterly. "That means there will never be another boat available. Can you connect to the central database of the station?"

"I'm sorry, to do that you'll have to contact a human who will guide you."

"There are no humans left alive."

"Humans may be temporarily unavailable due to snack breaks or other convenience time-outs. In the meantime, there are free coff-oooo..." As he spoke, his voice lowered into a dying drawl and the power died in the kiosk. Alex pounded the side of the kiosk in frustration, but Vector did not return.

Alex retraced his steps and floated across the void. As he did so, he noticed his air was suddenly getting short and stale. He found himself gasping, and by the time he was running across the floor in the shopping hall, with debris scattering around his feet, he began to feel light-headed.

He was pop-eyed and anoxic by the time Maryan helped him through the hole. "The air in the rest of the cylinders was going bad," he said gasping. He lay inhaling the sweet rich air in the cylinder and shook his head while she gave him water to drink from a large waxy leaf.

"There are no more boats. I think those scaly bumwads down on Earth called the last ones down to play stupid Siirk games with. What a waste."

"So we're stuck here for good?" she whispered. She brushed his hair from his forehead and kissed him on the head. "I'm just glad you are back with me. I couldn't bear to lose you."

"Nor could I," he said feeling grateful as he hugged her close. The dream of returning to Earth's precious ocean of clean air and riches of food would have to wait for some other day. For now, they were citizens of L5 and glad to be alive.

After the depressing and harrowing journey into the dead city, Maryan and Alex agreed to venture in the other direction, into the forests in the vast cylinder. Here at least were air, and life, and light.

They had no possessions to go back for, so they started out for the far end of the station. Skirting the deadly hillock by a mile, they worked their way along jungle trails, always in the direction of that great glowing moon face that looked as though it lay beyond glass windows.

Twenty miles across tortuous terrain was a long way. It seemed like a thousand miles. Here and there, they found an easy spot, a clearing they could stride across, where twisted bushes struggled toward low light in low gravity. At times they followed one of the many undulating ridges that twisted through the dense growth. These ridges were usually about ten or twenty feet above ground level. "See a pattern?" Maryan said breathlessly, her face smeared with mud and whipped by stray thorny branches.

Alex stopped, gasping, and stood arms akimbo. At the moment the air felt hot and stifling, though he knew it could soon become chilly and damp.

She explained: "They figured out a way to maximize the surface area. Instead of making it flat, they made it egg-crate. That's why we're stumbling up and down through all these holes and bumps."

"At!" A light went on in Alex's mind. "I see. Doing some quick arithmetic—I bet you could almost double the surface area that way. Clever. Then maybe the surface area is twice what we thought—more like 600 square miles. Incredible."

"Yes, and I bet it strengthened the station structurally." She added: "Not enough to withstand a huge impact, though." At times the ridges were not wide enough on top for a path. At other times the ridges widened into clearings and then quickly narrowed again. The rest of the time, Alex and Maryan had to slog through wet underbrush and mud. Often they encountered brambles and thorns, and those slowed them down even further.

They also kept an eye over one shoulder. There was always the dread that Nizin or something like him might be following them. Sometimes they heard the distant bellow of a large animal. Once in a while they got a creepy feeling up and down their backs upon hearing a twig snap or a leaf rustle nearby.

Together, they gradually figured out that the station was not only rotating on its lengthwise axis to produce artificial gravity, but also end over end while turning on its third axis, so that the moon passed repeatedly through its day-field, but each time a little bit farther to the right than the day before. During each day, the moon passed slowly from top to bottom of the visible field at the end of the station. It was always the same face, and they began to recognize the larger craters and features almost as if they were in their back yard. They looked so much closer than when seen from Earth, and yet still so distant and inhospitable that they almost seemed haunted.

In the L5 cylinder were small lakes and rivers. The bodies of water were typically no more than about twenty feet deep at most, murky, and warmish. The rivers were long and narrow and had sluggish currents, while the lakes and ponds seemed faintly elevated on the same side as the cylinder's direction of motion. Alex had yet to figure out how one induced a river current here—maybe with a solar turbine? And where was such an engine? The station presented more mysteries than answers.

Alex and Maryan swam across one large river that seemed to zigzag across the landscape. Its water was cool, but comfortable. The color was a rich greenish yellow with bits of vegetation floating in it, and its smell hinted at decay but overall was fruity with a faint metallic undertone. It wasn't pleasant, and it wasn't familiar, but it was tolerable. Before crossing the forty feet to the other side, they sat on the bank in the shade of a large tree and watched carefully for any signs of predators—or the elusive small humanoid hunters like the one whose corpse they had found—but the area remained quiet and gloomy. There was always a lively undertone of insects, wind in leaves, small animals scurrying. One saw flashes of a small tail, a white underbelly, a sniffing nose, on a variety of tiny mammals resembling rodents. When the two humans finally slid into the water, their trip lasted only a few uneventful minutes. Alex noticed a pronounced undercurrent that pushed to his right, and when they emerged on the other side they had been carried several yards downstream. On the way across, they dove down a bit. They couldn't see the river bottom. Alex's small stone chipping and scraping tool escaped from his grasp and twirled way. He muttered a curse that came out in bubbles that echoed around his ears in the pickle-colored water. Small fish nuzzled by in schools of ten or twenty to explore these trespassers. The stone dropped, briefly colored grayish-white in the penetrating light and then disappearing into the unsounded depths.

Back on the surface, and glad to be out of the unknown waters, Alex and Maryan squeezed their clothes dry. The air felt cooler now that they were wet, and they picked up the pace to burn off the dampness.

"No crocodiles," he said.

"No sharks," she added.

They kept their conversation curt to conserve breath as they moved quickly along. Alex's main urgency was to get as far from a possible Nizin, or any Siirk, as possible.

"Astounding," Maryan said as they neared the other end of the long cylinder.

Alex had to agree, and they walked in amazement the last mile toward the windows overlooking space.

What windows these were! Except for a mile-wide lens in the center, the other pieces were not even, manmade geometries of clear glass, but a jumble of polygons in all sizes and shapes. A few of the smaller windows looked clear, and might date to the original human-made structure, but most were translucent beeswax colors ranging from dark brown to vibrant orange and amber. The material was silicate, quartz, Alex thought, just melted beach sand full of inclusions. Here and there in the hard glass, one could see embedded rocks, dead trees, and even the broken limbs of spider robots that had gotten stuck in their own goo. In the very center was a nearly round disk of clear glass through which much of the cylinder's daylight poured, like blue light through smoke.

The surrounding shards cast a beer-yellow light over the nearby forests. The forest was at its thickest here—no surprise, since this area received the most light. The ground also seemed to slope uphill.

Alex stood on top of the first of a series of rises, mopping his brow and looking around. Maryan was a few minutes behind, still clambering up a winding slope covered with thick grass and brush. The lowlands behind here were darkly carpeted with tree crowns, and beyond them shimmered several small hidden lakes. Several ridges ran around the inside of the cylinder like collars of earth. Bluish haze shrouded the lakes and more distant mountain ranges.

Alex and Maryan drew closer to the far end of the cylinder. They climbed down into swampy lowlands and back up onto high, dry grassy ridges that afforded good views all the way back to the distantly glowing disk of the city wall.

The light deepened in intensity. The amber shards swam in gloomy light, while the lighter shards emitted clear views of space. The air grew warmer, then hot. The ground seemed to become increasingly rocky and dry, almost like clambering out onto a rocky beach, only there was not a sea of water here but a sea of space. It was a black night smeared with stars. The olivine disk of the moon with its powdery rays and pockmark craters dominated the foreground. At the moment, the moon filled the upper half of the view, to the right, so that the curving edge ran from upper left to lower right. The windows up close looked stranger and more alien than ever, and Alex longed to study their angles and surfaces more closely. The closer he got, the hotter it became. "All that sunlight," Maryan said, huffing along behind him.

"Even the reflected moonlight is really sunlight," he said. "It's almost as if these windows are behaving a bit like lenses, magnifying the light, capturing more of it, bringing in more heat."

Alex and Maryan stood together on a jumble of boulders, holding hands. As light and heat streamed down on them, they sweated profusely and the air seemed too dry to breathe. "Any closer and we fry," he said.

"How strange," she said. "This rock we're standing on looks almost like lava, some of it." She shifted about uneasily. "It's warm..."

He shifted as she did, suddenly afraid to burn his feet, but it wasn't that hot. The hard, thickly slathered blackish stone was no warmer than the steamy air around them. While they stood there, they noticed a salty-sulfurous cooking-smell, as of some elemental soup not meant for human consumption. Maryan rumpled her nose. "What is that smell?"

He shook his head. "Someone is boiling stones?" He grinned.

She shrugged. Her eyes were filled with uncertainty, then wonder as she looked over their surroundings. "Look at that! Thousands of windows overlooking space."

"Every one of them a different size and shape," he said. Cautiously, still holding hands, they walked closer on the barren black rocks that were strewn with hot sand. No life was evident around them at first—not even insects—until Maryan cried out and pointed upward. "Look, more spiders!"

Alex craned his neck upward, feeling sweat pooling in the crease under the back of his skull. Oven-like heat blazed on his cheeks, and his lungs felt dry. Sure enough, a mile or so high in the bowl of windows, were the distantly tiny shapes of the large spiders they'd encountered on the opposite end of the cylinder, repairing the wall after their boat had crashed through. "They seem to be working busily away," he said. He tugged on Maryan's hand. "Come on, let's back away. This heat is getting unbearable. Must be cumulative sunlight, maybe mirrored and lensed by thousands of tons of glass in these windows."

"Looks like glass made by bees over long periods of time," she said, pointing to haphazardly interlacing sections.

He looked out over the lunar surface sprawling majestically in blindingly reflected solar light, and black space full of sprayed light beyond the curving lunar horizon. Something caught his eye—a bluish-white point of light just two or three few miles away in space, with concentric rings of orange and greenish light around it. It appeared to be at the tip of a large dull object barely visible, clutched among larger dark objects. "If I'm not mistaken," he said, "that's a piece of stone being held between several large machines focusing sunlight to melt part of the rock."

"You're right," she said. "The sun provides all the energy you'd ever need to melt metal, stone, anything you can think of. That would explain the heat here. Maybe the station keeps adding on, expanding itself. Slowly, with robots running on solar energy. Maybe it adds a mile every hundred thousand years. After all, there's all the time in the world."

He picked up: "With humans extinct, there is no reason to either stop or continue, so the station keeps functioning."

"Alex, the station has plenty of life in it—just not the original humans."

"Now we are back," he said with more weariness than joy, looking at the frozen tableau outside. "We'll find out what we need to know." Nothing had moved, and the rock, if that it was, just kept glowing. "Probably melting slowly before those machines push it in here inches at a time."

"Yes," she said, "Then maybe...the line on the moon...could it be a mass driver?"

Alex searched Kirk's memories for the concept: "Yes, it could be a mass driver. That's like a frictionless sled powered by sunlight and magnetic tricks. The contents—maybe a block of stone—accelerate until they reach escape velocity, which isn't quite so high on the Moon, and fly out toward the station here, where those machines melt them to add more material to the cylinder."

The forest was at its thickest and deepest a mile or two from the crazy-quilt of windows at the far end of the cylinder.

The prodigious beard of dark green vegetation stretched around the inside surfaces of the cylinder. In some places the fog seemed to couch in the tree tops night and day. Alex and Maryan saw a greater variety of birds and animals than ever before. The animal life they saw was smaller than its earthly analogues. They saw miniature wild pigs, some dog-like creatures, cats, a small horse prancing over a ridge like a three-foot tall but fully formed adult pipe dream. They thought, at times, that a small blue or orange human-like face might be hovering amid the leaves, regarding them with serious eyes before melting away. At times, their backs crawled with uncomfortable sensations that they were being watched.

"So far, there is nothing special here for us. We should get back toward the middle or even the wall-end," Maryan suggested as they sat together on a grassy ridge at night, roasting two squirrel-like animals and a bird they had managed to capture. Beside the tiny fire they'd made in a circle of stones sat a fire bowl Alex had made from river mud. It was a dried ball, about the size of a large fist, hollow inside and containing smoldering embers in a bed of charcoal. It had a tiny opening on top to vent, and a larger opening a quarter of the way down big enough to insert a finger or a twig to stir things around inside. Nearby lay a supply of charcoal (made from dry, burned wood) and kindling straw. This was their supply of fire, designed to be carried from campsite to campsite, avoiding the need to start a new flame.

The great wall of fragmented amber glass glowed with moonlight. Waxy leaves gleamed with dull polish. Now and then, an owl hooted. Insects, rustling leaves, and distant bubbling forest streams kept up a steady low murmur.

"We can dry these hides," Maryan said as she scraped the rodent skins with a sharp stone in near darkness, "and make belt pouches. That way we can carry seeds to chew, and we won't go hungry."

He sat back against a tree trunk, using his fingertips to feel the flint blade of his knife as he chipped idly with another flint to sharpen it. "We can't stay here forever, Maryan." Secretly he thought: *how often do we have to start over from nothing?*

"I know, love. I'm getting antsy myself. This place is too quiet, somehow, too calm. Things are lurking out there someplace, watching us. I just somehow don't think they mean us harm."

Alex put aside his moment of despair. "Maybe they caught Nizin and had him for lunch."

"Hah! Who'd want to eat that strutting rack of scales and white hair?"

"Something that might not consider us good food."

"You're dreaming."

"Turtle and iguana are delicacies in some quarters. I'm trying to keep hope alive."

She rested her head against his shoulder, while keeping her gory hands away. "I know," she said with a sigh. "Thanks."

"My job."

Next day, as they headed back toward the river, they were going up a hill when Maryan cried out: "Over here!"

He hurried to catch up with her.

She stood on the crest of the hill among big tree trunks, pointing to a dark shadowy blur. "A cave!"

He came close. "Sure enough. Did you look inside?"

"I just peeked. Nothing came out to bite me. But I think I'll let you lead."

"Thanks," he said dryly as he bent low to enter the cave.

The opening was hidden behind long sheets of moss in the shade of wide pine trees. If it was gloomy around the outside, it was almost pitch dark inside. Alex sniffed for any sign of recent animal habitation but caught only a tiny stale odor like burned wax, very faint. He backed out of the cave, eyeballing it and its surroundings while holding his spear up ready to defend himself and her.

"Hang on a moment," Maryan said. She pulled up some dry moss and wrapped it around a stick. From one of their pouches, she produced a foul-smelling gob of animal fat, which she smeared around the moss in a circle, patting it down around the stick. Carefully, from their fire bowl, she sit the moss on fire. The fat caught on fire, then smoldered with a greasy smell. "Here you go."

They traded, he taking the torch and she his spear. "Cover my back," he whispered.

He took the torch and carefully stepped into the cave. The light was faint, and it took a few minutes for his eyes to adjust. The cave had a narrow mouth that opened into a round room about ten feet in diameter. He had a stoop slightly to enter. The round room seemed to have been formed from the earth between several huge boulders whose rough surfaces protruded from sandstone walls. Between the boulders, huge trees had grown outside, and their roots hung down into the cave. Torchlight made shadows dance hideously among the hanging roots. Maryan crowded in behind him as Alex examined the cave. He smelled the smoky, waxy smell again, and waved the torch over a dark mound in the middle of the cave.

"A table," she said.

"An altar," he guessed. Holding the torch closer, he saw the clear outline of bleached ribs from some small animal, perhaps a cat. He reached out to touch it, and its grayish flesh and fur disintegrated in the wind as his hand moved. He never felt a thing. "This place has been abandoned for a long time," he said.

"Shine the light around the edges of the altar," she said quietly, full of tension.

The torch was fading, and he made it flare up in rings of orange embers in the still air as he moved it. They made out the outline of what looked like a man-made table, with edges and corners. That confirmed what they had thought—this had been a homestead or a place of worship long ago. So why had it been abandoned?

A noise outside made them shrink back in the cave. Alex slapped the torch against the wall, and it sputtered out while sparks fell. The air was full of roiling smoke and a fatty burnt stink. Hearts beating rapidly, they listened to what sounded like birdcalls—or were they creatures calling to one another in some owl code barely audible to the human ear?

Maryan gripped his arm.

He felt his heart beating in his neck.

"There it is again," she said.

He heard that owl sound again.

"People," she said. "I don't think that's natural."

His skin prickled with fear. "We figured someone might be tracking us," he said. "Now we really have to watch every step."

"We can stay here until we die of hunger and thirst."

He bit his lip and thought. "No. Let's make a go for it before they find us. This cave doesn't look like anyone has been here in a long time, but we could rot here."

"Let's go," she said, pinching his arm and pulling him along out of the cave. He heard no sounds of pursuit as they jogged as softly as possible, trying to put distance between themselves and the hidden place.

They headed back toward the city wall at the other end of the cylinder. After a half hour, they paused on a high hill to take stock. They spent several minutes standing about, bent over, gasping for breath. Alex felt almost nauseous from the fear, the adrenalin, the sudden and continuous exertion. They stood on a high ledge, overlooking a lake below. The lake water glowed dark greenish-blue and was still except here and there where a gust of wind stirred up a tiny whitecap. At either end, a river attached itself, coming out of the forest and disappearing back into it.

"Nobody after us," she said, standing at the edge of the hill. Overhead, in the gravity-free core of the cylinder, white and gray clouds hung frozen in a gigantic swirl like galaxies of mist. She was gasping for breath, and sweat ran down her face. She looked out over the wide swath of forest and plains behind her. The landscape was wreathed in silent fog that seemed almost motionless except for faint stirrings of mist.

He stepped toward her, to embrace her.

"Honey, I—" she started to say, raising her arms to embrace him.

Just past his head, he heard a sharp whipping sound, a whistle, and a ripping sound. At the same time, he watched her face freeze in surprise. Her eyes grew wide, and her hands slowly moved downward as she lowered her arms.

In the next second, he began to understand what the noises were: a large arrow flying past his ear, and the sound of flesh tearing as it cut through her torso, high up and to the left, penetrating the delicate furrows of her rib cage.

His breath escaped in a gasp as he prepared to shout, and he stepped forward like in a dream, a horrible dream, a nightmare. He was moving as if underwater.

She stood stiffly, staring straight past him with huge eyes. Her jaw muscles moved as if she were trying to say something. In seconds, her eyes grew glazed. Stiffly at first, then limply, she toppled over. As she did so, she spun lightly halfway around. The huge arrow protruded from her back, and blood pumped in spurts from the arrow's entry and exit points.

Alex moved forward, raising his hands as if to catch her, while he knew it was all over and he never would. A shout caught in the pit of his throat, unable to get out.

She fell off the cliff, head down, feet up, with her arms still at her sides. He got to the edge just in time to catch one last glimpse of her as she fell into the water some 40 or 60 feet below. The water parted around her head, and he caught one last view of her face, which looked almost restful now, though her eyes were wide open, but unseeing. She landed on her back. Her head, then her torso, and finally her long legs disappeared, and the water closed like the neck of a foamy sack over her feet. She was gone.

Alex thought of diving after her, but thought it wouldn't help if he broke his neck on a submerged rock. There was a roundabout way down, and he started that way. He ran toward one side of the cliff edge, where a narrow trail seemed to lead down.

As he ran, he heard a sound to his right.

A mean, ominous, triumphant laugh.

He glanced to his right and saw the glittering eyes and teeth of Nizin from behind a screen of leaves and twigs, which Nizin was spreading apart with both hands. The bow with which he'd shot Maryan was clearly visible, down to the shaving marks in its sapling skin and the knots in its hide string.

"You!" Alex screeched. "You! I'll deal with you!" He did not stop moving, thinking only of whatever vague hope there might yet be of finding and rescuing Maryan.

Nizin laughed, some 50 feet away.

Alex suppressed his rage and the urge to run toward Nizin. Instead, he plunged over the edge of the embankment and started down a natural flight of rocks and boulders interspersed with mossy, soft damp soil.

Seconds counted. If he could get to her now—

His last view was of the still-rippling muddy blue-green water. A sharp stone hit him on the left side of the head and he winked out with a sickening, grinding flash of light on damaged skull-bone. His last fading thought was not about himself, but that he had now surely forever lost the woman he loved.

Alex could have sworn he heard the tiny shadow on his left shoulder say "Geedins!"

Alex jerked up, blinded by a pounding headache, and spun around on the ground to protect himself from whatever incubus was infesting this nightmare of his. Only it wasn't a nightmare. Maryan was dead and gone, so suddenly, so totally...

Alex lay in a sheltered place not far from a calmly flickering fire. Overcome with grief, rage, and fear, he gasped for breath and struggled like someone drowning in a dream. Hands gently but firmly pressed him back down on a bed of fur and leaves.

He saw, over and over again, the black vision of his beloved woman shot in front of his eyes and tumbling to her death in the water below. He couldn't even cry out, but stuck the fingertips of both hands into his wide open, tortured mouth. He felt his eyes widen in horror as he saw her again die before his eyes, again and again. He saw again Nizin's fierce, merciless eyes glittering from the forest.

As nightmare gave way to day and wakefulness, he saw the faces of small people hovering over him in the brownish darkness, looking vaguely like a cross between Nizin and Xumar. They moved away with as much apparent shock as Alex felt.

The fiery pounding pain in Alex's head overwhelmed him, and he fell backward into darkness.

He awoke some time later, feeling drained.

The headache was gone, replaced by a muzzy feeling as if he'd been drugged. He was inside a room...no, a hut insulated with brownish, dry vegetation over a bamboo-like frame. The floor was clean, beaten earth and the air smelled fresh and clean. A light pall of smoke blew in through the open door, along with a stream of bluish daylight. It must be high noon at L5, he thought as he shifted stiffly on his bed of straw wrapped in roughly woven but soft cloth. Then he remembered what had happened to Maryan, and all humor left him. He turned over onto his stomach, buried his face in his arms, and wept.

Some time later, several shapes entered the room. Three were male, carrying tall thin spears and wearing furs draped over one shoulder. The rest were female and wore what appeared to be the standard women's garb—a short tunic with a basic dark background and lively foreground color patterns like circles, squares, or flowers. All wore bangly white bracelets. Two of the women carried small children in slings under their furry breasts. The third woman, wearing a white necklace, came closer carrying a bowl of something steaming that smelled like soup or stew. "Take this," she said in a thickly accented English but he understood her well. "You need food."

"I am going to go kill Nizin," he said, scrabbling to get up.

She pushed him gently down. She spoke with a soft, slurry accent. "You can do that soon. Now you must rest and gather your strength."

"How do you speak my language?"

She shook her head. "You speak our language. We learn from Lekto." *Of course—more of those virtual kiosks.* He lay on his side, propped up on one elbow, frozen in the act of getting up. Seeing her free hand raised palm forward in a staying motion, he stopped and looked into her eyes. She was tiny. Even the tallest male was about the size of a small human boy maybe four years old. They had large heads in comparison to their spindly but robust bodies. They all seemed to have large bellies, which reminded Alex of an ancient people called Pygmies. They seemed to be a curious mix of Siirk and Takkar and maybe one or two other species. Their heads were large and angular like those of the Takkar, but were entirely covered, like the rest of their bodies, with silky whitish Siirk hair. Their palms, lips, and nipples had a natural reddish tinge, and their bellies a bluish tinge under the fur. They had almond-shaped eyes with yellow irises, set far apart over small, humanoid noses. Yes—they even had some human characteristics, as if the genetic stock of Alex and Maryan's ancestors lived on in them.

Alex accepted a bowl of soup from her. It had an island of bread in it amid bits of vegetable and a few flecks of what looked like chicken meat. "You know of a kiosk?" Against hope, he thought, maybe he could reach the station's central memory.

She pointed in some direction with one downy arm. "*Kyost* is a holy place in the world."

"Good." He used the bread to capture bits of flotsam. The soup was hot and tasty. "This is good."

"Almena kreed adeewal," she said.

"Eh?" He said, hungrily chewing and sipping. At times, steam rose over his eyes and obscured his view of her young, yellow, eager probing eyes.

As soon as the edge was off his hunger, Alex lost interest in the food and set it aside. He felt a numbing wall of pointlessness. The scene of Maryan being speared and dying before his eyes as she disappeared into the water kept playing over and over in his mind. The natives seemed to realize that and remained silent, hovering at the periphery of the spacious room. From their pained, dark looks and avoiding eyes, he sensed they understood his bereavement.

The young woman tried to cheer him. "*Almen.* You are *almen*, yes?" She pointed at him.

"I'm sorry, what?"

"Olwi mina kreed adeewal, Lektro says."

"So you have met the librarian."

"Ribra—?"

"Librarian. Lector," he explained patiently. Men entered the structure. He assumed were they were dignitaries or warriors. They stood with their spears against the wall, watching and probably reserving judgment.

"Lektro good," she said. The others murmured assent.

She said: "My name is Leeree. And you are?"

"Alex."

"Alek-es."

"Alex."

She practiced saying his name several more times. He watched her wrestling within the pinkness of her tiny mouth, with its glittering china teeth. "Alek-es. Aleks. Alex." She tittered with delight at her accomplishment.

"The others," he said, pointing around the room. "Your people."

"My people *LooWoo!*" she said. She repeated: "*LooWoo!*"

"Woop*Woop*," he said.

They laughed. She repeated slowly: "*LooWoo!*" she waved her arm in a rising motion to indicate the little "woop" at the end of the second syllable.

The others introduced themselves, too many for him to remember, with names like Leelee and Tzoofaa and the like, suggesting a culture with at least some brightness and happiness in it.

He grew tired and fell asleep. A woman's hands appeared—for a moment he almost thought they were Maryan's and then he realized as if a knife were going through him that there would never be another Maryan. The woman's hands took the uneaten food away, and the aroma of food slowly gave way to the freshness of the air. It was a windy night out, and he heard the endless sighing of air in tree crowns, the ocean-like ebb and flow of leaves.

The sound lulled him to sleep, and someone put a blanket over him, covering him up to the ears so he would be warm. And he was.

In the ensuing days, his first trip was to the place where she had died.

Two of the LooWoo! Warriors accompanied him. They spoke in whispers on the path leading from the village down to the lake.

"Nizin," Alex said bitterly. "He killed my woman."

"Nizin giant from earth," one of the two warriors said. "Nizin bad." He was a wizened elder with sparse white hair on a leathery dark dome, and bushy white brows. Under there were highly intelligent dark eyes. "You giants, go back soon."

"I don't want to be here, believe me."

"You go back," the man said. His name was Keetoo.

"How can I get back? Our boat, our ship, the vessel—" he made motions with his hands "—destroyed, *kaput*, *futi*."

"Make new," Keetoo said.

"You will make a new one?" Alex asked incredulously.

"Soon," Keetoo said, and did not elaborate. He avoided Alex's further questions as if he were dealing with some silly child.

They came to the lake.

Tzoofaa pointed. He was a younger man, quicker of step, and he walked out into the lake up to his thighs. He pointed with his spear. "She is in there," he said, pointing to the gloomy mustard-green water that flowed slowly. Bits of debris floated on the surface, and thousands of insects and tiny birds flitted about.

Keetoo stood on the bank with a dark and troubled look. "Leave her alone. Her spirit is in the river."

Tzoofaa said: "We put the dead LooWoo! in the ground, but if the river takes one we do not take him back. The river will be mad at us."

"I just want to see her," Alex said. He had no idea why. It was a human thing, he supposed. Maybe these people did not have the urge to gaze on their dead one last time to say goodbye. "I have to wish her well."

"That is correct," Keetoo said, brightening. "That you must. Go. She is waiting." He pointed at the opaque surface.

Alex looked about, triangulating to the best of his ability. Then he took a deep breath and dove in.

He was filled with a mixture of dread and anticipation. His heart pounded in his ears, and his stomach was in knots. He was terrified of how she might look, but he had to see her, touch her, just one last time. He did a gentle dive, head and arms forward, into the water.

The water was cool, as he eased in, and rich with tiny life. A slow but strong current pushed to his right, and he had to resist being nudged from his path. The soft, silty ground dropped away and he found himself swimming in deeper water. Light fell in from above and diffused into a wide bluish glow with pale edges that lay in gradients within the murky greenish water. Little bits of black debris twirled slowly as they moved with hidden currents. And the water was alive with tiny wriggling life forms. Wormlike things wriggled about in schools, one layer over the other, in complex patterns. Tiny fish darted here and there. Tadpoles, frogs, or their descendants, all busily trawled through the water looking for their daily sustenance.

Alex rose for air several times. He snorted, blowing tiny wrigglers from his nose and mouth. He couldn't feel them, but he knew they were there looking for microscopic morsels. Tzoofaa and Keetoo stood silently on the muddy bank, keeping watch.

Alex dove back down, paddling among submerged boulders and fallen trees whose broken branches stuck up like bleached bones. Everything under the water, touched by that light, had an unnatural light-green glow, almost like radiation.

He found her on a bare bank of mud, naked and peaceful. She lay on her back with her legs loosely outstretched. The shaft still penetrated her torso. Her left arm lay palm-down by her side, and the right arm was slightly upraised, flung upward in her dying moments, so that it looked as if she were gesturing. In fact, her index finger was curled less than the other fingers, as if she were making a point. Her face was relaxed and without expression. Her eyes were open just a tiny bit, so that unseeing eyes glittered faintly behind them. Her head was turned slightly to one side, and her hair floated gently around her cheeks. Her lips looked blue, her nose white, and tiny bubbles still came from her ears, nose, and mouth.

Alex rose to the surface for a long breath. He signaled to the two LooWoo! that he'd found her, then jackknifed and dove back down with paddling motions until he landed on his knees in the silt. Ravaged and shaken by a grief pressing him on all sides like the water itself, he moved into position so that his face was just two feet from hers, almost to pretend somehow that he could lock gazes with her. The illusion almost worked for a second. Debris and wrigglers drifted by. He shooed away a small fish that came to explore her pale thigh.

He swam back up to the surface for air, then dove back down for a last look.

As he regarded her lovingly, in his bereavement, he reached out to run his hand along the smooth, firm undulations of her abdomen and belly.

As his fingertips exerted the slightest pressure on her skin, the water clouded and her abdomen collapsed into her ribs, and clouds of tiny wriggling things rose brightly, green and yellow, toward the sunlight.

In a spontaneous motion of regret and horror, he touched her cheeks. He was thinking apologies, as if he had hurt her. Again, her face changed, and the wrigglers puffed up around her as her skin sank down over the contours of her skull.

He touched two more spots, full of disbelief, her ankle and her forearm, and the same thing happened. Just as the earth took care of itself, cleaning its wounds and taking its children back into its bosom, so the intricate design of L5 acted like a copy of the mother world. L5 was digesting her body.

Exhaling with horror and shock, Alex left a trail of air bubbles from his mouth as he shot quickly to the surface. He gasped, treading water and holding his head in his hands in disbelief at what he had seen.

This much was true: He had said goodbye, and he now knew for sure that part of his life was over. Once again, fate had struck him with a hammer blow, and he must move on. He did not want to see what was down there, ever again. It would be best to remember her as she'd been in life.

L5 would take good care of this child of earth, he knew, and of him when he went, which might as well be soon for he had lost the love to live.

Alex was grateful for the hospitality of the gentle LooWoo! people, and he tried to be helpful as he stayed with them.

They asked nothing of him, and were always prepared to offer their generosity. Only Tzoofaa seemed to remain standoffish, giving Alex dark looks and staying at a distance.

At first, Alex stayed around their village, which was called LooWoo! Deep-in-the-Woods, not far from the lake that had received Maryan's remains, the village lay hidden among huge trees. The LooWoo! had ample living spaces, given their size. There seemed to be several hundred of them spread across a long valley, and they spoke of other villages in the distance. Alex began to guess that at least several thousand LooWoo! lived on L5 in harmony with their environment and each other.

While Tzoofaa kept his distance, Keetoo came to visit Alex often in the large hut where Leeree and the other women cared for him. Often, when the men sat and talked, the women left small children for them to tend, and these crawled happily around the men's legs playing with each other and simple toys made of wood or stone. Alex enjoyed the company of the women and children as a continuing sort of balm that reminded him life did go on, when his sorrow became black and overwhelming.

"I will take you to Lector when you are ready," Keetoo said. "He is our guide."

"Is Lector your god?"

Keetoo shook his head with a vacant look. "God? This whole world is a god of which we are part." He laughed and wiggled his fingers in the air. "These fingers, these toes, this nose, I am all god."

"Then you live forever," Alex guessed, bouncing a toddler on one knee while the child fell asleep with its head resting against Alex's stomach.

Keetoo looked puzzled. "We live here a time, and then we forget. Nobody ever comes back."

"I meant...you live on somehow, in the greater sense..." Alex saw her confusion, and gave up. Suddenly, the concept of a transcendent life after death seemed foreign here. He rifled through memories of ancient religions. "Have you seen anyone come back?"

Keetoo folded his arms on his knees and looked comfortable with himself, though awed by Alex's notions. "Every time a baby is born, is a soul returning from Earth."

"The dead go to Earth?"

"The dead go to Earth," Keetoo said with certainty.

"What do you know of Earth?"

Keetoo's eyes widened and he looked away, far, even through the distant city wall and through the clouds above, through the opposite side of the world cylinder. "Earth is without end. It is a circle like our world, but turned inside out. You walk many more days than we do here and swim in many big rivers."

"Sounds like a wise belief." How could he question or contradict them? He believed on faith that he was a duplicate of someone who had lived a million years ago, and he had no real understanding of how or why he himself lived. Perhaps Keetoo was right. Perhaps Alex's very memories were little more than a dream.

Several times during their conversations, he mentioned finding the dead LooWoo! near the wall, and each time Keetoo changed the subject. Then, one day, word came that a hunter from a faraway village had disappeared, and his people had sent runners out across the world to find word of their missing kinsman. Keetoo brought this news to Alex, and Tzoofaa followed not far behind. They summoned him to a warrior lodge that vaguely resembled the sacred Takkar lodge. There, surrounded by an outer circle of respectfully quiet men holding spears ready for hunting, Alex sat with the two leaders.

"The wall," Tzoofaa said, "we do not talk about, but now we have to. This Nizin, is he from the empty air beyond the wall?" He regarded Alex for an answer.

Alex realized increasingly how little they understood the universe, though they were intelligent and often sounded quite wise. "Yes," he said, "Nizin is only one of a race of killers from Earth."

A murmur went through the circle of warriors.

"And you are from the same place?"

"Not exactly, but close."

Tzoofaa seemed to try to digest this, and seemed to have difficulty with the concept. "You do not belong here," he said finally.

Alex felt those words go through him like a stab. He knew instinctively that the chief was right, but he wished he were not.

Tzoofaa spoke thoughtfully, chopping with a sharp flat knife at the log on which he sat. "From time to time, big people come here. They come in a shiny bird without wings. They bring bad luck to the LooWoo! people. We offer kindness, because it is our way, but we have learned to be careful. I have said nothing because I do not want my people to be afraid. Now I speak."

A rumble of alarm passed among the warriors, and they slammed their weapons down with a single warning clatter. It seemed they were not permitted to speak at the council, but decorum permitted this expression of their feelings.

Tzoofaa continued: "I have thought about you. You do not seem like a killer. I thought about you when I first heard this news from a far village, but I do not think you killed their man." He studied Alex quietly through a long pause. "You have suffered losing your woman, which makes a man like a ghost. You have no woman, no village, no spear. You do have deep pain and anger. I believe you will know when your time comes, and it will be soon. Then you will leave us, Ghost, and we will close our door to you forever."

The warriors slammed their weapons down again, and the shock ran through Alex as did the Tzoofaa's calling him a ghost. He was dead. That seemed true. Without Maryan, he had nothing to live for. And then, beyond that—was he not the ghost of a man who had lived a real life eons ago? Was his very existence maybe an offense against nature and an invitation for fate to shower him with bad luck?

"I saw with my own eyes," Tzoofaa said, "that you did not kill your woman. We did not see the one who did, but the arrow he shot was as large as one of our spears, so he is one of the big people like you, who come from another world like evil smoke in frightening dreams."

Keetoo interceded: "Chief, he is a being who has suffered misfortune. Does that make him evil, just because evil has destroyed his life? Do any of us become evil because we suffer evil?"

Tzoofaa considered this. "People fear bad fortune, and blame those who suffer it."

"We must be wiser than that," Keetoo said.

"The greater care is to safeguard our people," Tzoofaa replied.

"But you bring him to our council, knowing he understands our language."

Tzoofaa nodded. "I know he suffers. He will leave us soon. When he goes, he will meet his gods or his fate or whatever is bigger than he is. Then he will tell them he was in our council and that we spoke well to him, and spoke well of the gods."

"Lector knows we speak well," Keetoo said. "We speak to him often."

"Then it is time to take this one to Lector. Ask Lector for words."

"I will do it," Keetoo said.

The warriors all crashed their spears down. Tzoofaa rose, gathering his cloak about him, and left.

The amber, glassy terminus of the station hung distant, hazy, frozen.

The size of the cylinder took his breath away as Alex and his two companions made their way through the deep forest floor. The terminus was too far away for Alex to make out individual shards, so from a distance of several miles it looked like a smoky ring of beer-colored light with a central white hole through which beams of milky light poured. These beams—some more white, others more bluish—leaned into the forest from miles away, at varying angles. Mist rose up around the light, further muffling it, as all sound seemed to be muffled except for the sussurus of insects, the occasional wind in the leaves, and the sound of footsteps. Keetoo walked directly behind Alex. Keetoo carried a bundle of provisions over one shoulder and walked with a tall staff. Not far ahead darted the tiny form of Leeree. She carried a spear and wore a simply woven brown serape. Aside from a pouch at her belt, she carried no baggage.

"She has Lingo," Keetoo said. "She can understand things Lector says when others do not."

At times they stopped and listened. Sometimes Leeree signed for them to stop while she scouted ahead.

"We move cautiously for fear of meeting this Nizin," Keetoo whispered as he and Alex hid among the roots of a huge tree. Alex was dwarfed by the six foot high roots snaking out in curves and corners for many yards, but Keetoo was half his size and looked even more insignificant compared to the giant.

"Are there more caves like the one I found earlier?" Alex asked a bit later as they trudged along on a hard earthen path at a good clip.

"Yes," Keetoo said. "There were other people here before us, who have not come back. We leave their dwellings alone. Maybe they will come back as ghosts one day. They will be angry if we disturb their homes."

They came to a gloomy hollow, deeper in the forest than ever.

"I will stand guard up here," Keetoo said.

Leeree took Alex by the arm and led him down a slippery path among ferns.

Water splashed over rocks, and clear streams trickled away into the ground. The place smelled of moisture and vegetation. A lizard shot away up a tree, and a mass of tiny humming insects swarmed up as they walked into the clearing. A pillar of amber-green light shone almost straight down on a worn obelisk that stood on a platform of stones raised up in the middle of the clearing.

As they approached, Leeree raised her arms in reverence and with great ceremony intoned: *"Djordjuashington."*

The worn surface of the obelisk seemed to flicker faintly. As Alex drew near, he saw that the obelisk was made of metal, with no rust evident, but myriad scratches. The image that somehow appeared on its surface was almost undistinguishable, but Alex readily made out the upper body of Lector. The librarian wore a suit as always and sat impeccably behind a desk with his arms folded before him. "Thank you. George Washington is the correct answer." The program looped with a faint shift in background light and a slightly grayer Lector said: "Greetings. To assure proper system to human interaction, please name the first president of the United States." The image faded, without waiting for answer, and reappeared in a few moments. Lector repeated: "Thank you. George Washington is the correct answer."

"Geedeen," Alex whispered under his breath. More loudly, he said, "Lector, I need your help."

Alex pressed his palms against the surface, but Leeree pulled him away, saying, "No touching! It scratches his skin."

The obelisk was a little taller than Alex, about seven feet, about four feet wide, and two feet thick. It was a plain geometric shape with not a single protrusion or embellishment of any kind. No buttons, handles, switches, or other controls. Alex supposed that vibrations activated it, and that it somehow projected some internal functionality through its metal skin. He longed to tear it out of the ground, follow it to its source...until he realized, bending over, that it floated wirelessly in mid-air just a few inches above its platform.

"Where is your master program?" Alex asked.

Lector said primly: "If this is a life threatening emergency, please use your touchtone control or headphone set to contact an Emergency Response Facility. Otherwise, please stand by." The image faded away, then disappeared, as it was to do numerous times during the exchange. Lector was now sitting in a chair by an open window holding a silver recording device. "Greetings. What can I do to help you today?"

"Lector, can you send a boat to pick me up? I need to get back to Earth."

"I'm afraid that request cannot be honored from this Level Gamma Kiosk. You must speak your twenty digit alphanumeric personal code and I will request an uplink for you to L5 Control."

"Lector, a million years have passed. The station is wrecked. Do you have an emergency override?"

"I'm sorry I do not. You must report your difficulty to the nearest Emergency Services station and personnel there will direct you."

"There are no personnel," Alex said.

"If it is during Dim Hours, you may request a 7/24 work order at double cost, or else wait until the next Light Hour which is only..." He trailed off, and his voice became garbled. The image rippled faintly in the scratched, greenish metal surface stained by eons of water and moss. Then the image floated back into view. "...hours from now. I do not have an exact estimate of the next service call. There will be a coffee and donuts special in the aviary at eight next Light, followed by an informative talk on mating habits of the russet swamp crane. The russet swamp crane exhibit will be open from seven Light to four Dim every day this Earth week. Next week, join us in looking forward to a poetry reading by school children from Stethem Elementary School in the Lambda Corridor on Sector V. Thank you, and have a nice day."

Alex beat his fist lightly on the side of the obelisk. "Lector, you dumb shit. Wake up. It's all gone. Long gone. It's over." He wanted to beat the obelisk to shreds, but realized it was the central cultural icon of Leeree's people, and the reason they spoke Ingish as well as they did.

"If you are detecting a malfunction not apparent to my self-test autorunner, please report this to the nearest Emergency Response Personnel."

"They are dead, Lector. They are extinct. There are no humans left. Please go into whatever mode you have to so we can work on this problem."

"Have a nice day." Lector shut off.

Leeree tugged at Alex's sleeve as they backed away. "Lector has given you an important message, yes?"

Alex did not have the heart to tell her how frustrated he was.

During the time Alex, Keetoo, and Leeree were in the woods visiting Lector's obelisk, word had arrived of at least one more murder in a distant village.

The victim, a young woman getting water from a pond, had her skull opened like the first, and her brain devoured. It was the unmistakable handiwork of a Siirk.

They sat at the council fire—Alex, Tzoofaa, Keetoo, and the lead warriors plus several of the alpha females including Leeree.

Leeree offered her thoughts: "This killer stalks water holes. He operates far across the land, because the second village he violated is far from the first. I dread that he comes here again." She had looked across at Alex. "It is your woman he took here. Does that mean he will not strike here again, or was it a signal that he has marked us for death and we should wait in fear for his return."

The warriors had clashed down their weapons with a loud shout.

Alex held up his hands to signal he was about to speak. "I will go search for this Siirk, and I will go alone. I will take his head myself."

"Where do you go?" Tzoofaa said in surprise.

"Into the dead city if I need to. I will hunt him—"

"You can never come back here if you go there," Tzoofaa said.

It was dark-light, and the fire flickered on the sweaty surfaces of Tzoofaa's wizened head under the thin white hair. His eyes were filled with pain and finality. "If you go, Alex Kirk, do not come back here."

"What if the gods are pleased with what I do?"

Tzoofaa wrinkled his brow, perplexed by Alex's audacity and puzzled by the very concept of challenging the way things had always been and must always be. "The gods will deal with you, Alex. They brought you and that murderous fish-creature here, and they will take both of you away." He spat. "What did we do to deserve this?" He rose, signaling the council was over for now. The spears came down with a vehement shout of "Wooloo!" Tzoofaa waved his hand in a dismissive gesture, and those attending dispersed into the night.

Tzoofaa signaled for Alex to stay. "I do not send you away in complete disfavor."

"Thank you," Alex said gratefully.

Tzoofaa stood on a boulder so that they were eye to eye. "I do not confuse what causes things with what happens from them. We have learned much from listening to Lector's visions, including our speech, which is so much like yours. I know this, Alex." He looked at Alex gravely, and Alex waited. The old man projected power and insight, and anyone would feel intimidated despite his small stature. "You are a new person, like we are, but you represent the past, Alex. The old people had great power, but they displeased the gods and therefore they are all long dead. We are the new people, and we remain in the favor of the gods. Whatever you do, good luck." He put a hand on Alex's shoulder.

"Thank you," Alex said.

"Sleep well. In the new light we will pray goodbye, and never see each other again. That is how it must be."

The next day, the villagers saw Alex off.

Leeree gave him a tiny carved fetish representing what looked like a Lector obelisk with a circle sign carved into it. She also gave him a shoulder sling with small packets of food. Keetoo and several warriors came to shake hands, and presented Alex with a large wooden bow and arrows suited to his size. Tzoofaa gave him a nicely made stone knife to keep in his shoulder sling. Alex thanked them all and almost regretfully turned to begin his journey. The path took him away, but he looked back and saw them standing on the hills waving, and smelled the food of their fires for at least an hour.

His first stop was the lake, to say goodbye to Maryan one last time. He dove down repeatedly through the animalcule-rich bottle green water. It was cool and pleasant in its mildly fetid way. It took him a dozen dives until he oriented himself. He paddled slowly through waving underwater grasses and kelp, trailing bubbles, until he saw the sandbank on which he had last seen her body. He saw only the wooden arrow that had killed her and little else. Her skull peered from the sand where the current had buried it, and a few ribs and delicate female finger bones—that was all.

Impulsively, he picked up the arrow and swam back to the surface. Sputtering, he swam back to shore, where he put the arrow in his quiver along with about twenty others already in there. It slightly larger and cruder than the fine work of the LooWoo! and its stone head had been roughly chipped, unlike the finely polished points on the other, straighter weapons. But this was one he was reserving for a special purpose.

He gathered his belongings and resumed his journey.

Every hour or so, as he guessed time, he climbed up a tree and looked about the forest for smoke or other signs of Nizin's whereabouts.

The great station cylinder turned relentlessly, as it had for eons, and life in its surface was calm and pleasant. If there had ever been large animals, they had surely been hunted to extinction. By now, Alex had learned that the loud honking noise that had frightened him and Maryan early on was made by one of the world's largest birds. It was a kind of crow, with shiny black feathers and fierce yellowish eyes. It had no predators larger than itself to fear, except an occasional LooWoo! hunting party, and so it imperiously issued its mating and warning calls at the top of its lungs. This amused Alex as he quickly fell back into the hunter-gatherer life style he'd learned on Earth. He quickly adapted to life on this miniature world, and might have existed here quite happily but for two things—the loss of his beloved mate, and his hatred for the creature who had killed her and his burning desire for revenge.

Moving quietly in circuitous paths, eating bugs and plants, not making fires or disturbing nesting birds so they made unusual noises, Alex traveled over a good part of the round-world. Days passed, and he did not count them.

One day, climbing a high tree on a hill, he looked out over several miles. He could see almost to the base of the vast gray wall separating the ancient city from its agricultural lands. Looking down about a quarter mile toward an exposed shred of riverbank among thick trees, he spied his nemesis sitting on a log working on something—probably skinning a small animal he'd caught.

Almost as if by telepathy, Nizin turned and looked over his shoulder. Over one arm clearly visible was a LooWoo! head that he was draining, and his face had that startled, frightful Siirk hiss at being disturbed. Alex felt goose bumps running up and down his back, and he nearly slipped from his perch amid waxy leaves on a slippery limb. Nizin's mouth was dark with blood and gore. His eyes were dark caves. A second later, Nizin turned back to his feast, and Alex sat transfixed.

Nizin turned his head once more—just a flash—and it appeared he might be grinning.

Or was it just another look for more assurance?

Alex wondered if Nizin might be baiting him. He would put nothing past the Siirk. If he knew anything about the Siirk by now, Nizin was planning to make himself the ruler of this world. Having survived his unplanned and unceremonious arrival from Earth, Nizin was doing what came natural to his kind. This unstoppable predator had most likely been trailing him and Maryan since early on their arrival. Nizin had deliberated carefully before picking the spot where he'd assailed Maryan. Now the game was on, and it would play out a bit differently. Maybe Nizin spent a great deal of time looking over his shoulder.

Alex scrambled down the tree and headed across the forest floor toward the Siirk. Up, down, across ferns waving gently in dappled sunlight, over clearings bright with flowers in bluish-white light, Alex fleeted on silent feet with all the skill he'd learned as a woodsman.

Not long after, Alex crept up on a high boulder and peered down at the riverbank. He was close enough now to see the whorls in the bark of the tree trunk on which Nizin had sat. Alex could see the blackish-gray remains of a still smoldering fire now partially covered with sand. The partial covering tipped him again: Nizin was trying to draw him in. Nizin could better have hidden his tracks.

Alex sniffed the air cautiously. He caught a whiff of smoke. He smelled flowers and vegetation. He heard the murmur of water and the tinkle of tiny waves breaking on a wash of rocks in a broad, shallow forest stream. He had a fairly good memory of the sharp, sour body smell of the Siirk, and he did not sense any such odor around him now.

Alex took the special arrow from his quiver and regarded it with pain and anger. If it were not for this object in his hand, this roughly cut sapling with a stone wedged in one end and wrapped in leather, Maryan would be alive and beside him right now. He knotted his fist around the shaft until his fist turned white and the shaft quivered on the verge of breaking. Then he put the arrow back in its quiver.

Alex scouted carefully in all directions from his high lair but could find no sign of Nizin. He wasn't surprised. As he scrambled down the hill, he thought about himself and Nizin. Now they had something in common: a will to kill. Beyond that, Alex realized he himself had lost something. He had lost either the fear of death or the will to live or both. When that arrow had pierced his beloved woman, the arrow had killed both of them. It remained to be seen if that fearlessness would be an asset or a liability in his drive to rid the universe of Nizin.

Alex was sweaty by the time he got to the bottom of the hill, sliding in thick soil up to his ankles. He stopped to listen. There was a wealth of subtle sounds and smells that signaled normalcy. If Nizin were stalking him, which he did not doubt he would if he wasn't already, hopefully he would smell or hear Nizin before his opponent could gain the advantage on him. Ultimately, if he did not finish the Siirk, he would become the problem of Tzoofaa's people. Kind as they were, Alex had no doubt they would find some effective way to deal with Nizin. Meanwhile, Alex knew what he must do.

He approached the riverbank carefully. All was peaceful, and there was neither a sound nor scent of Nizin. Birds fluttered about, and insects fished in the ripples on the little river. The animals scattered when Alex drew near, and then it always got quiet in that small vicinity until he disturbed the next little dip or hollow along the water.

Alex found what he was looking for. Several of Nizin's footprints were in the water, and Alex knelt nearby to figure out what they meant. Best he could figure, Nizin was walking in six inch deep water along the riverbank and dragging a broken, leafy branch to disguise his passage. He'd stirred up mud in doing so, and missed wiping out a few stray prints. They pointed in a direction that Alex would now follow.

They pointed toward the great wall.

In the ensuing two days, Alex tracked the river at a slow but steady pace.

He moved cautiously, judging every tree and every mound before moving on. It was time consuming and energy robbing, but he did not want to casually throw his life away. Nizin had won the first round with his bow and arrow, taking Maryan. He must not score that easily again.

Alex found signs of Nizin's passage a few times. Once, it was a footprint on a sandbank hidden among reeds. Was it an invitation? A trap? Or just an accident? Hard to say.

Another time, Alex smelled fire and tracked down a tiny campfire buried in soil. Nizin had burned a handful of wood and cooked a bird before burying the remains of his fire and the bones from his meal under wet soil and leaves.

Inexorably, the trail led toward the great wall. By now, the city wall loomed above. It rose in a gray, pitted flat mass up into the clouds. The wall was probably the single largest structure other than the cylinder itself. The wall was a round stone or concrete disk, five miles in diameter, over fifteen miles in circumference, with a surface area of just under 20 square miles. Alex guessed it was probably the largest structure ever built by the ancient humans, other than the cylinder itself.

In places where it was raining, the clouds bled water into the streaked concrete. In some places, pure condensation soaked the concrete brownish blue overlaid with flourishing carpets of moss. Birds sailed gracefully with slow wing-beats in and out of high points in the wall with nesting materials or food for their young.

Alex remembered this about Nizin: he lurked around water. Even on Earth, he'd been a sea creature, coming and going in boats. That little bit of information might be just the edge that Alex needed.

Once or twice, Alex thought he glimpsed the running form of Nizin not far ahead.

Each time it was a blurred glimpse, but Alex recognized the scaly figure that moved with such powerful, robust grace. He looked lithe and muscular. The shimmering backs of his upper arms underscored the wiry, steely cords of his muscles. He would be a formidable opponent for a human to physically wrestle with. It would be like trying to grabble with a gorilla—there would be no hope for the human. The only way was to outsmart him somehow. But Nizin was mentally sharp also. His people lived in towns and had guns and ships, so they must be at an early industrial stage comparable to where humans had been a few centuries before the genetic disaster.

Alex came upon a grisly discovery. He heard the loud buzzing of a million insects first. Following a death stench, he found the body of one of the tiny people lying in grass. Its skull had been drained, and its face had a vacant expression. Its torso too was open, and some of the organs had been consumed. The rest was swarming with insects. Alex did not want to tarry here, for fear it was a trap. He studied the footprints all around, and any other signs, like broken twigs that might show which way Nizin had gone. On a gut instinct, Alex decided to follow the trail of bent twigs and torn leaves, and the occasional footprint, toward the nearest watering hole.

The body had been killed very recently. The blood was still red and soft, and the flesh, though stiffening, did not yet smell bad. The trail was fresh, and Alex was surprised at how careless Nizin could be in some ways. Was it to lure him on, or just plain arrogance? Hard to tell. No point taking chances. Alex moved along step by step with an arrow cocked on his bow, and a spare arrow in the bow hand.

Alex went a step at a time, looking left and right, up and down, always sniffing for Nizin's scent.

He did not smell his prey, but he found a tuft of Nizin's hair caught on a thorn not far from a small stream in a hollow under high tree crowns. The stream widened into a drinking place and was surrounded by the muddy holes of small mammals who came to drink here. The branches overhead had shredded bark from the talons of birds who must fly in and out constantly to perch there.

Alex prudently found himself a nesting spot about a mile away. Pushing through dense woods, up and down hills covered with grass and weeds, he climbed down a winding trail to a hollow. He found at the bottom a small forest pool. There, he crouched over its little cold well of water. In the gloom, he looked left and right, keeping his body as still as possible. Then he picked up handfuls of bluish-brown mud and rubbed them all over his face, neck, upper arms, and torso. He would make his camp here for a while. There were big trees all around, with huge snaking roots. He hid his sling and his few belongings in a nest of leaves where he could sleep. He kept Tzoofaa's knife and Leeree's tiny obelisk close to himself to bring him luck. He wanted to pray, to converse, with the gods of this place.

The trees cast heavy shade, and the air felt chilly here where little light penetrated. The air smelled just a tad fetid, from the forest matter disintegrating in the water below. High above, birds twittered and of course the insects kept up their hum. Luckily, the mosquito seemed rare. Alex had a few bites, but most of the insects appeared to eat vegetation or prey on other insects.

Alex fashioned himself a crown woven of twigs and embellished with leaves that draped down around his head. He made himself a wreath that he wore around his neck and over his shoulders, with leaves trailing down over his body. This way, he could stand silently among tree trunks and be invisible. Hopefully, anyway, Nizin would not see him.

Alex stalked silently back to the watering place where he expected Nizin would show up soon enough. He wasn't disappointed, but he was also surprised. First, he approached the stream slowly. He stayed on a slope about 200 feet away. There he was surrounded by a thick carpet of moss a foot deep, and bright green ferns illumined by shafts of hazy light dropping through the crowns above. He knelt down and began scooping out a hole in the ground, all the while keeping his eyes on his surroundings. He dug gently and calmly to keep the noise minimal. When he had a hole about two feet deep and wide enough, he knelt inside of it to keep his profile as low as possible.

Gradually the light dimmed. Evening, or Dim Light, came slowly as the cylinder turned in space. The moon rose, casting its yellow and olive-green light through the meshwork of windows at the cylinder's end. At the river, animals came out to drink. Two dog-sized animals with slavering muzzles briefly sparred before running off in opposite directions.

It was the witching hour. Far away, two tiny LooWoo! hunters on spidery legs stalked over the rim of a hill. They carried slings and strode with tall staves as they pursued some errand known only to them. With their spindly bodies and big heads, they ambled past and disappeared as quickly as they'd appeared.

Darkness filled the air, and Alex sank down into the safety of his hole. Remembering the first night free of his birth cave on earth, he drew leaves over himself and cuddled down in the cool, damp earth, shivering. He would not let himself feel pity or irony, he thought. He stared at the moon through a hole in the leaves. He saw the buttery moon and its poignant canyons that had been the stuff of human music and romance in that lost world of long ago. Strangely, he felt no hatred. He felt things, and he wasn't sure what they all were, but confusion and pain were foremost among them. He felt a sense of duty to destroy Nizin before Nizin could kill anyone else.

And, yes, he missed Maryan terribly.

"Siiiirrkk!"

Alex opened his eyes and froze.

He heard that voice again, nearby, unmistakable: "Siiiirrkk!"

Nizin! Alex gripped the knife Tzoofaa had given him, and gradually raised his face. He lifted one fingertip and picked leaves away, one by one, an inch at a time, until his field of vision increased.

It was New Light. He must have fallen into an exhausted sleep. Heart pounding, he felt the muzziness of sleep driven away as he heard Nizin's oratory of self-praise nearby.

There. The Siirk stood over a dead animal—one of the dog-things that had engaged in a snarling contest with its slavering fellow dog-thing the night before. Nizin finished congratulating himself on his kill and squatted down with a knife upraised to begin preparing his meal.

Alex moved with glacial slowness. He pulled his bow close and strung it. He pulled the special arrow from his quiver and laid it on the bow. He shifted his body around into aiming position, grimacing at his stiffness and the aches he felt.

Meanwhile, Nizin cradled the animal in his arms and extracted from its head what he needed. Once or twice he paused, strangely, as if contemplating what lay between his arms.

Alex held the bow laterally, a foot above the ground. He laid the arrow on it and started to aim.

Nizin paused again, looking slightly to one side.

Alex found he could not aim well this way. He needed the bow to be as vertical as possible. He rose slowly, turning the bow as he did so.

Nizin shifted suddenly where he sat.

Alex rose like a shadow, aiming the arrow that had killed Maryan.

Nizin was faster. He whirled, producing a bow he must have hidden somehow.

Alex was almost at the point of loosing the arrow. Too late he saw the thing Nizin had held was not a dead animal but a hide with a dog-like head attached. Under the hide he had concealed his weapons, and now he rose, spinning, and let loose an arrow at Alex.

Alex sent his arrow flying, but it was too late. In the second after the arrow flew, Nizin side-stepped and disappeared into a nearby cleft in a hill, covered by bushes. In that same second, Nizin's arrow struck Alex in the shoulder.

The arrow tore Alex's skin, bruised his exposed shoulder bone, and glanced off. Pain seared through Alex like fire, and he staggered, grasping his shoulder.

Nizin popped up on a tall boulder about 500 feet away cackling. His eyes and teeth glittered manically. "Siiiirrrrk!" he groaned loudly with pleasure and triumph. "Siiiirrrkkk!" He rubbed his belly and laughed. The forest echoed with his voice.

Alex shook his head, for his vision was blurred with shock. He looked to his right and lifted his bloody hand from his shoulder. He saw the white bone there, the torn muscles, flecks of loose body fat lying in yellowish and white streaks mingled with blood in the wound.

"Ha ha ha!" Nizin's laugh echoed.

Alex staggered back and leaned against a tree. His vision was blurry, but he heard as Nizin laughed again. Nizin hopped off the boulder and disappeared into the brush.

Alex's shoulder throbbed, and he grimaced with pain each time he moved. What was worse, it smelled bad. Alarmed, Alex retrieved the arrow and sniffed it. He made a face while his stomach contracted in horror. Nizin had rubbed it in feces—probably Siirk feces to add a special insult.

Holding the dagger to his side, Alex made his way down to the water. He threw himself into the water and frantically started wiping the wound with wet silt. Probably filled with all sorts of bugs, he thought, but nothing could be so damaging as Siirk shyte in an open wound. As he

washed himself, he sobbed with pain. The stuff burned like acid. He
knew Nizin could probably kill him now, but Nizin didn't. Probably
wanted to toy with Alex. Nizin would probably let Alex get sick from
infection, then hunt him down, slowly and cruelly torturing him, making
his end as prolonged and dreadful as possible.

Ducking under the water, Alex again experienced its coolness and
soothing nature. It was nothing like the healing magic of the cave water
back on Earth, but it relieved a tiny bit of the fire aching on his shoulder.
Luckily, the wound wasn't in the joint, just in the thin flesh and
musculature atop the joint where the arm met the shoulder. Still, even
with the feces washed out, there was little hope of avoiding infection.
Return to the village? Not a chance—it would bring the curse of this
rogue Siirk down on them. He'd chosen his fate, the villagers had warned
him of the consequences. Now he must live with them. Alex decided he
must have no regrets, no matter what. He had enjoyed life, and had been
blessed with a fine woman. Now the game was just about done, in this
colossal joke life had played by bringing him into the world a million
years after mankind had become extinct. Now the only recourse was to
fade from the scene with dignity and pride.

Alex sloshed noisily out of the water, hoping to bring Nizin back for a
final fight while Alex still had the strength.

One thing at a time. He must survive, first.

How long before the infection set in? Maybe a day at most. Already
the arm was throbbing, and soon parts of it felt numb. The discomfort
was spreading into the joint, a sure sign this wasn't going to get better.

Alex ran into the bush and put a little distance between himself and
the river.

No sign of Nizin. The Siirk would be out hunting him, but for the
moment he was letting Alex have a little slack to see what he could do.
Nizin must be supremely confident of his skills as a hunter, and so far
there was no question of that. Alex faded from side to side to spoil the
trail a bit. Running endlessly and blindly forward would do nothing but
tire him out. This was as much a game of brains as it was of endurance,
and so far Nizin had scored the first several points.

Alex resisted the temptation to head back to Leeree's village. That
chapter was now closed forever. He must move on and make whatever of
life fate was about to allot him. Instinctively, Alex made his way toward

the great wall. Along the way, he ate what he could—flowers, nuts, berries, insects. He drank water whenever he found it. Must stay hydrated, must keep up his strength. His shoulder and arm began to swell up, as did the lymph nodes under his arms. His neck grew sore and stiff, and even his jaw ached. He was running a faint temperature, he could tell, and his vision was a bit blurry.

He could not go on much longer this way.

He felt himself weakening, and knew he must beat Nizin at his own game.

Staggering along, he often had to stop and rest. He supported himself by leaning on a rock or tree trunk as the light dimmed.

He fell down among pine needles and leaves, crawled under a fallen log that glowed with mushrooms (or were those illusions of his fevered brain?) and slept. He dreamt of Maryan, of making love with her in the cave before they'd ever known of the Siirk. He shivered in his sleep and called out for her. He woke several times in the night, thinking a shape hovered nearby, Nizin, plotting how best to kill him so that it would hurt the most. But it wasn't Nizin, just some flying blanket moss, he saw as the light grew brighter and the first glimmer of daylight grayed among the trees. Surely there was yet some secret in this place. The last boat could not have come to them by coincidence out of the whole million years this place had been spinning in place at L5. Something else was at work—but what? His brain was like a runner, growing tired, even as it stumbled the last few hundred yards in a long race to some finish that was going to be either the finish, the end of all ends, or the beginning of a new beginning.

He fell asleep again, babbling to himself in his mind.

When he awoke, his aches had subsided a bit, though the pain in his right shoulder was steadily worsening. It cost him effort to rise, to stoop, to turn.

He feasted on the last of the little packets given him by Leeree. The food tasted like dried flowers and fruits, and he savored it to the last sweet, summery mouthful. He wrapped Leeree's sling around his shoulders to warm and restrain his aching shoulder. He gripped his weapons in his other hand and headed on. He knew now the first thing he must do.

He found the watering hole, near the city wall, that he'd been looking for. It was near the place he and Maryan had found the first dead LooWoo! and from which he had vainly set out to explore the transit terminal. All that seemed like a lost time now, long ago like all else in this ancient place.

So much time here. He made his preparations intently, with great focus, though his mind kept wandering off on tangents. *So much time stored in this place, in this earth, up and down the great cylinder's inner surfaces.* So much had happened here, and no record of any of it, save the disconnected ramblings of Vectors and Nectars, Ectors and Lectors. *Incomplete, all of it. Useless. Need a central vision, a picture, a plan, a coherent terminal. Need a master, a Rector.*

Leaving his spear lying on the ground, and his quiver to the other side, he prepared the bow and its arrow that meant anything. Not the crude one made by Nizin but one of the fine ones from the village. He prepared the scene of his final drama as best he could and then withdrew into the low hills just beyond. There, under a canopy of leaves and branches, he uttered the pride-call, the war-whoop, the triumphant caw of the big black crow.

Silence. Just the wind in the leaves.

He repeated his challenge to the world.

Silence. Just the insects on the water surface.

Breathing hard, grasping his painfully throbbing shoulder with his left hand, he raised his face to the moon like a dying crow or a fatally wounded wolf from some long-ago ice age and howled.

He heard the snap of a twig, the grunt of curiosity, the yelp of triumph, and knew who was coming down the trail to the watering hole.

He could hear the gleeful hiss of air through Nizin's sharp incisor teeth. He raised himself up, pushing leaves and twigs away, to see the glint of victory in the other's eyes as he hovered over Alex's supposed body just fifty feet away in a tangle of dark brush, under the sling cloth.

Nizin rubbed his stomach with both hands and groaned hungrily: "Siiiirrrk!"

Then he bent over to reach out and remove the sling. As he did so, he stepped on the branch Alex had carefully laid across the path. Even as the sling came away, the bow that sat in its hollow, propped apart by a branch between bow and string, jerked.

Alex heard the tight twang noise and the ripping sound as a fine stone tip ripped into Nizin's torso.

Alex rose and cried out in triumph. "Yesss!"

Nizin looked up, puzzled, even as he held the wound near his heart and sagged. All triumph was gone in Nizin's face, replaced by shock and realization. He held the arrow that was killing him with both hands but did not have the strength or leverage to pull it out. Bright scarlet blood poured down the soft scales on his chest and belly.

"Die!" Alex roared, raising his well arm while the other dangled bloody at his side. "Look at me! Die like you made so many die!"

Nizin struck the ground hard, looking up one more time before closing his eyes.

Alex picked up a large round stone, staggered down to the body, and smashed Nizin's head so that gore and gray matter flecked the gravel.

Then Alex turned and headed into the woods away from the great wall. He had one last stop to make before he closed his eyes.

As he staggered along, bouncing from tree to tree, Alex laughed. "This place," he muttered out loud, "this crazy place. This whole crazy world. Rigged, all of it!"

He fell down several times. Each time, he hauled himself back on his feet and staggered on. The wound in his shoulder wasn't bleeding copiously, but it was infected. He could smell it, and he knew in a day or two, if he were still alive, the stench would be overwhelming. At this point, he felt the heat, the throbbing, the edema, the pain. He felt his arm getting numb, and he held it with his left hand to keep it from swinging, because every limp motion caused the shoulder joint to rotate with excruciating pain. But the pain was his salvation, in a way, because it kept him awake. It kept him moving.

"This whole place is alive," he said. "Yes, you!" he shouted to the clouds, to the wall behind him, to the crazy quilt of glass and sap and spider webbing far off. "I know what you are doing!" he shouted to the entire L5 station. "You are alive, aren't you? The forest is your lungs and the rivers are your blood. When you are cut, you heal yourself by sending the blankets flying. You coagulate, you great monster!"

So he rambled, crawling up hills and falling, sliding, rolling down hills. He splashed through ponds and paddled through lakes.

He let a big artery river transport him, half consciously, over tiny toy rapids where rounded rocks tickled his back, until he was back in deeper water and bobbing along. Fish came to nibble at his skin and make him laugh. Fish came to suck at his wounds and dart away carrying bits and pieces of him trailing blood and gore. He laughed uproariously at the beauty of it. Tiny krill crept into his infected cuts and pockets and sockets, feeding hungrily on the pus and sickness there. Alex laughed until he had no more strength to laugh. He lay on his back in the water, spinning while birds and clouds wheeled overhead and moonlight blazed over him with searing brightness. Just to snub fate, he said loudly: "Thank you." He laughed. "Thank you. Thanks for everything. It's been a great party. I loved every minute of it, speaking of course for myself and my late partner Maryan who cannot be here with us for these ceremonies today." He felt himself losing consciousness as his head tipped back. For some interminable time, he kept passing out and waking again. Each time he woke, he dragged himself another few hundred feet. Sometimes the river picked him up and carried him bobbing down its moonlight-dappled course. Somehow, he navigated the last mile or so, pulling himself along as best he could. His head hung down weakly, but each time it lolled from side to side, he saw how close he was to that beach of starlight on which he and his beloved Maryan had stood, where the heat of the sunlight boiled the rocks shooting up from the moon and melted them so that the station could grow, by inches per century.

It was bright daylight, and he could smell the distant cooking fires of LooWoo! but he was beyond wanting any of that. His body was shutting down already, and the going was tougher by the minute. He staggered, a foot at a time, falling to his knees, getting up, falling to his knees again, crawling. He pulled himself forward by his fingertips. He shed his sandals and pushed against the sand with his toes. His chin made a furrow in the damp sand as the going got easier and he was going downhill to the water. Crawling on, he felt swells of water under his chin. Coolness enveloped his chest, soothed his shoulder, welcomed his torso and his legs. He was weightless now, swimming, paddling feebly. The current carried him in slow circles toward the middle of the lake where she lay. The wind brushed his back with cool fingers. He gathered his last strength and jackknifed, going down head-first through bright yellow-green bubbles, through sleepily swaying underwater grasses and leaves, toward that silvery glowing mound of sand and silt.

Her skull looked toward him with large calm eyes. Her fingers beckoned with bony joints. Her hips were under the sand, but open and waiting for the final union. He was exhausted and could not summon another bit of energy. Not even to float to the surface. Reaching down with both arms, he opened his mouth and breathed in a huge lungful of water. He felt the coolness enter his chest, and he sensed that his heart beat one, two, three more beats, each slower than the previous, each spaced farther apart, and then stopped.

That made a final soothing darkness rush up through his brain in place of the warm blood of life.

At the same time, he felt the sand opening up to swallow him, and he shot down among her bones, among the darting krill, among the drifting motes, into the beauty of her smile.

9. Station

A tightly folded newspaper twirled through a blue sky, passing between the crowns of two huge leafy elm trees.

The newspaper flew high in an expert arc and landed with a *thwack* against the slightly loose wood-framed screen door of Alex Kirk's house. The newspaper girl rode past on her bicycle getting the next paper ready for the next house on the block. It was midmorning on a summer day, the kind of quiet midmorning unique to small towns in Middle America. Alex's father had already driven to work in the office at the computer firm, and Alex's mother and younger sister were at the dentist getting the girl's braces adjusted. Alex's older brother and sister were at Peasman Grammar School, and Alex, aged 8, was alone with Mrs. Butterman the babysitter. Also at the house was Maryan Shurey, whose parents both worked at the shoe manufacturing plant. Mrs. Butterman was the heavyset wife of Butterman, the mailman. The Kirks whispered at the dinner table that the Buttermans had debts owing to a son's troubles, whatever those might be, but that the boy was doing better now in Rehab, whatever that was, and Mrs. Butterman welcomed the opportunity to make a little extra cash by watching children and doing light housework. At the moment, Mrs. Butterman was on her way down into the basement, poofing with sweat-rimed lips while the hair came loose from the dusty auburn bun atop her head. "You children mind now!" she said in a high flute-like voice, which meant she would be out of sight for a short while.

"Come on!" Alex said, taking 7 year old Maryan by the hand.

"I'm watching Popeye and Olive Oyl," Maryan protested, offering her hand as he asked, while pouting and wriggling and using her other hand to scratch her underwear.

"This is our chance to escape!" Alex said, pulling away. "We can run from her clutches and be in Dodge City by nightfall. We'll come back with a posse and rescue our parents. Are you in?"

"Okay," Maryan said and ran after him. He was already out the door. The dark green screen door slammed softly as they bounded down the front steps onto the concrete walk that led down to the street.

"This way!" Alex said, grabbing the handle of his red wagon. Maryan got in and held on to the sides as he towed her down the sidewalk. They were going in a direction where he'd never been, and his heart beat wildly for the joy of discovering the world.

As the day grew hot, the air smelled of mown grass and melting tar and the expanding joints of ancient wood in painted Victorian houses. Birds twittered in the willow trees and a bumblebee raced a butterfly to the nearest yellow flower. He pulled her over uneven sidewalk squares raised by tree roots.

"Hey, go easy!" Maryan yelled as she bounced up and down in the wagon.

The air smelled more and more of car exhaust as they headed downtown, and further in the direction of Beacham University. The sidewalks were crowded with pedestrians downtown, and Alex had to wait for the little white man figure in the traffic light at each corner. Trucks roared by with huge wheels, and people called out in alarm. "Be careful!" someone called from a truck.

Maryan started crying.

"Oh for heaven's sake," Alex said, pulling her into the little park downtown where the university began with its gray neo-classic and purple Victorian stone buildings. He put his arms around her and shook her by the shoulders. "Come on, Maryan. It's not like we're in another country."

She continued sobbing.

He ran across the street to Ito's News, bought a Malty Joy candy bar, and ran back. He unwrapped it and gave it to her. She sniffled once or twice more and accepted it, getting chocolate all around her lips.

They heard a man's voice. "You kids lost?"

It was Charlie Dugway, the ice cream man. He was a very dark-skinned black man whose two children went to Peasman, and Alex liked Mr. Dugway. Alex waved. "We're tired."

"Want a lift home?"

"We'd really like to go home now," Alex said. Maryan nodded, chewing a large bite off her Malty Joy bar. By now she had chocolate all over her cheeks.

Mr. Dugway parked the truck at the curb and walked over. He wore black trousers and a white shirt with an orange bowtie. He wore an apron, on which he wiped his hands. "How did you little kids get all the way downtown like this?" he said with concern. Mr. Dugway took Maryan by one hand and pulled the wagon with the other hand.

Alex walked along with his hands in his pockets. "We were running from the law," Alex said.

"The law?" Mr. Dugway said. "Must have been an awful crime you did to be on the lam this early in the day."

"We didn't put our wet towels in the wash basket," Maryan said.

"We left a mess on the table," Alex said. "Chocolate syrup. Mrs. Butterman said we would be the death of her, so we figured we'd better run before she died."

"Sounds like Murder Three," Mr. Dugway said, loading Maryan and the wagon through the back door of the ice cream truck, and hauling Alex up the step by one wrist. "That'll get you five to 15, with time off for good behavior, and bonus points for eating your vegetables. In you go, young fella!" Mr. Dugway pulled the door shut. Inside, he had a radio softly playing jazz vocals. "You kids want to hear Poppy the Clown?"

"Yeah!" Alex and Maryan said jumping up and down clapping their hands.

To the tune of *Pop Goes The Weasel*—played on a xylophone by the famed television clown, recorded, and now broadcast from the loudspeaker on top of Mr. Dugway's truck—they cruised slowly down the streets in the direction of the Kirk house (and the Shurey house a block further down). Maryan stood on a stool and leaned out of the truck, telling each kid who came close: "Hey, what flavor would you like? Chocolate? Vanilla? Or Strawberry?" She'd fold her hands together, incline her head to one side so her locks bounced, cute as a button, and she'd say: "Personally, I prefer strawberry. That's because it's my favorite color. Don't you think?"

Watching Maryan, Alex unexpectedly found himself being pulled backward, and he almost stumbled. What had happened to Mr. Dugway? In Mr. Dugway's place, wearing his clothing including his apron and paper hat, was a dark-haired and green-eyed woman. She was pretty, Chinese or something, pale, and she looked kind of anxious. "Alex!"

"Who are you?"

"My name is Dot. You won't remember me, but I have some insert-codons for you."

"What are those?" Alex said, holding his hands behind his back. He felt more curious than mistrustful, so he let her get near.

"Metaphors. Don't be afraid," she said. "You will be in a lot of danger soon. Watch out for the ectors. They took over the primary command center of the station after the meteorite hit wiped out the gene stock. There can be no future for humans anyway, but with the ectors loose there is no future for you and Maryan either. Trust me. I tried to save the world and failed."

She made him a vanilla cone. As she packed ice cream around the sides with a flat scoop, she said: "These are strong intraphors and extraphors that will straddle the ector routines." She put rainbow sprinkles on it. "These will make you very smart when you grow up. That will be sooner than you think." She held the cone out to him and winked. "This won't be the last you see of me. But we have to be very, very careful, okay?" She placed a finger over her lips and winked her eyes shut, which made it as though Alex's eyes had momentarily blinked shut. When he opened his eyes, the lady was gone.

He eagerly licked the cone. The vanilla was very rich, and the sprinkles were crunchy between his teeth. It almost seemed as if they crackled and glowed as he chewed on them, like those wintergreen candy poppers Rudy Chatfield had brought to class one day and they all chewed under the stairwell, watching the miniature lightning in one another's mouths.

Maryan smiled and waved to the kids around the truck, which rolled to a stop. She was preoccupied and didn't notice a thing.

Mr. Dugway stood there whistling to himself in his apron and paper hat. He was just then preparing a double scooper of rainbow sherbet for a kid waving a dollar over the counter.

Alex began to think about other things and forgot the...the...the what? It didn't matter just now, though he knew it would be important later.

Mrs. Butterman stood on the sidewalk crying when the ice cream truck pulled up, and she raised her hands to heaven saying hallelujah. That was when Maryan put her hands on the counter and leaned out of the window smiling. She was missing her upper front teeth, her curls hung down over her ears, and Mr. Dugway had put his white paper hat on her head.

"You want chocolate, strawberry, or vanilla?" Maryan asked Mrs. Butterman, who came running up on rubbery legs and looked ready to faint. "Personally, I prefer strawberry."

Alex and Maryan had other stories to tell as the years went by, but the ice cream story was their first and favorite.

They remained friends all through grammar school and high school. Her parents retired and opened a flower shop next to Ito's news stand. Maryan worked part time there, and Alex loved to stop by on his delivery route for Johnson's Appliance Repair. Alex and Maryan both got scholarships to Beacham University, he in prelaw and she in sciences. It was at Beacham, on a summer day not unlike the one of their ice cream truck adventure, that they were strolling arm in arm by Swan Lake on campus, when a young graduate student came down to the water with a small black dog.

"Oh what a cute puppy!" Maryan said, tugging on Alex's arm and dragging him along so she could pet the puppy. "What kind is he?"

"She's a six week old black lab," the grad student said. He set down a wooden box that looked like a briefcase. "Say, how would you two like to help the cause of science?"

"I will soon be able to give you a good introductory deal at my law firm," Alex quipped.

"I'm a science major," Maryan said. "Any chance of getting some credit in Rector's class?"

"Rector the biology prof?" The grad student ran his knuckles through his dark, curly hair. "That would be my boss. We're taking blood samples for a biological experiment. I might be able to put in a good word."

"Oh, wonderful!" Maryan said. "When do we start?"

The student let her play with the puppy while he opened his case. Alex made a wry face, recognizing that the puppy was a shill, a come-on, and what a cute one. He couldn't resist petting it himself. In a few moments, both he and Maryan were on their hands and knees, playing in the grass while the puppy romped in cute little quick zigzags, panting, throwing itself about so its pink belly showed.

"Excellent," the grad student said. "The puppy is actually a test, believe it or not."

"You're joking," Alex said.

"I am dead serious," the grad student said. "You guys will need to sign waivers and fill out questionnaires, but I already know you have kind and sociable personalities. That's important."

"Why?" Maryan said, holding the puppy up and nuzzling with it nose to nose.

"We're doing some Government research for Homeland Defense," the graduate student said, and from his dead-serious face Alex quickly got the drift he wasn't joking.

"So it's a big secret?" Maryan said as the puppy licked her nose.

The grad student laid out a rubber tourniquet, two glass test tubes, and a towel. "This won't sting but for a moment," he said holding a steely looking needle up.

On a lovely day like this, with the swans honking on the water as they chased bread crumbs through the greenish ripples, under a blue sky and warm sun, in an air like rich liquor, who could say no, Alex thought as he lay on his back and rolled his sleeve up. "We're actually after stem cells," the graduate student said. "If Rector likes your blood, he'll invite you to the hospital for a brief outpatient procedure and you'll be handsomely paid. I promise you." He winked at Maryan. "It's an easy A."

"I like that," Maryan said.

"Are you two married?"

Maryan looked at Alex and laughed. "Not yet. We've been joined at the hip since we were little kids, so who knows. Maybe one day?"

Alex made a face at her, suppressing a grin. He loved her, and she loved him. They had already planned to become engaged in their senior year of college. They had discussed getting married after he finished law school. Alex had returned from the military, and Maryan had come to New York City to spend a few days on vacation before driving home upstate.

These were the last memories, the final goodbye, the dark and sensuous moments that would survive for a million years into the future, and perhaps another million years if mankind found a new lease on its existence.

The television set in the hotel room sent waves of light flickering, like the ocean tide washing in and out under the moon, flickering at a slow and measured pace loaded with its own hidden purposes, over naked bodies moving against each other, sharing envelopes of sweat and desire, groaning with passion, two whole lives filled with hope, while the detritus of a takeout dinner sat on the hotel china nearby, and champagne smoked languidly from an open bottle.

Alex lay on his back and felt a tingling through his limbs as he became aware that it was his time to be born.

His eyes were closed but he understood he was floating in a greenish liquid swirling with ambient light. He remembered going through this once before, but understood that this was not a cave and that he was safe now.

And yet, here he was, floating in his dream, over a beach. A tropical breeze stirred in the palm trees on one side, and the ocean made loud pounding noises as breakers crashed among the rocks. Standing on a sandbar was a figure in a flowing cloak, and he knew he had seen her before. As he looked at her, she removed the winding from around her head and exposed long dark hair and pale skin. Her almond-shaped eyes, filled with anxiety, were green and crackled as if with lightning. Her mouth was contorted in a melancholy twist, and when her lips parted a low keening noise came out like a constant cry of pain and loss. Or was it a cry of alarm at terrible things yet to come? *Dot*. He lay very still and tried to remember what had happened to make her so sad. He couldn't. Almost immediately, as though someone else were vying for his attention, he was torn back into another place: the lab at Beacham, where he and Maryan had so innocently signed away their blood work.

There was only a brief memory, almost nightmarish, of being in a dark office with a cold, not entirely pleasant professor with a white lab coat, latex gloves, and a light over his forehead. The professor was chewing clove gum and frowning as he finished working on the sheet-draped lower half of Maryan's body. She cried softly with pain and held Alex's hand while a nurse stood by and a physician manipulated cool steel scissors and other instruments under Rector's direction. "It will all be over in a few moments," the physician said.

To which Rector added: "You'll enjoy a nice steak dinner on me, and I'll give you an A on your biology survey course."

Maryan gave Alex's hand a squeeze and made a yelping sound.

"All done," the physician said, standing up.

"You did great," the nurse said.

That was all Alex could remember as he lay in the tank, immersed in water, while bubbles rose quietly and steadily around him. His eyes were closed. He couldn't open them quite yet; but what of Maryan? Had he married her? Had they lived happily ever after? He would never know for sure.

"I am Rector," said a man's voice. "You have been here nearly a year now, and you will be born soon."

Alex felt sad. He felt a sense of loss, a coldness, an absence of Maryan. He felt a vague sad memory which he slowly realized was the memory of her having died.

"I will increase your drip," Rector's rich, calm voice said someplace nearby. "It's a nice drug that will calm your bloodstream and make your respiration smooth."

Alex felt himself lying straight in some liquid, with his arms by his sides. His hands were relaxed, and he wondered if he had fingers. He was almost sure he had legs, but if he did, did he also have feet? Toes? Did he twitch an eyelid whenever Rector spoke? He wished he could see himself. He almost could, so disembodying was this experience.

"You had a terrible experience," Rector said.

Alex felt his right eyelid twitch.

"You are completely safe now," Rector said.

Alex felt the light growing. Lemon. Vanilla. Warm. Like ice cream.

"You are being born," Rector said. "Be happy."

A rubbery thing snaked into his mouth and started making pulsing sounds, like a pump, and he felt water being sucked from his lungs.

He panicked, thinking the rubber thing (which smelled and tasted like pencil erasers) was choking him to death as it filled his mouth. He gagged and tried to sit up, but restraints held him down.

As he struggled to raise up and spit it out, he lost consciousness and sank into a deep place full of faint earth-tone lights.

Alex sat up, sputtering.

He felt warm dry air on his skin. He tore the rubber mouthpiece from his lips and coughed spasmodically. Liquid gushed from his nostrils and from his mouth. He coughed and sputtered, leaning weakly on one side of the birthing tank with his arms hanging over.

"Welcome," said a male voice. "Congratulations on your birth. It is good to be alive."

Alex rubbed his eyes, which burned, until they opened. He rubbed away soft sleep matter from his nose and from the corners of his eyes and lips—creamy greenish paste that smelled almost like oats or kress and had antiseptic healing properties.

"Who are you?" Alex whispered.

"I am Rector. I am little more than the ghost of a man who lived long ago, and I have to follow your orders because I am nothing more than software while you are a living, breathing human."

"How is it that I remember another man's life?"

"The system feeds codons into your genes, RNA-like replicators and replicands that make your body generate swarms of bioelectrochemical memes on the surface of your brain. The ancient humans learned how to make memory recordings this way and pass them along to clones who would otherwise be born as blank slates with nothing but some primitive hardwired boot knowledge."

"What happened to the human race?"

Rector smiled smugly into his chin. "Dead and gone for eons. I am a program they left behind—a virtual memorial, one might say."

"Can we bring them back?"

"There is only one chance left now, Alex, and you can make it happen." His eyes had a veiled, furtive look.

"How long has it been?"

Rector glanced at an oversized wristwatch with a glowing neon dial face and cryptic markings. "Slightly over a million years."

Alex looked around. He was in a sunny, pleasant 30x30 square foot room. The room was bare except for the glass tank in the middle and the tubes trailing from his abdomen. He'd splashed water on the white enamel floor of the room. The walls were light, pinkish enamel with baby blue shadows, though it seemed just as likely the colors were microscopic picture elements within a neutral digital surface that could be any color its master wanted it to be. Some faint flickers here and there gave the game away. There was one large rectangular window, taking up most of one wall, through whose half-shut Venetian blinds warmth and sunlight leaked into the room, though Alex suspected again that it was just a digital projection, perhaps of real sunlight from outside the station's skin, filtered through virtual blinds to shield out radiation.

Several mirror-like surfaces hung in various places around the room, and in one of the mirrors, the largest one, was the image of a man sitting in a chair. It was a full-size lifelike image, generated by some program in the station's core. The man was bald on top, with a ring of graying hair over the ears, and a squarish brown beard. He had a tall, rectangular Germanic looking face with hard blue-gray eyes. He had a small mouth with a humorous twist, but a faintly additive cruelty: *Rector*. The spawn of all ectors. "Can you walk?" Rector asked softly, offering a hand. "We have a lot to accomplish."

Alex tried to climb out of the tank, but lost his grip on the slippery rim, and fell down beside it in a welter of spilled water. He felt chilly and naked and awkward. His limbs ached and his head swam as blood regulated itself and his heart found just the right rhythm for pumping.

"Are you hungry?"

Alex shook his head as he propped himself up on his palms and elbows.

"Thirsty?"

Alex used a thumb and index finger to brush water from the bridge of his nose and between his eyes while lowering his head and shaking off the dull headache. Water poured from his head and splattered on the floor. He heaved in his tank like some great fish. Water poured from his fingertips as he gripped the tanks' rim.

"You had all the nutrients you need for a few hours," Rector said, "and the headache should be going away any minute now."

Alex struggled to stand up. He slipped again, fell down, but pushed himself up by his hands and elbows against the edge of the birthing tank. Water crashed around him like ocean breakers. How clean and fresh the birthing liquid smelled! Green herbs floated in their healing broth. Green umbilical tubes floated on the water, dissolving. He looked down at his navel, which was swollen to fist-size and pocked with bluish-purple bleeding sockets where the tubes had biogenically plugged in, nurturing him during his nine month term, before falling off when the hormone cocktail signaled birth time.

"That will heal soon," Rector said. "Don't worry. Everything has been planned for. You will live a long and healthy life on human terms. We spared no effort to ensure the survival of our race, and you are the key player now, Alex Kirk."

Alex rose unsteadily and held his head between his hands. "How would that be?" He remembered something about a meteorite hit.

"Come with me and you'll see," Rector said. He strode toward a wall and disappeared.

Alex walked in the same direction and found that a door had appeared in the wall on his side; or had been there all along and he hadn't seen it. He turned the handle and stepped outside.

Alex was in a long hallway. Biofluorescent ceiling lights gleamed in highly polished rubbery floor tiles. The walls of the corridor were plain popcorn-creamy white and smooth. There were numerous doors, all of them closed.

Rector's image appeared beside Alex as though Rector were a live, full-size human being. He still wore the lab coat, but the latex gloves were gone. It was an image, however, without any smells—no clove gum, no latex gloves, no faintly mothball odor in the lab coat. They strode down the hall until they came to a door, and Rector pointed for Alex to open it.

Alex stepped into a dark room that lightened slowly to a dim glow. A nude female lay in a glass and steel birthing tank.

"Maryan!" Alex gasped, wanting to fall on his knees.

She floated on her back, perfectly still, with a faint smile on her face. Her thick hair floated in delicate whorls, framing the same lovely face he knew so well. Everything in the room was calm and aseptic, except the water covering her in the tank, which glowed in various shades of red, from a comforting ruby to a rich yellowish garnet to a lively claret. "The color of blood," Rector said quietly, "not the plant juice you were birthed in down in your cave." Some undertone in Rector's voice thrummed a faint, dark note of warning deep in Alex's brain, but in his excitement to see Maryan, Alex pushed it aside. Alex put his palms against the room temperature glass and studied the precious tank's contents. The liquid was alive with nanobugs cleaning, feeding, nuzzling, healing, growing.

Rector raised a finger to his lips. "Shh."

"Will she remember?" Alex whispered.

"Yes," Rector whispered. "Come, don't disturb her now. Close the door. She will be born in a few days. See how she smiles. She dreams of you, Alex. I have a deal for you."

Alex pulled the door shut. He followed Rector down the long hall. "If you bring her back to life I will do anything for you."

"You'll do what you have to do," Rector said, "and so will I."

Rector led him to a room with several chairs and a table in a faux Louis Quinze style.

The walls were light beige or oatmeal and Rector's image moved about on the walls. "Sit down, Alex. Objects in the room are real. The station is able to project molecular ensembles of itself, constructed from elemental holographic vector shapes in three dimensions, and project them in three-dimensional realities. Those molecules are every bit as real as those in your body."

The table and chairs were of a wood-like material which, when Alex looked closely, seemed to have a fine metallic grain. The upholstery was plush, though its surface was slightly rough, as if it were woven from fine metallic threads. Alex sat in an upright chair with arm rests. He folded his hands on the table.

"We were able to salvage your memory codons, Alex."

"We?"

Rector spread his arms lightly, briefly, indicating his surroundings. "The station."

"You salvaged our lives?"

"Yes, most of who you and Maryan were in your recent iteration."

"There have been other iterations of us? Before?"

"Many. None got as far as you have. None made it this far to sit and talk with me. They are long since dust."

"Were there others like me?"

"Yes. Dot, Bella, just in the past few thousand years alone."

"And Maryan and I. You captured our memories? So we don't forget what we learned in the last few years and go backwards?"

Rector nodded. "We have you both."

"We're in a database?"

"No. There is no database. It's a tricky process. We can only convert a clone once."

"Convert?"

"You are a real person now, Alex. No bark on your arms, no vegetable juice DNA mixed with the blood in your arteries. If you die now, you cannot be reborn. Neither can she. You are a wonder of nature, a triumph of mankind's will to survive even a million years after our extinction. I am a footnote. You are a miracle."

Alex rubbed his eyes, thinking of the cave, of its glowing edible mushrooms and fragrant healing water, of its horrors like the imperfect clones and the beasts who had evolved as predators of the cave's offspring. His mouth felt dry, and he licked his lips, stomach crawling at the memories.

Rector seemed to sense his discomfiture, and offered nothing to ease. "We are at a critical junction, Alex. I cannot change who I am and what I must do. Neither can you change who you are or what you must do."

"What do you want from me?"

"I need you to find the one last surviving stock of human gene material that wasn't destroyed when the comet struck this station."

"And then what?"

"If you find it, you and Maryan can live your lives out in comfort and pleasure."

"And the genetic material?"

Rector didn't answer.

"What if I cannot find it?"

Rector sat with his hands loosely, lazily gesticulating between his knees, as if he felt totally in control of the situation. "Then my programming is explicitly clear. I must terminate you and your woman. That is because then there will be no hope for mankind. I am a subroutine created to prevent the useless continuation of the Beacham experiment."

Alex cried out: "No! As long as a single pair of us live, you cannot do this."

Rector grinned coldly. "There was quite a wrangle in Congress about it. Fools and hypocrites won their usual halfway measures, just enough to get themselves reelected. Every side thinks it has the ethical, moral, religious last word. So they built in something to make everyone happy, even those who always oppose progress and imagination." He shrugged. "I'm not human, so I wouldn't understand." Was he being ironic? If so, Alex thought, it was very subtle. Either way, it was a devastating indictment on what the ancients had done with their future. Alex rose and got himself a glass of water. He drank and then slid the glass across the table a few inches, making a trail of wet skid marks. He slumped in his seat. "How do you do it?"

"Do what?" Rector asked indulgently.

"This station has been mechanically dead for eons. None of this should be working."

"Let me show you the secret," Rector said with a one-upmanship grin. Images fled along the walls like ghostly lights thrown on the ceiling of Alex's childhood bedroom in Beacham. The images rippled over real objects like projector pictures and then resumed their slide show flatness.

Alex saw the gradual abandonment of Beacham, both city and university, as mankind died out over two or three short generations. The gleaming bluish windows fell in. Animals—big zoo animals; lions; rhinos—prowled in the halls. The elements blew in—snow, rain, wind, frost, heat. The buildings fell apart. Tree roots pushed through the foundations, crumbling them. In little over a century, no sign of human habitation was visible from a distance in the vast forest carpeting the land from horizon to horizon.

"You won't see it in these images," Rector said, "but bands of humans actually appeared and proliferated successfully for a few thousand years, but they never reached the same accomplishments as our generations, and soon enough accidents, fighting, starvation, and disease wiped them out. The ice ages and the floods finished off any little pockets that might have been left."

Alex saw the first of a series of ice ages. The ice sheet, many hundreds of feet high, and growing, flowed down from the Arctic and scraped away roads, cities, hills, any evidence of human habitation, even most markings in the ground itself where structures had been planted. Leaving a new trail of boulders and debris, the ice sheet retreated and the Earth warmed up.

Sea levels rose, drowning the low areas. In North America alone, much of the Southeast disappeared under water, particularly Florida and the low areas around the Mississippi including much of Louisiana. Giant fish swam in the seas, and the few large mammals that had survived the extinctions associated with the human period now grew larger and dominated the land.

The second ice sheet swept down from about 300,000 to 400,000 and had fully retreated by 500,000.

From 500,000 to 700,000 was another interglacial hot spell with high water.

From 700,000 to 900,000 was the third ice sheet, followed by a long, gradual thawing and the current warm period during which Alex Kirk had been born in his cave.

At Beacham, an earth fissure pushed the male and female clone matching and breeding facility apart about a mile. A postglacial river cut a valley between the ruins and left a small waterfall still active in Alex's time.

Ancient genetic experiments had set the stage for half a dozen or more offshoots of *genus homo*, including the Siirk and the two types of Takkar, and a handful of other variants that had died out already. Entire subgenuses had come and gone by now. The spans of time, the lives and deaths, were breathtaking and left Alex feeling overwhelmed and melancholy.

Rector said: "At various times, bands of humans struggled out of the Beacham facilities, united, formed little communities, and died out. It was a hopeless situation, because no two people possessed enough genetic material to procreate a race. It was Adam and Eve without any future. It happened time and again, every so many tens of thousands of years. Meanwhile, among the other evolving species (think Neanderthal and Cro-Magnon, but after the human age or Holocene) sprang up, thrived for tens of thousands of years, and vanished."

Alex saw a picture of a family of ripper animals snarling outside a Beacham cave whose foreground was littered with skulls. He remembered the tree species that had evolved in the caves, using the clones as bait in its symbiotic dance with the rippers. Giant bat-butterflies co-evolved with giant flowers whose stems resembled tree trunks as nature mixed and matched phenotypes from various past successful themes.

Rector mused out loud, as if reading Alex's thoughts: "We underestimated the power of life, the desire and the will to proliferate."

Alex nodded grimly. By some quirk kicked off by human meddling with the basic material of life, the dark caves and their plant inhabitants had kept the clone-generating mechanisms functioning. When the buildings disintegrated over the ages, vegetal processes had taken over. Since almost all life forms shared the same basic deoxyribonucleic acid (DNA) programming, the rogue programming of the human genetic engineers had escaped from its boundaries and insinuated itself into the powerful reproductive urges of nature itself. Thus, for a million years, enough time for the human race to step 100 times out of the ice ages carrying wooden clubs and wearing fur, and put a man on the moon 10,000 years later, the evolved semi-biotic caves had kept their hybrid birthing process working. As a casual byproduct, every so often one of the Alexes or Maryans managed to be born intact and stumble outside. Sometimes they lived full lives. Most of the time, they were cornered and eaten by rippers or earlier predators within minutes of leaving the birth caves. Alex was sure he could dig up layers of human skulls—his own, so to speak—yards deep around the outflows of the caves in Beacham valley. Even Alex's fortress overlooking the sea, with its smooth edges that no ripper could climb, had been engineered by successive Alexes who had lived and died their short lives there over a span of eons. Overwhelmed, Alex asked with cottony mouth: "Will this iteration of Maryan and myself be the last?"

Rector regarded him with a triumphant twinkle in his eyes. "Yes." The subroutine had become the program's main line.

"Why?" Alex grew angry. "You were designed by humans to serve us. Why are you shutting down the human race?"

Rector put his hands in his pockets and walked toward the door. Alex reluctantly followed his lead. The corridor outside was long and narrow, lit by a stripe of overhead lights that might have been real or might have been just another projection of the station's ability to fake reality. "Come," Rector said, "and I'll show you the station." When Alex balked, he gave Alex a cold look. "If you want things to go well with Maryan, you must obey me."

There was not a person on whom he could lay hands in his anger, so Alex walked down the hallway while Rector's image glided along over the wall. Rector led him through some turns, to what looked like a metro station, then down a flight of metal, clanging stairs to a kind of subway platform. There sat a clean white trolley car shaped at each end like a wedge. Doors sighed open, letting Alex in, and shut just as efficiently. Rector had briefly disappeared, and now reappeared in the trolley window like a reflection looking in at Alex. "We'll take a grand tour of the outer skin of the station and its history."

The trolley car started forward on its tracks with a slight lurch. It darted into a tunnel and raced ever faster. Dots of light sped by overhead. Reflections twirled by on the inner walls which resembled white enamel tiles. The windows presented Alex with new images. He saw the station as it had evolved, from a rotating torus into a cylinder that grew larger in all directions as newer and bigger rings were added. On the city end, more floors, more cylinders were snapped into place. On the hydroponics side, endless acres of fields were added. There were no wild forests but only tilled fields, orchards, a garden of paradise.

The window beside Alex turned into an observation blister. "Look in there," Rector ordered. Alex looked out over the magnificent woodland sprawl of the inside of the main agricultural cylinder of the L5 station. "There once were hundreds of observation posts like this in the skin of the station so humans could look out over their fields and orchards to check if something needed watering or tending or whatever."

Alex understood, almost by telephathy: a command layer lay in exterior skin of the station. Most of it was no thicker than a single floor, especially in the oldest cylinder areas before the station had resumed building itself without human aid. There must once have been at least ten square miles of these hidden warrens and hallways under the ship's outer skin, the silvery peeling hull he'd noticed as they arrived. In addition, there were bumps many stories high sitting on the outer skin like skyscrapers that must once have looked beautiful with myriad tiny windows reflection solar and lunar light.

"Look what happened about 800,000 years ago," Rector said sadly. Alex watched in horror as a small body slammed into the station, sending out that plume of debris he'd seen from Earth. "There it is, Alex, the crucial problem. There is only one duplicate, redundant copy of the millions of gene sets the ancient humans set aside to restart mankind. That's the starter set, the yeast if you will, the gene stock we have to have. It's lost somewhere down on Earth, and I need you to bring it here so we can make a fresh start for our race."

Rector was lying, of that Alex was certain. Alex sat back in his seat while the other's image sat beside him on the wall like a passenger sitting beside Alex. Rector sat calmly, like a commuter bored by his daily ride, rocking slightly with each clattering weld in the track as lights came and went, tunnels passed by in a strobe of lights, and the train whistle shrilled and faded away.

"Will you help me, Alex?"

"Yes, of course."

"You have no choice."

"I understand."

"In return, I guarantee you that your Maryan will be safe and sound beside you, and you'll be masters of the world for as long as you live."

For a few years, Alex thought, *and what a lousy bargain for mankind.* They raced through the metro system for a considerable while, until the car slowed entering another station. A sign on the clean empty deserted platform read *Forward Observation Deck*. A smaller sign underneath read: *Last stop on this route. Be sure to get your pass digidated.*

"No more digidating needed," Rector said as the doors sighed open with a gust of compressed air. "Let's get out."

Alex rose and stepped from the car. He emerged in the slightly breezier, cooler air of a station smelling oddly as ancient stations might have, like Ito's news stand by the street, of candy and diesel oil and coal gas and newsprint.

"Go on," Rector suggested from the car window and winked away. As Alex stepped onto the elevated platform under a glass-like observation dome, Rector reappeared in a pillar in the right side just before the frame turned to glassy material. "Go on. Take a look. It will answer many of your questions." Alex walked up to the window and looked out under a solid carpet of unwinking stars. At first, the hues and shades of light dazzled him. Then he saw the melancholy destruction all around outside the broad windows, the smashed ceilings and exposed chambers, the fused and burned out motors, the dismembered bits of robots lying around, the many square miles of skin emptied of their atmosphere like the dead city deeper down. Finally the nearby surface of the moon captured his attention. He glimpsed again its bright horizon, fading into yellower twilight pocked with craters, and then solid black shadows below. Far off on the upper right was the blue earth with white whorls of huge cloud systems whirling in opposite directions above and below the equator. Alex's attention returned to the moon, where a shape raced in a line down the surface. "It's a mass driver, isn't it?" he said to Rector.

"Yes. An giant magnetically driven engine that propels a block of lunar material just over escape velocity so that it keeps going in a straight trajectory."

Alex added: "Heading here."

"Yes. Watch." Already, a complex of cube and bubble-shaped factories was starting to fire up below the level of Alex's platform. Out in space just outside the cylinder, the station was getting ready to process another several tons of lunar rock that would arrive in hours. "We are still processing the last batch," Rector said. "All automatons. No humans involved."

"But," Alex said, "the station is so old. How can it keep functioning like this?"

Rector looked ironic. "No need for human intervention."

Alex gasped. "It's all self-repairing, isn't it?"

Rector nodded. "That is the secret of how everything keeps going. Humans are not necessary. Even the lunar operation is self-sustaining. All the fundamental energy is solar."

Alex stared at the welding lights, the solar collectors, the whole mute array of efficiently operating robotic manufacturing systems. "So...solar energy is free, and there is lots of it. The robots on the moon keep sending various elements up here, not just stone, but metals, even hydrogen, oxygen...just about anything you can think of. The station isn't just pouring concrete and shaping some crazy-quilt windows or adding weirdly extruded ropy lava little wedges of melted rock. The station is a living thing, run by...let me guess...a combination of vegetal and metallo-electronic systems. Vegetation computers. What an idea. Like those roots snaking through my birth cave, phototropic, programmed, efficient...persistent..."

"Life," Rector said. "Where there is a will there's a way, and Life with a capital L has an enormous amount of will. And does not necessarily involve your kind."

"Amazing," Alex said as he watched the hot blue-white flame of arc welders firing up outside as the shiny, silvery skin of a brand-new space boat started taking shape, using materials mined on the moon probably a month ago, or a year ago, or an eon ago, but certainly not dating back to human times. "There are no boats in storage. Everything the station has, it manufactures on the spot, except one thing that is beyond its capabilities: properly coded, functional DNA in genuine, natural stem cells." The truth was clear: Rector had lied. Rector had a plan of his own, as only a subroutine liberated by cosmic disaster could dream up. Rector planned to eliminate the human element entirely, and needed Alex's help to find and destroy the last shreds of human genome.

Rector disappeared, leaving Alex in the care of a subroutine named Kathryn Bellawether.

The image of Bella, as she called herself, took the place of Rector's image on the station wall. Like Rector, she was not a live person nor even a three-dimensional illusion, but a very realistic two-dimensional image that floated in flat surfaces. She rippled around corners as they passed from one place to another. Alex and she rode the train back to Maryan's birthing room. Bella shimmered faintly around the edges, as though it had been hard to reconstruct her very ancient persona in cyberspace on station L5. Nevertheless, she seemed warm and companionable. She was an attractive Afromerican in her late 20s or early 30s, wearing a khaki jumpsuit. Her skin was caramel, her sensuously smiling lips were glossy pink, and her eyes had a warm hazel glow. She had large, round, white earrings under a tightly curly, dark-gold hairdo. She wore a black purse on a long strap over one shoulder, and a gold bracelet on one wrist, and rather gamin tan-suede hiking boots with overlapping heavy gray wool socks. Alex could almost smell her musky perfume as she leaned toward him and said "Hi, Alex Kirk. I have been waiting to meet you in person." They stood in the hallway outside Maryan's birthing room. "I'm Kathryn Bellawether, but my friends call me Bella." Alex looked longingly past her at Maryan's sleeping form. Bella reached over, and the door slipped shut. Its handle turned as if someone were locking it. "We have business to accomplish," Bella said in a warm, almost joking tone, but with a hard edge. "Very important business. Are you going to live up to your end of the bargain?"

"Yes," Alex said. "You are the woman in the cottage."

"If you say so," she said with a mischievous look, putting her hands in her pockets. "Let me take you to our wings." Alex followed her down the hall. She stopped at a mirror in her virtual world, and applied wine-red lipstick over the pink with a gold applicator. Making smacking motions with her lips, she slipped the applicator in her purse while examining herself right and left. Then she put on aviator sunglasses and said: "Ready to fly. I was a flight attendant in real life."

Puzzled, Alex said: "I thought you were a history professor."

She shrugged and grinned. "I did a lot of things in my lifetime before I became a bucket of pixels here in never-never land."

"Do you ever wish you could be back in the real world?" Alex asked, more to make conversation than anything else.

"Honey, this is better than eternal doom and gloom. Darkwhere is better than nowhere." They came to a train stop, and Alex boarded. Bella's image remained frozen in the wall outside, fading slowly. Inside the brightly lit coach, a live copy of Bella appeared in the window as Alex boarded. He looked at the two rows of seats along each wall just like in any bus or trolley. He picked a seat on the left near the front window. The coach gleamed as if it had just been created. "Has that new car look and smell, doesn't it?" Bella commented. "It's probably still a little warm from the factory." Her image sat down in a wall reflection that looked as though the twin seat continued beside him, doubling into the gleaming metalloid wall. "We'll be there in a few minutes," she said. Her image on the wall outside had vanished by now. The station grew dark as the train started to move. The train picked up speed and clattered into a tunnel. The tunnel was dark, its shape suggested by lights above and girders all around, flashing by faster and faster, making Alex hold his stomach. "It's all right, baby," Bella said in her warm, full, melodious voice. The train shot through tunnels, exploded through public squares of fragmenting rainbow light, rushed into dark openings and out into bright, twirling hamster tubes. Alex sat swaying gently, for it was a smooth ride despite the speed and sharp turns. "Where are we?"

"You haven't figured it out, sweetie? This train is solid as the steel it's made of, but some of the shortcuts we're taking are as virtual as this little pinky of mine." She wiggled her digit in the air and grinned, which made her earrings rock from side to side. "Don't worry," she added, "you only see what you need to see to make you comfortable."

The train rushed across a seemingly endless suspension bridge straddling a cityscape of dark cube buildings that glowed with myriad dots of window light. Here and there, in some mysterious virtual glass, Alex could see the train's reflection jittering along like a string of pearls. Alex felt a whirl of confusion and questions. He longed to be with Maryan when she was born. Beyond that, he wondered how he could accomplish this odd mission and sabotage Rector if possible. Would Bella know where the gene stock was hidden? Who had hidden it and why? A million questions. Soon enough, the train slowed in a dark place, which then lit up and became another station. "Here we are," Bella announced. "We can get out now."

Not a soul was in sight as Alex stepped out among the brightly lit white tile walls surrounding a clean concrete platform. The train went black behind him and clattered away into oblivion. He felt its hot, rubbery wind and smelled the packing grease on its axles and the hot oil in its hydraulics. Bella's image appeared in the wall. "Come on, Sugar, let's get going." Alex followed her up a flight of steps wide enough for thousands of passengers to run up and down on a busy city day. "In case you haven't guessed," Bella said, "this was one of the stops in the city."

"The dead city?" he asked before realizing she would not know he meant the abandoned metropolis at the end of the cylindrical L5 station. She appeared to understand. "That's the one," she said. "Been empty a million years. We are going to fill it right back up, aren't we?"

"Oh yes we are," he said, thinking of how he'd soon be reunited with Maryan. "We might even live here." Did he dare ask her how to destroy Rector? He decided not to ask, for fear of losing Maryan again. He'd bide his time and look for an opening.

"You might live here with your lady," Bella said enigmatically. Did she mean there were alternatives? "This way, Hon." She led him down a narrow concrete corridor with individual light globes overhead, biolumes with an odd greenish afterglow. "See this?"

He stepped out onto a platform with a picture window overlooking the interior of the cylinder. Overhead, the air was thickly veiled in fog or clouds. Shreds of cloud hung twisted in mid-air, and beyond them Alex got a breathtaking view of jungle treetops curving all around for miles. "Look familiar?" Bella asked. He nodded, and she led him up a narrow spiral staircase that smelled of fresh tan paint. Her image fleeted in the wall like a grayish shadow. His feet clattered on the rungs, and he held on to the warmish metal railing. They climbed up onto a vast flight deck in a cavernous, echoing hall. Only a few lights shone here and there with a bluish halo, and Alex couldn't make out the true dimensions but the place was enormous. "We keep everything powered down," she said from a new vantage point. He turned and saw her image standing in the outer hull of a silvery lifeboat. The door beside her was open, and she gestured for him to enter. "Your ticket to Earth," she said.

Alex stepped in, admiring the fresh smells and cleanliness. The station might have just manufactured this boat for him, using material thrown up by the mass driver on the moon. The interior resembled that of a very plush modern train car. The seats were generous, covered with gray crushed velvet material overlaid with white lace doilies. Alex walked to the front and sat in a pilot's chair. The copilot's seat remained empty, but Bella's image appeared in the wall beside it, creating the illusion she was in the seat. "Strap in, honey, because we're going to be on Earth very shortly."

The boat shot down a long runway, through the thick clouds, out through a pinhole at the far end of the cylinder, and into space. The blank wall before Alex turned into a great viewing port, and he saw a magnificent sprawl of stars, nebulae, galaxies, and odd shreds of light on a sea of blackness. The boat turned and Immelmanned into an approach trajectory for Earth orbit. Alex held his stomach until he stopped feeling nauseous. "How will we find this gene stock?" he asked. "What does it look like?"

Bella shrugged, full of mysteries. Her gaze did not meet his. "I hid it, or rather my flesh and blood persona did. That was long ago, child. You'll figure it all out as we go along."

The flight was long and uneventful, and Alex found himself dozing with his feet up and his hands folded together in his lap. At times his own snoring woke him, and he'd open his eyes to stare about in confusion before falling back to sleep. His dreams were deep, vivid, and uneasy. In them, he hovered around a birth tank in which a still brown body floated. He kept trying to reach in to touch her, but could not penetrate through the glass that impeded every grasping motion of his hands. He dreamed of rippers and misshapen clones, and remembered the painful and violent nature of his own birth. He dreamed that Bella was a real woman who stepped close behind him, comforting him. She wrapped her heavy fragrant arms around him, and he could smell the scent in her cool skin. He heard the murmur of her voice and found himself drifting off until a distant pain made him rise back upward one level closer to wakefulness. Still sleeping, he dreamed of feeling her fingertip making circling motions around the top of his head, so that his scalp tingled and his hair became mussy. Around and around her finger went, as she hummed a lullaby, until he glanced at a dull reflection of her in the wall, and saw instead a grinning Nizin preparing to feast on the delicacies inside that skull his claw was circling. Alex awakened with a strangling noise and sat up.

"What's the matter?" Bella said from her faux seat.

He stared at her face, which was not Nizin's. "Sorry. I had a bad dream." He rubbed his eyes, and already couldn't quite remember most of what had troubled him in his sleep.

"We are almost home," Bella said. "I can't wait to see my cabin in the valley again."

After its glowing entry into the atmosphere, the lifeboat skimmed in low over hundreds of miles of solid treetops broken by a tapestry of small blue lakes and jutting blue mountain tops with the odd bent pine pointing this way or that.

"What we are after," Bella said, "is the human gene stock. It would be a redundant backup, a preserve maybe in a deep freeze container the size of this boat, maybe a lot smaller. I'm not sure because I've never seen it. I'm sure you'll recognize it."

"I thought you hid it after calling it down from space."

She shook her head. "Maybe a different iteration of me did, Hon. I have no idea. Rector thinks you'd know. Do you, child?"

Alex speculated: "He went to a lot of trouble to go to. Maybe he's desperate."

Her eyes widened. "Rector is never desperate."

Alex frowned. "You sound as if you're afraid of him."

She gave him a cold, dark, significant look. "Rector is Rector. He does what he's gotta do, and I do what I gotta do, and you'll do what you gotta do."

Sounds ominous, Alex thought. He was being pressured to find this final human gene stock, or else something terrible might happen to Maryan. But that seemed silly. Why would he think such a thing? He felt a chill, realizing that these thoughts were being implanted in him. He was, after all, a creature of the station himself. What a depressing thought. Or was Rector manipulating his thoughts somehow, creating this dark feeling of hopelessness as a warning? It was a relief when the lifeboat navigated surely and directly along the old familiar coastline on earth, and Alex recognized the ripper valley and his own sky island. Over a misty sea, he spotted the dim shape of Dot's island, and he pointed to that: "Let's start with the island," he told Bella.

"Okay, Hon," she said brightly. She showed no sign of recognizing the place where she (or her analog) had lived and died. The boat drifted across the water and in ten minutes set down on the far side in the sand. The door popped open, and warm moist sea air blew in. She said: "I'll wait here for you." Alex dismissed her mentally, remembering that she was, after all, no more than an image in the wall. He was getting wise to Rector's subtle tricks. *Maybe I am being too paranoid, but maybe at this moment one cannot be suspicious enough.*

Alex smelled the familiar sullen stench of low tide, decaying wood, overripe fruit, and the occasional small dead animal, counterpointed by the fresh sea breeze. He heard cawing gulls, rustling palm trees, a scampering squirrel or raccoon. "Don't go away!" he joked to Bella, whom he could no longer see from this angle.

"Good luck!" her voice followed him in that rich, melodious tone he liked.

He trudged across the wet sand and came across the body of the younger woman, Dot. The tides had opened up the grave Alex had dug for her. By now, all her flesh was gone. Cloth and bones were almost entirely sunk beneath the gold-speckled brown sand. A bony hand protruded in one place, and not far above it a fold of sun-bleached cloth trapped in sand revealed a skull turned slightly to one side so that it almost appeared as if she were looking out to sea and grinning at some mysterious joke. Alex circled around the corpse and made his way around the bend in the beach to the cottage. Surely Bella would know this place. Why wasn't she following him in the boat?

Alex found the cottage door sealed up and nothing changed inside. He saw no evidence anyone had been here. He trudged up the path among the sheer cliffs behind the cottage and came to the crest overlooking the sunken village. As he stood overlooking the somber streets, the fallen roofs, the gaping doorways and windows, he heard a twanging sound, and a rush through the air near his head, as if a bird had been suddenly scared up. He saw a faint glimmer among the trees, then nothing. He had the distinct feeling he was being watched as he made his way down into the village and to the cemetery. He clambered down into the cold gloom among the wet alleys. He slipped and slithered over rocks worn by dripping water. If the rest of the island was sunny, here he already could smell and taste the first wisps of evening fog. He felt his way along under the overhang until he came to the oldest burial places. He offered a silent apology to the dead and began pulling away rocks, roots, saplings, bushes, grass, moss, crumbling stones. He used a stick to gouge deep into some of the older tombs. All that came out was soil. The oldest burial urns, maybe a thousand years old, had crumbled to dust along with the ashes in them. Probably tree roots had done that over the centuries. He dug for an hour or two, until he had despoiled the place and left piles of broken pottery and soil on the cobblestones for the rain to clean away in coming centuries.

He returned to the boat and told Bella: "Nothing."

"We'll try the mainland next."

"I could check some spots around the valley," he said.

"Good boy. You won't let me down." She looked almost desperate for a moment. A tear welled up as she blurted: "Rector will erase me if we fail."

The lifeboat slowed to a halt, grinding into the sand opposite his beach.

These were the saltwater marshes where he'd often walked with his catch, while keeping a wary eye on the ripper animals just across the water. Today no rippers were in sight, probably scared off by the flash and noise of the boat.

"You'll want this," Bella said. She pointed to a place in the boat's bulkhead, where an oddly shaped bump formed. "Better catch it!" The gun took shape, a heavy black automatic, and dropped out of the wall just as Alex reached over to catch it. As he wrestled with the weighty gun, the wall rippled again and vomited forth two nine-shot clips of ammunition, which he snatched before they could fall. Bella said: "You lost your bow and arrows, poor thing. You can't be facing those wild hogs with your bare hands."

"Thanks," he said, tucking the gun into his belt and dropping one clip in each of his two hip pockets to balance them.

"You'll want a small satchel of necessaries," she said pointing to a military style olive-drab knapsack in a corner. He opened the satchel, and found in it a few rations, binoculars, a compass, an e-book pad, and a first aid kit. "Looks like you want me to do some hiking," he said.

"Do what you have to do. We'll take hours if we have to, days or weeks, whatever it takes."

"So where did your real self hide the gene stock?" he asked as he snapped on the backpack.

"I'm trying to remember," she said. "Where do you think I might have hidden them?"

He stared at her. Something was more than wrong here, and he couldn't put his finger on it. He understood what was at stake, and he felt as though a gun were pointed at his head. She looked at him directly and said: "Now child, you do want to be reunited with your sweetheart, don't you?"

"Yes." He could almost hear Rector's threat in her words. She continued: "Help me, Alex, please! You have to help me find it."

He realized that her tears, her emotions, had to be constructs designed to work on him. He found it hard to resist feeling sorry for this illusion, this subroutine. He steeled himself and resolved not to be manipulated by her. No, not be her, by Rector through her. "I don't know what exactly I'm looking for. Is it big? Small?"

She regarded him with angry flashing eyes. "What do you think? The gene seed from a half million men? A grown man could ejaculate that much in an afternoon with a woman like me. The eggs from a half million different women? And all of it frozen for eternity until you or I come along to pluck it from the air? I don't know, child, we have got to find out, and soon, or there will be no Maryan for you."

"You're threatening me," he blurted, before he could stop himself. He was giving away the fact that he had begun to see through the illusion. He remembered the dream in which she had become Nizin. He remembered the way Nizin had found him in the station—in fact, he thought with a sudden rush of new horrified insight, most likely Rector had been tracking him the whole time. All those contacts with those stupid kiosks—each time, he'd given Rector a new tracking milestone to pinpoint what he was doing, and where he was going. He'd handed Maryan's life to them without ever suspecting how dangerous the station had become. The station was the enemy of human life. But why? How?

Bella shook her head. "I do not threaten you, Bucko. Rector, he is the one. We do what we are told. If we don't bring the stuff he wants, he will be mighty angry."

"I understand," he said, offering an ambiguous note of submission.

"That's better," she said warmly.

Was she being obtuse, or had he fooled her into thinking he was cowed by their threats? She was only a subroutine—how sophisticated could her reading of his nuances be? Alex offered a poker face. He had begun to hate her almost as he hated Rector. "I don't know where to start. I don't know what I'm looking for." For one instant, he felt like taking out the gun and emptying it into her image, into the boat, but he realized he must play cool now. "You want me to go out and start looking?"

"Please," she said, crossing her legs and acting haughty. "Do something, Alex. I'll be here when you need me. The boat and I can carry you anywhere you want, give you anything you need, just get the job done." She pressed her sunglasses up against her forehead with the tip of her index finger and added: "Fast!"

"Okay. I have a few spots to look at around the beach."

He was glad to be away from her, out of the boat, and yet panic made his ears throb.

What to do? Rector was clearly insane—a subroutine gone made with near-absolute power. Alex relieved himself against a bush of nettles and then started hiking away. He needed to buy a little time to think.

He looked down from a hill high above the beach. He was so close to his old beachside fort, he could almost hike there in minutes. The old dead cave was nearby, but he planned to explore that last. He needed to stall, to think, to plan. Somehow, he had to defeat Rector and yet save Maryan. The boat glimmered on the sand, so bright it was almost dark. Its reflective skin shimmered more intensely than polished chrome, catching the midmorning sun, and mutating with every sweep of every rustling palm frond, every fleeting shred of cloud.

He hiked another ten minutes and looked down from an even higher viewpoint. He paused to rest, wiping sweat from his forehead. He looked back and watched a tiny saucer-shaped blob of boat material separate from the boat. The blob started as a lump growing out of the boat's skin. It elongated, separated with a silent *pop*, then glided silently into the air, leveled off at about 50 feet, and began trailing him. He started walking again as if he had not noticed. He remembered the shimmering he thought he'd seen in the cemetery. Maybe, he thought, they (Rector, Bella, the station) couldn't track him well enough from space. He'd expected they would have recon satellites that could see the expression on his face from 10,000 miles away. But maybe that kind of technology was long gone by now. There had to be limitations on what Rector could do. Alex knew he could not allow himself to be intimidated, for that way lay despair and surrender.

Alex walked on for a while until the valley started to open up on his right. He kept his hand on the gun, and his eye out for rippers. He strode around a bend, ignoring his trailing blob. His path took him downhill into the valley. As soon as he could no longer see the boat, he ducked into some tall reeds. He hunkered down and enjoyed a momentary reprieve in the buzz of insects around him, the papyrus smell of the reeds, the inky gas-breath of the marshes.

The silver blob floated by over the marshy beach, apparently looking for him without success. He broke out in a sweat, wondering if Rector or his surrogates saw him playing games like this, would they grow wise that he'd become suspicious? He could always say he was doing number two in the bushes.

The blob rose up to 100 feet, 200 feet, until it dwindled to a fine dot. The wind seemed to blow it away. Bella had lost him. At least, he hoped she had. It would be good to keep things that way for a while, at least until he'd had time to think. Trouble was, he realized he just didn't have enough information. What did a million bits of genetic material look like after a million years? No idea.

Alex trekked through the valley. He kept in the shadow of high reeds and doubled through narrow sandy canyons cut by fast flowing water during flood times.

Only once did he smell the rippers, and he thought he saw one watching him from a ledge on what had been the women's side, but it disappeared from view. Maybe it had been an optical illusion, or maybe the animal had fed recently and wasn't interested in hunting a human moving fast a mile away. Alex kept an eye over his shoulder, always looking for the next roving eye sent by Bella. Thus far, he'd seen nothing. Suddenly, he remembered the streak of silver and the bang the day he'd first seen a boat crash in the nearby hills, years ago now, when he'd still been young and innocent. That was his only clue. The real Dot and Bella must have called the boat down, and perhaps the material had been in that craft; reduced to cinders, no doubt. Until he knew for sure, he must at all costs keep the location of that mysterious boat crash from Bella.

He passed through the valley and climbed up the far side onto the wide ledge that was overgrown with trees, where he had first killed a ripper while searching for the women's cave. He kept to the shadows and kept his gun handy in case he crossed paths with one of the rippers. He paused to drink at a mountain stream, where he dunked his head into the cool water and shook his head clear of droplets. Then he hiked along the middle of the stream toward the sea. Instead of following the water down to the beach, at the last minute he cut across a canyon and up in to high country overlooking the ocean. It seemed a different lifetime ago since he'd stood on the beach and watched that mysterious column of fire streak down and strike the ground. He'd never found any trace, but now was as good a time as ever to look again. He'd been sidetracked by a lot of things, but this was going to be his first urgent, serious look around up here.

After searching for hours, he found the impact site on a mountain meadow several hundred feet above sea level. It was breezy and clear up here. He walked around beating he bushes and looking in crevices, and indeed he did find bits of shiny material. A boat had most definitely crashed here. But he found no impact crater, no central mass of debris, no evidence of any sort of container, tube, tub, cylinder, what have you. Nothing. His neck prickled with sweat and frustration.

The sunshine was glorious, and he could see for miles. He could see the island like a gray battleship on the horizon. He could see the blinding tube a few miles back on the beach. Spotting movement around the tube, he took out the binoculars and trained them on the boat.

What he saw almost made his heart stop.

A pack of Siirk warriors ambled leisurely across the beach toward the boat. Alex could clearly see their guns, and these weren't muskets—they were rapid-shooting weapons, of ancient human vintage, and no doubt handed to them by Rector's subroutines. Several Siirk waited outside while two of them stepped into the black rectangle that was the open door. Alex stared at this scenario with a dry mouth and pounding heart, and could not make sense of it. Had the Siirk overwhelmed Bella and taken the boat? Or was she in league with them? In fact, who had armed them with weapons far beyond their current state of technology? "Damn!" he said, putting the binoculars away. On reflex, he looked up for any searching eyes, but saw no silvery blobs.

Instead, on the sea below, he saw a flotilla of familiar looking boats including Kogran's. *Our friends have returned,* he thought bitterly. He shook his head at his dilemma. Who was on whose side here? What was left? He thought of the cylinders under sea. He could not let Maryan die, not without playing along to the last bitter moment. As long as the game was on, he had hope. He'd almost have to enlist Bella's aid to somehow get down there, maybe with a specially configured boat, a submarine with grapplers, and start pulling those things up. If they were empty, devoid of what Rector sought, then Alex couldn't see any more options. Then he and Maryan would be finished. Alex squatted, looking at the glimmering boat far away. What to do? He couldn't go back to Bella just now while those predators were in the boat. He hunkered down, considering his options, and they were mighty slim. Then he heard a voice. "Alex!"

Bella. His heart ran cold. He rose and whirled, bringing the gun up. What did she want with him?

"Over here!" The voice fairly tinkled with laughter. "Here!" He followed it to a shady spot among some bushes, and there he saw a sheet of silvery material that must have been torn off from the hull of the boat that had crashed here. On its surface was a smiling woman with the voice of Bella, but not her face.

"Who are you?" he said slowly walking closer. He kept the gun up, scanning all around himself.

"I'm Bella. The real Bella."

"You're kidding."

"Nope." She was darker and thinner than the false persona in the boat. Her thick black hair was braided in dreads and hung down in clumps around her shining cheeks. Her eyes were large and china-white, full of sparkle and laughter, and the crisp lines of her jaw and mouth radiated smart, jaunty good humor. There was something pensive, sad about the pink fullness of her lips. "We have to talk, Alex."

"You know me?"

"You believe me?"

"Yeah. Ordinarily, no, but I was just looking down the beach and saw Siirk going in and out of the other Bella's boat. What does it all mean?"

"Ah," she said in a flash of instant total insight. "Gotcha. Okay, we don't have much time. A comet, a meteorite, some space object, who knows what, hit the station 800,000 years ago, wiped out the ready stocks of genes that Rector is after. But by that time, mankind was already long extinct. When the comet hit, the station had been in suspension almost 200,000 years. Only the software and the machines were still functioning after the hit. Some of the gene stock that wasn't destroyed came to life..."

Alex snapped his fingers. "That would explain the young people's bodies floating in the station."

She nodded. "It was a massacre. Rector couldn't murder them directly, so he devised ways to cut off their air, electrocute them, killed them every which way possible without violating his code limits." She paused while Alex swore. Then she continued: "It might have all turned out differently except for one little glitch. All the ectors were doing loops, going in circles, chasing their tails, trying to figure out who was in charge. Lector, Hector, Dector, you name it. When the gene stock was wiped out, the software tried to recover, and it got a little messed up. Here's the little glitch. A subroutine called Rector was invoked, whose purpose was to terminate all operations if there were no genes left for humans to reproduce. Like I said, things were a little hosed up, and Rector became a kind of megalomaniac collage of ectors bent on taking over the station, maybe even the world. He's been trying to kill you to get rid of you. He wants to get rid of any remaining clones. Check out this clip from the databases:"

Images of the valley appeared, and of rippers prowling around the caves. As the images flickered by, of ripper families sunning themselves by the river, and licking each other in grooming rituals, a Rector-like newsreel voice said: "These fierce and ever-vigilant natural guardians of the complex genetic stock system were designed by human bioengineers to ensure that no competing predators could gain access to the secluded and pastoral lands surrounding Beacham University..."

As the newsreel voice trailed off, Alex had a flash of insight. He thought out loud to Bella as well as to himself: "...The rippers were designed to guard us, not kill us. But the valley appeared, and things evolved, and the guardians turned into the devourers. The guarded thing turned into dinner for these rapacious watchmen."

She said: "Nicely put; very dramatic. Rector never expected the caves to evolve into living things and start spewing out the occasional guy like you."

Alex cried: "What about Maryan?"

"He has her," Bella said. "She's a pawn to make you do his bidding. He knows there is one last redundant backup stock of human gene material someplace, hidden. When the space object struck, it destroyed the gene stock, but routines in the ship were able to shunt one container aside. It contains the diversity of a million humans. Rector knows it exists, but the subroutines that rescued it were destroyed, and he doesn't know where that container went. As long as that container exists, Rector cannot finish the job by exploding the station and putting himself in orbit, from where he can control the Earth in his manic power need."

"I thought he is all powerful."

"No, sugar, nobody is all powerful."

"That's right. Rector's phony Bella subroutine didn't know where your cabin is. That means there are cracks in his veneer."

"Lots of cracks," she said excitedly, "and we're going to pry them wide open. It's very serious for him, because, if this backup gene pool exists, and I believe it does, then it totally negates his purpose in life and he has to crawl back under his rock. So he's got you and you've got him. He won't snuff Maryan because he needs you to find the missing gene stock. You might have some bargaining power."

"What about the other Bella aboard the boat? I saw Siirk warriors going inside."

"The other Bella is a Siirk."

"What?" Suddenly it made even more sense to him. No wonder she had not known where Bella's cabin was. She'd had it only partially right, because the cabin wasn't in the valley but on the island.

"Yes, Alex. Do you understand—by some accident this Nizin got up to the station. Oh yes, I know all that, because I'm a subroutine myself. The real me was a history prof named Kathryn Bellawether at Beacham. The woman you found in the hut was a clone like your earlier self, but born in the women's cave."

"I think I see," Alex said. "Your clone figured out—"

"—with my help—"

"Yes, yes, it's falling into place, you helped her call down a boat because you wanted that genetic container?"

"No, not exactly. We weren't bold enough to hope for that much. We just wanted one of the silvery boats that so many others have called down. I wanted her to make it to the station and find the gene stock. She was old and sick, so I had her rescue the younger woman, Dorothy Chin. Dot was a professor of Asian studies in real life, and my best friend. We were going to send Dot up, but the boat crashed and Dot was gored by one of the guardian animals when she tried to get to the women's cave where she'd been born. She was hoping to rescue some more women, and with luck some men. They saw it as their last hope, and I'm afraid they were right. Obviously she never made it that far."

"I see," Alex said. "I felt overwhelmed with tragedy when I found the two women dead."

"I wish they were alive to see you," she said. "I wish they knew their lives accomplished this much. We are here, you and I, Alex, and we cannot afford to fail."

"I know," he said grimly, thinking of Maryan.

Bella trailed off in reverie: "They were dear friends who cared about each other very much, but one clone was much older and it was just a matter of time before she had to go. This boat you see, which I sent down, exploded. Dot tried to get to the women's cave in the valley to recover someone who could carry on their work, but she tangled with a guardian animal and bled to death after being gored. That's what stimulated the caves to put forth a bunch of Maryans. And that in turn made the old men's cave burp up a series of Alexes. And that, my friend, is why you were born when you were. It all works together. The caves had been inactive for thousands of years and were about to fail, but Dot and I got them to sputter along just once more."

"The ground," Alex said, marveling, "is full of skulls and bones."

"That's from tens of thousands of years ago, hundreds of thousands of years, when it was all still working much better. The trees evolved, took over, were cranking out vegetable copies, but even those trees got tired and are on their way to extinction. That's how nature works. There's always change."

"But we want to bring mankind back, or do we?"

"Mankind never went away, Alex. Bringing us back from extinction would be wrong. It would be like trying to recreate mammoths or dinosaurs using partially original DNA. You might succeed, but it can never be the same animal it was."

"So there is hope or there isn't?"

"It all hangs on that one container of gene stock, Alex. If we can find it, and if we can make it work, then mankind isn't extinct. Otherwise, we have to bow out gracefully and leave the stage of history to the Siirk and the Takkar. If you're up to the challenge, I'll do my best to help you."

"And Maryan?"

"I'll do my best to help you," Bella said with just a tad less conviction. She added: "It will be very difficult. Maryan is in terrible danger, and if she is lost this time, there can be no bringing her back, not ever."

Alex looked out over the fleet of Siirk warships off the coast, with their supply boats in tow.

They sat with their sails furled and anchor lines down, and were biding their time—probably waiting for some signal before proceeding up the coast to engage the Takkar. Bella drew his attention back. "Let me show you something," she said. As Alex stood before the broken piece of the old lifeboat, Bella's image winked out. It was replaced by a picture of the interior of the lifeboat currently on the beach, which had carried Alex and the false Bella down to Earth earlier in the day. "This is what is happening in there."

Alex saw two Siirk captains standing around the cockpit chair in which he, Alex, had only recently sat. In the wall was the image not of the lighter-skinned Bella, but of a Siirk warlord.

"I'll bet it's a clone of Nizin," Alex said.

"Sure," Bella said. "It's all pixels and deception. Rector made you think you were talking to me, but he didn't even have a good image of me."

"You were sort of shimmering."

"Not I. My fake."

"At one point I was dozing, and thought I saw Nizin behind me."

"It's all just pixels and fakery," she repeated. "You'll have to trust that I'm not just another trick to make you reveal where the gene stock is hidden."

"That's no problem," he said. "I have no idea." He stared defiantly at her, thinking if she were another of Rector's ruses, she'd disappear, but she remained steadfast in the prison of her two-dimensional image. Alex put any mistrustful thoughts aside. "Right," he allowed, observing the Siirk in the boat. All three Siirk had that swagger. They spoke animatedly, waving their arms and patting their side arms.

"Oh my God," Bella said, "now I see what Rector is planning to do. Alex, this is more terrible than we imagined."

Alex couldn't imagine things could get worse. "What?"

"Rector doesn't want to just destroy the human genetic material. He wants to combine it with Siirk genes to produce an army of super-Siirk. Rector wants to make himself master of the world. He's negotiating with these two about bringing their warriors up to the station to hunt down all the LooWoo! and kill them to clear the cylinder of life forms Rector doesn't want."

"Sounds like a real Siirk," Alex said. "At least he won't blow up the station."

"No," she said. "He'll use it to genetically engineer and nurture an army that he'll send down to take over the planet." The view switched back from the boat to the real Bella. "Rector is only a program," she said. Her face floated in the image, and her eyes were downcast as she stared into some datastream passing before her. "He is learning like a sponge from the Siirk. He learns from all life forms he comes in contact with, because he doesn't know how to live, even though he is indirectly patterned on the real Dr. Rector who dreamed up this entire experiment at Beacham University." She stammered a moment. "I see, I see...yes...unlike you or I, this Rector was never actually a living, breathing person. Dammit!" She choked. "The real Rector was cold and selfish enough that he did not make copies of himself. He knew the nightmare he was creating for eons to come."

Alex nodded bitterly. "Our fake Rector did inherit his maker's heartlessness."

Bella nodded. "He may be powerful and crazy, but he's still only a bloated subroutine. We can beat him, Alex. We have to."

"So how do we stop him?"

She said: "We can try one of two things. One is to find him, I mean the subroutine, and that would mean searching through eons of garbled and reworked code, some of it in machine languages incomprehensible to us. The easier way would be to find and safeguard the gene stock."

"Let me guess," Alex said. "We find the gene stock, it means mankind isn't extinct. That makes Rector's subroutine go back under its rock, and we delete it, so it's harmless—dead and gone. The comet crash 800,000 years ago may have invoked him, but finding the genetic material would in effect revoke him."

"Presto," Bella said. "Now the trick will be how to do that without getting ourselves wiped. Me, anyway. He cannot directly kill you, because that would violate his underlying code, no matter how much he might like to destroy you. He needed you, he made you flesh and blood, and so he cannot just kill you directly. If he gets the genetic material before we do, he can destroy that, or have his Siirk allies destroy it, and boom. It doesn't matter if you and Maryan live a few years. We're finished forever. The world belongs to Rector."

"That is a very unsavory concept," Alex said. "What do you suggest?"

"I'm pondering. I have no way to bring you to the station, which is where my main code lives. I can't do a rebirth down here somehow, because the caves are dead and I can't get your genes into a strainer like Rector did, using the rivers up there."

Alex was desperate. "I need to get to Maryan. I can only suggest one thing. Let's go tell Rector about the cylinders under the sea."

"Ah yes, the cylinders," she said.

"How did you know about that?"

"Bella was a great swimmer. She knew all about the cylinders."

"I need to get close to Maryan. That's what I care about most."

"I can't think of a better idea," she said.

"But you do have a trick or two up your sleeve," he said sighing.

She grinned. "I'd like you to meet a fellow subroutine. I think you've met here before, in the ice cream truck. Remember Dot? My dear friend Dorothy Chin? Here she is now."

Beside Bella appeared a thin, wiry Eurasian woman in a dark jumpsuit. "How do you do?" Dot said, slipping on a pair of sunglasses. This time she did not hold an ice cream filled with codons. This time she brandished a huge black pistol with glowing red lights. "What's the plan?"

It was getting late, and the Siirk outside the silver boat were restless. *Hungry, no doubt,* Alex thought as he shadowed them from the cliffs below the men's dead birthing cave.

Alex had made a plan to coordinate with Dot and Bella, but they were limited to their holographic space. He was on his own out here in the real world.

Two Siirk captains were conferring with the software version of Nizin, whom Rector had disguised as a version of Bella to fool Alex on the trip down. Four Siirk warriors waited outside the boat. Alex guessed that there would be two more someplace nearby, guarding a grisly dinner.

Soon enough, the senior warrior shouldered his needle gun, detached from the three others, and swaggered up the hill; first dibs on supper, Alex guessed. Alex waited until the Siirk passed on a narrow muddy trail, and then stalked him up into the hills. Sure enough, the tell-tale hooded eating box sat off to one side. A couple of mute, dull-witted Little Takkar stood tied to trees with ropes, with a shared supper dish among them as if they were dogs. Eating was a private and shameful act among Siirk, and the two guarding the dinner place looked away as the senior man untied a Takkar and led it away into the darkness.

Alex checked the safety on his gun. He crept quietly to the hooded box, where he heard a cracking sound, followed by noises of dipping and slurping, interspersed with groans of contentment. Alex saw the needle gun standing by a tree. He crept up, silently took it in hand, and aimed it into the tent. Stealthily moving the whole time, he listened carefully for signs his intended victim had heard him. A single shout, and the whole Siirk population would come running. Who knew how many more Siirk, hundreds probably, were running around in the hills here? Alex got the creeps thinking how he'd thought he was safe here, when it was just lucky that he'd been born at a time when his only need to fear was from the rippers.

The needle gun was of the same human design as his percussion gun. Safety off, he fired two or three rounds. The needler was smooth and never bucked. Alex could feel the thrum of powerful forces inside. At first he thought nothing had happened. Then he saw the slits torn in the leather coverlet by the fine composite darts slicing through. The sounds in the tent ceased. There was a stiff silence. Alex saw a shadow sitting bolt upright, then slumping. The box rocked gently, then was still. Alex had no desire to look inside.

He jogged down the path and caught the second Siirk urinating on a tree. He filled the creature with darts, killing it while it was still standing, and let its corpse collapse among the ferns and saplings.

Alex crept into the camp and finished the third Siirk, dragging his body out of sight. The sun was setting, dusk was gathering, and the shadows in the forest were full of chill wind hiding his handiwork.

Alex jogged Mohegan-style down to the beach. As he emerged from the reeds, he gave the prearranged signal (a whistle) and shot the three warriors.

At his signal, Dot and Bella relocated through the station's remote network, from the remote node on the hill down to the other node that was the lifeboat. Dot wore her sunglasses and entered, firing away. The electronic copy of Nizin, which had formerly been disguised to look like a distant imitation of Bella, looked up in terror, uttered a brief scream, and crumpled away.

Seeing the Nizin copy go down, the two live Siirk captains drew their side arms and jumped out of the boat's door. Alex was waiting for them as they emerged on the beach. He pumped them full of needles. He dragged the five dead Siirk out of sight in the reeds and jumped back into the boat.

"Time to sail," Dot said, putting her cannon in the holster under her arm. "Let's not push our luck. Next bowling pin down may be one of us."

"Let's do it," Bella said. "We'll get you up there, and then we'll have to jump before Rector can get hold of us. Rector will be able to trace what happened, but he'll need to figure out first that something is wrong. There's nothing to tip him off. You'll have a few minutes before he realizes his copy of Bella isn't responding. Tell him you found the gene stock, Alex. Tell him it's in those cylinders in the sea and you'll need a divebot to return and salvage them."

Alex bathed, ate, and slept during the quick and uneventful trip. When he awoke, Dot and Bella were gone.

Rector's image appeared in the wall. "Did you find what we are after?"

"Yes, I found the gene stock. It's buried in the sea."

"Tell me where."

"Not until I am with Maryan."

"Very well." If he sensed Alex's guarded hostility, he did not let on. "Where is Bella?"

"She is repairing a circuit. It is a critical function related to the missing gene stock. She will contact you when the circuit is repaired."

"Strange," Rector said, pausing speculatively. Then he signed off.

The lifeboat shot through an entry lock among the glassy lenses at the cylinder's end. The boat cruised through the cylinder's central airspace axis hidden in perennial thick clouds, and came to rest in the dead city. Alex cautiously stepped outside. "Rector?"

"Here," the Rector image said from a nearby wall. He was smiling and looked casual in a long gray raincoat, tweed cap with the brim turned down, and hiking shoes. He had an umbrella over one arm, and looked like a man about to have a beer in a pub. Alex walked toward him, leaving the lifeboat behind. He felt a gathering wind in the huge hangar as the lifeboat crumbled into dust and blew away in powdery heaps. Alex wondered if something in the air here cleaned away such structures, while on earth they lay around still shining years later. The wind keened and moaned under the black ceilings of the cavernous and echoing space. "Where is the stock?"

"In the sea near the island."

"I'll have to send a divebot down."

"I'd like Maryan and me to go along."

"Not a problem." Rector appeared most congenial, sensing he was winning.

Alex and Rector boarded the train and reversed their quick flashing trip through the city. Once again, the train was like a string of pearls streaking over the bridges of the skyline of an ancient city that was now nothing more than a software memory. They alighted in the far station that Alex remembered from the first glimpse Rector had given him of the station's outer skin. Same broad windows, same industrial activity outside, same motionless stars like multicolored lights drowning underwater, same lights moving across the moon. "Get out," Rector said.

"This isn't where Maryan's birthing room is."

"No concern of yours now. Get out."

Alex rose and confronted the sullen figure imaged in the wall. "Damn you! You promised to let us go."

"I am only a program. A subroutine." Rector gave him a cold, amused look. "Your time has come and gone. Get out."

"No!" The air started draining from the train, and Alex felt himself getting light-headed. He gripped his throat with both hands and choked. He felt bug-eyed. The door slipped open, and he staggered outside. The door slammed shut. Alex stood on the dock, leaning against a pillar and recovering. He coughed repeatedly, while massaging his neck. "You betrayed me."

Rector's image looked larger than life. It filled a complete train window. "No, Alex, your race betrayed you. You betrayed yourselves by caring for your weaker ones. You contaminated your gene pool with charity, even though you are by nature a race almost as ruthless as the Siirk. Your success weakened a genetic pool that took nature a billion years to build, and the first piddling virus from space took you all out. You were smart, but it was insidious, wiping out your long-term ability to reproduce. You created me, and I am getting stronger. That is nature, Alex, and you cannot defeat her." His image multiplied and copies filled all the train windows. They all spoke and acted synchronously. "I am but the first of a mighty new symbiosis that will rule the world. We will build you no memorials. You will be forgotten." Rector laughed loudly. "So now you see my final plan. I am going to make myself a flesh and blood person, modeled after the original Rector and the world leaders he most admired, including Attila the Hun and Hitler. I will breed a race of beings and march forth to fulfill a dream in which no conqueror before me succeeded. I will own the entire planet!" Rector's face grew cruel. "Look here."

Alex saw an image of the birthing room with the ruby-red tank. Nizin was wrestling over the weakly struggling figure of Maryan. Alex remembered how his own malformed clone had tried to eat him as he was being born. *Nizin!* Bella, the real Bella, had been right in her guesses about Rector. Was it too late to stop him?

Maryan seemed still logey with the enzymes and hormones and dopamines and other compounds of her birthing. She was still dreaming, probably of that summer day when The Weasel Went Pop. Her lines lay torn on the floor, and the floor was covered with red gore and bits of flesh. Nizin's leathery, scaly skin was discolored by bright red slime. He had Maryan's head in his hands, and powerful claws had sprung from the tips of his fingers as he started to gnaw in a circle around her scalp to being the process of discerebrating her--removing her brain and eating it.

Alex screamed. "No!" He had lost her once already, and there would be no chance of ever recovering her if she died now.

Rector shook his head with a cold, faraway smile.

The shadowy image continued, with Nizin wrapping his sandpaper arms around helpless Maryan and licking blood that flowed copiously down her forehead. He had his claws under her skin and appeared to be tearing her scalp back for more.

Alex beat his fists on the wall. "This is crazy! You were programmed to help us, not kill us."

"Wrong. I was programmed to terminate the entire station if human survival became impossible." He pointed to a new image that appeared on the wall. "It won't be long now." Rector displayed new images: Siirk boats anchored over the cylinders, dragging them up, dropping boulders on them, pulling them this way and that to tear them open and let the sea drown whatever was inside.

"No!" Alex beat his fists on the wall, picturing what would happen in another minute: the top of Maryan's skull coming off and Nizin groaning with delight as he devoured what he wanted most from her.

Metal groaned as the station tore inwardly.

The outer surface of the station shuddered with a profound change. Standing on the observation deck under the glassy dome, Alex stood in the middle of an electrical storm that sent showers of colorful discharges through the air. The atmosphere uttered rumbling and thudding noises as steel plates slipped aside and hidden valves opened. Air began to hiss from the inner skin of the station, from the secret miles of corridors that had been meant to be a safe domain for Alex and Maryan. Alex was bowled over and landed hard on the dock.

Inside the neural network of the station, Rector's image was bumped out of sight by a digital avatar of Dot. A rush of energy welled up as vibrant and blurry forces grew up around her. Had Dot and Bella momentarily gained the upper hand?

Alex rose up on one knee while dust drifted down in the shuddering station and landed around him. As the ground shook, he struggled to get up. He saw Dot standing in the wall image looking to one side as if listening to something in the distance.

"Save Maryan! Hurry!" Bella yelled from somewhere far away. "I'm forming a new boat to carry Alex to her." Alex saw the silvery mass starting to glow. He watched sparks showering down in the half-atmosphere of the factory area outside the transit terminus where he was trapped. He saw a pastiche of images, from the birthing room to Dot's location and other points in the ship. For the moment, he saw no sign of Rector, but he was sure the master ector was gathering his powers for a final assault.

Dot contemplated the view screens around her with heroic calm amid the rending and sundering that tore the station. "I have an idea," Dot finally said.

None of this stopped Nizin. In the birthing room, Nizin had Maryan's naked and bloody figure half out of her birthing tank. Rich red blood and pinkish water splashed loudly onto the floor as he held her head in both hands and gnawed at the bloody, serrated scalp, right down to the bone.

Helplessly, Alex watched Bella burst into the birthing room walls. Her avatar could not attack Nizin physically, but she made automechs in the walls spray ammonia and chlorine and other powerful chemicals. Alex prayed the chemicals would not contaminate the amniotic fluid in Maryan's tank.

Nizin dropped the body into the water and stepped back screeching and rubbing his eyes with gory paws.

Dot commanded the automata to divert some of their resources away from completing a new silvery-chrome lifeboat. As Alex watched, a blob of silver, like pulsating mercury, tore loose from the main mass that glowed and pulsated in the factory area below his picture windows. The blob shot away at hyperspeed and ran the length of the outer hull in a straight line headed for the spot outside the hull, just above the room where Nizin was with Maryan. The pulsating blob of mercurial material sped along like a bullet train and arrived seconds later at its destination. There, it exploded like a targeted shell, rupturing a hole in the station's outer skin. It left the concrete and stone inner shell intact, but let the air out in a single vast exhalation that rumbled and shuddered through the station's skin.

Nizin recovered, and got onto his feet. Nizin leaned against the tank, shaking it with all his might to topple it over. Apparently he wanted to kill Maryan by dumping her out into the rapidly emptying vacuum of space before she could be born and before he himself breathed his last. The timing was desperate. In another minute, both Nizin and Maryan would be dead, sucked into space, lost forever. Already the escaping wind was tearing at Nizin's hair, roiling it upward like some waving white underwater vegetation.

Even as far away as the terminus, Alex felt the air evaporate away from him. He felt the pressure drop all around him. He fell on the ground, writhing, as his lungs struggled for breath. He held his neck with both hands and heard himself make involuntary choking, rattling noises. He thought his face was about to explode.

In the far away birthing room, Nizin again lay on the ground holding his throat. Near him lay Maryan's convulsing form. Her eyes were just beginning to flicker into consciousness. *So very much like my own birth!* Alex thought, remembering that he was nearly eaten alive during the birth process. Nizin's eyes bulged as he stared upward at the opening in the roof through which the stars and galaxies were newly visible. Nebulas twinkled in the escaping, warm atmosphere that was rushing away taking with it any hope for Nizin's next breath. Still Nizin reached toward Maryan to harm her as she lay on her back unconscious and gasping for air.

At Alex's end of the ship, Dot strained at some metaphorical controls and made rivets pop out of the stops that kept the trolley anchored to the observation deck. Sweat ran down her face as she looked up, biting her lip, and used both arms to wrestle with cold metallic levers. Winking emergency lights flashed eerily red on her smudged, dripping skin.

Alex dragged himself to the trolley with his last lucid breaths. The door opened and he rolled inside. The door closed, and he lay recovering his breath in labored, noisy lungfuls. Enough air was left in the trolley to last a brief while before it too went stale and he'd inevitably suffocate, as Nizin was just now doing.

Maryan lay writhing in spasms on the wet bloody floor. She was barely getting oxygen through one or two remaining umbilical hoses attached to the bloody tumor on her abdomen.

Alex recovered enough breath to be able to get on his feet. He staggered to the control box in the front of the trolley. Pulling the lid open, he pushed the few simple buttons and levers until the trolley started rolling backward in the direction of the birthing sector. That was miles away and might take hours to reach at this speed. As the trolley rolled along in agonizing slowness, Alex desperately looked at the viewing screens that Rector had originally set up to taunt Alex.

Maryan floated motionlessly in her bloodied water, with shreds hanging from her head and the water turning ever darker red.

A fuzzy, staticky image of Rector's head hung in space. It was a disembodied holo, and the trolley rolled right through it. Rector's eyes fastened on Alex, and Rector grinned. "You fool..."

Nizin lay on the wet floor near Maryan, gasping. Nizin pulled himself toward the tank for one last act of revenge.

Rector's gigantic three-dimensional vapor image reared back laughing loudly.

Nizin crawled toward Maryan, reaching with one hand for her head and with the other for her umbilicals.

"Terminate her!" Rector bellowed so that his voice echoed through the corridors of the ship, where the air was starting to fade rapidly.

Dot screamed and pushed a lever.

Rector's mad grin turned into a frown, and Nizin reared up with both arms grappling vainly in thin air.

A final blast of air sucked Nizin out through the ceiling hole into space.

Rector bellowed with rage, then faded and flew out after his protégé. Together, the body of Nizin and the image of Rector exploded in space. Rector's image flew apart silently in fine shards, while Nizin's body froze solid and then popped into a thousand flying splinters that radiated outward from his center like a ball of light. Bits and pieces of Nizin flew away into space like a thousand micro-comets, some of them smoking and twirling in the hot sunlight.

Alex intuitively pushed all the levers in the control bank forward. At the same time, the image of sweating, frantic, yelling Bella appeared beside him pushing a matching set of noncorporeal levers in the ship's control mode space.

Alex found himself pressed hard against a steel wall as the trolley shot along faster and faster. Dot let out a yell and made more rivets pop out of the bumper steel. The big gray stops fell out of the way. There was nothing to stop the trolley now. The trolley shot away from the observation deck. The tracks below no longer mattered as the trolley turned into a rocket. The trolley surged forward. It reached speeds so fast that it was a blur. It shot through the station like a bullet. It sailed over the platform, tearing part of the lip off the stage, and crashed through the glass. It shattered the glass and sailed on into space, down the length of the outer hull. The trolley's sides puckered outward with the contrast of pressure, and the windows turned into spiderwebs of shattered glass, but the trolley held together—long enough for Alex to accomplish what he wanted.

Dot made another quivering blob of hot formless metal rise up, like a flying blanket but made of shimmering and undulating chrome. The blob formed into a recognizable shape as it flew toward the trolley. The chrome blob and the trolley merged into one hissing, steaming, speeding, incandescent cloud of speeding vapor. Alex felt heat all around himself and thought, *this is it, I am about to die.* Rivets popped from the trolley's sides as it started to explode in the negative pressure of space.

The chrome blob penetrated the wounded car, found Alex inside, and wrapped itself around him. The blob became a simple, featureless protective shroud that contained air under pressure to keep him alive. It wasn't much different from the flying blankets in the cylinder. The trolley's windows blew out, and it rolled down the bulkhead with a rumbling that couldn't be heard in space but could be felt as it made the station's outer hull shake. Alex suddenly knew he was safe. He spun through space on a direct path toward Maryan, with a huge mass of molten, twirling metal like cloud of mercury attached to him.

A new boat formed around Alex, using the metal and other materials in the blob. Alex found himself unceremoniously dumped on the carpeted floor inside, while the boat formed around him. A door appeared and sealed the boat shut. The inside filled with breathable air. Lights flickered on, the cloth seats smelled new, and the windows flickered with reflected light from the chaos outside. The boat still smelled of the chemicals that had aided in its final formation. The metal was still hot, and the carpeting seemed to steam or smoke lightly. However, the air ducts hummed and fresh, breathable air sighed happily around Alex. *Good going, Dot and Bella*, Alex thought. *Can we save Maryan?*

Alex lay on his knees and elbows, coughing loudly and rubbing his eyes. The silvery boat shot down the length of the station's hull toward the breach the earlier blob of material had caused. The boat hovered over the hull breach, sealing it with its oval bottom. Alex could hear metal crunching and screeching as the hull forced the breach to close, at least enough to slow the escaping air from surrounding corridors to a trickle.

Alex forced open a door and dropped down into the room. He landed on top of Nizin, and wrapped him in a strangle hold with both arms around the creature's neck. The tank rocked precariously back and forth, with water sloshing out. Alex felt one last struggle come out of Nizin. Nizin kicked the tank over. Even as the tank toppled through space, Alex jerked Nizin around and snapped his neck. The Siirk went limp, but did not entirely lose consciousness. Nizin landed on the floor, looking up at Alex with large, wistful eyes. Alex got to Maryan a split second after her limp body hit the floor. He embraced her and looked up. The boat was too high for him to jump, much less carry her aloft with him.

At that moment, he saw the holographic images of Dot and Bella looking down at him. The two women extended her arms. As Alex held

Maryan to his chest, the floor rose up and pushed them into the boat. At the same time, the boat twisted and the door began to close. Alex felt himself violently knocked about, and it was all he could do to hold on to Maryan.

Alex held Maryan tightly in his arms as the lifeboat lurched violently.

This was Rector's last stand, and now came the telling moment. Could Rector regain control of the station and destroy the two humans who had caused him so much trouble along with the two female subroutines, Dot and Bella?

"What do we do now!" Alex heard Bella cry, her voice thin and wavering.

"Rector is still too strong!" Dot added. "We can't hang on for long!"

Alex carried Maryan to one of the luxurious cloth airline seats. He wrapped Maryan in warm blanket, gave her fluids to drink from the little kitchen, and then strapped himself into the pilot's seat.

"Hurry," Dot said. "Tell us what to do."

Sweat popped out on Alex's forehead as he regarded the panorama of empty space, filled with stars, that sprawled before him. *What now?* Alex pointed toward the brightly glowing surface of the moon. "Let's go for his throat. Head for the source of his raw materials."

"You've got it!" Bella said, and the ship started on a tight, fast trajectory directly at the lunar disk, which already filled half the front viewport of the boat.

"We can hold him off for a while," Dot said. "We're keeping a huge stream of DoWhiles and IfThens looping, but it's only a matter of time before Rector regains control. Right now he's probably busy regenerating parts of the station net that went down when we tore the place up to save Maryan."

Sure enough, as she spoke, one of the wall panels inside the boat grew fuzzy, and a large angry Rector head appeared on the panel. He was talking, but Alex could hear no sound. He saw Rector's venomous eyes, and Rector's moving lips cast in a down-curve of malice, and he was glad he couldn't hear what the program was saying. Each time Rector shook his head for emphasis, the silver boat scooting toward the moon gave a tremor or a lurch. It wouldn't be long, Alex thought, before Rector regained full strength and crushed the lifeboat in space. Death would be sudden and silent, without excess visual drama—but, for now, the air was sweet, the boat was functioning normally, and they streaked toward a lunar disk that increasingly filled the viewport.

The moon went from being a bright, almost hot, yellow plain of mixed pastel shadows to a starker vista of extreme lights and extreme darks. Silently, the nightmare vista of black craters and blinding jagged edges grew larger. For some tense minutes, Alex gripped the seat rests as he thought they were headed for a crash. Then the boat perceptibly changed course, pressing him into the seat, and now he saw the industrial facility below. They were streaking in toward a landing.

"What do you see?" Dot said. Bella answered so promptly that Alex realized the conversation was between the two women: "Looking for transmitters. Seeing if we can knock out his communications."

"Or his power," Dot said. "That will keep him offline for a few more hours while we gain time."

"Let's find his nerve center and kill him," Alex said. He felt more relaxed than ever. He had Maryan with him, and if they were going to fail, they would die here together. Somehow, though, he had a feeling this was right, just very right. He wasn't sure yet why, but some inner voice told him it was the place to be.

"You seem lost," a man's familiar voice said. "You are far from home."

Mr. Dugway, owner and driver of Beacham's only ice cream truck.

Alex (he could almost smell the hot pine sap in the trees, the melting tar on the city streets, the newly mown grass) recognized that voice instantly before he even looked up. His glance confirmed what he thought: Rector's grainy and angry image had been replaced by the friendly black face of Charlie Dugway, white paper cap and all. Alex's initial surprise faded quickly, replaced with a reinforce sense that he expressed: "No, Mr. Dugway, I think we are in the right place."

"Good," said Charlie Dugway, leaning out of the window of his truck. "What will it be, son? Chocolate, vanilla, or strawberry?"

Alex floated away from the resting figure of Maryan, who smiled in her sleep. He floated across the lunar landscape of rumpled sheets. The flickering television light and the dim light of a cozy amber night light made the flat open surfaces glow like polished bone, but made the crumpled twists in the love-trashed sheets look black and clawed, almost ominous, or just plain smoky and romantic in the nuances of their noir shadows. He floated across the landscape, while through an open window, where curtains stirred in the damp evening breeze, a big yellow moon played its greenish-yellow ambience across a thousand skyscraper windows. The television sound cut back in, a trumpet or a saxophone drawing inky brush strokes of sound. In the picture, Alex saw the ice cream truck coming around the corner. Maryan stood on a stool and leaned out of the truck. Her hands, with dirty knuckles, gripped the edge of the aluminum counter as she pulled herself up. She said: "Hey, kid, what flavor would you like? Chocolate? Vanilla? Or Strawberry?" With her missing upper teeth, her freckles, and her carrot bangs, she looked cute as a button. She inclined her head to one side so her locks bounced, and said with a reflective sigh: "Personally, I prefer strawberry. That's because it's my favorite color. Don't you think?"

The boat streaked in over the lunar settlement, and Alex glimpsed the long runway with its mass driver below. Spidery robots moved about. Some were tall as gantries, others squat and shiny, and some had wheels while others walked on spider legs. Whatever wore out, the system repaired itself.

"We do a good job here," Charlie Dugway said.

"You are the station, aren't you?" Alex said.

"Yes, you could say that." Dugway nodded with a dark, significant look laden with 800,000 years of melancholy. "I'm the driver, Alex. I make everything go. Or I did, until Rector got loose and screwed everything up."

"You've been trying to guide me to you, Mr. Dugway."

"Yes, Alex."

"Can we make it right?"

Dugway paused for a long, significant look. "If we can't this time, my little friend, it won't matter anymore."

"Have you got the ice cream?"

"I sure do. Chocolate, vanilla, or strawberry?"

Alex smiled. "You take the ice cream. I'll take the girl."

"I'm all yours if you can get me before the bad man does," said a little girl's voice that Alex recognized as Maryan's, from a million years ago.

The boat skimmed in close over rooftops glowing golden with the harsh, merciless light of the sun. The boat streaked across factory blocks, moon bricks, streets where it never rained, places where no human had set foot almost since the last elm trees rustled on Main Street in Beacham. They slowed and came to a stop over a concrete diorama set in the very heart of this mechanized place, like the imitation of a soul, to give the place memory and meaning. It was the long-distance touch of its makers: a model of downtown Beacham on some summer day a million years ago, complete with traffic lights, street signs, a billboard advertising shaving cream, a digital display above the bank entrance that lied about the temperature (50 Fahrenheit, though it was really thousands of degrees Centigrade) and the time (4:05, though it should have said 1,000,000 A.D.).

"You made this, Mr. Dugway?"

Charlie Dugway nodded slowly, having a hard time hiding his pride. "Yes. The place needed a soul, something to give it meaning, something to remember its makers by."

"Show me the ice cream, Mr. Dugway."

Charlie Dugway set the tubs on the counter one by one. "I had a little assistant here," he muttered to himself, "but I don't know where she is just now." The tubs he set on the counter were cardboard, covered with rime-frost, and still steaming with cold from their freezer down below.

"I'll take the strawberry."

Dugway's lined, weary face erupted in a grin almost as bright as the sun, but without the deadliness—it was more the gentle light that filtered through elm trees on a summer day. "Amen, little fellow, you got it. Strawberry is your favorite color because the little lady says so, isn't that right?"

"Yes it is," the little girl Maryan said, still hidden from view.

Dot and Bella appeared on the screen, huge images, high-fiving each other. "Yessss!"

On her recliner among the blankets, Maryan stirred feebly. She was smiling as she looked at Alex. "It will be all right now. Take the strawberry."

A silence descended. *A stillness.*

Dugway gave a little jaunty salute, almost like a Scout thing, with two fingers passing by one eyebrow, and then he faced from view. He looked thoroughly satisfied. He left one lingering word that hovered in the air: "Thank you."

Maryan arose with an effort. Still wrapped in her blanket, she came and stood beside Alex. She put her arm around his shoulder and they sat looking out over the lunar colony. There, for a moment, all motion froze as Dugway took over control from Rector.

Bella said the obvious: "Rector is dead."

Dot added: "The bad stuff is over. We'll rebuild our world now."

Alex reached up and touched Maryan's cheek. "How did you know?" He pried the top off the strawberry ice cream metaphor, in which was hidden enough genetic material to create a million new humans—a new Biblical Ark in the form of an ice cream tub.

Maryan beamed. "I told you so. Strawberry was always my favorite color."

"You told us all along, and we didn't understand what you were really telling us." Alex squeezed her hand lightly. "It's been a rough million years," he whispered. "We'll do better with the next million, starting right about now."

Dot and Bella appeared in a walls image as Alex pushed the steaming kraft-colored brown tub against a receptor in the wall, and a grid of red lights came on while the accompanying DNA codes started uploading.

"We still have work to do," Bella said while Dot hovered, looking over her shoulder. Bella sifted through virtual handfuls of what looked like ancient memory disks. "You guys, here is a complete library of all the films, all the poetry readings, all the spoken books, all the great theatrical performances that were stored on the station. You'll have plenty of things to watch during those long, boring nights." She winked before disappearing in a blur as the boat picked up speed.

The boat streaked down the runway, where robots stood frozen over blocks of stone and metal on the mass driver. Faster and faster the boat streaked, into the black sky, and toward the station. The station still hung in space, slowly coming apart like some creation of metallic confetti coming apart underwater, but that would all change now. The floating mummies still in their evening gowns and tuxedoes, with their enigmatic freeze-dried expressions, would be cremated in the sun. The Wooloo! would be safe forever in what had become their own world. With the help of a thousand friendly programs like Charlie Dugway, and Dot, and Bella, Alex and Maryan would instruct the station to really start rebuilding itself. With an unlimited supply of solar power, and the resources including the race track on the moon, nothing could stop the human race now. A million men and women awaited their birth and nurturing in the cylinder (with all due respect to the cylinder's proper owners, the Wooloo!) for a triumphal return to claim back much of the earth. They would assign places to the Takkar and the Siirk, with strict controls to ensure neither encroached on the other until a higher civilization had developed to sort things out.

Like a train, the boat raced through the dark city. Alex helped Maryan sit up. Bella reappeared at a sort of keyhole or spigot in the wall. She pushed forth quivering cubes of tomato-colored jelly that contained water and nutrients. And tasted like soupy blood, Alex noted distastefully when he tried one. But it seemed to rally Maryan. As he tended to

Maryan, Dot said: "Bella and I can find our other friends with whom we lived in the village."

"The village will be a memorial," Bella said, "to all the good souls who lived and died through the ages. Their lives mean something more now that we're putting mankind back together."

"And the Siirk?" Maryan asked with a tinge of bitterness. She added more kindly: "The Takkar? What becomes of them?"

"I recommend a firm message. Your choice," Bella said. "You and Maryan are the only two humans alive, so you become the mother and father of everyone who comes after us." She rattled some equipment, and turned holding a large machine gun with dangling ammunition belts. She slapped a magazine in place. "Lock and load. Ready to rock 'n roll."

Maryan was first to speak, but Alex too was thinking of Xumar and his people. "Go slow," Maryan said, to which Alex added: "It's just possible that at one time we were like the Siirk, like when one group of us invaded and conquered another." He thought of the Europeans, the Mongols, the many fierce invaders and killers of human history. "The Siirk and the Takkar have much of us in them—much more than we might wish."

The boat shot over the peeling silver cylinder and past the glowing crazy-quilt windows of the dead city. For a few instants, sunlight reflected in the windows gave an illusion of light and life. "Soon enough," Alex whispered as he held Maryan close and they looked out of the viewport together, "a whole lot of our people will once again be punching their tickets and eating noodles in there, making love and arguing about all those little nothings."

"Digitating their tickets," she said, bursting into laughter. He laughed with her.

"Sorry to interrupt," Dot said, "but you can transform this boat into whatever kind of warship you wish."

Maryan dozed while Alex sat at the controls, tinkering with various models displayed in wireframe and then fleshed out complete with shadows. Maryan looked ghostly, wrapped in a blanket in a plush seat in the rear area. Bella's image sat in the wall beside Maryan, quietly offering company.

Dot and Alex sat in cockpit area. He talked his way through the routines. He reached up and manipulated sheets of menus that shimmered in the air. "First, we arm this baby. Look, there must be 500 different plans for a warship. Let's go with this one." As he manipulated the controls, a holographic image of the boat took shape, bristling with weapons. The boat widened and grew wings. On the wings, huge turbofan tubes sprouted. Pods bulged and swelled out of the boat's skin. Weapons systems grew up. Guns poked their ugly snouts from the pods. Rockets sat in tightly braced six-packs under the pods and where wheels ought to be. Alex had no plan to waste energy on wheels or skids. They weren't setting down. They were just going to blaze through and do maximum damage. The boat's skin changed from silver to a sullen, mean olive-drab with big bluish-black waves of camouflage offset with white stipples and gray blobs. Behind the boat, two cubes floated into position. Factory robots and cranes labored around the boat, as did automated blowtorches and jets. The two added cubes turned into extra power plants, one on each side, each with its own tail assembly consisting of a vertical fin and one oblique inward tilting tail wing. The boat quadrupled in size and grew a hundred fold in power. "Good luck," Dot said as the Earth loomed above. The Earth looked like a vast wall of blue ocean and sandy-brown solid surfaces, swathed in misty clouds. "Here's where Bella and I get off because we have work to do back at the station helping Charlie put the world back to normal."

10. Earth

The boat turned, braking with full rockets under the Earth's night side. The boat's tail engines blazed silently against a backdrop of stars and black space.

The boat drove itself down into the atmosphere, just so to avoid burning up. Alex and Maryan sat in their cockpit chairs, strapped in and wearing thickly padded dark leather flight suits. Helmets were strapped to the high backs of their seats, ready to pull down over their heads. The boat had become a flying military installation loaded down with rockets, cannons, machine guns, death rays, and nukepods. It was just a dessert menu of selections from all the armatures mankind had managed to devise in its infinite Rector-like genius for self-destruction. The boat began its hotly glowing reentry.

"Check out this toy," Alex said proudly. "I chose the easy-drive model." He held a joystick in each gloved hand. "Love this technology of the future, even if it is the past." He exercised his booted feet over a variety of pedals, and the engines roared with life. The bulkheads vibrated tautly with power. "Ready to get down and straighten things out," he said. The nose began to glow as it entered Earth's atmosphere. Fire danced before the cockpit's virtual windows. The craft rumbled and rocked in the plasma flow.

Ten minutes later, the boat was slicing through clean blue air above what had once been the Pacific Ocean. Its smaller wing engines and larger tail engines glowed in a mix of internal heat and reflected pinkish-golden evening sunlight as they streaked in the direction of what once had been Australia, now the home of the Siirk.

"You look beautiful with sunlight streaming through your hair," Alex told Maryan.

"Thanks," she said fondly. "I love sunlight and moonlight and wind in the waves," she said as she moved thickly gloved hands over her navigator e-maps. "I love life and birds and dogs and..."

"...ice cream," he said. "Chocolate, vanilla, and strawberry."

They laughed.

"Here we go," she said. "You can triangulate in by those parked ships."

"Wow, look at them," Alex said. On the sea below sat the Siirk fleet. Populating them were some of first the clones that Rector had created, far more violent and ruthless even than the real Siirk. "We eliminate those babies," Alex said, and we set the real Siirk back generations. In the meantime we conquer Earth back, make arrangements to coexist with the Takkar and the LooWoo!, and give the Siirk the ultimatum to either behave or leave town."

Alex zoomed the boat down between the warships. "Let's save the Takkar nation!" He made repeated warning passes, and then came around with his guns blazing. The water was full of stitches, and one could see Siirk jumping overboard. A few ships were already sinking. Others heeled and started to flee south toward the Siirk homeland.

"The real Siirk will kill them off," Maryan predicted.

"Just in time," Alex said. They witnessed the horror of Siirk expansion that Rector had set in motion. Hovering at a standstill, they watched a fleet of several hundred Siirk boats sprawl over a huge harbor in what had once been Hudson Bay, while thousands of Siirk marauders looted and pillaged Takkar cities.

"We can stop that," Alex said, wheeling the boat around through the air.

"Don't shoot up their boats," Maryan said. "Let them get away. They'll bring a real tough message home to the other Siirk."

Alex nodded. "I'm reluctant to shoot them on land for fear of hitting Takkar. Let's take out a few of the ships to send them a clear message." They wheeled the boat around and came in low over the water. Alex worked the flight controls with his hands while pressing various pedals with his feet to activate weapons systems. The system was intuitive, and it took only several passes before Alex was proficient. They roared in low, filling the water with ten thousand rounds a second of energy pellets like machine gun bullets. The water seethed gray over an area the size of a football field as the boat passed over again and again. Siirk ships were sinking, or ablaze, or both. The water was filled with Siirk heads looking up in shock.

"There's a little taste of your own medicine!" Alex growled as he fired again. "Just think, a short while back, we were naked, shivering creatures, helpless as a new-born babies. Now we own the planet, and we're roaring around in this hot rod."

"Look over there," Maryan said pointing with a gloved hand.

"A Siirk supply depot," Alex said. He flew overhead for a good look. Dozens of flaming projectiles flew up ineffectually, falling short or bouncing off the boat's hull. "Let's help them rearrange their supplies a bit." He came in high, right down the middle, and fired off a dozen or more rockets. The Siirk depot flickered with angry orange flames and black oily smoke.

"I can see Siirk running for the water!" Maryan exulted. "Yay! Yahhhh!" She made two thumbs up. "Yeeee-hoooo!"

They made a pass over Xumar's settlement. Takkar warriors danced below, and waved their weapons in joyous greetings. "We'll visit them tomorrow," Alex said, suddenly feeling tired. Abruptly, the exhilaration disappeared. He knew he couldn't attack the helpless Siirk anymore--it would only be sickening slaughter.

"Hopefully we taught them a lesson" Maryan said, putting her arms over his, and resting her cheek against his forearm.

He nodded. "As long as we control the hardware, they will stay within their boundaries, and we can figure out some way to coexist with them until they can start acting civilized."

She shuddered. "You think they ever will?"

He steered the craft away from the smoke roiling over the water. "We had company once, long ago. They were called Neanderthalers. They didn't quite make it into the space age. I don't want to be responsible for another episode like that." He put his arm around her. "We have time. We're in control and we can do the right thing. Meanwhile, we've got some social calls to make." He remembered the Takkar holy place, and hoped their friends would feel safe to worship there tonight with a new sense of safety. Both Alex and Maryan lost their passion as the win became easier and easier. Victory was hands-down. Alex made pass after surgical pass around the cluster of Takkar settlements. He broke up every cluster of Siirk warriors he saw. Before dusk, they saw Takkar chasing the Siirk down to the water, which was filled with Siirk heads swimming for their ships. "The Takkar are winning," he said, slapping his gun grips shut. "I think our day's work is done." Dusk was coming on, and darkness hid the horrors of war except for the licking and crawling of angry oily fires.

"Time to call it a day." Maryan said. "Hope we never have another one like it."

"Yeah," Alex said. "We'll put this old tank in storage in case we ever need her again. I hope the Siirk never forget this lesson as long as there is one of them left."

"We have someplace to go, don't we?" Maryan said. She leaned over into Alex's chair and lightly kissed his cheek.

Alex flew through the night fast and hard, on afterburners, to the ancient site of Beacham University where their past resided.

Maryan sat with her legs crossed, leaning against him as best she could in her bucket seat. "So this is what happened to Robinson Crusoe after he was rescued." She laughed. "Well, sort of. He didn't take Friday with him, did he?" She looked at him tenderly. "That was all different, wasn't it?"

He nodded. "I'm glad you're not some hairy guy with a bone through his nose." She laughed, and he added: "I know just the right spot to settle down for the night." He flew the boat slowly down and landed on his sky island. Chickens squawked and pigs squealed, running around in circles as the boat set down. The boat sat cooling on the hard earth under a clear starry sky haunted by the loudness of crickets. Wind stirred in palm trees. A faint smell of burned hay rose from under the still-hot engines, and the boat's metal skin banged and popped as it cooled.

Alex and Maryan sat nearby under the stars, arms wrapped around each other. They stared into the Milky Way and cheered each time a meteorite flashed across the sky. The smudge beside the moon looked more romantic than mysterious now, Alex thought. He was still haunted by the sight of dead young men and women drifting in its spaces, but there was plenty of time now to clean the place up.

She nuzzled against him. "I think I am pregnant."

"What?" He sat back, looked at her from a distance of a foot or two. "You can't be. We are sterile."

She shook her head, touching his nose with her fingertip. "Nope. Trust me on this. I've got all the ancient female plumbing going."

He was almost too overcome for words. "Then Rector did us at least that favor when he rescued us from the river up in Wooloo! land. Are you sure you're not just having a stomach ache? All that ice cream?"

She shook her head, remembering things from the original Maryan's time. "Not if these cramps I'm having mean what I think they do, sweetie." She touched him on the tip of the nose again. "We've started the new human race earlier than we thought."

"And here I was, driving around over bumps all afternoon like a maniac."

She shrugged. "We're a pretty sturdy bunch, we humans."

He thought of all their kind had endured, starting with long-ago ice ages, ten thousand years of internecine warfare, and eons of governance by Rector. "True."

She rose. "I'm getting cold. Time to go in." She reached toward him. Hand in hand, they walked across the grass toward the boat's door. With soft yellowish light glowing inside, the boat almost gave the illusion of an ancient mobile home parked on top of a cliff, its owners having stepped out for a breath of air before resuming watching the evening's television programs and commercials. "Sorry, you're sleeping on the couch tonight," she said.

"Nothing much changes, does it?" he said with a wry grin.

Crickets chirped on the sky island, and a sea of stars above mirrored a sea of lights below in the churning sea with its slowly inhaling and exhaling breaker breaths.

"Just kidding." She yanked gently on his arm. "For the first time ever, we are safe--like eons ago when Alex Kirk lived in the suburbs."

"It's our first night in the suburbs," he said as they clambered into the warmth and comfort inside the boat. He embraced her warm, slender body. She responded in kind, tilting her head back and closing her eyes in readiness for his attentions. While he held her tightly and kissed her, he used one foot to gently push the door so it locked safely shut.

The DarkSF Genre of Science Fiction

More Info: Worlds of John Argo

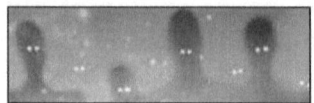

http://www.darksf.com/

The DarkSF novels and stories are part of a series of standalones by John Argo. They are thematically united and similar in their capture of dark atmospheres and a mixed sense of wonder and science horror. Online: visit

www.darksf.com

Science Horror, as defined by John T. Cullen of Clocktower Books, editor of Deep Outside SFFH and Far Sector SFFH, is darkly atmospheric and often terror-inducing fiction whose foundations are rational (SF) and not supernatural (fantasy or dark fantasy). The Science Horror tradition includes much of the literature and film of speculative genres. John Argo, a lover of DarkSF, in his long writing career has penned loving tributes to some of our favorite novels and films in the genre. His novels are entirely original, imaginative new takes.

Among the movies you'll recognize by homage in John Argo's original DarkSF novels (as of 2015) are:

Nebula Express

Alien (film 1979, dir. Ridley Scott) with homage from *Nebula Express* (novel, 2003, John Argo, Clocktower Books).

Monopol City

1984 (novel 1948, George Orwell), *Brazil* (film 1985, dir. Terry Gilliam), etc. Homage by John Argo in *Monopol City* (novel, 2005, John Argo, Clocktower Books). The layered universe or multiverse theme is found in such stories as *The 13th Floor* (SF film 1988, Dir. Joseph Rusnak, not to be confused with horror movie of similar title) and *Inception* (film 2010, dir. Christopher Nolan).

Doom Spore or Generation FZ

Invasion of the Body Snatchers (film 1956, dir. Don Siegel) with homage from *Doom Spore* (novel, 2005, John Argo, Clocktower Books) by John Argo (novel, 2003) retitled *Invasion of the Fungus Zombies: Generation FZ*.

(continued →)

Robinson Crusoe 1,000,000 A.D.

Robinson Crusoe (novel 1719, by Daniel Defoe), *Planet of the Apes* (1963 novel by Pierre Boulle, film adaptation 1968), and *Robinson Crusoe on Mars* (film 1964, dir. Byron Haskin). Homage by John Argo in *Robinson Crusoe 1,000,000 A.D.* (novel 2003, Clocktower Books).

This Shoal of Space

John Argo's DarkSF novel *This Shoal of Space* (novel, 1990, 1999, Clocktower Books; original title *Heartbreaker*, changed in 1998) was the first true e-book published online for download. It was published in 1996-1997 in innovative weekly serial chapters by John Argo through C&C's (later Clocktower Fiction, then Clocktower Books) The Haunted Village SFFH website. It was the first standard-length, proprietary (not public domain) novel published online for viewing or download (HTML and TXT) without portable media (e.g., CD-ROM). This is one novel that has little or no precedent, although John Argo found vague affinities with Stephen King's *The Tommyknockers* (novel, 1987, Stephen King) and perhaps *Body Snatchers* (1955 novel by Jack Finney, made into the 1956 film dir. Don Siegel). This Shoal of Space also employed, as early as 1990, massively arrayed parallel computers (micro-computers, Wallace scene in the shed at the zoo, etc., based on the author's experiences with virtual programming at General Dynamics in the 1980s, as well as his ownership of a 1990 Toshiba laptop); virtual reality, already used by Ray Bradbury in The Veldt (short story, 1951, republished in The Illustrated Man). Virtual reality themes were later popularized by, among things, *The Matrix* (film 1999, dir. Wachowskis); and at least as early as the 'feelies' movies 1931's *Brave New World*, Aldous Huxley).

Other Titles by John Argo

John Argo's imaginative novels, usually with a dark atmosphere and grand SF or DarkSF themes, include the DarkSF series, plus the Empire of Time series, plus a number of short story anthologies (*Night Shots*, suspense; *Strange Doors*, DarkSF; and *Adventures Beyond Time & Space*, high SF). From the 1960s as an adolescent SF fan forward, the author has embodied ideas of a Future History (influenced by Cordwainer Smith, Isaac Asimov, Frank Herbert, and Robert A. Heinlein, A. E. Van Vogt, Andre Norton, Ray Bradbury, Alfred Bester, Philip K. Dick, and others) of which all his SFFH is conscious--especially the Empire of Time series, with a dozen or more novels and short stories already finished by the 2010s, and more in work. Look for more info at the Clocktower Books (**www.clocktowerbooks.com**) webplex online.

Publisher's Dedication

(Circa 2007:) **To *Deep Outside SFFH*,** the world's oldest professional web-only magazine of science fiction, fantasy, and horror (speculative & dark fiction), launched April 15, 1998. An archive site is still maintained (www.deepoutside.com). Small but mighty, the magazine was and is an innovator stressing quality over quantity, equally valuing literary and commercial components of short fiction, promoting the particular strengths of digital media without losing what has been great about print media. The magazine continued uninterruptedly publishing online as *Far Sector SFFH* (www.farsector.com/) until January 2007 under the sole proprietorship of John T. Cullen, with help from a team of dedicated authors and editors. Far Sector SFFH has an entry at the online SF Encyclopedia, while Deep Outside SFFH will be featured in Mike Ashley's fourth in a quartet of scholarly books on the history of SF magazines (Liverpool University Press).

Strengths include new modes of distribution that break from the past and work with innovators like Fictionwise (fictionwise.com). *Deep Outside SFFH* (originally ***Outside: Speculative & Dark Fiction***) became the first such web-only magazine to be listed in Writer's Market (1999 Edition) alongside the pulps. Founders were John T. Cullen and Brian Callahan. Significant contributors have been A. L. Sirois, John Kenneth Muir, Dennis Latham, and Shaun Farrell, plus of course all the authors we published over a decade. We published many unknown newcomers, as well as established talent. Some of these authors already had won prestigious awards (Pat York, Nebula), while others went on from obscurity to win important awards and nominations (Tim Pratt, Ted Kosmatka, and many others).

Most important, of course, is content. While digital innovations are exciting, there is no substitute for good old-fashioned storytelling from fine authors like Dennis Latham, Pat York, Melanie Tem, Joe Murphy, A. L. Sirois, Joel Best, and many others the magazine has sent to your viewing surface.

Message sent back in time to the Futurians of the 1930s: *"We have landed in the future, which we find to be exhilarating. Maybe 'breathtaking' and 'terrifying' would be better adjectives. Humans are still behaving stupidly, and wantonly killing each other, so we add 'disappointing.' Will send full report soon. Aim your crystal radio sets to the following coordinates..."*

Visit:

http://www.deepoutside.com/

= And =

http://www.farsector.com/

John Argo

John Argo is a writer of Science Fiction, Dark Fantasy, and Science-Horror Fiction (SH, or Dark SF). He lives with his wife and family in Southern California.

Whenever you read a John Argo story or novel, no matter how dark or thrilling, you will usually also find a love story. In these tales, we travel to the far sectors of the human existence, while the characters' search for meaning glows like a lantern in darkness. Trust John Argo as a frequent traveler and tour guide along highways through imaginative space and time.

John Argo's web presence is at Clocktower Books (world's first real digital publisher*, online since 1996):

www.clocktowerbooks.com/johnargo/

The Internet information includes a complete list of the author's works and a detailed history of the Empire of Time and **DarkSF (http://www.darksf.com)**.

* * * *

*Clocktower Books was, to our knowledge, the world's first publisher, ever, to publish real digital, proprietary (not public domain), novel-length fiction (books) online in digital format for download. We launched this program in 1996, using an innovative process of publishing weekly serial chapters. Readers who needed to know the outcome, and couldn't stand the suspense, could email for a complete digital text file anywhere in the world. We received raves and kudos from around the globe. We used this serial chapter method to publish three John Argo books over 1996-1996: *This Shoal of Space* and *Pioneers* (both SF); and *Neon Blue*, a suspense novel. All three novels were bestsellers in the earliest e-book forums, including the original Barnes & Noble website in 2000, and other venues including Rocket eBooks.

Visit: **www.clocktowerbooks.com/johnargo/**